John Cordy Jeaffreson

The Real Lord Byron - New Views of the Poet's Life

Vol. I

John Cordy Jeaffreson

The Real Lord Byron - New Views of the Poet's Life
Vol. I

ISBN/EAN: 9783743337312

Manufactured in Europe, USA, Canada, Australia, Japa

Cover: Foto ©Raphael Reischuk / pixelio.de

Manufactured and distributed by brebook publishing software
(www.brebook.com)

John Cordy Jeaffreson

The Real Lord Byron - New Views of the Poet's Life

THE REAL LOR[D BYRON]

NEW VIEWS OF THE [LIFE OF LORD BYRON]

BY

JOHN CORDY JEAF[FRESON]

AUTHOR OF

'A BOOK ABOUT THE CLERGY,' 'A [BOOK ABOUT DOCTORS,']

'A BOOK ABOUT LAW[YERS,']

&c. &c.

IN TWO VOLU[MES]

VOL. I.

LONDON:

HURST AND BLACKETT, PUB[LISHERS,]

13 GREAT MARLBOROUGH STREET.

1883.

LONDON:
Printed by STRANGEWAYS & SONS, Tower Street, Upper St. Martin's Lane.

LONDON:
Printed by STRANGEWAYS & SONS, Tower Street, Upper St. Martin's Lane.

CONTENTS.

CHAPTER I.

Byron's Temper—His Personal Characteristics—His Freedom from Aristocratic Insolence—His Early Friendships—Homage to Rank—Leigh Hunt's Malice—Familiar Pride.

CHAPTER II.

Mediæval Buruns—Sir John the Little with the Great Beard—Filius Naturalis—Thoroton's 'Nottinghamshire'—Elizabeth Halghe's Slip—Knight of the Bath—The Byron Barony—Byronic Fecundity and Longevity—Thomas Shipman's Patron—The Byron-Chaworth Duel—The Berkeley Strain—Taste for the Fine Arts.

CHAPTER III.

Admiral Byron—'Foul-Weather Jack'—Mad Jack Byron—The Marchioness of Carmarthen (Lady Conyers)—Augusta Byron's Birth—Miss Gordon of Gight—The Poet's Birth—His Lameness.

CHAPTER IV.

Holles Street, Cavendish Square—Augusta's Grandmother—'Baby Byron'—Mad Jack in Scotland—Catherine Gordon's Characteristics—Mad Jack's Death.

CHAPTER V.

The Widow's Poverty—The Poet's Childhood—May Gray's Calvinism—Catherine Gordon's Treatment of her Boy—His Scotch Tutors—His Lameness—Banks of Dee—Heir Presumptive—Aberdeen Grammar School—The Fifth Lord's Death—Byron's First Love: Mary Duff—His Temper in Childhood—His Girlishness—'Auld Lang Syne.'

CHAPTER VI.

The Sixth Lord—His First Visit to Newstead—The Abbey—Tutor at Nottingham—Lavender, the Bone-setter—Dulwich Grove—Dr. Glennie—A Very Troublesome Mamma—Guardian and Ward—Byron's First Dash into Poetry—His Second Love; Margaret Parker—His Later Attachments—His Sensibility, Memory, and Imagination—Malvern Hills and Scotch Mountains.

CHAPTER VII.

Dr. Drury—'Good-bye, Gaby'—The Fat Boy—His Hatred and Love of Harrow—'All the Sports'—Cricket and Rebellion—Passionate Friendships—Girlish Sentimentality—Tender-hearted Harrovians—The Poet's Affection for his Schoolmaster—'The Butler Row'—'Little Latin and Less Greek'—Declamations—Lord Carlisle's ' Indeed !'

CHAPTER VIII.

Lady Holderness's Death—'Baby Byron'—His Sister Augusta—Her Plain Face and Sweet Nature—Life at Southwell—Mary Anne Chaworth—Matlock and Castleton—Annesley Hall—Who was Thyrza?—'The Dream'—Its Falsehood and Malice.

CHAPTER IX.

Despondency—Eddleston, the Chorister—Dr. William Lort Mansell—College Friends—Hobhouse on Byron's Nature—

viii   CONTENTS.

THE REAL LORD BYRON.

CHAPTER I.

MISCONCEPTIONS ABOUT BYRON.

Byron's Temper — His Personal Characteristics — His Freedom from Aristocratic Insolence — His Early Friendships — Homage to Rank — Leigh Hunt's Malice — Familiar Pride.

IN great things and small things it was Byron's lot to be misunderstood during his life, and misrepresented after his death. With the exception of the few, perhaps the few hundred, persons who, with sufficient discrimination for the task, have taken care to separate the few facts from the many fictions of his numerous biographers and the many facts from the few fictions of his published letters and journals, and out of the reliable data to make a memoir of him for themselves, the man is still almost as little known to the students of his poetry as he was to the people who on the eve of his withdrawal from England frowned at him in London drawing-rooms or murmured against him in the London streets.

After all that has been written about him, readers have still to learn the qualities of his temper, the real failings of his nature, the peculiarities of his manner, and even the most conspicuous points of his personal appearance. They have been taught to regard him as a man of mysteries, tortured by remorse for crimes too terrible for confession and guarding secrets too revolting for avowal ; whilst in simple truth he went through life from first to last with his heart and all its frailties upon his sleeve, and lived from boyhood to his last hour under glass, that, whilst it magnified all his faults, put all his virtues in miniature. With all his perverse and baneful delight in mystifying people about trifles, this man of mystery could not to save his life, or what was far dearer to him—his fame,—hold within his own breast a single secret that vexed it seriously. Inspired at times by vanity to make himself the enigma of his period, even in his most perplexing moods he was nothing more than a riddle to be solved by any one of ordinary shrewdness with a brain clear of romantic fancies. What marvellous stuff has been written of the stern and cruel spirit of the misanthrope, who with the sensibility and impulsiveness of the gentler sex could not in his softer moments see misery without weeping over it and seeking to relieve it ! Who has not been invited to ponder on the habitual melancholy of the man, who in his brighter time brimmed over with frolic, and even in the sadness of his closing years made the world ring with laughter, and delighted in practical jokes? Who has not heard of his gloomy brow, black locks, dark eyes, and club foot? And yet, his face was not more remarkable for the beauty of its features than for the brightness of its smiles ; his hair, light chestnut in childhood, never darkened to the deepest brown of auburn ; his eyes were grey-blue ; and he hadn't a club foot.

One of the fictions is that, valuing himself inordinately on his birth, he was less proud of the genius that gave us 'Childe Harold' and 'Don Juan,' than of the accidents that made him a Lord of the Upper House. Due in some measure to the biographers who, like Leigh Hunt and Tom Moore, could never lose sight of his patrician quality, this misconception of a nature, innocent of all such miserable weakness, is referable chiefly and in an equal degree to the simplicity and obsequiousness of the many readers, who would have honoured him for being an insignificant peer, even if they had not reverenced him for being a great poet. It is not usual for those, who plume themselves on their ancestral advantages, to attach themselves strongly to persons of inferior extraction. Though he may admit persons of plebeian birth to his intimacy, the noble, who is greatly prouder of his pedigree than his natural endowments, never fails to draw a line between the acquaintances who are beneath him and the friends who are his equals, and whilst cultivating the former for the entertainment they afford him, to give his warmest affection and perfect confidence only to those who are of his own order. With the single exception of Lord Clare, Byron's closest comrades were found in ranks something or greatly beneath his own.

There were times, doubtless, when Hobhouse was justified in thinking his friend gave too ready an ear to flatterers whom he should have kept at a distance. But there never was a time of his whole career when the particular insolence, that biographers are pleased to call 'pride of race,' precluded Byron from sympathising cordially with his social inferiors. In boyhood, whilst composing some of the weakest lines of the 'Hours of Idleness' to the honour of those 'mail-covered Barons who proudly to battle led their vassals from Europe to Palestine's plain' (ancestors, by the way, who are not known to have donned armour in the Crusades or set foot in the Holy Land), he cherished a romantic fondness for the son of one of his Newstead tenants. At Cambridge he conceived a similar affection for the college-chorister (Eddleston), of whom he wrote in his nineteenth year to Miss Pigot of Southwell, 'During the whole of my residence at Cambridge we met every day, summer and winter, without passing *one* tiresome moment, and separated each time with increasing reluctance.' Though they were gentlemen by birth, culture, taste and purpose, Hobhouse, Hodgson, Scrope Davies, Charles Skinner Matthews and the other members of his particular set at Trinity, were not the persons, to whom he would have attached himself, had he rated his descent at more than its proper worth. The pleasant terms on which he lived during his Cambridge vacations with the Bechers, the Pigots and the other modest gentry of a small provincial town, are evidence that the youthful peer was not so largely animated by a sense of his patrician magnificence, as some of his biographers would have us believe. In later time this aristocrat with all his overweening arrogance took for his peculiar intimate the son of a Dublin tradesman. Though the main purpose of his almost unpardonably spiteful book was to render Byron contemptible and ludicrous by magnifying his weaknesses, and putting them in the strongest and fiercest light, Leigh Hunt was held to truth on this matter by enmity that was even keener and more rancorous than his animosity against the author of 'Don Juan.' Smarting under the slights put upon him and the injury done him by the men who were of opinion that Byron would suffer in dignity and reputation from his connection with the Hunts, the author of 'Rimini' remarked in a vein scarcely consistent with his affectation of a republican superiority to aristocratic prejudices, 'The manner of such of his lordship's friends as I ever happened to meet with were in fact, with one exception, nothing superior to their birth . . . . It is remarkable (and, indeed, may account for the cry about gentility, which none are so given to as the vulgar) that they were almost all persons of humble origin; one of a race of booksellers; another, the son of a grocer; another, of a glazier; and a fourth, though the son of a baronet, the grandson of a linen-draper.'

Nor can it be fairly urged, though it has often been unfairly suggested, that Byron surrounded himself with men beneath him in rank, because they rendered deference to his social superiority, and fed him with flattery. Now and again sycophants approached him, as they never fail to approach men of eminence; now and again, in a season of weakness, he yielded more than he should have yielded to their addresses; but the weakness was always transient, and the ascendancy so gained over him was never lasting. Vehement in all things, Byron was especially vehement in his friendships; and despite all that may be urged to the contrary, on the strength of cynical flippancies uttered to astonish his hearers, and bitter words spoken or written under the spur of sudden resentments or the torture of exasperating suspicions, it may be averred stoutly that in choosing his friends and dealing with them, he was altogether controlled by his heart. As for the way in which his friends treated him, it is not more unjust than ludicrous to attribute subserviency to the men who were wont to criticise his writings severely in words spoken to his face, or letters sent to him through the post. Tom Moore certainly 'noble lords' and 'noble friends' him through six rather tedious volumes, in a fashion that to readers of the present day is not a little laughable and offensive. But in fairness to the biographer it should be remembered that what offends us in this matter was less due to the writer's idolatry of rank than to the etiquette of the period in which he figured as a man of fashion, and first warbler of aristocratic drawing-rooms. In the first twenty years of the present century, when rank was honoured at least verbally in a degree not easily imagined in these last twenty years of the same epoch, it was the mode of our grandfathers to seize every occasion to remind lords of their nobility. The Irish ballad-writer was not singular in this respect. Himself the heir of an ancient and dignified family, and a man whose way of living and thinking had altogether disqualified him for courtly service, Shelley — absolutely devoid of respect for mere conventional nobility — was no less careful to give Byron his title in the written page, and like the author of 'Lalla Rookh' refers to him in letters as his 'noble friend.' Had the author of 'The Cenci'

employed himself at Pisa in writing six small-octavo
volumes about his 'noble friend's' life and adventures, the performance would have contained almost
as many 'lords' and 'noble lords' and 'my noble
friends' as may be counted in Moore's occasionally
dishonest pages.

Whilst literature honoured peers in this obsolete
and curious fashion, and the world at every turn
bowed before hereditary rank far lower than it bowed
to rank of any other kind, it was not in the nature of
things that Byron should be indifferent to the distinction that, coming to him from his ancestors, made
him a personage before he had laid aside his Highland petticoats. Naturally it pleased the child to
listen to brave stories of the Byrons of olden time,
who may (for all any one can say) have led their
vassals to the Holy Land, and certainly might have
done so for pay or piety had they been so disposed.
On taking a poetic turn in his boyhood, it would
have been strange had he not written verses on the
four brothers who fell at Marston. Nor is it wonderful that, towards the close of his short career, when
art required of his pen the picture of a lordly English
home, he travelled in memory from his Italian vil-
legiatura to the old familiar abbey (from which
Childe Harold had so few years since set forth on his
pilgrimage) and sung again, tenderly as in former
days, but far more strenuously, of

> 'The gallant cavaliers, who fought in vain
> For those who knew not to resign or reign.'

This wholesome pride in his domestic annals peeps
forth now and then in all his writings, from his

earliest boyish verses to his last dying song, but
it never made him insolent or in any other way
foolish. Though it was powerless to save him from
many errors and much avoidable misery, he had, with
all his waywardness and perilous sensibility, too
liberal a store of 'saving common sense' to commit
the blunders of a pure simpleton. Possibly his arms
were set in Italy over his bed, in the manner described by Mr. Leigh Hunt, who records the unimportant fact in the spirit of a discharged valet. Fifty
years since beds of state were often. so adorned in
England, as well as Italy, just as spoons, and hall-
chairs and carriage-panels are still ornamented in like
manner by owners who have not gone crazy with
ancestral insolence. Though Hunt's malice inspires
him to reproduce a piquant story of the anger with
which Byron returned a box of pills to an apothecary,
because the packet was directed to 'Mr.' instead of
'Lord' Byron, the malice of five hundred detractors
would induce no discriminating reader to believe so
egregious and manifest a fabrication. If family
pride had been inordinately strong in Byron, he
would not have sold Newstead, for the sake of adding
a few hundreds yearly to an already sufficient income. Nor was the sentiment in him a peculiar and
distinguishing characteristic. In the fulness of its
force it was nothing more than a fair share of the
almost universal sentiment that causes many an
ordinary, undistinguished English gentleman to
resemble General Braddock of 'The Virginians,' in
being as proud of his no family in particular, as any
peer can well be of his particular family.

CHAPTER II.

Mediæval Buruns—Sir John the Little with the Great Beard—Filius Naturalis—Thoroton's 'Nottinghamshire'—Elizabeth Halghe's Slip—Knight of the Bath—The Byron Barony—Byronic Fecundity and Longevity—Thomas Shipman's Patron—The Byron-Chaworth Duel—The Berkeley Strain—Taste for the Fine Arts.

OTHER considerations discountenance the notion that the poet regarded his pedigree and the annals of his house with unqualified complacence. For though the Byrons of Newstead co. Notts, and Rochdale co. Lancaster, were a family from which a modest squire of George the Third's England might well have been proud to trace his descent, their annals were deficient in lustre, and their pedigree was not stainless. There are peerages and peerages,—those that contribute to our national glory, and those that are mere affairs of county history. There are peers whose several dignities are the memorials of their ancestors' achievements in the successive generations of successive centuries. There are also peers whose nobility, instead of growing in honour and gathering lustre from the flying decades, has acquired nothing but age from the time that has slowly obscured the services for which it was created. To say of the Byron barony that, on coming to the poet at the close of the last century, it was a specimen of this fruitless, leafless, lifeless nobility, is not to say all that could be urged to its discredit. It is recorded by his not invariably accurate biographers that Byron's school-fellows nick-named him 'the Old English Baron,' in derision of his practice of vaunting how superior his ancestral dignity was to modern creations of a higher grade. If he was guilty of such boastfulness, the boy knew strangely little about the matter.

Too old to be called a mushroom peerage, his dignity was far too young to be rated with ancient baronies. Given in 1643 by Charles the First to Sir John Byron, in acknowledgment of the knight's zeal and devotion, and in the hope that it would lure other gentlemen to their sovereign's standard, it had not completed the hundred and fifty-sixth year of its existence, when it devolved on Catherine Gordon's son; and it certainly had not grown in social esteem during its passage from its first to its sixth possessor.

Against the antiquity of the Nottinghamshire Byrons nothing can be urged, with the exception of a certain matter to which the reader's attention will be called in another minute. The poet may have had no better authority than his fancy and Collins's 'Peerage' for the precise number of his ancestors' manors when he wrote in Don Juan's '10th Canto,'

> ' .   .   .   .   . a sort of doomsday scroll,
> Such as the conqueror William did repay
> His knights with, lotting others' properties
> Into some sixty thousand new knights' fees.

> · ' I can't complain, whose ancestors are there,
> Erneis, Radulphus— eight-and-forty manors
> (If that my memory doth not greatly err)
> Were their reward for following Billy's banners:

> And though I can't help thinking 'twas scarce fair
>   To strip the Saxons of their *hydes*, like tanners ;
> Yet as they founded churches with the produce,
>   You'll deem, no doubt, they put it to a good use.'

But whilst there is sufficient evidence that the Byrons came from Normandy in William's train, it is certainly 'as true as ever truth hath been of late' that Erneis de Burun got from the Arch-Invader a grant of lands in Yorkshire and Lancashire, and that Ralph with same surname found his proper share of real estate in Nottinghamshire. Nothing more can be told of this pair of rather mythical adventurers. Nor is history much more communicative respecting those of their descendants who were the first Byrons to acquire possessions in Derbyshire, and in later time (under Edward the First) yet more land in Rochdale co. Lancaster. Save that they were great land-holders, little is known of these fortunate Byrons during the next eight or nine generations. If any of them went to Palestine they missed the poet to celebrate their achievements until the dawn of the present century, when all their descendant could say of them was that they went thither, arrayed and attended in the manner already mentioned. Now and again one of the broad-acred clan shows himself for a moment, and then passes from the cognizance of history. The name appears in the records of the siege of Calais under our third Edward. Byrons fought at Cressy, and a Byron was at Bosworth on Richmond's side. From the general silence of the chroniclers about their doings it is not unfair to assume that these descendants of Ralph and Erneis were more intent on keeping their old lands, and adding to the number of their manors, than on winning new honours. And this inference from their historic unobtrusiveness is countenanced by their good fortune in retaining their acres in their hands and keeping their heads on their shoulders, in those troublous times that were so disastrous to adventurous men and ambitious families. Anyhow it is noteworthy how much oftener a Byron is mentioned in connection with a stroke of peaceful acquisitiveness than with an essay of martial daring. Their good fortune in getting and keeping was, however, coming to an end when, on the suppression of the religious houses, Sir John Byron—styled more familiarly and picturesquely ' Sir John the Little with the Great Beard '—received from Henry the Eighth a grant of the church and priory of Newstead : a property that after remaining for something less than three centuries in the hands of the Byrons passed by sale and purchase from the poet to his former schoolmate, Colonel Wildman. With this parting benefaction, fortune seems to have turned her back on the family who had enjoyed her favour for so many years, whilst doing so little to deserve it. Hitherto they had been rich and undistinguished. Henceforth they went to ruin and nobility.

Had Sir John the Little with the Great Beard either inherited or acquired an hereditary dignity, the honour would not have passed from him to his son, for the simple and sufficient reason that this son— through whom the poet and the five preceding Lords Byron traced their descent from the Norman Buruns —was a bastard. On this point there is no uncertainty. The record of the Herald's visitation of the County of Lancaster (1567 A.D.) leaves no room for doubt on this matter.   Here is what the Elizabethan record says of Sir John the Little with the Great Beard, the poet's direct lineal ancestor :—

'S^r. John Byron of Clayton aforesayd Knight, sonne and heire to S^r. Nycholas, maried to his firste wiefe Isabell daughter to Peter Shelton of Lynne in Norfolke, and by her had no yssue.   After · the said S^r. John maried to his second Wiefe Elizabethe daŭr to W^m. Costerden of Blakesley in Com Lanc and Wydowe to George Halghe of Halghe Com Lanc Gent, and by her hathe yssue John Byron, his eldest sonne and heire *filius naturalis*.   John Byron of Clayton in Com Lanc ar, sonne and heire by deade of gifte to Sir John Byron knt., maried Alyce daughter to Sir Nycholas Strelley of Strelley, &c.'

This is explicit and altogether devoid of ambiguity.   Sir John Byron, the great-grandfather of the first Lord Byron, was of illegitimate birth ; and the Norman blood on which the poet unquestionably reflected with complacence, though never with the absurd pride attributed to him by his biographers, was tainted with the defilement of bastardy, — a matter of no moment to the physiologist : but a matter of high moment to churchmen, heralds, and lawyers, and to all persons who accept the doctrine of churchmen or the sentiment of heralds.

Though he is not in possession of the facts that countenance his opinion, Dr. Karl Elze (Byron's German biographer, and the best of all the poet's biographers) declares it inconceivable that the author of ' Childe Harold ' was ignorant of this serious defect of his Norman pedigree.   On the other hand, Dr. Elze's anonymous English translator insists that

Byron may be presumed to have been ignorant of a circumstance that was mentioned in no Book of the Peerage or other genealogical work published during his life. Hence the translator argues that the poet should be acquitted of the meanness and imposture of vaunting his Norman blood, whilst he was well aware of its defilement, and of its consequent inability to bring him honour or estate from any of his ancestors preceding the son of Sir John the Little with the Great Beard. It happens, however, that this disqualifying incident of the Byron lineage is alluded to by Thoroton in the 'History of Nottinghamshire' (1677 A.D.), a work that certainly was not unknown to the poet, and probably afforded him his earliest knowledge of the main features of his ancestral story, and even his first acquaintance with those prime heroes of his house—Erneis and Radulphus. In Thoroton's notice of the Nottinghamshire Byrons, it is observed with quaint caution and delicacy that Sir John the Little with the Great Beard took to him a second wife, 'on whom he begot (soon enough) Sir John Byron of Newstede, who married Alice, the daughter of Sir Nicholas Strelley, of Strelley.' On reading the bracketed words, Byron could not fail to see their meaning. If he needed further enlightenment, he could have obtained it from his lawyer, who was well aware that instead of holding Newstead by inheritance from Sir John the Little with the Great Beard, his client inherited it from Alice Strelley's husband who acquired the estate by *deed of gift* from his father, from whom he could, as a bastard, have inherited nothing. Or the poet might have gained the needful information from the officers of the Heralds' College, his

neighbours of the county, or the curate of Hucknall-
Torkard.   In Nottinghamshire there were scores of
people capable of informing him of the matter that
was no secret.   If the Newstead Byrons of Charles the
Second's time were unaware of the blemish in their
pedigree before 1677, none of the family can be suspected of the same ignorance after the publication of
Thoroton's Nottinghamshire—a book to be found in
every library of the county.

Whilst he is right in maintaining that Byron
cannot have been ignorant of this dark page of his
familiar history, Dr. Elze errs in imagining that the
poet was meanly sensitive and discreditably reticent
on the subject.   Byron was not the man to attach
undue importance to sacerdotal sanction of any kind.
Had he lost an estate or a dignity through Sir John's
libertinism, he would have thought himself unfortunate, and spoken angrily of his ancestor's morals.
Of course he would have preferred a stainless roll.
But it was not in his nature to trouble himself
seriously about such an accident, or to think less
honourably of himself because one of his remote ancestors loved his wife something too soon, and sought
the priest's blessing on their union something too late
for decorum.   Instead of reflecting upon it from the
priest's point of view, or the herald's point of view,
he regarded his Norman descent from the physiologist's stand-point, which was not affected by the
naughty behaviour of Madam Elizabeth Halghe *née*
Costerden (or *Constantine*, as the lady's maiden surname is spelt in Thoroton's book).   It was enough
for him to know or fancy that the pluck, and energy,
and chivalric sentiment of the Norman Burons had

come to him through twenty or more generations. It was enough for him to know that Alice Strelley's husband was his 'father's son.' Of course he was not perpetually calling attention to the awkward affair. When he talks of his pedigree, a man is under no obligation to proclaim its blemishes, or speak of the black sheep of the family. Thus far Byron may have been, and was reticent ; but so far was he from trying to conceal under falsehood a matter that was no secret to the antiquaries of Nottinghamshire, and all persons curious in aristocratic genealogies, he could allude to the affair with lightness and pleasantry in pages written for the amusement of any one who cared to peruse them. Few persons will question that Elizabeth Halghe's slip and its consequences were in his mind when, after condensing his view of Catherine the Great's character and conduct into one of the most pungent and notorious couplets of 'Don Juan,' he wrote :—

> ' But oh, thou grand legitimate Alexander !
>   *Her son's son*, let not this last phrase offend
> Thine ear, if it should reach—and now rhymes wander
>   Almost as far as Petersburgh, and lend
> A dreadful impulse to each loud meander
>   Of murmuring Liberty's wide waves, which blend
> Their roar even with the Baltic's—so you be
> *Your father's son, 'tis quite enough for me.*
>
> To call men love-begotten, or proclaim
>   Their mothers as the antipodes of Timon,
> That hater of mankind, would be a shame,
>   A libel, or whate'er you please to rhyme on :
> But people's ancestors are history's game ;
>   And if one lady's slip should leave a crime on
> All generations, I should like to know
> What pedigree the best would have to show ?'

The sixteenth century did not end before the Nottinghamshire Byrons had felt the annoyances, if not the humiliations of pecuniary embarrassment. After living at Newstead with profuseness and ostentation, Alice Strelley's husband left a mortgaged estate and costly establishment to his heir, who was made a Knight of the Bath on the occasion of James the First's coronation. 'I do therefore advise you,' the Earl of Shrewsbury wrote to the young man, immediately after his father's death, 'that so soon as you have, in such sort as shall be fit, finished your father's funerals, to dispose and disperse that great household, reducing them to the number of forty or fifty at the most, of all sorts ; and, in my opinion, it will be far better for you to live for a time in Lancashire than in Notts, for many good reasons that I can tell you when we meet, fitter for words than writing.' Being good, this advice was probably not taken. Young men are apt to think lightly of counsel supported by sound reasons. Lancashire was further than Newstead from the Court where the Knight of the Bath had friends and hopes of preferment. At Rochdale the young man would be amongst comparative strangers ; at Newstead he was surrounded by friends who had known him from boyhood. It may, therefore, be taken for granted that the new Chief of the Byrons was slow to act on the Earl's suggestions of prudence, and never acted on them with resoluteness and perseverance. Anyhow, it is certain that the estate, which came to the Knight of the Bath burdened with mortgages and liabilities, passed to his heir under still more disadvantageous conditions ; and that when troubles grew and thickcned about Charles the First, troubles were also growing and thickening about the Byrons, who could barely pay their own rather stately way, on being invited to raise money as they best could for the king's use, and help him with their swords and men to prostrate his enemies.

For staking heavily on the Crown, and venturing their all in its service, the Cavaliers of Newstead were rewarded with impoverishment and a peerage. It would have been better for them if they had received only the former part of the reward, and missed the barony, that was only an incumbrance to them in their fallen fortunes. Without their nobility they might have recovered from their poverty; but with it, as things went in the later half of the seventeenth century, they were doomed to go from bad to worse; and when it has gone half the way to ruin, nobility usually finishes the journey. The Byrons were singularly unfortunate when once Fortune, after befriending them so long, deserted them for ever. Crippled with a peerage they scrambled on for something more than a century and a half, to be broken up and extinguished by a man of rare genius—the only man of genius they ever produced. The poet killed the family of which he was abundantly proud. There is still a Lord Byron; for generations to come there will doubtless be gentlemen and gentlewomen of the name figuring in the peerage, and playing minor parts on the social stage; but for all practical purposes the family perished, territorially and historically, with the man who made it famous.

The first Lord Byron having died without male issue, the barony went to his brother, whose long epitaph, telling nearly all one knows or wants to know about him, is still to be read in Hucknall-Torkard Church, where the poet was buried, after the Dean's refusal to give him sleeping-room in Westminster Abbey. One of the poet's quite erroneous notions about his own people was that they had nothing to do with longevity or livers. 'The Byrons,' he used to say, 'die early and have no livers.' Another of his fancies about them was that they were not prolific—a failing for which he used to console himself by reflecting that the fiercer and nobler animals had few cubs. The family had, upon the whole, sound livers and big broods of babies; and its members went to the proverbial threescore and ten years and upwards, like the men and women of other families, when they steadily eschewed late hours and excess in drink. On all these points he was mistaken. Byron himself had a good liver till he destroyed it, and it certainly was due to no constitutional weakness that he was not the father of a numerous family. The second lord of the family is an example that it was not impossible for a Byron to live long and beget a numerous progeny; for he had ten children by his first wife, and survived his seventy-third year, after 'repurchasing part of the ancient inheritance' of the seven Byrons (himself and his six brothers), who 'faithfully served Charles the First in the Civil War, suffered much for their loyalty, and' (the epitaph adds with some obscurity of expression) 'lost all their present fortune.' This worthy gentleman's eldest son, who became the third Lord Byron, is chiefly memorable for having written some execrably bad verses to his poetical friend,

Thomas Shipman, and for being the nobleman, whose marriage with a daughter of the Viscount Chaworth was accountable for his famous descendant's consanguinity with Mary Chaworth. If this Lord Byron was not a foolish and stupid person, his wretched doggerel in Shipman's 'Carolina or Loyal Poems' (1683) does him gross injustice. The fourth lord does not seem to have been a man of brilliant parts or any force of character ; but he played with the fine arts, and together with other children he begat two sons, who in very different ways distinguished themselves enough to be much talked about,—the fifth Lord Byron who killed his cousin and neighbour, Mr. Chaworth, in a duel of so singular a kind, that he was tried for wilful murder by his peers, who acquitting him of that gravest offence, found him guilty of nothing worse than manslaughter ; and Admiral John Byron, the hardy and daring sailor, to whose misadventures at sea the poet referred in the familiar lines of the 'Epistle' to his sister, Augusta:—

> 'A strange doom is thy father's son's, and past
> Recalling, as it lies beyond redress ;
> Reversed for him our grandsire's fate of yore,—
> He had no rest at sea, nor I on shore.'

. In the remarkable · letter, which he wrote at Genoa to Monsr. Coulmann in July 1823, shortly before his departure for Greece, the poet observed, 'As to the Lord Byron, who killed Mr. Chaworth in a duel, so far from retiring from the world, he made the tour of Europe, and was appointed Master of the Staghounds after that event, and did not give up society until his son had offended him by marrying in a manner contrary to his duty. So far from feeling any remorse for having killed Mr. Chaworth, who was a fire-eater (spadassin), and celebrated for his quarrelsome disposition, he always kept the sword which he used on that occasion in his bedchamber, where it still was *when he died.*' From these statements, the accuracy of which has never been questioned, it appears that the fracas and subsequent trial did not cause the survivor of the two combatants so much discredit as successive writers have represented; and that had he lived with ordinary prudence and decency during the subsequent three-and-thirty years of his time in this world, no great amount of posthumous obloquy would have been put upon him for the affair, that created prodigious noise and excitement at the time of its occurrence.

In fairness to a man, who has no especial title to charitable consideration, it may be admitted that notwithstanding its irregularity and several suspicious circumstances, the fatal duel would not have justified society in sending the survivor to Coventry. The blame seems from the evidence to have been equally divided. The quarrel arose out of a trivial dispute — no uncommon thing in duels. Both of the combatants were so quick-tempered and vehement in passion, that they may be presumed to have been alike captious and offensive. As to the statement that Lord Byron thrust his adversary into the fatal room, Mr. Chaworth was not a man to be pushed about like a little boy. He entered the room, and entered it with the intention of fighting. The absence of seconds and the darkness of the chamber, lit with only a single candle, were features of the case to be regarded as matters for which the enemies were alike accountable.   Lastly, the duel was fought with swords, Mr. Chaworth being well known to be a much better swordsman than his antagonist.   The first impression that Lord Byron took his adversary at a disadvantage, and slew him in a dark corner without warning, was removed by the evidence.   In short, it was a case of two practised duellists flying at one another in the fierceness of rage, begotten of much wine and mutual insolence.   Had Lord Byron fallen, there would have been an outcry against Mr. Chaworth, whose superior swordsmanship would, in that case, have been produced in testimony that he pushed the quarrel to an immediate issue, in order to fight with the weapon of which he was a consummate master.

But though he was less culpable in this ugly business than people have been led to imagine, the fifth Lord Byron deserved the evil fame that covered him in his old age as with a garment, and still clings to him, though he has been entombed for more than eighty years.   A morose husband, tyrannical father, hard landlord and harsh master, he was detested by the peasantry of Nottinghamshire, who spoke of him habitually as the 'wicked Lord Byron,' and sincerely believed there was no enormity of crime of which he was incapable in his darkest and most vindictive moods.   Of course, things were said of him that on inquiry were found to be untrue.   But when due allowance has been made for exaggeration, it is certain that in his closing years his nature was detestable and his position pitiable.

He did not, as rumour averred, shoot his coachman in a sudden frenzy of rage, and then throw the man's dead body into the carriage, whilst Lady Byron was seated in it.   He did not, as it was reported, throw his wife into one of the Newstead ponds with the purpose of drowning her ; but he drove her from Newstead by ill-usage ; and when she had fled from her proper home, he called to her vacant place a common woman who was styled ' Lady Betty ' by the satirists of the village.   His solitude, even to the last, was not so complete as successive writers have represented, for his niece, Mrs. Leigh (General Leigh's wife), never ceased to visit him ; but the Nottingham-shire nobility avoided him, and it was seldom that any of the minor gentry of the county called upon him.   Having quarrelled with his heir for marrying a cousin whom he loved, this curious old reprobate let the Abbey go to ruin, and cut down the timber on the estate.   Always in straits for money, though he spent little on hospitality, he replenished his empty exchequer by making an illegal sale of Rochdale property, to the serious injury of his successor. After losing his son and his son's son, the miserable old man transferred something of his aversion for them to ' the little boy at Aberdeen,' as he invariably styled the future poet and sixth lord.   There are grounds for the opinion that he was entreated to con-tribute something towards the charges of the educa-tion of this little boy at Aberdeen.   If the prayer was made, it was unsuccessful ; for the old man never sent a doit to the widow, who, rearing the child in the poverty to which a Byron had reduced her, lived through a hard time at Aberdeen.   And when at last this little boy came to Newstead, in the company of his irascible mother and pious Scotch nurse, he found the

Abbey in ruins and its only tenantable rooms empty of furniture. And yet the 'old lord,'—the 'wicked old Lord Byron'—had to the end of his wicked existence one or two innocent pastimes. Having built mock forts about the lake in his park, and put a fleet of toy gun-boats on the water, he used to amuse himself, like the big, hoary-headed baby that he was, with mock-fights of a naval character—the toy-ships firing away at the forts, which returned the fire in gallant style. And when he was weary of this ridiculous game, the old man used to lie on the ground and gossip with the crickets, whom he loved far more than 'the little boy at Aberdeen.' When the crickets were troublesome, he used to whip them with a wisp of hay; and the crickets are said to have left the Abbey in a body, as soon as their one friend of human kind was dead, and never to have returned thither.

On the death (19th May, 1798) of this Lord of evil fame and miserable nature, 'the little boy at Aberdeen' became the sixth Lord Byron of Rochdale, co. Lancaster, the master of the dilapidated Abbey of Newstead, and the Hereditary (?) Chief of all the descendants of Erneis and Radulphus, when he was just ten years and four months of age, and when the Barony—that had not illustrated itself by winning a higher rank in the peerage—had been in existence just one hundred and fifty-five years.

The family was certainly an ancient one; but whilst houses may be eminent without being ancient, for families to be illustrious it is not enough that they should be old. Had the Byrons of Rochdale and Newstead possessed higher claims to reverence, the poet would have said less of their antiquity. With the single exception of Admiral John Byron (the fifth Lord's brother), who seems to have derived his pluck and devilry and delight in adventure from the Stratton Berkeleys, the Byrons. had lived in the land for upwards of seven hundred years without producing a man of conspicuous natural eminence. When the most favourable view is taken of the soldier and political partisan, who won the Barony from Charles the First, he is seen to be a person of merely respectable endowments. On a greater field, and under more auspicious circumstances, he might have figured in history as a considerable soldier ; for in addition to the fidelity, which is his strongest title to honourable recollection, he was well endowed with energy, courage, and common sense. But it would be simply ridiculous to rate him with men of genius.

So much arrant nonsense has been written about the poet and his remote forefathers by literary charlatans —whose only dispute amongst themselves turns on the question whether his genius should be referred altogether to his Norman extraction or should be regarded as the result of a felicitous fusion of Norman force and Celtic sensibility—it is well for readers to be assured how little countenance is lent to such fanciful theories by the history of his progenitors in this country. Till Byron's genius broke suddenly upon the world, and captivated it almost in a single hour, no one ever thought of looking to his peculiar people for any signal exhibition of intellectual power. In the whole peerage no family appeared less likely to produce a poet who would make a new period in the history of English literature. Not that the family was exceptionally wanting in refinement and taste. On the contrary, from Charles the Second's restoration the Newstead Byrons had taken an interest in letters and the fine arts. Though the third Lord's poetical performances were contemptible, his friendship for Thomas Shipman indicates a creditable concern for literature and its followers. The fourth Lord Byron inherited a taste for painting from his mother (a Chaworth), and produced some landscapes, which Sir William Musgrave reproduced in etching. One of this Lord's sons—Richard Byron, who took holy orders—has a modest niche in the Temple of Fame for copying Rembrandt's famous landscape of the 'Three Trees' so skilfully, that the copy was mistaken and bought by a connoisseur for the original work. And though the earlier book exposed him to charges of imaginative exaggeration, and even to a suggestion of inaccuracy on matters about which he was especially bound to be precisely truthful, Admiral Byron's famous 'Narrative' of his adventures on the coast of Patagonia, and his scarcely less famous 'Voyage round the World,' are performances of no common merit, and deserved, on literary grounds, to be favourite reading with the author's grandson, who, after throwing Don Juan on the sandy fringe of Haidée's charming island, says of the adventurer's troubles from shipwreck,—

> 'And need he had of slumber yet, for none
> Had suffered more—his hardships were comparative
> To those related in my grand-dad's "Narrative!"'

CHAPTER III.

BYRON'S NEAR ANCESTORS.

Admiral Byron—'Foul-Weather Jack'—Mad Jack Byron—The Marchioness of Carmarthen (Lady Conyers)—Augusta Byron's Birth—Miss Gordon of Gight—The Poet's Birth—His Lameness.

To argue that a man of the nineteenth century derives the strongest elements of his nature from a man of the eleventh century, because he is known to have descended from one of the knightly 'followers of Billy's banners,' without making any account of the influence of the twenty and more infusions of blood from other stocks, each of which must have modified, or at least should—in the absence of evidence to the contrary—be assumed to have modified the characteristics of the Norman progenitor; and to dress up this marvellous inference with much jargon about the 'influence of race,' is to play the part of a pedant without common sense, or of a fool with just a little learning, and no more.

Of two-thirds of the families with which Byron's ancestors in the direct male line intermarried, and from which some modifying influences must have come to the Byron nature, nothing is known or can be known. And even if one could obtain precise information respecting all these families, and more especially of the particular women of them who mated with Byrons, it would be impossible to say how far so many and various influences changed the moral and mental qualities, which passed. to his descendants from a Norman of whom nothing is known beyond his name, the number of his manors, and the fact that he took part in a great military movement. It will contribute more to the purpose of those, who would account for the peculiarities of the poet's temper and intellect, to examine the natures of his parents, his father's parents, and his grandfather's (Admiral Byron's) mother.

In marrying Frances, the second daughter of the fourth Baron Berkeley of Stratton, William the fourth Lord Byron took a wife who seems to have transmitted to his and her descendants the vehemence, and impulsiveness and waywardness which were characteristics of her race. It is certain that her descendants differed in these qualities from any earlier Byrons of whose tempers we have sure information. It makes also for the point to which these remarks tend, that Lady Byron's sister, Barbara, married John Trevanion of Caerhayes, Cornwall, and had by him a daughter, Sophia, who by her marriage with her first cousin, Admiral Byron, became the mother of that brilliant scapegrace, Jack Byron, and grandmother of the poet. It follows that Jack Byron of the Guards, who seduced the Marchioness of Carmarthen, and then despoiled Catherine Gordon of Gight, took the Berkeley blood and nature from both his parents, each of whom was the offspring of a Berkeley. It is more reasonable to refer the impulsiveness and vehemence of Jack Byron and of his son, the poet, to these ladies of the great House of Berkeley, than to account for those qualities of the father and son by reference to the absolutely unknown natures of Erneis and Radulphus of the eleventh century.

Greatly though they differed in several respects, there was a strong resemblance between Frances Berkeley's two sons,—the fifth Lord Byron and his brother, the Admiral. In the former, the Berkeley vehemence changed to violence, and in his later years degenerated into unsocial moroseness and malignity. In the latter, it was a generous fire that animating the sailor for a career of adventure was attended with a sweetness of disposition by no means uncommon in emotional natures. But in both brothers the Berkeley fire showed itself, burning with poisonous fume in the one, and blazing out cheerily in the other.

Fortunate on shore, John Byron was luckless at sea. It would be an exaggeration to say that he never went to sea without encountering disaster; for the affair of Chaleur Bay—when with three ships he destroyed three French ships of war, with twenty schooners, sloops, and other armed vessels,—was no less successful than brilliant. His 'Voyage of Discovery' accomplished its objects, in spite of unlooked-for difficulties. But on returning to England after his indecisive engagement with D'Estaing, in which he displayed more intrepidity than tactical adroitness, the sailor, whose significant nickname in the Navy was 'Foul-weather Jack,' had weathered more storms than any other Admiral of 'the Service.' Sailors and ministers being alike distrustful of unlucky men, it is possible the intrepid navigator's proverbial 'bad luck' was the reason why he was never employed again in the way of his profession, after his return from the West Indies in 1779. His biographers erred in supposing the Admiral never again desired active service.

If he did not *seek* employment, there is evidence he would gladly have taken another command, and suffered from chagrin at the Admiralty's neglect to offer him a ship. He was smarting under this disappointment in the spring of 1782, when the prospect of an immediate peace made him despair of ever again getting employment. Four years later the gallant and luckless sailor encountered a worse enemy to naval ambition than even the longest and most exasperating peace. On 10th April, 1786, he died in his sixty-third year, leaving two sons—John, who was the poet's father, and George-Anson, who distinguished himself in the Navy, and was the father of the poet's successor in the barony—together with three daughters, one of whom (Frances) married General Leigh (Colonel of the 20th Regiment of Infantry), whilst another (Juliana Elizabeth), by her marriage with the fifth Lord Byron's only son, became the mother of the heir-apparent to the barony, through whose untimely death at Corsica, in 1794, the poet succeeded to his place in the Peerage.

Like his uncle the wicked lord, and like his son the poet, the Admiral's eldest son John—nicknamed 'Mad Jack' by his brother-officers of the Guards—was the subject of many scandalous stories that originated in the malice and imaginative humour of gossip. As Byron justly remarked in his letter from Genoa to Monsieur Coulmann, 'it is not by "brutality" that a young officer of the Guards seduces and marries a marchioness, and marries two heiresses.' Instead of being remarkable for harshness and grossness, as posthumous scandal represented him, 'Mad Jack Byron' was a gentleman of elegant figure, charming address, and winning smile. Even to the last of his scarcely honourable days he retained much of the facial beauty that had distinguished him in his youth, and reappeared in the lovely lineaments of his only son. In her frequent fits of fury with her boy, Catherine Gordon used to upbraid him for being a Byron all over; and in her no less frequent fits of tenderness for him, she used to put hysterical kisses on the eyes that reminded her of his father. But though he was irresistible in drawing-rooms, by virtue of his riant beauty and musical joyousness, Mad Jack was from his boyhood a sad libertine, and, after falling into poverty, a pitifully mean fellow.

Educated first at Westminster School and then at a French military academy, where he learnt to prefer life in France to existence in England, he served with his regiment in America whilst a stripling, and on his return to London lost no time in winning the affection of the Marchioness of Carmarthen, the wife of the heir to the Dukedom of Leeds, to whom she had already given three children. At the beginning of this *liaison* with a woman whose beauty surpassed even her rank, and who had not completed her twenty-third year, John Byron was under age; his years numbering no more than twenty-two when he married the lady immediately after her divorce from her first husband in May 1778, the year in which she became Lady Conyers (Baroness Conyers, in her own right), on the death of her father, the fourth Earl of Holderness. After resting for a brief while at the lady's house near Doncaster, where the poet was a visitor thirty-five years later, the young people went to France, to escape from English obloquy and English creditors. Never returning to her native country, after she left it under these painful circumstances, Lady Conyers died abroad in 1784—from her husband's cruelty, it was whispered in Mayfair : or, as the poet assured Monsieur Coulmann, from her imprudence in accompanying her husband to a hunt before she had completed her recovery from the accouchement which gave birth to Augusta (afterwards the Honourable Mrs. Leigh), the second, but only surviving, issue of her father's first marriage. Apart from rumour, there is no evidence that John Byron treated his first wife with harshness or neglect. Certainly he had good reason to wish her long life, for she had an estate for life that yielded her 4000*l.* a-year—a revenue that enabled him to pass his time pleasantly in the gayest and, in the last century, perhaps the cheapest capital of Europe. On her death, the young man of luxurious tastes and considerable debts was penniless.

Returning to England in search of an heiress, whose possessions would extricate him from his pecuniary difficulties, he found one at Bath—not so rich as he could have wished, but still rich enough for his immediate requirements. In money, land, and bank-shares this heiress (Miss Gordon, of Gight, in Aberdeenshire) had about 23,000*l.*, a fortune that rumour had doubled. To the widower, only twenty-eight years old at the time of his wife's death, Miss Gordon's actual and unexaggerated estate would have seemed so inadequate to his necessities, that it is difficult to believe he would have embarrassed himself with so unattractive and uncongenial a companion had he not, at the time of marrying her, been under a misconception as to the magnitude of her possessions. Drowning men, however, catch at straws; and 'Mad Jack Byron' may have persuaded himself that 23,000*l.* would, with clever management, put him in easy circumstances. Anyhow he married the lady in March, 1786—*not* at Bath where Moore believed the marriage to have been celebrated; *but* in Scotland whither she was followed or attended by her suitor from the fashionable resort of idlers and invalids. If there was an elopement in the affair, it must have been a merely formal elopement from the Somerset wells, that was arranged to gratify the lady's desire for a romantic passage into matrimony, and also to preclude inconvenient demands for a nuptial settlement of her property; for when she determined to give them to Captain Byron, Miss Gordon was mistress of her person and worldly goods. Her father having already committed suicide, there was no guardian with power to stay her on the way to ruin as she was of age. In Medwin's book, Byron is said to have spoken of his father's elopement with Miss Gordon; but if the poet did not talk loosely to Medwin, the author of the ' Conversations ' was a strangely bad listener and careless reporter. The marriage took place in Scotland, and early in the summer following the date of the matrimonial contract, 'Mad Jack' carried his bride to Paris and Chantilly, where they soon made away with the 3000*l.* which the heiress possessed in ready money at the time of the wedding, and the 600*l.* obtained from the sale of her two shares of the Aberdeen Banking Company. Just one year and ten months after her marriage, Catherine Gordon Byron, having returned from France to Great Britain *viâ* Boulogne and Dover, was in Holles Street, Cavendish Square, with a babe in her arms, and heaviness at her heart. During her brief stay in that street she was for days together without money in her purse. Since her marriage she had discovered that her husband had married her only for the sake of her fortune ; and in Holles Street she learnt that when the needful arrangements had been made with his creditors, she would be left with only a pittance, barely sufficient for the subsistence of herself, her husband, the infant in her arms, and his child by Lady Conyers.

Hitherto there has been a question whether the poet was born at Dover, or Holles Street, Cavendish Square, London. That his sister believed him to have been born in London is shown by the inscription of the mural tablet which she placed to his memory in the chancel of Hucknall-Torkard Church; and all the other witnesses to the point, who agree with the inscription, may be presumed to have gained their information directly or indirectly from her. But Dallas—the author of ' Recollections of Lord Byron ' (1824), who might be thought more likely than the Honourable Mrs. Leigh to have known the truth of the matter—had a strong opinion that Catherine Gordon's boy first saw the light at Dover. Mr. Dallas received the lady at his house in Boulogne when she was on her way to England ; and he certainly was not without grounds for his impression that she was taken with pains whilst crossing the Channel, and was delivered of her child at the English sea-port. It is however certain that Dallas was mistaken, for there exists conclusive evidence that the birth took place in London, and that Mrs. Byron was attended at her accouchement by the famous surgeon, John Hunter, who, before her departure from London for Aberdeenshire, gave the young mother instructions respecting the kind of shoe her child should wear on coming to need shoes. At a later date (towards the end of 1790, or in an early month in 1791), Hunter wrote to Dr. Livingstone, of Aberdeen, on the same subject; but either through misapprehension on the part of the Scotch doctor, or through the inexpertness of a Scotch shoemaker, the result of the directions was so unsatisfactory that it became necessary for Mrs. Leigh (General Leigh's wife)—then living at 39 Brompton Row, Knightsbridge—to call upon the London surgeon for more precise guidance. This application to Hunter for further counsel was in May 1791; and when a shoe had been made in accordance with his orders, Mrs. Leigh sent it to her sister-in-law in North Britain.

And here it may be remarked that the lameness, which occasioned the poet so much discomfort of body and mental distress from his childhood to his last days, was due to the contraction of the tendon Achilles of each foot, which, preventing him from putting his heels to the ground, compelled him to walk on the balls and toes of his feet. Both feet may have been equally well formed, save in this sinew, till one of them was subjected to injudicious surgery; the right being, however, considerably smaller than the left. Instead of being congenital, the slight contraction of the left tendon Achilles may have been the result of the patient's habit of stepping only on the fore part of the foot, so as to accommodate its movements to the action of the other extremity. But though it may not have existed in the earlier years of his childhood, the contraction of the comparatively normal sinew was noticed by Trelawny when he made the *post mortem* examination of both extremities at Missolonghi. The right tendon, however, was so much contracted that the poet was never able to put the foot flat upon the ground ; always using for it a boot made with a high heel, and fitted with a padding inside under the heel of the foot. This foot was also considerably distorted so as to turn inwards—a malformation that may have been caused altogether by the violence with which the foot was treated by the less intelligent of the boy's surgical operators, and more especially by Lavender, the Nottingham quack.

It is therefore manifest that Byron's lameness was of a kind far more afflicting to the body and vexatious to the spirits than the lameness of such an ordinary club-foot as disfigured Sir Walter Scott. With a club-foot to plant firmly on the ground, Byron could have taken all the bodily exercise needful for the natural correction of his morbid tendency to fatten. He would have moved about awkwardly, and to the derision of his least generous playmates ; but he would not have been debarred from participation in all of their manlier sports. Instead of musing or moping for hours together on the famous tombstone, he would have distinguished himself in the Harrow playing-grounds at cricket and even at leap-bar. A few years later, instead of standing sadly in the corners of London ball-rooms, eyeing enviously the young men whirling round with fair partners, he would have fatigued himself in the gallopade and delighted in the waltz, which he affected to abhor, as unfit alike for men and women. Better still, instead of taking most of his out-door exercise in the lazy yacht or easy saddle, he would have been a bold climber of mountains.

To the question why Byron did not bear his lameness as bravely and cheerily as Scott bore his lameness, one answer is, that whilst the Scotch poet suffered from nothing worse than a club-foot, the author of 'Childe Harold' endured a lameness far more trying to health and spirits. Had Sir Walter been constrained to pick his way through life on his toes, 'hopping' about like a bird (to adopt Leigh Hunt's way of sneering at a comrade's grievous afflic-tion), he would certainly have been less happy. And had Byron been able to walk about like a man, albeit with a club-foot, he would have been less often stricken with melancholy and moved to breathe the fierce breath of anger.

CHAPTER IV.

MORE OF 'MAD JACK BYRON.'

Holles Street, Cavendish Square — Augusta's Grandmother — 'Baby Byron' — Mad Jack in Scotland — Catherine Gordon's Characteristics — Mad Jack's Death.

THAT Captain and Mrs. Byron returned from France to England without having fully realised the magnitude and urgency of their pecuniary difficulties may be inferred from the character of the quarter in which they took a furnished house on their arrival in London for a term of three months, ending on the 8th of April, 1788. Another indication, that the lady, on coming to Holles Street, still regarded herself as a gentlewoman, who might spend money freely, is found in the engagement of the first surgeon of his time to attend at her accouchement. Before she left the street, the poor lady had reason to take a different view of her position. Her land and all its appurtenances having been sold during her residence in France, Captain Byron's creditors clamoured for a speedy settlement of their claims on the money coming to him from the sale of his wife's estate; when, instead of sending him the means of pacifying these eager claimants, the Scotch lawyers were even reluctant to remit enough money for his current expenses. Had it not been for his sister, Mrs. Leigh,

who gave him more of her pin-money than she could
well afford, 'Mad Jack' would have been without the
guineas needful for his simple amusements about
town. On coming from the seclusion of her chamber,
poor Mrs. Byron, when she was not nursing her
baby, found her principal employment in writing
letters to her Edinburgh lawyer. Possibly the writer
to the 'Signet' was moved by his client's pitiful epistles
to push matters forward to a final arrangement, but
to the miserable gentlewoman he seemed to act with
exasperating slowness ; and before she received the
remittance which enabled her to journey northwards,
she had been for the greater part of a fortnight without a penny in her pocket.

Before she returned to her proper country, the
burden that had come to her from her own want of
prudence was lightened by the Dowager-Countess of
Holderness (Captain Byron's whilom mother-in-law),
whose blue eyes and golden hair, with a score of other
charms beseeming 'the belle of the Hague,' had won
an English coronet for her nearly half a century
since, when Lord Holderness was the British Pleni-
potentiary to the States-General of the United Pro-
vinces. At Chantilly little Augusta had lived under
her father's roof, and she was one of the party entertained by Mr. Dallas at Boulogne, when he had occasion to observe that Mrs. Byron would soon become
a mother. But as the time neared for her brother's
appearance on the scene, little Augusta (in her fifth
year) was packed off to stay with her grandmother,
who had tender yearnings for the child, though little
reason to like the child's father. And now, to Captain Byron's lively contentment, the Countess de-

clared her wish to undertake the child's nurture, and
to provide for her.   Catherine Gordon must also have
received the Countess's proposal with satisfaction.
In justice, however, to the gentler side of a nature by
no means altogether loveable, it should be recorded
of Mrs. Byron that she could not surrender unregret-
fully the child who had been her best companion
many a day at Chantilly, when her husband was
amusing himself in Paris.   There was another reason
why Mrs. Byron cared for the child, whom she had
nursed in France with exemplary tenderness and devotion through a severe illness, that for several days
promised to end in death.   Thirteen years later, when
Augusta and her stepmother came together again,
there was small need for Mrs. Byron to remind her
husband's daughter of this passage of her childhood;
for Byron's sister had never forgotten the service of
love.   Still it was not in the nature of things for
Catherine Gordon to resist the Countess's proposal.
So the brother and sister, whose mutual love is recorded in deathless song, went different ways—
'Baby Byron' (as Augusta used to call him after
he had risen to universal celebrity) journeying slowly
northwards to the land of mountain and mist,
whilst she went to the roof of the Countess,
who, growing mightily fond of her grandchild, used
to tell her acquaintances, in her own peculiar
Dutch-English, that the girl would be her 'residee-
legatoo.'

Though she no longer possessed a patch of land in
the county, Catherine Gordon was 'going home' as
she travelled towards Aberdeenshire; but to her
husband (when a year and half later he set out to

join his wife in Scotland), the journey to Aberdeen where Mrs. Byron after staying for a while with some of her relations, had settled herself in lodgings, was a journey into exile. It was a dismal prospect for the man of luxurious tastes, who, more French than English in his appearance and habits, delighted in the sunshine and mirth and vintages of the land, where he received the more important part of his earlier training ; the land that, instead of crying 'Fie!' at his naughtiness, had welcomed him all the more cordially for having carried a peeress in her own right away from her lawful husband. In France he had lived intimately with the great Marshal Biron, who hailed him as a cousin. In Paris his elegance, beauty, gallantry, horsemanship, had won the admiration of *salons*, whose wits, men and women alike, held precisely his own views on questions of religion and morals. The gentleman shuddered at the imagination of what lay before him in Scotland—a land of bad cookery and worse manners, of bleak winds and dismal skies, of boors and fanatics. He shuddered again as he mentally compared the beauty and cleverness and gaiety of Lady Conyers, with the homely aspect, provincial style and intolerable temper of Mrs. Byron, to whom he was going reluctantly ; the peeress who had 4000*l.* a-year, with the petty laird's daughter whose fortune had dwindled to a pitiful 3000*l.*

The comparison would have been unfavourable to Mrs. Byron had he compared her with a woman of ordinary attractiveness. For though she had royal blood in her veins, and belonged to the superior branch of the Gordons, it would not have been easy to find a gentlewoman whose person and countenance were less indicative of ancestral purity. A dumpy young woman, with a large waist, florid complexion and homely features, she would have been mistaken anywhere for a small farmer's daughter or a petty tradesman's wife, had it not been for her silks and feathers, the rings on her fingers and the jewellery about her short, thick neck. At this early time of her career, she was not quite so graceless and awkward as Mrs. Cadurcis (in Lord Beaconsfield's 'Venetia'), but it was already manifest that she would be cumbrously corpulent on coming to middle age; and even in her twenty-fifth year she walked in a way that showed how absurdly she would waddle through drawing-rooms and gardens on the development of her unwieldy person. In the last century it was not uncommon for matrons of ancient lineage to possess little learning and no accomplishments; but Miss Gordon's education was very much inferior to the education usually accorded to the young gentlewomen of her period. Unable to speak any other language, she spoke her mother tongue with a broad Scotch brogue, and wrote it in a style that in this politer age would be discreditable to a waiting-woman. Though she was a writer of long epistles, they seldom contained a capital letter, or a mark of punctuation, to assist the reader in the sometimes arduous task of discovering their precise meaning; and though she could spell the more simple words correctly, when she was writing in a state of mental placidity, she never used her pen in moments of excitement, without committing comical blunders of orthography. To Captain Byron, however, the lady's temper was more grievous than her defects of person, breeding, and culture. It should, however, be remembered by readers, who would do her justice, that Mrs. Byron was by no means devoid of the shrewdness and ordinary intelligence of inferior womankind, and was capable of generous impulses to the persons, whom in her frequent fits of uncontrollable fury she would assail with unfeminine violence — and even with unnatural cruelty.

On the road to Aberdeen, where for his own gratification he could arrive none too late, Captain Byron paid a visit to one or two agreeable houses, and so long as he was the guest of hospitable lairds, who gave him the best wine of their cellars and the best sport of their domains, the man of pleasure found life in Scotland endurable, and could pay himself compliments on the address and philosophical cheerfulness with which he accepted the usages of a semi-barbarous people, and like a consummate man of the world accommodated himself to the habits and humours of his associates. But when the visits had all been paid, and the time came for him to settle down in an Aberdeen lodging, and live on oatmeal and inferior whiskey in the society of a wife, who was perpetually upbraiding him for having reduced her in so short a time from affluence to penury, he lost his gaiety, and showed his victim the sternest and meanest qualities of his nature. With proper sentiments of pride and honour, Mrs. Byron was bent on living within the income of 150*l.* a-year, still coming to her from the 3000*l.* in the hands of trustees — the income that was now the only certain means of subsistence for herself, her husband, her child, and the single servant, who whilst acting the part of nurse to the future poet, discharged also the duties of housemaid and cook. Captain Byron decided that, instead of filling himself with 'haggis,' he would at least dine daily as a gentleman of ancient descent and high fashion ought to dine. 'Supplies would soon be coming to him,' he said, 'from his kindred in the south, and his old friends in France; and in the meantime wine and meat must be bought for him on credit.' The altercations and noisier quarrels of such a husband and such a wife may be imagined. To escape from the woman, who scolded him from morning till night, he withdrew from her lodging at one end of Queen Street and took a lodging for himself at the other end of the same thoroughfare. Money coming to him soon afterwards from the relative, who had already helped him so many times, the Captain withdrew for a while from Aberdeen, to the sorrow even more than to the material relief of the wife who, overflowing with animosity against him when he was at hand, could still love him passionately when he was out of her sight.

A few months later, in 1790, he reappeared in Aberdeen, to wheedle his wife out of a little money that would enable him to get away to France. But Catherine Gordon (though she eventually yielded to his importunity) told him roundly that she had not a penny in her pocket, and that even if she had fifty guineas in hand she would not give him one of them. Perhaps this answer seemed to him a hint that a *single* guinea might still be squeezed out of her. Anyhow the man actually had the meanness to write to her, imploring her to give him a guinea—a begging letter that came in the course of years to the poet, who, preserving it as a curious domestic record, could still think of the writer with tenderness. It is certain that Captain Byron was not wanting in affectionateness to the little boy, who on one occasion shared his father's bed for a night. Whilst 'Mad Jack' and his wife were occupying separate lodgings in Queen Street, Aberdeen, he used to waylay the child and his nurse in their daily walks, so as to have the pleasure of playing with the little fellow. The poet's memory was very retentive of kindnesses rendered to him in childhood; and though imagination had doubtless much to do with his affectionate recollections of his father, there is no reason to think them *mere* fancies. 'I was not so young,' Byron said towards the end of his life, 'when my father died, but that I perfectly remember him.'

The poet, however, cannot have been more than three years old when he saw his father for the last time; for Captain Byron withdrew from Aberdeen at least as early as the first month of 1791, on obtaining the means—partly from his wife and partly from Mrs. Leigh—to fly to France beyond the reach of his creditors. A few months later he died at Valenciennes in his thirty-sixth year.

Conflicting accounts have been given of his death; one of them being that he died by his own hand, a statement that at least accords with the man's character and the desperate circumstances to which he brought himself by numerous acts of imprudence. To Harness, Byron more than once asserted that ' 'his father was insane, and killed himself;' but on coming to grounds for attributing the death to natural causes, Harness came to the astounding conclusion that the poet in so speaking said what he knew to be untrue, and in a mere freak of morbid humour 'calumniated the blood flowing in his veins.' The information which caused Harness to take this view of his friend's behaviour came to him, doubtless, directly or indirectly, from those members of the Byron family who were of opinion that Captain Byron died, as the phrase goes, 'in his bed,' and in the ordinary course of nature. Even if Byron told a wilful untruth in this matter, it is extravagant to charge him with thereby 'calumniating the blood in his own veins;' for some of the most amiable and altogether virtuous persons have gone mad and killed themselves. The gloomy misadventure may occur to-morrow to the wisest and mildest and best of living men. Byron's statement, true or untrue, was nothing more than a statement that his father died in a peculiarly mournful manner. But what is the evidence that the statement was discordant with fact? At the most, it can have been nothing more than the strong and reasonable opinion of certain persons that Captain Byron did *not* die by his own act.

But the strongest evidence on such a matter is sometimes illusory, and the reasonable conclusion from it erroneous. Many a man has committed suicide in such a manner, that he has expired in his bed, and that his death has been assigned sincerely to natural causes by his nearest kindred, and all the members of his household, ay, and by a coroner's jury specially appointed to ascertain the cause of death. Lastly, even if it could be shown that Captain Byron was not guilty of suicide, why should Byron be accused of falsehood in the matter? The poet of strong, at times morbidly strong, imagination, after long brooding over his father's melancholy story may well have come to a wrong conclusion about his death, and having once accepted the ghastly fancy for such fact, may have sincerely believed what he certainly said to Harness. The man, who was known throughout life as 'Mad Jack Byron,' may be presumed to have been a person whose eccentricity bordered upon insanity. This man of vehement feelings had fallen to a condition in which men of strong passions and unsettled faith are apt to meditate on self-murder as a means of escape from their humiliations and exasperating troubles. Going abroad with a few guineas in his purse—just enough money to keep him for a few weeks—he died in his thirty-sixth year. That he killed himself in despair was no unnatural opinion for his son to entertain long afterwards. It is a melancholy example of the injustice dealt out to Byron during his life and after his death, alike by his friends and his foes, that so amiable and worthy a gentleman as Harness could attribute falsehood to his friend, because his account of his father's way of dying was contradicted by persons who seemed to know the real truth of the matter. Surely Harness might have been content to charge his friend with nothing worse than mere morbid misconception, and to pity him for the sorrow that came to him from so dismal a fancy. It never seems to have occurred to Harness that, as the chief of his house, Byron might have had surer and fuller information about this doleful business than all the members of his family.

On the open question, whether 'Mad Jack Byron' died by his own hand, no opinion is here offered. At this distance from the event, the question is of no great moment to readers. But a very strong opinion is given that the poet did not utter those words to Harness in mere levity and wickedness, and that one of the causes of the melancholy that ever followed his joyous moods like a shadow was a conviction that the father, whom he recalled lovingly and pitied profoundly, killed himself to get away from his misery.

On receiving the news of her husband's death at Valenciennes, Catherine Gordon's grief vented itself in screams that were audible to her neighbours in the same street. The poor woman had small cause to weep for the event that stirred her to so characteristic a display of strong emotion. For *her*, at least, it was well that the libertine, who had wasted her wealth, and with cruel words had whipt her into many a fit of fury, could never again approach her. Even though he had lived to put a coronet on her head, she would have had small reason to thank God for so bad a husband. It was also well for the little boy, already observant and clever enough to think it strange his mother should be so wildly wretched for the death of the man, whom she had so often upbraided in his hearing for being a prodigy of masculine wickedness.

Byron was a school-boy, stricken with illness from which he did not expect to recover, when in one of the most interesting and thoughtful of his youthful poems, he wrote the familiar lines—so touchingly prophetic of the troubles that were soon

to come upon him through the want of wise parental
control,—

> ' Stern death forbade my orphan youth to share
> The tender guidance of a father's care.
> Can rank, or e'en a guardian's name, supply
> The love which glistens in a father's eye ?
> For this can wealth or title's sound atone,
> Made by a parent's early loss, my own ?'

He had endured what these early lines predicted,
and was fast moving onwards to the rocks that
wrecked him, when in more strenuous verse but in
the same strain of feeling, he wrote,—

> ' The chief of Lara is return'd again :
> And why had Lara cross'd the bounding main ?
> Left by his sire, too young such loss to know,
> Lord of himself ;—that heritage of woe,
> That fearful empire which the human breast
> But holds to rob the heart within of rest !—
> With none to check, and few to point in time
> The thousand paths that slope the way to crime ;
> Then, when he most required commandment, then
> Had Lara's daring boyhood govern'd men.
> It skills not, boots not step by step to trace
> His youth through all the mazes of its race ;
> Short was the course his restlessness had run,
> But long enough to leave him half undone.'

To those who have learnt from the admitted facts
of his youth and earlier manhood, how gentle, affectionate, and manageable a creature Byron was at life's
outset ; how quick to respond to kindness, and render
homage to those whom he respected ; how ready to
profit by sympathetic admonition, and sacrifice his
self-love to his sense of right ; how full of loyalty to
all who had a moral title to his allegiance ; and how

devoid of even a leaven of vicious wilfulness,—it appears, at least, more than probable that had he been watched and guarded, from his sixteenth to his twenty-sixth year, by a proud, sagacious and loving father, he would have been saved from the catastrophe, in which he lost his domestic happiness, and every-thing that was really dear to him, with the excep-tion of his sister's love, a few friendships, the fame that could not be taken from him, and the genius that was destined to make him still more famous.— But under no conceivable circumstances could 'mad Jack Byron' have sobered down, and mellowed and ripened into such a father.

CHAPTER V.

ABERDEEN.

The Widow's Poverty—The Poet's Childhood—May Gray's Calvinism
—Catherine Gordon's Treatment of her Boy—His Scotch Tutors—
His Lameness—Banks of Dee—Heir Presumptive—Aberdeen
Grammar School—The Fifth Lord's Death—Byron's First Love:
Mary Duff—His Temper in Childhood—His Girlishness—'Auld
Lang Syne.'

DURING her residence in Aberdeen, from an early
day of 1790 to the end of the summer of 1798, Mrs.
Byron had three different places of abode;—the first
in Queen Street, the second in Virginia Street,
and the third in Broad Street. In the two first-
named streets she had small furnished lodgings,
but on moving to Broad Street she took an 'entire
floor,' which she fitted with the furniture that on her
migration to England was sold (with the exception
of the plate and linen) for 74*l.* 17*s.* 7*d.*

What with her inexperience in the arts by which
a little money may be made to go a long way, and
what with the consequences of ' the Captain's wicked
extravagance,' which so often stirred her to equally
reasonable and unreasonable outpourings of indignation, Mrs. Byron found it impossible at first to live
within her narrow income of 150*l.* a-year. At the
time of the Captain's second visit to Aberdeen she
was in debt at least to the amount of 100*l.* And

creditors had put 'arrestments' on her modest
revenue, when in the first quarter of 1791, she felt it
incumbent on her honour to promise certain of the
Aberdeen tradesmen, that she would herself pay those
several little bills which the Captain, of course from
pure forgetfulness, had omitted to settle on the eve
of his withdrawal from the city.   But when she had
taken heart to borrow 300*l*. at 5 per cent., in order to
wipe off all claims on her estate and sense of dignity,
and to pay the charges of needful furniture for her
Broad Street 'flat'—a financial re-arrangement that
reduced her yearly revenue by 15*l*.—she passed to a
more tranquil period of her monetary experiences.
Henceforth she contrived to live without owing aught
to any-one ; and on the opportune death of her
grandmother, by the cessation of whose already
mentioned annuity the 135*l*. per annum rose to 190*l*.
a-year, Mrs. Byron could face her liabilities as they
rose, and at the same time lay by enough for those
unforeseen occurrences that are so likely to prevent the
ends of a small income from meeting.   When George
suffered from measles in 1792, there may not have
been money in hand for medicine and subsequent
change of air ; but in 1796, on his convalescence from
scarlet fever, Mrs. Byron had no occasion to debate
with much anxious casting of accounts, whether she
could afford to carry him forty miles up the Dee to
that pleasant farm-house at Ballatrech (near Balla-
ter), where he would breathe the purest air in all
Scotland.   It should be borne in mind that a guinea
in George the Third's time had a much greater buying
power than twenty-one Victorian shillings.

. Whilst Catherine Gordon, who preferred her

maiden surname to the one she had acquired by marriage, was graduating in the arts of domestic economy, and seizing every occasion for impressing on her boy how vastly superior the Gordons of her branch were to the Gordons of any other branch, and how immeasurably inferior English Byrons (albeit of a noble race) were to every variety of the Scotch Gordons, she maintained a correspondence with the child's London aunt (Mrs. Leigh, of 39 Brompton Row, Knightsbridge), who seems to have taken a womanly interest in the 'little boy at Aberdeen,' and from her heart to have compassionated her sister-in-law. The sisters may not have had many subjects in common, or much to tell one another. But to the widow a letter from England must have been welcome, if it caused her to think of the lordly Abbey her boy might some day inherit. Perhaps the ladies were the better friends for the distance between them. As fellow-tourists in France they would soon have fallen out. For whilst Mrs. Leigh pitied '*that* poor French king,' and wept her eyes red over Marie Antoinette's troubles, Catherine Gordon Byron was on the side of 'the people' whose sufferings in her opinion fully justified the strong measures they were taking to 'crush out the tyrants.' Whatever else may be said against her, it cannot be denied that Mrs. Byron had just then the courage of her opinions. Declining to be called whig or liberal, or by any other milk-and-water name, she avowed herself 'a democrat,' and in the very ears of Aberdeen tories prayed for the time, when kings and all other oppressors would be called to account and punished according to their deserts. Whilst little George was instructed in theology by Mary, shortened affectionately to 'May' Gray (his pious Scotch nurse, the sister and successor of his first nurse), he was taught by his mother to abhor tyrants and regard the poor as extremely ill-used people, who would be as prosperous and virtuous as any philanthropist could wish them to be, if despots would but leave them alone. The child, who from the one teacher learnt to fear God, was inspired by the other with distrust of kings and a romantic concern for 'the people.' May Gray was the better teacher, but the mother also had a share in the formation of the child's character.

The nurse taught the child his first prayers ; and before he could read, he learnt from her lips to repeat passages of the Sacred Scriptures ; the first and the twenty-third Psalm being amongst the selections from the Bible, which were thus planted in his memory in his earliest infancy. And when one recalls how, in later time, he not seldom listened to the counsel of the ungodly, and stood in the way of sinners, and sat in the seat of the scornful, it is pitiful to think of the little fellow repeating the first Psalm to his attendant ere he bade her 'good night' and lay his curly pate on the pillow. At this tender age, the nervous child accepted with the trustfulness of infancy all the nurse's Calvinistic views on matters of religion. It is more than probable that, had it not been for May Gray's enduring influence on her pupil, Shelley would not have had occasion to extend his arms towards his wife in a way expressive of astonishment mingled with sorrow, and shriek excitedly, 'By what he said last night in talking over his "Cain," the best of all his undramatic dramas, I do believe, Mary—I do believe, Mary, that he is little better than a Christian!'

Whilst the Scotch servant, with her strong Calvinism and narrow intellect, was thus mindful for the spiritual welfare of her 'charge,' Mrs. Byron was no less watchful over his morals and deportment. A more exasperating and injurious ruler for a sensitive and sometimes violently passionate child, cannot be imagined than this vehement and undisciplined woman, who fell daily into as many fits of ill-temper as there are hours in the day, and rarely passed a week without a wild outbreak of hysterical rage. Abundantly lavish of kisses to the child when he was in her good graces, she was no less lavish of blows when he incurred her capricious displeasure. Now covering him with caresses and now seizing him to give him a beating, she was no mother for such a child to love,—but an equally perplexing and appalling fact for him to study, ponder over, and dread. In a later stage of his infancy, instead of fearing her, he hated and ridiculed her. At least, on one occasion, after pouring half-a-hundred abusive epithets upon him, and even swearing at him, she mocked this issue of her own body for being 'a lame brat!' At this unnatural gibe a fearful light came from the child's eyes,—the light that so often flashed from them in the coming time. The boy's visible emotion was not lost upon the mother, who probably expected it to be followed by words no less violent than her own. But the child surpassed the mother in self-control. For half-a-minute, whilst his lips quivered and his face whitened from the force of feeling never to be forgotten, he was silent; and then he spoke five short words, and no more. ' I was born so, mother!' he said slowly, before he turned away from the woman who dared not follow him. The words were in the poet's mind when, in his early manhood, he told the Marquis of Sligo the several reasons that made it impossible for him to feel towards Mrs. Byron as a son ought to feel for a widowed mother. The scene, which ended with these words, came to his mind on his return from Greece (where he had taken the young Marquis into his confidence), when the intelligence came to him of Mrs. Byron's death. At Pisa, just three years before his death, the scene was in his mind when he wrote the first words of ' The Deformed Transformed :'—

> ' *Bertha.*   Out, hunchback !
> *Arnold.*   I was born so, mother !'

Whilst receiving lessons in religion from May Gray and lessons in demeanour from Mrs. Byron, the boy acquired the rudiments of other knowledge from one or another of the three pedagogues who successively directed his studies before he was sent to the Aberdeen Grammar School in 1794, and for each of whom he had a kindly word, when in his twenty-sixth year he put on paper his recollections of his childhood in Scotland ; the first of the preceptors being Mr. Bowers, whose pupils (of both sexes) were pleased to christen him ' Bodsy,' in reference to his dapperness. Having, for the modest fee of one guinea, spent a year (from November 1792 to November 1793) under the tuition of Bodsy Bowers, whose method of imparting knowledge did not save his pupil from having his ears boxed in Broad Street for knowing just nothing, the boy was placed under the charge of Mr. Ross, the 'very devout, clever little clergyman,' whose 'mild manners and good-natured painstaking' rose years afterwards to the poet's grateful memory; when standing on the heights of Tusculum, he looked 'down upon the little round lake that was once Regillus,' and recalled how his imagination had in childhood been taken by the story of the Battle of Lake Regillus. As he 'made astonishing progress' under the good minister's care, and had a strong liking for his master, he should not have been removed from so excellent a teacher, and placed under the strictly limited authority of the 'very serious, saturnine, but kind young man, named Paterson,' who was a rigid Presbyterian, and the son of his pupil's shoemaker. It is not, however, surprising that he was taken from so worthy and efficient a preceptor as Mr. Ross; for the boy's tutors never pleased Mrs. Byron, who was at all times quick to hold them accountable for his faults of demeanour, and more particularly for his obvious want of affection for herself.

In perusing the biographies of the poet, alike in the pages that refer to his earlier time and those that relate to the successive periods of his manhood, readers should be mindful of what has been said in this volume of his lameness, or they will be misled by the passages which speak of his excursions up the Dee and his 'solitary rambles,' as though he were a fairly good pedestrian. 'In early life,' says Trelawny, a sensible writer and the best authority on this subject, 'whilst his frame was light and elastic, with the aid of a stick, he might have tottered along for a mile or two; but after he had waxed heavier, he seldom attempted to walk more than a few hundred yards,

without squatting down or leaning against the first
wall, bank, rock, or tree at hand, never sitting on the
ground, as it would have been difficult for him to get
up again.' Fashioned for strength in his neck,
shoulders, and arms, he could at Aberdeen and afterwards at Harrow acquit himself well enough in a
pugilistic combat, so long as he could hop and spring
about on his toes, but in a long fight he was sure to
be worsted, through the weakness of his feet. Fierce
and resolute as any of his successive bull-dogs, he
won several fights at Harrow, but in every case he
won them by rushing at his adversary with the *élan*
of a French foot-soldier, and making a short business
of each round by putting in quickly two or three
blows with his singularly muscular arms. When he
could not snatch success in this manner he was beaten,
and had to bide his time for another opportunity of
' paying off ' an enemy, as he paid off his schoolmate
at Aberdeen on the occasion mentioned by Moore.
In later time he boxed with Jackson (the famous
pugilist) and Jackson's pupils in the same manner.
During his brief and brilliant career in London, it
was noticed by his friends that to hide his lameness,
he always entered a room quickly, running rather
than walking, and stopt himself suddenly by planting
his left (the comparatively sound) foot on the ground,
and resting upon it. On the rare occasions when he
was seen walking in the streets, it was observed that
he moved with a peculiar sliding gait rather than the
easy lounge of a fashionable saunterer,—in fact, with
the gait of a person walking on the balls and toes of
his feet, and doing his best to hide the singular mode
of progression. Passages may, indeed, be found in

his diaries and letters, that do not accord with this account of his pedestrianism. But they must be regarded as the venial misrepresentations of a writer who wished to divert attention, even his own attention, from the infirmity respecting which he was acutely sensitive. Just as the blind sometimes talk about 'seeing things,' and even go to picture galleries to 'look at' works of art, the lame are often heard to talk vauntingly of their achievements in walking. It was so with Byron. Rather than reveal his infirmity, he would endure serious discomfort. When the sudden shower of rain fell upon the prison garden (*vide* Hunt's 'Lord Byron and his Contemporaries,' Vol. I. p. 298), Byron could have run in his peculiar way for the length of the enclosure, as fast as Moore who had left him in the wet ; but as he could not run without revealing his infirmity to a person, whom he thought ignorant of it, he continued to move slowly to cover, at the risk of getting wet through.

Suffering from his lameness in childhood and youth, no less than he suffered from it in his earlier manhood, the Aberdeen 'laddie' was, of course, incapable of taking the amount of exercise on foot that is usual with children of his age. His excursions on the banks of the Dee, and other rambles, were made with the help of a pony, whether he went by himself or with a playmate. His days were nearing the end when, in a note to one of the brightest and heartiest passages of 'Don Juan,' he recorded his clear recollection of 'Balgounie's brig's black wall,' and of the fear that thrilled his nerves lest in crossing the river on the back of his pony, he (an only son) should fulfil the prediction of the terrifying lines :—

> ' Brig o' Balgounie, wight is thy wa';
>   Wi' a wife's ae son on a mare's ae foal,
>   Down shalt thou fa'.'

There is also a sufficiently attested story that, on approaching the same bridge with a companion (another only son), whose 'turn' at 'riding and tying' had placed him in the saddle, little George Byron insisted on remounting the pony and riding to the other side of the stream, whilst his friend waited behind to see the result of so hazardous an experiment; the argument by which the future poet carried his point being that, whereas he had only one parent to mourn for his death, his friend had both father and mother to weep and wail, should their boy be killed from the falling of the bridge. If it should be proved to be as fictitious as biographical anecdotes are sometimes found on critical examination, this story would still accord with the way in which the ' little boy at Aberdeen ' made excursions in the neighbourhood of the city, and brought himself face to face with the picturesqueness of more northern scenes. It was well for the youthful poet to sing in the ' Hours of Idleness,'—

> ' I would I were a careless child,
>   Still dwelling in my Highland cave,
> Or roaming through the dusky wild,
>   Or bounding o'er the dark blue wave.'

Even when she plays the part of her own autobiographer, Poetry is permitted to be inaccurate in details. The 'careless child' roamed 'through the dusky wild' on the back of a Shetland pony, and was no more accustomed to foot it about the Highlands than to 'dwell in a cave.'

If it were safe to trust the biographer (Dallas),

who, notwithstanding his connexion with the Byrons, certainly was in error as to the poet's birth-place, and even wrote about his ' fine *black* hair,' it would be recorded on this page that the boy, whilst living at Aberdeen, acquired the elements of French—a language he never spoke or wrote with correctness or facility—at Monsieur De Loyauté's academy.

In 1794, the year in which her son entered the Aberdeen Grammar School, Mrs. Catherine Gordon Byron had reason to think her husband's family paid her less attention than she might fairly expect from them. That Mrs. Leigh, who had been her helpful friend in several emergencies, allowed several months to pass without writing to inquire for her nephew, was a circumstance that troubled Mrs. Byron not a little, and filled her with suspicion that enemies had intercepted the letters to her which General Leigh's wife, now living at Sandgate, near Folkestone, might be presumed to have written and sent up, in packets of similar notes, to London, whence they could be ' franked on ' to Scotland. No coldness to account for Mrs. Leigh's silence seems to have risen between the ladies. This silence was the more remarkable and vexatious to Mrs. Byron, because it not only prevented her from having the pleasure of surprising her neighbours with a most exciting piece of intelligence, but also exposed her to the humiliation of being indebted to some one of them for the information which should have been sent promptly to her from Nottinghamshire or London, and of course would have been so sent to her, had the Byrons made much account of ' the little boy at Aberdeen ' and his mother.

The fifth Lord Byron's grandson had died in

Corsica, and weeks had passed since his kindred in England donned mourning for him, before Mrs. Byron of Aberdeen knew of the event, which put her little boy next in succession to Newstead and the barony ; and when the intelligence reached her, it came in a manner that declared to all Aberdeen how little she was esteemed by her husband's people. For the news, which should have been sent promptly from Newstead, she was indebted to the gossip of a neighbour. If she received the astounding intelligence at a tea-party, it is not difficult to imagine the resentment and humiliation that qualified her delight, when an eager demand for her informant's authority for the staggering announcement provoked expressions of lively astonishment at her ignorance of a matter, that had been known for more than a month to every one else. Such an incident could not fail to ruffle the always emotional lady.

But if the way by which it came to her was galling, the intelligence was very gratifying to her pride. It was so good that, to guard herself from bitter disappointment, she tried not to believe it, till she should receive confirmatory letters from the South, putting it beyond question that her boy had really and truly become his great-uncle's heir-apparent. On learning in due course that the talker at the tea-party had spoken no more than the truth, poor Mrs. Byron began to chatter about leaving Aberdeen, and withdrawing George from the Grammar School which, though a most respectable seminary and quite good enough for the sons of mere lairds and writers to the signet, was no fit place for a young gentleman who a few years hence would be a lord of the Upper House.

The news, of course, raised Mrs. Byron considerably in the regard of her neighbours in Aberdeen, and revived the waning affection of her kindred throughout the county. Persons who for years had thought lightly of the ruined heiress, and declared her temper insufferable, now discovered in her good qualities, for which no one had heretofore commended her. Cousins, who had neglected her ever since her husband's death, now sent her pressing invitations to visit them, and bring her boy with her. Mr. Ferguson, a leading gentleman of affairs in Aberdeen, who had stood staunchly by her in her darkest hour, was of opinion that Lord Byron might, by judicious treatment, be induced to make her an allowance, or at least to pay for the education of his heir at one of the great public schools. Mr. Ferguson was also of opinion that if her case were submitted to the consideration of His Most Gracious Majesty by the Prime Minister, a pension of at least 300*l.* a-year would be granted her on the Civil List. And this last matter was one on which Mr. Ferguson was the more justified in speaking strongly and hopefully, because he had himself been instrumental in procuring from the King's gracious benevolence a pension for a lady of quality, who like Mrs. Byron was suffering from straitened circumstances. Knowing the strings to be pulled and how to pull them, Mr. Ferguson would have much pleasure in acting for Mrs. Byron in the matter, *if* he could only have Lord Byron's written authority to bestir himself for the accomplishment of his desire. Without authority from the chief of the Byron family, it was obvious that Mr. Ferguson could not move effectually or safely in the lady's behalf. Lord Byron was known to be a person of a singular temper; and it was conceivable that he might denounce for a meddler any person who, without his sanction, should venture to submit a statement of Mrs. Byron's necessities to the minister who at that time enjoyed the sovereign's confidence. The lady was therefore urged to put herself in communication with Lord Byron on the subject. If she did not like to write to his lordship at once, it was suggested by her discreet counsellor that she should consult Mrs. Leigh, who was believed to enjoy her uncle's favour, and through her get access to the Lord of Newstead.

Whether the 'wicked Lord Byron' was ever applied to on the subject, there is no evidence. Possibly Mrs. Leigh knew her uncle too well to trouble him with talk about Mrs. Byron and the 'little boy at Aberdeen.' Anyhow his lordship contributed nothing to the widow's means, and never authorized Mr. Ferguson to pull official strings. Instead of offering to send his heir to Eton or Harrow, the eccentric nobleman made the illegal sale of Rochdale property, which resulted in the long and costly lawsuit that was one cause of the poet's financial embarrassments in the earlier stages of his career, after coming of age. This lawsuit was the principal legacy for which the author of 'Childe Harold' had to remember his great-uncle.

In default of the requisite sanction, Mr. Ferguson took no steps to introduce the widow to the King's benevolent consideration; but five years later, when her son had become Lord Byron, on the death of his great-uncle (who died on the 19th of May, 1798),

Catherine Gordon Byron obtained the long-desired pension of 300*l.* a-year on the Civil List;—an exhibition of royal benignity, that placed the democratic lady in sufficiently easy circumstances, and perhaps caused her to be more cautious in declaring her disapproval of kings.

At the Aberdeen Grammar School, Byron 'threaded all the classes to the fourth,' as he himself states the case in one of his autobiographical journals. But in thus rising from the place appropriate to the 'little fellow' of the school to the place where a boy in his eleventh year would be looked for as a matter of course, he displayed neither aptitude nor liking for his lessons. Sometimes indeed he was at the top of his class, but on those occasions the top, as an Irishman might say, was the bottom. To pique the ambition of the superior scholars to recover the places which they had lost without disgrace, and to spur the less apt scholars to retain the dignity they had not won, it was the practice of the masters of the school to invert the order of their classes, so that for a moment the knowing boys were placed lower than the ignorant ones. On these occasions Byron, after walking from the bottom to the top of his form, more than once heard his master say in a bantering tone, 'And now, George, man, let me see how soon you'll be at the foot.' The judgment of the masters about him was the judgment that has been accorded by pedagogues to so many children, who have distinguished themselves honourably in later time:— 'Quick enough, but wanting in application!'

Whilst he neglected his lessons, the lame boy, though scarcely to be described as studious, was a reader of books (seldom perused by lads of his age), when his mates were at leap-frog. On the margin of a leaf of the elder D'Israeli's 'Essay on the Literary Character,' Byron in his mature age made this memorandum respecting the authors he had read before leaving Aberdeen:—'Knolles, Cantemir, De Tott, Lady W. M. Montague, Hawkins's translation from Mignet's 'History of the Turks,' the 'Arabian Nights'—all travels or histories, or books upon the East, I could meet with, I had read, as well as Ricaut, before I *was ten years old.*' And in connexion with this account of the desultory studies of his earlier years, it should be remembered how much evidence is afforded by his writings, that his memory was strongly retentive of the matters picked up from books perused in his infancy. Dr. Moore's 'Zeluco' (1789)—a novel in which he delighted in his Aberdeen time—gave the poet his first conception of 'Childe Harold.' All that is most pathetic in the incomparably beautiful account of the 'two fathers in this ghastly crew,' in the Second Canto of 'Don Juan,' is referable to the impression made upon him by the 'Narrative of the Shipwreck of the "Juno" on the coast of Arracan, in the year 1795,' which he read with quickened pulse and tearful eyes in the year following his withdrawal from Scotland in 1798. In the whole range of literature, one would look in vain for a genius of the highest order, whose mind was more notably influenced throughout life by the food on which it fed in the earliest periods of its development.

At Aberdeen, also, Byron received his first lesson from the greatest and most ennobling of human teachers. One may smile for a moment at the thought of so young a child's first passion for a companion of the opposite sex. But no one who remembers Dante's passion for Beatrice (a love that warmed him in his tenth year), and Canova's quickness to fall in love at a much earlier age, will regard as 'mere child's play' the sentiment with which the boy of meditative moods and almost morbid sensibility regarded Mary Duff—the little girl with dark-brown hair and hazel eyes, whose charm of face, and voice, and form, and manner, gave him many a sleepless night, when he was only nine years old. That he 'could neither feel *passion*, nor know the meaning of the word' at the time of this love's warmest fervour, Byron was certain when he recalled the affair and wrote about it in his twenty-sixth year ; but for months together it was happiness to the shy boy to be allowed to gaze at this girl, to attend her in her walks, to sit by her side in the playroom of the old house hard by the Aberdeen Plain-stones, sometimes even to caress her. And all through the same months, it was misery to him to be away from her. Unutterably happy in her presence, he fretted and pined in her absence. This is not playing at love, but the passion itself, so far as a child, incapable of the peculiar desire to which perfect love owes so much of its colour and warmth, is capable of the sentiment. It is love, felt perhaps by one child of a hundred thousand, but quite unknown to the others. In Byron this sentiment was so enduring,—or (to speak more precisely) so capable of being revived— that in his seventeenth year he experienced an hysterical agitation, that nearly occasioned him one of those convulsive seizures to which he was liable throughout his life at moments of supreme emotion, on learning suddenly that his 'old flame' was well though most unromantically married to an Edinburgh wine-merchant.

One of the poet's journals contains a passage which shows that though he could recall his own childhood he was imperfectly acquainted with the nature of ordinary children. After describing his infantile devotion to little Mary Duff, he writes in his twenty-sixth year, 'In all other respects, I differed not at all from other children, being neither tall nor short, dull nor witty, of my age, but rather lively— except in my sullen moods, and then I was always a devil. They once (in one of my silent rages) wrenched a knife from me, which I had snatched from table at Mrs. B.'s dinner (I always dined earlier), and applied to my breast . . . just before the late Lord B.'s decease.' The 'rages,' that Byron regarded as peculiar to himself in his childhood, are not unusual in young people; and there was nothing very remarkable about the ways in which he displayed his occasional passionateness. It is not surprising that the child, whose mother often vented her fury in his presence by destroying pieces of her wearing-apparel, should in one of his earliest fits of fury have torn his new frock to shreds; and the behaviour of a ten-years-old boy, in seizing a knife under a sudden impulse of wrath and threatening to kill himself, was less extraordinary than the autobiographer imagined. On the other hand, it is certain that, apart from amatory precociousness, little George Byron differed from the majority of children in several respects. Especially he differed from them in retentiveness of memory and in intellectual receptivity. The knowledge, largely qualified with error as childish knowledge must ever be, that came to him in his infancy, passed into his soul and never left it. When it is remembered how needful for their happiness it is that persons who feel acutely should be capable of forgetting their annoyances, Byron's retentiveness of memory may be described as terrible. He differed also from the majority of young people in the delicacy of his sensibilities, and also in his morbid shyness, that far exceeded the shyness of proud children, exposed to mortifying circumstances.

A story is told of his behaviour in his eleventh year, which is noteworthy for its evidence that the bashfulness from which he suffered at this time and for several subsequent years,—indeed, in some degree throughout life,—was less the weakness of a sheepish boy than of a timid girl. On being required for the first time to answer to his name in the school roll-call by the title of ' Dominus,' a robust boy would have answered ' Adsum ' in a clear voice, and would have replied to the astonishment visible in the countenances of his school-fellows, by looking them proudly in the face, whilst his own glowed with excitement. But Byron was unequal to the ordeal, that certainly would not have tried severely the self-possession of an ordinary child of his age. Overcome by the novelty of the position and the gaze of his staring class-mates, he stood silent and fell into tears. The girlishness of his emotion on this occasion was characteristic of the boy,—whom Hobhouse in later time used to regard as a wayward and irresistibly charming woman, rather than as man, and whose sister to the last used to call him her dear ‘ baby Byron.’

Notwithstanding the pain that came to him from his mother’s capricious harshness and violence, from incidents vexatious to his pride, from the terror begotten in his strongly imaginative mind by May Gray’s calvinistic concern for his spiritual interests, and from the feminine sensitiveness of his highly nervous temperament, it is, however, certain that Byron’s childhood was not upon the whole chiefly remarkable for its unhappiness. In many respects the circumstances of his infancy were unquestionably favourable to the health of his peculiar bodily constitution, the formation of his character, and the development of his genius,—or rather let it be said, to the development of those germs of feeling and faculty that were destined to result in his genius. It was well for the nerves of the delicate boy that in his earlier childhood he breathed the bracing air of his mother’s native county. It was well in later time for the poet, who was a peer and (without being so foolish about it as his biographers have asserted) prided himself none too little on his rank, that without having been subjected to the dwarfing and embittering conditions of extreme penury, he could recall a period when he lived in the ways that lie between affluence and poverty. It was well for the aristocrat to have been reared amongst the people, and to have learnt from personal experience how closely humble folk resemble the children of luxury and grandeur. If it abounded with trials to his pride and with incidents peculiarly afflicting to his sensitive and impetuously affectionate nature, his childhood afforded him pleasures which he remembered no less vividly than its vexations. When his days were speeding onward to ' the yellow leaf,' the man, who had drained a bitter cup to the dregs, could still write cheerily and tenderly,—

> ' As auld Lang Syne brings Scotland, one and all,
>   Scotch plaids, Scotch snoods, the blue hills and clear streams,
> The Dee, the Don, Balgounie's brig's black wall,
>   All my boy's feelings, all my gentler dreams
> Of what I *then dreamt*, clothed in their own pall,
>   Like Banquo's offspring ;—floating past me seems
> My childhood in this childishness of mine :
> I care not—'tis a glimpse of " Auld Lang Syne." '

The heart's music rings out too unmistakably in these lines for any one to question their sincerity. It matters not that he had often spoken of Scotland and her people in a different strain. When the great Jeffrey with his review tried to crush him, the young poet wrote savage things of the critic and his clique; and in later times he visited Scotland with his wrath because a few of her writers were worrying him. When the saucy girl twitted him with the Scotch note, that was faintly perceptible at times in his musical voice, he could say pettishly, ' I would rather hear that the country was sunk in the sea than believe you to be right.' People could in his careless moods amuse him by ridiculing Scotland, and he would take part in the banter, but only with the playful malice which a humourist reserves for his best friends, and delights to pour upon them *because* they are his best friends. In his heart he loved ' the land of mountain and of flood,' and was grateful to her for the childhood that, without being an altogether joyful one, had left him with many a joyful memory.

CHAPTER VI.

NOTTINGHAM AND LONDON.

The Sixth Lord — His First Visit to Newstead — The Abbey — Tutor at Nottingham — Lavender, the Bone-setter — Dulwich Grove — Dr. Glennie — A Very Troublesome Mamma — Guardian and Ward — Byron's First Dash into Poetry — His Second Love; Margaret Parker — His Later Attachments — His Sensibility, Memory, and Imagination — Malvern Hills and Scotch Mountains.

In language suitable for his purpose Moore tells how in the summer of 1798 Lord Byron 'left Scotland with his mother and nurse, to take possession of the seat of his ancestors,' and how on their arrival at the Newstead toll-bar 'they saw the woods of the Abbey stretching out to receive them;' when Mrs. Byron, feigning ignorance, asked the woman of the toll-house to whom the Abbey belonged. On being informed that the late owner, Lord Byron, had died some time since, the proud mother inquired who was the late lord's heir :—a question that elicited the reply, 'They say, it is a little boy who lives at Aberdeen;' whereupon, May Gray, no longer able to control her feelings, ejaculated, 'And this is he: bless him!' at the same moment 'kissing with delight the young lord who was seated in her lap.' This pleasant story had probably a foundation of fact; but the sceptical reader will question whether the young lord—in the middle of his eleventh year, and a rather fleshy boy for his age—entered his ancestral domain sitting on the nurse's knees.

Modest truth would have been content to say that Mrs. Byron, with her son and maid-servant, travelled by stage-coaches to Nottingham; whence, on the day after their arrival at the town's best inn, they drove in a post-chaise to Newstead, to look at the place, which it was hoped the young lord would some day inhabit, after finishing his education, and marrying a lady with enough money to restore the ruinous mansion, and set the spits turning in its kitchens.

Though the woods extended their arms to receive the heir, the house was in no state for the entertainment of his mother. Had the house been tenantable, Mrs. Byron (not yet in possession of the Civil List pension, and with no other means than the small income on which she had lived at Aberdeen) was in no position to dwell in so grand a place. The young lord's estate (already in Chancery) was no property from which his mother could hope to get an allowance of three or four thousand a-year for the charges of his education at Eton or Harrow, and the maintenance of so stately a home for him during the holidays. The most being made of the rental, and the least of needful expenses, the few farms pertaining to the Abbey yielded a revenue of from 1200*l.* to 1500*l.* per annum. At Rochdale there was the property of which the late lord had made an illegal sale. To recover that property would be a work of time and expense; and on its recovery, should it ever be wrested from the people in possession, it might be worth some twenty thousand pounds. In the meantime, there was no fund for carrying on the law-suit, apart from the few hundreds a-year of the Newstead rental, that should not be needed for the young peer's education. The most valuable part of the boy's Newstead property was the part that yielded no income, beyond what the pasture of the park was let for, and moneys from the sale of timber. The entire property was valued by the land-agents at 90,000*l.* A statelier and more picturesque place of its particular kind could scarcely be found in the midland shires; and fortunately there was no entail to preclude the new lord from selling, as soon as he should come of age. But of course, so long as he should be a minor, all thought of sale would be out of the question.

It can be imagined how Mrs. Byron, daily growing stouter, waddled her way, under the guidance of an aged care-taker, through hall and corridor, through galleries and chambers, through neglected gardens and crumbling ruins, speaking querulous truth at every turn of the wicked old Lord who had suffered so noble a place to fall into such dilapidation. It can be conceived how, long before the hour appointed for the repast, May Gray was sharply ordered to unpack a certain basket, which the excursionists from Nottingham had brought with them, unless she would see her mistress faint away for want of luncheon and a glass of sherry. It may be imagined how the young Lord, heedless for the moment of his lameness and the pain of walking, slipped away from his mother to the eminence of the park that gave him the best view of the fair domain and venerable pile, whose beauties he described some twenty years later in his greatest poem :—

' An old, old monastery once, and now
Still older mansion,—of a rich and rare
　　Mix'd Gothic, such as artists all allow
Few specimens yet left us can compare
　　Withal : it lies perhaps a little low,
Because the monks preferr'd a hill behind,
To shelter their devotion from the wind.

' It stood embosom'd in a happy valley,
　　Crown'd by high woodlands, where the Druid oak
Stood like Caractacus, in act to rally
　　His host, with broad arms 'gainst the thunderstroke ;
And from beneath his boughs were seen to sally
　　The dappled foresters—as day awoke,
The branching stag swept down with all his herd,
To quaff a brook which murmured like a bird.

' Before the mansion lay a lucid lake,
　　Broad as transparent, deep, and freshly fed
By a river, which its softened way did take
　　In currents through the calmer water spread
Around : the wild fowl nestled in the brake
　　And sedges, brooding in their liquid bed :
The woods sloped downwards to its brink, and stood
With their green faces fix'd upon the flood.

' Its outlet dash'd into a deep cascade,
　　Sparkling with foam, until again subsiding,
Its shriller echoes—like an infant made
　　Quiet—sank into softer ripples, gliding
Into a rivulet ; and thus allay'd,
　　Pursued its course, now gleaming, and now hiding
Its windings through the woods ; now clear, now blue,
According as the skies their shadows threw.

' A glorious remnant of the Gothic pile
　　(While yet the church was Rome's) stood half apart
In a grand arch, which once screen'd many an aisle.
　　These last had disappear'd—a loss to art :

The first yet frown'd superbly o'er the soil,
   And kindled feelings in the roughest heart,
Which mourn'd the power of time's or tempest's march,
In gazing on that venerable arch.

' Within a niche, nigh to its pinnacle,
   Twelve saints had once stood sanctified in stone ;
But these had fallen, not when the friars fell,
   But in the war which struck Charles from his throne,
When each house was a fortalice—as tell
   The annals of full many a line undone,—
The gallant cavaliers, who fought in vain
For those who knew not to resign or reign.

' But in a higher niche, alone, but crown'd,
   The Virgin Mother of the God-born Child,
With her Son in her blessed arms, look'd round ;
   Spared by some chance when all beside was spoil'd ;
She made the earth below seem holy ground.
   This may be superstition, weak or wild,
But even the faintest relics of a shrine
Of any worship wake some thoughts divine.

' A mighty window, hollow in the centre,
   Shorn of its glass of thousand colourings,
Through which the deepen'd glories once could enter,
   Streaming from off the sun like seraph's wings,
Now yawns all desolate : now loud, now fainter,
   The gale sweeps through its fretwork, and oft sings
The owl his anthem, where the silenced quire
Lie with their hallelujahs quench'd like fire.

*   *   *   *   *

' Amidst the court a Gothic fountain play'd,
   Symmetrical, but deck'd with carvings quaint—
Strange faces, like to men in masquerade,
   And here perhaps a monster, there a saint :
The spring gush'd through grim mouths of granite made,
   And sparkled into basins, where it spent

> Its little torrent in a thousand bubbles,
> Like man's vain glory, and his vainer troubles.

> ' The mansion's self was vast and venerable,
>   With more of the monastic than has been
> Elsewhere preserved : the cloisters still were stable,
>   The cells, too, and refectory, I ween ;
> An exquisite small chapel had been able,
>   Still unimpair'd, to decorate the scene ;
> The rest had been reform'd, replaced, or sunk,
> And spoke more of the baron than the monk.'

Taking charge of the young lord's estate, Chancery committed his person and education to the Earl of Carlisle, said by Moore to have been ' connected but remotely with ' his ward's ' family.' A son of Isabella Byron,—scarcely less famous for eccentricity than her brother, the ' wicked lord,'—Lord Carlisle was first cousin (one degree removed) to the poet, who, had it not been for his mother, would probably have lived on pleasant enough terms with his guardian, instead of quarrelling with him bitterly.

Settling herself at Nottingham, where she resided for about twelve months, Mrs. Byron found a sufficient tutor for her son in Mr. Rogers, a worthy schoolmaster of the town, who without ' grounding ' the boy in Latin, so as to prepare him for a public school, led him on to construe loosely certain parts of Virgil and Cicero. Of the lad's life at Nottingham little is known save that he conceived an affectionate regard for his tutor, suffered much at the hands of the bone-setter, Lavender, and was goaded by an old lady of Swan Green, one of his mother's gossips, into writing the four lines of puerile doggerel which have been noticed seriously by some of the poet's biographers as his earliest effort in satirical literature. On the bone-setter, for whom he conceived reasonable contempt and aversion, the boy is said to have played a childish trick, that from time immemorial has caused merriment in the nurseries of children. Arranging the letters of the alphabet in gibberish words, he asked his tormentor what the language was; when the pompous impostor declared the words Italian. A more characteristic and agreeable story is told of the sufferer's intercourse at this time with his teacher of Latin. 'It troubles me, my lord,' said the tutor, pausing in a lesson, 'to see you sitting there in such pain.' 'Never mind, Mr. Rogers,' was the answer; 'you shan't see any signs of it again.'

There is small need to describe the bone-setter's way of treating the foot. Blind to the nature of the case, the man did precisely as any other pretender of his kind would have done. He rubbed the foot with oil, twisted it about with violence, and fixed it tight in a wooden machine, constructed for 'screwing' and 'torturing' bone and muscle into better behaviour. Day after day this barbarous process was repeated; the result of the treatment, of course, being that the foot suffered more injury from bad art, than unkind nature.

In the following year—when Mrs. Byron on getting her pension, moved from Nottingham to London and took a house in Sloane Terrace—the patient was taken at Lord Carlisle's suggestion to Dr. Baillie, who of course saw at a glance the character of the mischief, for which surgery could do nothing more than what John Hunter had prescribed years since. The foot having been provided with a shoe, made by an expert mechanician on the lines ordered by the famous surgeon, Dr. Baillie told the boy and his mother that it must be left to nature to overcome or modify the unfortunate consequences of hurtful treatment. The physician's counsel, that the comfort of the foot should be studied whilst nature was left to her own way of dealing with the distorted bones and injured tissues, was henceforth acted on, with a result that certainly justified the advice, though it scarcely fulfilled the doctor's moderate anticipation of amendment. On going to Harrow, Byron wore a shoe, that announced his infirmity to all observers of his costume; and he had been several years in England, before he could write to his first nurse (May Gray's sister) that he could wear an ordinary boot.

Mrs. Byron having moved from Nottingham to London, May Gray returned to Scotland, where she married a worthy man and died some three years after the death of the famous poet, in the formation of whose character she had been a considerable influence. On her departure for the North the boy, remarkable in later time for kindness to his servants, bade May Gray farewell with characteristic expressions of gratitude for her care of him during his long affliction; his parting gift to her being the first watch he ever possessed, the watch that after the nurse's death became the property of the kind doctor who attended her in her last illness. The boy had already given his nurse the little full-length portrait of himself 'standing with a bow and arrows in his hand, and a profusion of hair falling over his shoulders.' As her tide of life ebbed away, the loyal servant delighted in talking to the doctor of the great man, in the drama of whose history she is so characteristic an actor.

Whilst his foot was recovering from Lavender's mal-praxis, Byron was a pupil in the excellent preparatory school, kept by Dr. Glennie at Dulwich,—a preceptor whom the poet would have remembered no less affectionately than Mr. Ross of Aberdeen and Dr. Drury of Harrow, had it not been for misunderstandings arising from his mother's foolish behaviour. Finding the boy well acquainted with the historical parts of sacred scripture, Dr. Glennie was struck by the intelligence and earnestness with which he spoke on matters of religion. From the doctor's evidence on this subject it seems that Byron's acceptance of his nurse's doctrine can have been troubled by no sceptical considerations so long as she was his daily companion. There is indeed a story that, before he left Scotland, the boy had given his first nurse's husband cause to speak of him as 'a particularly inquisitive child and puzzling about religion.' But this goes for nothing against the abundant evidence, that it was during his later time at Harrow or his earlier time at Cambridge, that Byron became a sceptic.

At the same time Dr. Glennie's attention was arrested by the boy's fondness for reading good literature : and at Dulwich Grove the lad had the means of indulging this taste; for sleeping in the doctor's library, he was encouraged to amuse himself with certain of its books, that comprised a set of the British poets from Chaucer to Churchill, which he was believed to have read from beginning to end. Whilst there is sufficient evidence that the schoolmaster, a gentleman of no ordinary culture and amiability, was abundantly considerate for his pupil's welfare and indulgent to his humours, it is on record to the doctor's honour that eighteen years later (in 1817, at Geneva) he had the courage and generosity to declare his disbelief of the stories with which society resounded to the poet's discredit. The more, therefore, is it to be regretted that no testimony can be produced of corresponding good-will on the poet's part. Byron's silence about Dulwich Grove, where he remained for two years, is significant. Had he remembered the meritorious master with kindness, there would certainly have been some exhibition of the feeling in his published journals and letters. On the other hand, had there been good reasons for his want of grateful regard for the preceptor, he would have put them on record. The fair inference is that, whilst he could not recall the doctor pleasantly, a sentiment of justice forbade him to write a word to his discredit.

The terms in which Glennie wrote to Moore of Mrs. Byron, whilst he had only the kindest words for her son, would of themselves show that Mrs. Byron was accountable for the disagreement of the master and pupil. 'Mrs. Byron,' he wrote with an asperity, that is the more remarkable, because the Scotchman would naturally have been lenient to the lady's northern peculiarities, had she not incensed him greatly, 'was a total stranger to English society and English manners; with an exterior far from pre-possessing, an understanding where nature had not been more bountiful, a mind wholly without culti-vation, and the peculiarities of northern opinions, northern habits, and northern accent, I trust I do no prejudice to the memory of my countrywoman, if I say Mrs. Byron was not a Madame de Lambert, endowed with powers to retrieve the fortune and form the character and manners of a young nobleman, her son.' If these plain words expose the writer to a charge of something like a breach of professional confidence, it can be pleaded in his behalf that he had endured extraordinary provocation from the lady, who treated him as contemptuously as it was in the nature of such a woman to treat a gentleman who was ' only her son's schoolmaster.'

Of course the disputes and conflicts, that arose between Dr. Glennie and Mrs. Byron, related to small matters; for the life of a school, more especially of a preparatory school for quite young gentlemen, is made of small matters. Complaining of the slowness of her boy's progress, Mrs. Byron acted as though her chief object was to make the progress slower. Instead of leaving George to his studies, she was continually driving over to Dulwich to take him out for the afternoon; to carry him off to a theatre or children's party. To the doctor's earlier and milder protests against these interruptions of his young friend's studies, Mrs. Byron answered with promises she failed to keep. But when the doctor became firmer and somewhat less conciliatory, the lady's brow clouded. There were scenes, in which the schoolmaster showed displeasure and the lady became angry ;—followed by still stormier scenes that ended on Mrs. Byron's side with hysterics. Mrs. Glennie tried with her gentle voice to manage this ungentle and exceedingly troublesome mamma. But Mrs.

Glennie succeeded no better than her husband. Not
once or twice alone, but repeatedly, the boy's guardian intervened between the belligerents, at the instance of the tutor, who of course knew the Earl
would be on his side. By the Earl it was decided
that Mrs. Byron's inconvenient visits to Dulwich
Grove should cease, and that George's studies should
not be interrupted during the six working days of
every week. With due regard for the mother's feelings, and not a little to the schoolmaster's disappointment, it was, however, decided by Lord Carlisle that
Mrs. Byron should receive a weekly visit from her
son from the Saturday to Monday, on condition he
was sent back to school on Monday in time for
lessons. When Mrs. Byron had shown her regard
for this stipulation by keeping the boy with her till
Monday afternoon, till the middle of the week, and
even on one occasion for an entire week beyond the
time appointed for his return to Dulwich, the Earl
was again entreated to speak in the interest of tutor
and pupil.

By this time Lord Carlisle's power over Mrs.
Byron was at an end. The gentlewoman, whose
insolent speech in the doctor's study and Mrs.
Glennie's parlour had often been audible to the servants in the kitchen and the boys in the playground,
was no gentlewoman to stand in awe of an earl.
Of Lord Carlisle's last interview with Mrs. Byron
nothing is known, save that he left her presence with
a determination to see as little as possible of her in
the future. Confessing himself beaten by the virago,
with whom he never again condescended to bandy
words, the Earl said to Dr. Glennie, ' I can have

nothing more to do with Mrs. Byron,—you must now manage her as you best can.' That the guardian had good cause for this resolve no one has questioned; and it is more than probable that he had reason for extending his displeasure to the boy, who, though he is not to be blamed for his mother's bad temper, might have done something to check and moderate its outbreaks. The boy may even have been guilty of impertinence to the guardian, who from the time of these rather ludicrous and very unfortunate occurrences regarded him with disfavour.

'Byron, your mother is a fool!' one of the boys remarked bluntly to the future poet.

'I know it!' was the gloomy reply.

But though he 'knew it,' Lord Byron wanted the spirit to beg her to behave less unreasonably. Without showing any lack of filial respect, the twelve-years-old boy might have entreated Mrs. Byron out of her maternal care for his feelings and interests, to have more regard for the wishes of his schoolmaster and his guardian. At least he might have shown both the Doctor and the Earl, that he was sensible of their goodness in taking much trouble and enduring many annoyances for his advantage. The boy who failed to show this feeling by words or manner, seemed of course to be taking Mrs. Byron's part in the unseemly contention. In siding thus far with such a mother the schoolboy was, of course, actuated by no higher motive than a desire for as many holidays and as much pleasure as possible. Though quick enough to resist his mother when she thwarted his wishes or stung him with bitter speech, it is conceivable that in his girlishness—the girlishness that set him ' crying for just nothing ' before his Aberdeen schoolmates—he shrunk from provoking a conflict with her, when she seemed to be overflowing with affection for him. Under these circumstances it is not wonderful that Lord Carlisle thought too unfavourably of the boy, of halting gait and clouded brow, heavy features and sullen look, who spoke with his mother's brogue, and could not enter a room without dropping his eyes to the carpet, from a shyness, in no way distinguishable from the shyness of rusticity. Indeed, who could have predicted thus early and thus late in his story that this sheepish, awkward, thankless little fellow, after almost surviving his Scotch accent and learning how to conceal his lameness, would, ten short years hence assume a shape of singular elegance and a face of peculiar loveliness, and break upon the world almost in the same instant as the greatest poet and brightest coxcomb of his generation? Is it wonderful that, when the brown bud had changed to perfect blossom, Byron never cared to talk of the Dulwich school, which he remembered only as a place, where his mother had made herself more than usually contemptible, and he had played the part of a young cub rather than of a young nobleman?

This least satisfactory period of Byron's boyhood —the two years preceding his entrance at Harrow— covered, however, two passages of feeling in which he figures more agreeably and creditably. The season which a great poet recalls as the time when his feelings first passed into song, and the season when he is known to have been deeply stirred for the first time by the beauties of scenery, are points of interest for his biographers and admirers. Though Dr. Elze attaches some importance to the four lines of satirical doggerel, on the old woman of Swan Green, most readers will be content to rest on the poet's assurance that his 'first dash into poetry' was made in 1800, from the inspiration of the love—the second of the 'grand passions' of his boyhood—which he conceived in that year for his cousin Margaret Parker; the girl, whose dark eyes, long eyelashes, Grecian face, and transparent beauty went to the grave some two years after the poet fell in love with her. In the summer of the following year (1801), the boy accompanied Mrs. Byron to Cheltenham, where he found inexpressible pleasure in watching the Malvern Hills 'every afternoon at sunset,' whilst his foolish mother pondered over the words of the fortune-teller who, after winning the lady's confidence by telling her that her son was lame (a piece of information that of course could only have come to the prophetess through divination) went on to predict that the lame boy 'should be in danger from poison before he was of age, and should be twice married—the second time to a foreign lady.'

Because he was deeply stirred by the news of Mary Duff's marriage, it does not follow that the lad's passion for his cousin Margaret was nothing more than one of those transient states of feeling that arise in young people from ordinary flirtations. On the contrary, he was terribly in earnest; and so was the gentle girl, who returned his affection with the fervour and sincerity of a loving and guileless nature. Having declared his worship of her in the verses, which he had forgotten, and possibly had done well to forget, before his twenty-sixth year, he honoured her when she was no more with the elegy (written in his fifteenth year) beginning,—

> ' Hush'd are the winds, and still the evening gloom,
>   Not e'en a zephyr wanders through the grove,
>   Whilst I return, to view my Margaret's tomb,
>   And scatter flowers on the dust I love.'

The attachment was so genuine and strong on either side that it is conceivable, if Margaret Parker had lived, the world would never have heard much of the poet's other cousin, Mary Chaworth, or been invited to sit in judgment on the domestic trials of the lady who, to every one's misfortune, became the poet's wife. It does not follow that the poet differed from most other men in being able to love two women passionately at the same time. What is most curious in Byron's personal story before his marriage, and also in his personal story after that lamentable event, will be missed by those who persist in regarding the ' passions ' of the earlier period as nothing more than so many exhibitions of sentimentalism, and in regarding the ' attachments ' of the later period as nothing more than so many exhibitions of libertinism. Of the later attachments something will be said hereafter, but only enough for the requirements of honest biography, certainly nothing in the way either of defence or palliation. Of those ' attachments ' (there is no need to call them by a harsher name) no Englishman, reared in the ways of domestic virtue and altogether fortunate in his domestic circumstances, can think without feelings of repulsion, to be equally divided between astonishment and disgust. But the real Byron will never be known to readers who cannot be led to see that, even in the most deplorable stages of the later period of his career, he never made a profession of love without being for the moment inspired by it, or without for the moment believing himself to be completely dominated by it.

In the domain of the affections, he was from boyhood till his hair whitened a man of so acute a sensibility that it may well be termed morbid. To this excessive sensibility, and the various kinds of emotionality that necessarily attended it, must be attributed the quickness with which his 'passions' succeeded one another. Fortunately for society, such sensibility is rare. It is even more uncommon for such sensibility to be united with the singular retentiveness of memory that was another of Byron's most remarkable endowments. Still more unusual is it for so perilous a sensibility and so strong a memory to be found in co-operation with an even stronger imagination. It is only by considering these three several forces, and thinking how they could not fail to act and re-act upon one another, that the reader will realise how it was that even in his early boyhood, when they were only nascent, Byron could in two years survive his first love for little Mary Duff, so as to be capable of a stronger passion for Margaret Parker, and yet be so deeply affected on hearing that the object of the earlier attachment had passed by marriage to another worshipper. That the second love followed so soon on the first was due to the boy's sensibility. His agitation at the sudden announcement of Mary Duff's marriage was due, in the first instance, to the quickened memory that brought before him every one of the child's loveable endowments ; then to the imagination that heightened all the charms which captivated his childish fancy ; and then again to the sensibility that occasioned an instantaneous renewal of the affection, though it had been followed by the stronger attachment to another object. Though two 'passions' could not co-exist in the breast of a man so exceptionally constituted, it was natural for several 'passions' to occupy it successively, and to follow one another with perplexing rapidity. In a being so swayed by feeling, memory, and fancy, a passion, long dead, might at any moment revive. And it was because they knew him to be so constituted that a few of the poet's closest friends, knowing little of Lady Byron, even to the last regarded it as possible that he and she would survive their mutual animosity, and resume the affection that for several months unquestionably existed between them.

To the same forces may be referred what was most remarkable in Byron's love of beautiful scenery. To afford him all the gratification he was capable of deriving from the study of nature's aspects, it was necessary that a landscape should remind him of scenes that had filled him with admiration and gladness in his childhood. It was at Genoa, when he was almost on the threshold of his life's last year, he wrote no inconsiderable portion of his biography in the lines,—

'He who first met the Highland's swelling blue,
Will love the peak that shows a kindred hue,
Hail in each crag a friend's familiar face,
And clasp the mountain in his mind's embrace.
Long have I roam'd through lands which are not mine,
Adored the Alp and loved the Appennine,
Revered Parnassus, and beheld the steep
Jove's Ida and Olympus crown the deep;

> But 'twas not all long ages lore, nor all
> *Their* nature held me in their thrilling thrall ;
> The infant rapture still survived the boy,
> And Loch-na-gar with Ida look'd o'er Troy,
> Mixed Celtic memories with the Phrygian mount,
> And Highland linns with Castalie's clear fount,
> Forgive me, Homer's universal shade !
> Forgive me, Phœbus ! that my fancy stray'd ;
> The north and nature taught me to adore
> Your scenes sublime, from those beloved before.'

In this respect the man was faithful to the boy. In the pleasure, which came to him first at Malvern and afterwards at Cheltenham, in his fourteenth summer, from the hills that reminded him of the Highland mountains, delight at the scenery offered to his gaze was curiously and characteristically blended with delight at the scenery which quickened memory brought before his mental vision. Moore may have been guilty of sentimental extravagance in urging that—' a boy, gazing with emotion on the hills at sunset, because they remind him of the mountains among which he passed his childhood, is already, in heart and imagination, a poet.' Countless boys,—without a single thread of imaginative force, and with no feeling more poetical than the home-sickness, that causes the dullest Swiss exile or any brainless Savoyard organ-grinder of the London streets to pine for his native scenes,—have experienced similar emotion under similar circumstances. But it cannot be questioned that, in thus passing in Fancy's freedom from the distant hills to the heights of Lachin-y-gair, this particular boy made a distinct step towards the domain of feeling, in which he was destined to spend his brief and unrestful manhood.

CHAPTER VII.

HARROW.

Dr. Drury — 'Good-bye, Gaby' — The Fat Boy — His Hatred and Love of Harrow — 'All the Sports' — Cricket and Rebellion — Passionate Friendships — Girlish Sentimentality — Tender-hearted Harrovians — The Poet's Affection for his Schoolmaster — 'The Butler Row' — 'Little Latin and Less Greek' — Declamations — Lord Carlisle's 'Indeed!'

Soon after this visit to Cheltenham, Byron went to Harrow, a school that has been repaid in lustre for its beneficial part in the formation of his character. Entering the school in the middle of his fourteenth year, he was a 'Harrow boy' for four entire years, from the summer of 1801 to the summer of 1805, when, after passing the holidays at Southwell where Mrs. Byron had taken a house (Burgage Manor) in the previous year, he went into residence at Cambridge. A better school than Harrow, or a better master than Dr. Drury, could not have been found for the lad of neglected education, undisciplined temper, and unprepossessing manners, who, sorely needing the discipline of such a seminary, would have rebelled against any government, that was not at the same time firm and sympathetic.

The personal characteristics of the 'wild mountain colt,' in whose eye Dr. Drury detected mental force, and in whose exhibitions of temper the sagacious master discerned a spirit to be more easily led by a silken string than by a cable, differed greatly from the young Lord Cardurcis whose 'long curling black hair and large black eyes' arrested little Venetia Herbert's attention on her first survey of his pale face and slender form, when he was still in his twelfth year. Whilst it is improbable that he retained to his twelfth year the curls which are known, from the miniature given to his nurse, May Gray, to have fallen about the shoulders of the Aberdeen child, it is certain that the poet's eyes were blue-gray (though their long lashes *were* black), that his chestnut hair at its darkest period just missed the deepest brown of auburn, and that from infancy to manhood's threshold he was remarkable for the 'tendency to corpulence' which he is said by Moore to have 'derived from his mother.' The boy, who was led in his fourteenth year to Dr. Drury's presence by Mr. Hanson (the young gentleman's solicitor) was a decidedly plump youth. To the dissipation of romantic visions of a certain tombstone with a handsome stripling in a recumbent posture upon the moss-grown slab, it must even be recorded that, towards the close of his school-days, the boy whom Dr. Drury governed so wisely was a *fat* boy. The hateful epithet comes to this page not from the pen of a rude writer, but it came to him through an ultra-polite writer from the lips of the charming gentlewoman, Miss Pigot of Southwell, who recalled for Tom Moore's advantage, how the 'fat bashful boy' looked and demeaned himself on entering her mother's drawing-room, when he had just finished his third year at Harrow. With cheeks encased in fat, and his hair combed straight over his forehead, the young poet looked such a perfect 'gaby' that the narrator in her girlish sauciness actually told him so. The talk at the poet's first interview with the young lady, who was for some years his most familiar friend of the gentler sex, having turned on the character of Gabriel Lackbrain in the play lately performed at Cheltenham, she responded to the formal bow he made on rising to go, by saying ' Good-bye, Gaby.' To his credit it should be added that, instead of blushing and looking wrathful at the sally, he acknowledged it with a bright smile, and stayed for a few minutes longer, to show how well he could talk on getting the better of his shyness.

To know the real Byron, instead of the unreal and rather absurd Byron of romantic biography, and realise the difficulties under which he fought a painful way to a premature grave, readers should be duly mindful of his morbid propensity to fatten as well as of his lameness, and should also realise how the two afflictions worked *together* in a curious way for his discomfort. In a later chapter of this narrative, attention will be called to the painful measures he employed to correct this disposition to fatten, which the infirmity of his feet prevented him from fighting in a natural and healthy way. But as he did not become unwieldily corpulent, till he ceased growing in height, it is enough to remark that one could not have found amongst his Harrow schoolmates a stouter boy than this young gentleman, who a few years later was remarkable for delicacy of face and elegance of figure.

Whilst they are comical for their remoteness from the truth, the mistakes respecting Byron's appearance are interesting to connoisseurs of evidence for showing by turns how soon people may forget the personal characteristics of their familiar friends, and how likely people are to be misled in matters of detail — especially on questions of colour — by those portraitures in black and white, on which they rely chiefly for information respecting the semblance of individuals they have never seen. Known only to a few dozens of his fellow-countrymen before the morning on which he awoke to find himself famous, and then known to few persons outside the world of fashion, Byron, after shining for a few seasons in London drawing-rooms, left England for ever in early manhood, without having been beheld in the flesh by so many as ten of every thousand English people who, fascinated by the writer, were curious about the man. Wherever he dwelt in foreign lands, his life was one of comparative seclusion — especially of seclusion from natives of his own land. Henceforth his aspect could only be known to the majority of his readers by the black-and-white portraits, exhibited in the windows of printsellers or in his published volumes:—the pictures that, whilst affording a more or less inadequate notion of his profile and the beauty of his mouth and chin, tell nothing of the sweetness and gaiety of his smiles :—the pictures that caused even his former acquaintance to think of him as a dark man. Since Dallas, who knew him intimately during the perfection of his personal attractiveness, was brought by these portraitures to think he had 'fine black hair,' it is not surprising that the younger Disraeli, who never saw the poet, made the same mistake.

From the fantastic things to be found in the biographies of the poet about his life at Harrow, one would suppose that the discipline which did him much good, afforded no sharp trials to the proud boy who had never been taught to obey,—the sensitive boy whose Scotch brogue provoked derision,—the ill-taught boy who entered the school so badly prepared for its studies that had it not been for Dr. Drury's consideration he would have been placed in a class of little fellows greatly his juniors,—the shy boy whose shyness made him uncouth,—the quick-tempered boy whose ' rages ' only stimulated his tormentors to worry him more maliciously,—the sullen boy who was ordered about like a servant and then licked for obeying orders sullenly. Is it not written in Mr. Moore's book that his noble friend ' rose at length to be a leader in *all* the sports, schemes, and mischief of the school?' and does not Dr. Elze follow the lead by applauding the youth ' for excelling in *all* games and sports?' There is something pathetic in the commend-ations thus poured on the poor boy whose lameness debarred him from even participating in some of the games of his comrades. The passages of the poet's jour-nals that speak of his ' cricketing,' and the line of the ' Hours of Idleness ' that refers to ' cricket's manly toil ' as though he had himself ' joined in ' it with pleasure, are mere ' bits of bounce,' to be read betwixt laughter and tears, and ticketed together with the similar pass-ages relating to the poet's pedestrian exploits.

These little essays of ' make-believe ' excepted, Byron himself is frank and truthful enough about the darker side and sterner experiences of his time at Harrow. Far from pretending that from the first he enjoyed the school which he loved so cordially at last, he admits that he detested the place for the first two years and a half,—that is, till time had given him the privileges, and immunities, and authority of an upper-form boy. It is a curious instance of Moore's carelessness, that reduces by exactly two-fifths the period of the poet's dislike of his school. 'Accordingly,' says the biographer, 'we find from his own account, that, for the first year and a half, he hated Harrow,'—a way of misstating the case, in which the Irishman is followed by Dr. Elze. The words equally precise and emphatic of Byron's journal are, 'I always *hated* Harrow till the last year and half, but then I liked it.' Elsewhere in the same reminiscences he says, 'I was a most unpopular boy, but *led* latterly.' From the considerable quantity of information about his life on the Hill, it is sufficiently clear that the period of his extreme unpopularity was identical with the period of his hatred of the school and misery in it. As an underling he was pugnacious, resentful, and in general disfavour; but when he had risen to a position to give the word of command, and indulge his characteristic and essentially amiable, though slightly vain-glorious, taste for protecting little fellows and patronising his juniors, he ceased to provoke enmities and gained a reputation for kindliness. And it cannot be questioned that as a junior he had reason for disliking the school where even the infirmity, of which he was so sensitive, exposed him to insults. When, in later time, the coarser of his assailants in the press sneered at the bodily as well as mental deformity of the wretched rhymester, who not content with maligning Christianity had even presumed to lampoon the Prince Regent, the poet remarked with affected indifference that he had not gone through a public school without learning that he was deformed. 'Unfortunately,' Leigh Hunt observes respecting his friend's lameness, 'the usual thoughtlessness of schoolboys made him feel it bitterly at Harrow. He would wake, and find his leg in a tub of water.' Such indignities, which were largely accountable for his long dislike of Harrow, came to an end in 1804, when he was in the proud position to record in one of his note-books: 'Drury's Pupils, 1804. Byron, Drury, Sinclair, Hoare, Bolder, Annesley, Calvert, Strong, Acland, Gordon, Drummond.' As one of 'Drury's Pupils,' the youthful poet could be benignant to 'juniors,' such as his 'favourites' Clare, Dorset, C. Gordon, De Bath, Claridge, and J. Wingfield, whom in his loftiness and superabundant lenity he even, to use his own words, 'spoilt by indulgence!' His tombstone became a throne, with courtiers regarding him reverentially from a distance. These also were the days of the 'cricketing' referred to in his journal with curious self-complacence; when he could amuse himself for half-an-hour with the bat, whilst juniors did the bowling and fielding, and a fag made the runs for him.

One would like to know what grounds the poet had (if he had any) for writing in February 1812 to Master John Cowell, on that young gentleman's departure for Eton : 'As an Etonian, you will look down upon a Harrow man; but I never, even in my boyish days, disputed your superiority, which I once experienced in a cricket match, where I had the honour of making one of the eleven, who were beaten to their hearts' content by your college in *one innings*.' Though cricket eighty years since was no such arduous sport as the cricket of this year of grace, it is scarcely credible that Byron, whilst 'leading' his school, took the part his words imply in the match. If he did it is not surprising that Harrow was badly beaten in a single innings.

His choice of familiar associates at Harrow certainly justifies Moore's remark that 'it is a mistake to suppose that, either at school or afterwards, he was at all guided in the selection of his friends by aristocratic sympathies.' But few persons will concur with the same biographer in thinking that he was actuated by *pride* in surrounding himself with 'favourites' who, from being his inferiors in age and strength, looked to him for protection ; the delight in patronising being referable to vanity rather than to pride.

The most remarkable and characteristic features of Byron's intercourse with these 'favourites,' is the girlishness of the sentiment he lavished upon them and the girlishness of the regard with which they repaid his affection. 'L'amitié, qui dans la monde est à peine un sentiment, est une passion dans les cloîtres,' is an aphorism, that he adopted from Marmontel, and put into one of his note-books in his third year after leaving Harrow,—doubtless because it struck him as peculiarly applicable to his enthusiasm for his friends at school and afterwards at the university. 'My school friendships,' he wrote in the journal, that may be called the 'Autobiography of his Boyhood,' 'were with *me passions* (for I was always violent), but I do not know that there is one which has endured (to be sure some have been cut short by death) till now. That with Lord Clare began one of the earliest, and lasted longest—being only interrupted by distance—that I know of. I never hear the word ' *Clare* ' without a beating of the heart even *now*, and I write it with the feelings of 1803–4–5, ad infinitum.' The record is the more interesting, because of the approximate date, given to the commencement of this peculiar development of sensibility and affectionateness. The friendship for Lord Clare, which began in 1803 (the poet's sixteenth year), having been ' one of the earliest,' the Harrow ' passions ' may be regarded as the affairs of the later half of his school life.

But if they were ' passions,' these school friendships were the ' passions ' of a girl, rather than of a boy endowed with the robustness appropriate to his sex. They were girlish in their tenderness, tearful vehemence, and incontinence of emotion. They were girlish (on both sides—but especially on Byron's side) in the jealousies, suspicions, and piques that attended them. Sometimes it is scarcely less exasperating than diverting to observe the ' tiffs ' and reconciliations of these tender-hearted Harrovians who, when least girlish, are so many sentimental French lads, wearing their hearts on their sleeves, rather than stout English boys, holding their hearts in their breasts. The misunderstandings of these mutually ' loving ' and ' beloved ' youths arose out of the absurdest trifles, which caused them to mope, and shed tears, and write ' tiffy ' letters to one another because they were not so much ' loved ' as they ought to be. Byron is in his last year at Harrow, when he is aggrieved by the cruel coldness of a school-mate, who has positively had the inhuman hardness to address the poet in a letter as ' My dear Byron,' instead of 'my dearest.' At another time the Harrow 'leader' is fretting because the same correspondent, instead of loving his dearest Byron more than any-one else, seems to care less for him than for John Russell. To another school-mate who has wounded his sensibilities, the Poet of the Hill writes in the following strain of anguish and indignation :—

'You knew that my soul, that my heart, my existence,
  If danger demanded, were wholly your own ;
You know me unaltered by years or by distance,
  Devoted to love and to friendship alone.

'You knew—but away with the vain retrospection,
  The bond of affection no longer endures,
Too late you may droop o'er the fond recollection,
  And sigh for the friend who was formerly yours.'

That the poet's influence at Harrow during his last year was considerable, and that he was in a certain way the leader as he afterwards boasted of the school, is shown by the fact that, whilst living in a small set of sentimental worshippers--for whose peculiar sentimentalism he was himself altogether or at least chiefly accountable, he was still so far accept-able to the majority of the upper boys, as to be made the chief director of their comical demonstration against the election of Dr. Butler to be Dr. Drury's successor. But it cannot be said that the influence, which disposed a considerable proportion of the cleverer and more sensitive boys to play the part of 'friendship-sick maidens,' was a wholesome in-fluence. One can readily believe, as Dr. Butler seems to have believed, that it was by no means conducive to the manliness that should distinguish the sons of English gentlemen,—and, indeed, the sons of Englishmen of every class. Of course, the influence, so completely resulting from sympathy with the single boy of an exceptional constitution and peculiar temperament, was transient. It was not in the nature of things that,—on the disappearance of the Apostle of Friendship with his power of verse and the set of admirers to whom he communicated his peculiar sentimentalism,—the boys of a great public school should continue to cherish 'passions' of friendship for one another, and turn tearful at being styled 'dear' instead of 'my dearest' in the heading of a letter. It was not even possible for the boys, whom Byron had infused with his peculiar girlishness, to continue in the way of feeling to which he introduced them. On contact with the world these Byronized schoolboys became men of common sense ; and the Apostle of 'passionate friendship' was deserted by his disciples. All this is told by Harness, where he says of his former patron at Harrow,—'Of his attachment to his friends, no one can read Moore's " Life," and entertain a doubt. He required a great deal from them—not more, perhaps, than he, from the abundance of his love, freely and fully gave—but more than they had to return.'

But there was another side to the boy's Harrow life, to which it is a relief to turn, after thinking of its girlishness. If they are honourable to the master, the poet's feelings for Dr. Drury throughout his school days and to the end of his life are no less creditable to the pupil. Nothing more is required to show how gentle, and docile a creature Byron would have been in his childhood under proper management, and how amenable he was in his older infancy to authority, that commended itself to his sense of right and justice, than his consistent and unwavering gratitude to the great schoolmaster, who governed him for four years with sympathy and at the same time with firmness. 'Dr. Drury,' he says in the autobiographic Journal, 'whom I plagued sufficiently too, was the best, the kindest (and yet strict, too) friend I ever had—and I look upon him still as a father.' The letter, in which the poet announced his acceptance by Miss Milbanke and his approaching marriage to his old master, is in the same vein of filial confidence and affection.

Of the other examples of the poet's regard for his famous preceptor, there are two that may not be omitted from these pages. The schoolboy had become a man ; and the man had almost in an hour mounted to a giddy eminence of celebrity, and was still in the full enjoyment of his first intoxicating triumphs, when, on being asked by Dr. Drury why he had not sent his old master copies of his works, he answered with unaffected modesty and simple truth, 'Because, sir, you are the only man I never wish to read them.' Years later,—when he had withdrawn from his native land for ever, under the thunder of the loud calumny to which he grew by degrees comparatively indifferent, and the fire of 'the speechless obloquy,' that never ceased to work like poison in his soul,—on putting into the Fourth Canto of 'Childe Harold' some lines to the discredit of the system of education that prevails in English schools, he was careful to guard the verses with a note of homage and reverential explanation, so as to spare his dear old master the pain that might come to him through misapprehension of the author's purpose. The words of the poem, thus guarded from misconstruction, are—

' .   .   .   . not in vain
May he, who will his recollections rake
And quote in classic raptures, and awake
The hills with Latian echoes; I abhorr'd
Too much, to conquer for the poet's sake,
The drill'd dull lesson, forced down word by word
In my repugnant youth, with pleasure to record

'Aught that recalls the daily drug which turn'd
My sickening memory; and, though Time hath taught
My mind to meditate on what it learn'd,
Yet such the fix'd inveteracy of thought
That, with the freshness wearing out before
My mind could relish what it might have sought,
If free to choose, I cannot now restore
Its health; but what it then detested, still abhor.'

The note runs thus, 'I wish to express that we become tired of the task before we can comprehend the beauty; that we learn by rote before we can get by heart; that the freshness is worn away, and the future pleasure and advantage deadened and destroyed, by the didactic anticipation, at an age when we can neither feel nor understand the power of composition which it requires an acquaintance with life, as well as Latin and Greek, to relish, or to reason upon. For the same reason we can never be aware of the fulness of some of the finest passages of Shakespeare ("To be, or not to be," for instance), from the habit of having them hammered into us at eight years old, as an exercise, not of mind but of memory, so that when we are old enough to enjoy them, the taste is gone, and the appetite palled. In some parts of the Continent, young persons are taught from more common authors, and do not read the best classics till their maturity. I certainly do not speak on this point from pique or aversion towards the place of my education. I was not a slow, though an idle boy: and I believe no one could, or can be more attached to Harrow than I have always been, and with reason;— a part of the time passed there was the happiest of my life; and my preceptor (the Rev. Dr. Joseph Drury) was the best and worthiest friend I ever possessed, whose warnings I have remembered but too well, though too late—when I have erred, and whose counsels I have but followed when I have done well or wisely. If ever this imperfect record of my feelings towards him should reach his eyes, let it remind him of one who never thinks of him but with gratitude and veneration—of one who would more gladly boast of having been his pupil, if, by more closely following his injunctions, he could reflect any honour upon his instructor.'

Notwithstanding all this evidence of the affectionate dutifulness, which distinguished Byron's conduct to his principal school-master, both during his stay at Harrow and throughout the years of his manhood, there exists a notion that he was chiefly remarkable at Harrow for unruliness and a taste for rebellion. The people, whose ingenuity has especially delighted in drawing indictments against him from scraps of his writings and in dealing with the figures of his poetry as though they were facts of his personal story, have even found testimony of the poet's naughtiness at school in the following lines, of 'The Address to the Duke of Dorset,'—

> Ah ! though myself, by nature haughty, wild,
> Whom Indiscretion hail'd her favourite child ;
> Though every error stamps me for her own,
> And dooms my fall, I fain would fall alone ;
> Though my proud heart no precept now can tame,
> I love the virtues which I cannot claim.'

Evidence of a sensitive conscience and spiritual modesty, rather a strong propensity to evil, evidence especially interesting to biographers for showing at how early a date Byron's practice of magnifying his own misdeeds began—these words of an imaginative boy, playing the part of a stern moralist, should scarcely be taken as a culprit's confession. The witness against himself should at least be allowed the benefit of his avowal of 'loving the virtues.'

Apart from the misdemeanours of which he was unquestionably guilty towards Dr. Butler, there was as little reality in the 'rebelling' as there was in the 'cricketing,' to which the poet refers so jauntily in his journal; and on examination, even those misdemeanours are found altogether insufficient to sustain the grave charge of a propensity for rebellion. The whole business of 'the Butler Row' grew out of a trivial affair. When Dr. Drury retired from the Mastership of Harrow in 1805, there were three candidates for the office,—Mark Drury, Evans, and Butler; and naturally enough Byron came to the fore of the boys, who from affection of their old master entertained a strong opinion, that the office which a Drury had filled so honourably ought to descend to a Drury, who, of course, *as* he was a Drury, would fill it with equal honour. Each candidate had his party of well-wishers amongst the boys, who—of course, without seriously supposing their voices

would or should determine the issue of the contest—
behaved as though the election rested with them.
The parties lampooned and hooted one another, and
worked themselves into a prodigious excitement
about a matter, that was no more their affair than
the choice of the next President of the United States.
On the election of Dr. Butler, the beaten parties
united in imagining themselves very badly treated.
In the excitement Byron behaved badly, and was
guilty of at least one overt act of rebellion, for which
he would of course have been severely punished, had
not the new Head Master wisely determined to take
a lenient view of misconduct, committed without
calm deliberation and in consequence of his own
success. Byron (a boarder in Dr. Butler's house)
pulled down the gratings before some of the Master's
windows, and on being called upon to answer for his
conduct, had the impudence to say without a word of
apology, that he tore down the gratings 'because
they darkened the hall.' On the other hand, the
poet ranged himself on the side of order, when some
of his confederates proposed to burn down one of the
class-rooms,—an outrage from which they were withheld by their leader, who reminded them that in
doing so they would destroy the desks, illustrated
with the names of their fathers and grandfathers.
But though he saved the class-room, he persisted to
the last in showing disrespect to Dr. Butler; even
going the length of declining at the end of the term
to accept the invitation to dinner which the Doctor
sent to him as an upper boy, in accordance with
etiquette of ancient usage. Moore even goes so far
as to assert, on the authority of one of Byron's school-

fellows, that on being asked his reason for declining the invitation, the poet replied to his interrogator, 'Why, Dr. Butler, if you should happen to come into my neighbourhood when I was staying at Newstead, I certainly should not ask you to dine with me, and therefore I feel that I ought not to dine with you.' As Dr. Butler, on seeing this story in Moore's 'Life,' assured the biographer that the anecdote had very little foundation in fact, it may be assumed that the explanation was worded less offensively. Byron's worst act in the whole of this puerile business was the last of his offences. Instead of dismissing his dislike of Dr. Butler on leaving Harrow, he was so wrong-headed as to publish in the 'Hours of Idleness' some offensive verses against the Master, who had given him no grounds for enduring displeasure.

But though Byron cannot be acquitted of behaving badly in this affair, much may be said in palliation of his misbehaviour. Devotion to his old master was the cause of his strong feeling about the election, that occasioned so much excitement in the school. Instead of being the originator of the riotous movements, that arose in the school immediately after the election, he was actually holding aloof from his party when he was entreated to command it. Indiscretion is venial 'even in an Upper Boy,' whose pride is tickled by an invitation to 'lead his comrades.' There is no doubt he believed the new Master to be unworthy of his office, and conceived he was under no moral obligation to accept the ruler who had been imposed upon him. His most mutinous acts resulted from the heats of contention. The sensitive and quick-tempered boy imagined he had been insulted by a chief, who in order to humiliate him had exceeded the limits of his authority. The offensive verses were inserted in the 'Hours of Idleness,' when the poet was under the exasperating impression that the Master was in the habit of holding him up to the reprobation of his former schoolmates, as a dangerous companion and a discredit to the school. Under these circumstances the indignant boy may be pardoned for behaving for a while with the perversity and vehemence of youth. Anyhow, to wipe out every speck of the discredit put upon his character by the affair, it was only needful for Dr. Drury's tractable and loyal-hearted pupil to repent of his folly, and express the feeling to Dr. Drury's successor. Byron did both. On coming to his right mind, the young poet hastened to Dr. Butler and made him an ample apology. Before leaving England the poet was on good terms with his former enemy; and he started for Greece with the purpose of withdrawing the offensive lines from the 'Hours of Idleness' in the next edition of the poems. In the same spirit, on coming to review his life in his twenty-sixth year, he wrote in the Journal of reminiscences, 'I was a most unpopular boy, but *led* latterly, and have retained many of my school friendships, and all my dislikes—except to Dr. Butler, whom I treated rebelliously, and have been sorry ever since.' These are the facts of Byron's misbehaviour—a passage of boyish effervescence, followed by ample atonement and generous repentance —to which some of his calumniators have pointed in evidence that he was from his youth an ill-conditioned fellow.

Note 40 to the 4th Canto of 'Childe Harold'

tells how little Byron profited by the classical instruction of the school, that is so largely indebted to him for its celebrity. Had he come to the school at an early age and after better preparation the note would probably never have been written, and the poet would probably have taken a more favourable view of the educational method of England's public schools. He might not have entertained the ambition of editing Greek and Latin classics, but it is more than possible he would have been delighted to—

> '. . . quote in classic raptures, and awake
> The hills with Latian echoes.'

Coming to the school in a state of ignorance, that put him at a disadvantage with class-mates, greatly his inferiors in natural quickness, he never had the heart for the steady labour that could alone enable him to compete with them for the honours of the term. Perhaps no boy ever brought less Latin and Greek to Harrow, or after rising to the highest form carried less of those learned tongues away with him to his university. The very volumes of Greek plays, which he gave to the library on his departure for Cambridge, afford evidence in his own handwriting of the insignificance of his ' classical attainments ' at the time when, in the technical and strictly scholastic sense of the words, they were at their highest. To mathematics he had a strong repugnance ;—his natural inaptitude for even the most familiar processes of arithmetic being so unusual that, in the later period of his life when it was his humour to watch his domestic expenditure with a jealous eye, he experienced no little difficulty and distress of brain in ' auditing ' his ' weekly bills.' Had he distinguished himself in the

Latin and Greek classes, it would have been less remarkable that he went to Cambridge without having acquired facility and exactitude in the spelling of his mother-tongue ; for in the earlier years of the present century, it was almost a point of honour with a public-schoolboy, who knew Homer well, to spell his own language indifferently. The bad spelling of the Harrovian, who prided himself on his considerable knowledge of English literature, deserves notice ; for whilst it may be regarded as indicative of the *literal* carelessness with which he perused the pages of his favourite authors, the deficiency may also be regarded as evidence that he was not altogether free from the particular kind of intellectual indolence, that is often united with mental sprightliness and seldom fails to characterise in some degree the poetic dreamer.

But if he was weak in his Latin and still weaker in his Greek, Byron distinguished himself at Declamations,—a scholastic exercise in which the elder boys of the school delivered as orations, in Dr. Drury's presence, the essays which they had previously written on given subjects. In these exercises, so excellently designed to qualify the youthful orators for one department of public life, Byron was successful in attitude, gesture, and vocal address ; and on one occasion he distinguished himself in a way that greatly impressed his most critical hearer. After delivering the earlier part of his composition with his usual address, he suddenly broke away from the restraint of the written words, and no less to the Doctor's surprise than sympathetic apprehension for the boy's failure passed to extempore utterances that, without any kind of impediment, flowed through well-balanced periods to a felicitous conclusion. 'I questioned him,' Dr. Drury told Moore, 'why he had altered his declamation? He declared he had made no alteration, and did not know, in speaking, that he had deviated from it one letter. I believed him ; and from a knowledge of his temperament am convinced, that, fully impressed with the sense and substance of the subject, he was hurried on to expressions and colourings more striking than what his pen had expressed.' Byron had probably displayed this power of strenuous speech, when Dr. Drury said of him to Lord Carlisle, 'He has talents, my Lord, which will add lustre to his rank ;' praise that, to the Doctor's disappointment, only drew from the Earl a look of surprise and a significant 'Indeed !'

CHAPTER VIII.

HARROW HOLIDAYS.

Lady Holderness's Death—'Baby Byron'—His Sister Augusta—Her Plain Face and Sweet Nature — Life at Southwell — Mary Anne Chaworth — Matlock and Castleton — Annesley Hall — Who was Thyrza ?—' The Dream '—Its Falsehood and Malice.

HOWEVER. good his school may be, and however efficient his tutors, they are seldom the most important, never the only, forces of a boy's education. To observe the influences that are usually more powerful over his nature than his official and recognised teachers, one must follow the lad of quick feelings and lively intelligence from the class-room and the play-ground to his home, and be the sharer of his holidays.

In Byron's case it is the more necessary to do this, because the pleasures of his Harrow holidays were more influential in the development of his affections and genius, than they would have been, had the shy, sensitive, meditative boy been strongly interested in the severer pursuits of his school. In those holidays he learnt to love his sister, and conceived his passion for Mary Chaworth. In those holidays he explored (in the saddle—*not* on foot, as his biographers suggest) some of the loveliest parts of Nottinghamshire, and during hours of solitary gladness studied the tranquil beauties and stately aspects of Newstead. In those times of vacation he had also larger opportunities for reading novels,—those toys of the frivolous, those comforters of the aged, and those powerful teachers of the young.

Immediately after her son's departure for his first term at Harrow, Mrs. Byron went to Brighton for several months. She was still breathing by turns the sea-air and the breezes from the downs, when, on the old Countess of Holderness's death, she came to the opinion it would be well for her boy and his sister to come together. So long as he remained at Aberdeen, no painful question arose respecting the separation of the children. But it was otherwise when on coming to Sloane Terrace, Mrs. Byron discovered that, though the Countess had no disposition to refuse Mrs. Byron's boy occasional access to his sister, she had no wish for Mrs. Byron's acquaintance. It is not surprising that the aged lady, with little cause to think tenderly of Mad Jack Byron, had no intention to be troubled with visits from his second wife, whose least agreeable qualities were not unknown to the dame of high degree. And had Mrs. Byron been a sensible woman, and more thoughtful for her child's welfare than her own dignity, she would have waived a few points of social etiquette, in consideration of the Dowager's age and infirmities, and· have allowed the boy the pleasure and benefit of associating with his sister on terms, to which the Countess could consent. But Mrs. Byron, after speaking proud words of the Gordons and scornful words of the Dutch woman's presumption, determined to keep the children asunder. This state of things, however, came to an end in 1802 ; and henceforth Byron had, in his holidays, sufficient though by no means frequent opportunities of associating with his sister, who during their separation had never ceased to think of him as 'the baby' that he was when she last kissed him in Holles Street, and who for that reason, as well as from a humorous perception of the poet's least manly though by no means least agreeable qualities, used to call him 'Baby Byron' after he had become famous. When the fourteen-years old boy began to know and love his sister (the only person of her sex, whom he ever regarded for any considerable period, with deep, steady and unchanging affection), she was eighteen years of age, and it is probable that he was at their first interview disappointed by her appearance, which cannot in a single particular have accorded with his boyish conceptions of feminine loveliness. For even at the age, when girlish charms are most apparent, the Honourable Augusta Byron would have been rated as a decidedly plain girl, or overlooked altogether on account of her insignificance. Notably wanting in beauty of feature, her appearance —from the day of her presentation at Queen Charlotte's court, to which she was in later time officially attached—was chiefly remarkable for the want of 'style' and of taste in dress, that made her (to use Mrs. Shelley's well-chosen expression) 'the Dowdy-Goody' of all her acquaintance. It speaks not a little for Byron's affectionateness that, from the first hour of his intercourse with her, he was the fond brother of so unattractive a sister. In one respect only was Augusta Byron fortunate in her personal endowments. Her not unintelligent countenance had

an expression altogether accordant with the sweetness
of disposition, the womanly goodness and the unaffected piety, that, unaided by any kind of cleverness,
made her from first to last the chief influence for
good in her brother's life.

From Brighton Mrs. Byron moved to Bath, where
she was joined by her son during the summer holidays of 1802 ; when in the costume of a Turkish boy,
with a diamond crescent in his turban, he attended
her to Lady Riddle's masquerade. Returning soon
after the Bath season to Nottingham, where she
resumed her former lodgings, Mrs. Byron resided
there till she moved to Southwell in the later half of
1804, and established herself at Burgage Manor, a
pleasant roomy house on 'the Green,' and drew
about her the neighbours, amongst whom the poet
made several congenial acquaintances. A better place
of abode could not have been found for a gentlewoman
in Mrs. Byron's rather peculiar circumstances than
this pleasant little town, with its collegiate church
and picturesque vicinity, its public coffee-room with
papers and gossip for the gentlemen, its assembly
room for concerts and dances, and its coterie of clergy
and other local gentry — such as the Pigots, the Leacrofts and the Housons — who, in their simple
contentment at finding the youthful peer within their
borders, were lenient to Mrs. Byron's want of refinement, and concealed their disapproval of her vagaries.
Near enough to Newstead, for its story and beauties
to be known to every inhabitant of the town, the
Byrons enjoyed at Southwell all the homage due to
their patrician quality and territorial greatness.
Before his Cambridge career, Byron had of course

seen enough of the town's provincial pettiness, and spoken sharp words of its dullness and delight in scandal; but after his return from Greece, when needy Mr. Dallas was looking out for a place of cheap and agreeable seclusion, the poet wrote to him from Newstead Abbey (Oct. 11th, 1811). 'Now I know a large village, or small town, about twelve miles off, where your family would have the advantage of very genteel society, without the hazard of being annoyed by mercantile affluence ; where *you* would meet with men of information and independence ; and where I have friends to whom I should be proud to introduce you. . . . . My mother had a house there for some years, and I am well acquainted with the economy of Southwell, the name of this little commonwealth.'

Mrs. Byron, however, was still in the lodgings at Nottingham, when, in the summer of 1803, her son came to her from the school, which he had not yet ceased to 'hate.' How the boy must have enjoyed his solitary rides about Nottinghamshire on his clever horse,—in the fleckered shade of green lanes and in the sun that was never too hot for him ; far away from those ungenerous enemies to his peace of mind, who thought meanly of him for his lameness and imperfect acquaintance with the Greek irregular verbs! It was a memorable vacation (this year) for the boy who, in its course, put himself on pleasant terms with Lord Grey de Ruthen, the tenant under chancery and occupier of Newstead, till the heir was on the point of 'coming into his own.' That the schoolboy might have some present enjoyment of the property, that would be in his hands six years hence, Lord Grey de Ruthen gave him a standing invitation to the Abbey, and even assigned him a room in the mansion, for his use at pleasure. At the same time the doors of Annesley Hall, the home of his cousins— the Chaworths, were thrown open to the young peer, who had already seen the heiress of the fair domain in London.

Little thinking what trouble would come of it, Miss Mary Chaworth—with her sweet voice, piquant air, strangely beautiful face, and all the gaiety of girlhood in its eighteenth year—covering the boy with kindness and filling him with gladness, inspired him with his third grand passion. She was all the more benignant to him, on the first occasion of his crossing her threshold, in order that he should be the less likely to remember that hideous duel which had now for nearly half a century kept Chaworths and Byrons asunder. A bed at Annesley was put at the service of the visitor, who was already provided with a sleeping apartment at Newstead. So the young peer passed the hours pleasantly between the two houses, spending however less time under the shadow of the ancestral ruins, than in the drawing-room where the young heiress sung again and again, for his particular delight, the song (with a pleasant air) of 'Mary Anne,'—a name of witchery and music, surely, to any poet loving a particular Mary Anne. The heiress made up a party for a trip to Matlock and Castleton, and invited the schoolboy to join it. Of course he joined it ; and the young people—four girls, two gentlemen, the young lord from Harrow, with a chaperon of suitable years and complaisance— went off to the Derbyshire springs, and did as people used to do at Matlock and Castleton, and at the delightful spots round about them. At Matlock there was much dancing that afforded the lame lad poignant misery ; for in his inability to dance, he could only stand or sit in a corner of the ball-room, whilst his goddess danced with the partners who were eager to lead her out. Still he would rather endure anguish in the corner of the hot room, than vainly seek happiness where she was not. For he was possessed with a passion,—the third and greatest of all his grand passions.

On her return from Derbyshire, Miss Chaworth was attended by the schoolboy, who, having slept at Annesley before the trip, resumed the room, which had been assigned to him. Instead of availing himself, at first, of the permission to pass the nights under his cousin's roof, he preferred to sleep at Newstead, because of a fancy that the portraits of the departed Chaworths would in the hours of silence and darkness descend from their frames, and as restless ghosts disturb the slumber of the Byron, who had ventured to enter the house long closed to the bearers of his name. But after encountering ' a bogle ' on his darksome way from Annesley to Newstead, he thought he might as well speak with ghosts at home as with ghosts at large. Though trivial, this story deserves notice, as it points to a nervous weakness that attended Lord Byron throughout life. In his weaker and more indolent moods, Byron was superstitious. A believer in presentiments and unlucky days, in apparitions and ghostly warnings, he would sometimes discover prophetic significance in strange coincidences, and refer to supernatural agency what he should have referred to indigestion.

It is not surprising that Miss Chaworth was slow to detect her young visitor's ' passion,' and that for a moment she found it difficult to refrain from laughter, when the shy boy, of ' rough and odd' manners (if Moore may be trusted), blurted out his staggering proposal for the union of their hearts and their ' lands rich and broad.' In their pity for the boy, who suffered so long and acutely from his entertainment of a preposterous hope, people have felt less than proper concern for the feelings and embarrassment of the young heiress, on finding herself with so strange a suitor on her hands. Divided between the fear of giving pain by treating the affair too lightly, and the fear of causing the boy deeper and more enduring distress by treating the affair too seriously, she may well have been perplexed, and in her perplexity must more than once have wished the lad at—Harrow. The care she had for his feelings is the more commendable, as there was nothing in his appearance to win from her even the kind of favour, with which bright and well-looking school-boys are usually regarded by grown women. If his countenance, ' notwithstanding the tendency to corpulence derived from his mother,' already ' gave promise of that peculiar expression into which his features refined and kindled afterwards,' the faint indications were accompanied with an air that betrayed he was more than duly conscious of them. Moore learnt from several quarters that, at this point of his boyhood, the young Lord of Newstead was ' by no means popular among girls of his own age ; ' and it was less due to his want of personal comeliness than to his self-consciousness and vanity that the young ladies found him 'insufferable' and a 'perfect horror.' In truth, the lad who appeared a laughable gaby to Miss Pigot in the summer of 1804, must have seemed an egregious gaby to Miss Chaworth in the summer of 1803. The very devices, by which he sought to plant himself in the heiress's affections, were more likely to offend than to conciliate a young woman with a proper sense of her own dignity, and a fairly quick sense of the ridiculous. In his egregious vanity, he tried to play the part of a lady-killer, and to pique his coldly benignant mistress into loving him by a boastful exhibition of a locket, given him by a fair adorer, whom the heiress of Annesley was thus invited to regard as her rival. If this locket was given him, as Moore suggests, by his cousin Margaret Parker, the use to which he now put it shows how completely his latest passion had for the moment driven from his breast all generous tenderness and chivalric regret for the girl, whose elegy he had written some eight or nine months since,—and whose image some eight years later became the chief, if not the only, inspiring force of the 'Poems to Thyrza.'

But however droll and amusing they may be to cynical spectators of his proceedings, the absurdities of a boy's fierce love, whether it be for the high-born heiress of a great estate or for an obscure actress of a provincial theatre, are little calculated to assuage the first anguish or lessen the subsequent annoyances of the failure of his suit. It did not comfort Arthur Pendennis for losing the fair Fotheringay, to think how his uncle was chuckling in his sleeve, and to know that even Emily's papa thought him a simpleton. Though he may be presumed to have ordered his pony and ridden off to Newstead, instead of 'darting out of the house' and making at full speed for the Abbey on his feet, in the fashion described by half-a-dozen different historians, no one with sympathy for the griefs of beardless boys—certainly no man who can recall how he himself sickened long syne and all but died of 'calf-love'—will suspect the biographers of exaggeration in recording that the fifteen-years old peer carried away from Annesley a heart full of scalding anguish, after hearing either from the young lady's lips, or from the tongue of a spiteful tale-bearer, those torturing words—'Do you think I could care anything for that lame boy?' The disappointment was followed quickly by clear and agonizing recognition of all the folly of his futile suit, as well as of the madness of his baffled hopes. Quick to wound its possessor long before it taught him how to wound others, the boy's sense of the ludicrous, acting like acid on the etcher's plate, helped to bite Mary Chaworth's picture deeper into his memory. The recollection of his ignoble hunger for her 'lands broad and rich' and the gold that could restore the ruinous mansion in his park, intensified the torture of reflecting on his brief, insane, ennobling desire for her beauty and love. Turning his pale cheek scarlet, and in an instant covering his brow with cold beads of wetness, as it came to his mind, that mean desecration of Margaret Parker's love-token, gave sharper point and surer poison to the stinging words—'Do you think I could care anything for that lame boy?' Possibly this cruel misadventure was largely, if not altogether, accountable for the fervour with which the boy, on his return to Harrow, in his strong yearning for sympathy and in his despair of being loved by womankind, threw himself into those 'friendships' that were so curious a feature of his later time at school.

In the ensuing summer—the holidays of 1804, which he passed chiefly at Southwell—the boy visited Annesley, and wrote in one of Miss Chaworth's books the set of verses, for which he was indebted to another poet,—

> 'Oh Memory, torture me no more,
>   The present's all o'ercast;
> My hopes of future bliss are o'er,
>   In mercy veil the past.
> Why bring those images to view
>   I henceforth must resign?
> Ah! why those happy hours renew,
>   That never can be mine?
> Past pleasure doubles present pain,
>   To sorrow adds regret,
> Regret and hope are both in vain,
>   I ask but to—forget.'

Soon after he transferred these verses from a printed book to the leaf, that would be almost certain to come again under her gaze, Byron (now in the middle of his seventeenth year) bade Miss Chaworth farewell on the hill (near Annesley), to which 'The Dream' had given the twofold interest of poetry and history,—

> 'the hill
> . . . crown'd with a peculiar diadem
> Of trees, in circular array, so fix'd,
> Not by the sport of nature, but of man.'

It can readily be believed that, though his countenance was calm, the feelings which he held well under control at this interview were feelings of unutterable misery and hopelessness.

'The next time I see you, I suppose you will be Mrs. Chaworth?' he said at the moment of parting.

'I hope so,' was the lady's only answer.

In the August of the following year (1805), when Byron—no longer a Harrow *boy*, but a *man* who had already chosen his university and college—was staying at his mother's house on Southwell Green, Mary Anne Chaworth was married to Mr. John Musters, a handsome man and notable sportsman, who after taking the bride's name on the occasion of the marriage and bearing it for a few years, resumed his former surname. Perhaps a more foolish story never passed from a mendacious prattler to a serious biography than the anecdote told by Moore of the manner in which Byron was informed that this marriage had taken place, and of the self-possession he displayed on the unexpected announcement. It runs thus, on the authority of some person who was of course present at the scene that can hardly have taken place:—'His mother said, "Byron, I have some news for you."—"Well, what is it?" "Take out your handkerchief, I say." He did so, to humour her. "Miss Chaworth is married!" An expression very peculiar, impossible to describe, passed over his pale face, and he hurried his handkerchief into his pocket, saying, with an affected air of coldness and nonchalance, "Is that all?"—"Why, I expected you would have been plunged in grief." He made no reply, and soon began to talk about something else.' Is it credible that even Mrs. Byron (with clear recollection of the painful agitation she had in former time caused her son by an abrupt announcement of Mary Duff's marriage) behaved in so cruel a fashion to her boy, whilst he was still suffering from

the disappointment of his passion for Mary Chaworth?
A woman must be far worse-tempered and worse-bred
even than Mrs. Byron to behave so brutally to a love-
stricken son.   The woman, who, in a fit of passion
with the child, could swear at him, and call him
'lame brat!' could not amuse herself thus malignantly
with the bitter anguish of the man.   Even when full
account is taken of the propensity, which made Mrs.
Cardurcis so eager for just ' one glass of' Lady
Annabel Herbert's ' mountain,' there is no evidence
to justify even a suspicion that Catherine Byron
could *without provocation* act so atrociously.   Again
is it conceivable that the news of Mary Chaworth's
marriage came in this fashion as a surprise to the
young lord, who was living within twelve miles of
her park-fence.   The heiress had been engaged to
Mr. Musters for two years: Mr. Musters had obtained
Letters of Licence to take the name of Chaworth
before the marriage ; all Nottinghamshire had been
talking for weeks over the arrangements for the approaching wedding ; the Byrons themselves would
have been at their kinswoman's marriage, had not
delicacy forbidden Miss Chaworth to invite her discarded suitor to the celebration.   In the name of
whatever little common sense may be found in this
mad world, outside lunatic asylums, is it conceivable
that under all these circumstances Byron can have
first heard of the wedding in the alleged manner?
The whole story is nothing more than a clumsy re-
production (with variations) of the story of the way
in which Byron was suddenly informed of Mary Duff's
marriage,—which took place in the year before Miss
Chaworth's marriage.   Either the narrator who was

present at the scene ' mixed the two Maries,' so as to substitute the wrong one for the right one ; or Moore was himself the maker of the mistake. It is quite conceivable that Moore muddled the story, which ' the narrator ' told correctly.

Byron did not see his cousin Mary Chaworth after her marriage, till he dined with her at Annesley, at her husband's invitation in 1808 ; when he was deeply stirred by the appearance of her little girl,—the infant and the incident alluded to in the lines, dated from Newstead on 11th October, 1811 :—

> ' I've seen my bride another's bride,—
> Have seen her seated by his side,—
> Have seen the infant which she bore,
> Wear the sweet smile the mother wore,
> When she and I in youth have smiled,
> As fond and faultless as her child :—
> Have seen her eyes, in cold disdain,
> Ask if I felt no secret pain ;
> And *I* have acted well my part,
> And made my cheek belie my heart,
> Return'd the freezing glance she gave,
> Yet felt the while *that* woman's slave ;—
> Have kissed, as if without design,
> The babe which ought to have been mine,
> And show'd, alas ! in each caress
> Time had not made me love the less.'

And now comes the question who was ' Thyrza,'— to whose spirit in heaven Byron penned the five poems (to be found in the ' Occasional Pieces '), during the deepest gloom of the sorrow, that covered him in the closing months of 1811 and the earlier months of 1812 ? Moore says that Thyrza was a creation of the poet's imagination, and that the poems addressed to this 'imaginary object' of the poet's affection 'were the essence, the abstract spirit, as it were, of many griefs.' On the other hand, the Editor of Mr. Murray's one-volume edition of Byron's works is of opinion that Thyrza was the person, to whose death the poet referred in a letter dated October 11th, 1811 (the *exact* date assigned to the first set of verses to Thyrza), in the following words, 'I have been again shocked with a death, and have lost one very dear to me in happier times; but "I have almost forgot the taste of grief" and "supped full of horrors," till I have become callous; nor have I a tear left for an event which, five years ago, would have bowed me to the earth.' Surely the death (just heard of), for which Byron had not a single tear left, cannot have been the death of the person to whom the first poem to Thyrza—a poem written in tears and not to be read with tearless eyes—was addressed. The identity of the dates is not important :—for the dates assigned to their performances by writers may not be taken too precisely. The same date (October 11th, 1811) is also given to the 'Epistle to a Friend,' containing the last quoted verses about Mary Chaworth. But it can scarcely be supposed that the 'Epistle to a Friend,' the first poem to Thyrza, and the long letter to Mr. Dallas were written on the same day.

Moore speaks so confidently on the question, which had for years stirred the curiosity of Byron's admirers, that he may be presumed to have good reasons, possibly even Byron's own assurance, for the statement that Thyrza was an imaginary being. But even if Byron was himself the authority for the biographer's statement, it does not follow that Thyrza was *mere* creation. *If* she was the offspring of the poet's tender recollections of two separate objects of his affection in former times,—say of two girls, each of whom had died after inspiring him with love,—he would be justified in speaking of the heroine of the poems as a thing of imagination, and certainly would not be justified in speaking of her as the poetical portraiture of a single individual. In that case Thyrza, though a creation, would not be a *mere* conception ; and the question would remain,—of whom was the poet thinking alternately or together when he wrote the successive sets of verses?

In one of Byron's journals reference is made to 'a violent, though pure love and passion' that possessed him in the summer of 1806, the summer of his first year at Cambridge, and co-existed with his vehement friendship for Edward Noel Long, who three years later was drowned on his voyage for Lisbon with his regiment. After speaking of the pleasant hours he spent with Long at Cambridge, the poet says, ' *His* friendship, and a violent, though *pure*, love and passion—which held me at the same period —were the then romance of the most romantic period of my life.' Nothing more is known of this passion. Its cause and object may have survived the sentiment, and also the man whose pulses it quickened. It is not known whether Byron had on his departure for Greece survived the passion—in so far as a young man so strangely constituted could survive any vehement affection. It is, however, conceivable that the love was fervid when he started for the East, that he thought of this (to history nameless) girl often during his travels, and that she died in England during his pilgrimage. But even if all this and other things could be shown in a way to make it obvious that she was an inspiring force of the poems to Thyrza, it would still remain certain that Margaret Parker was also an inspiring force of the same unutterably tender and pathetic poems.

Thyrza is dead; so is Margaret Parker.

Thyrza died when the poet was far away from her; so did Margaret Parker.

Thyrza had been the poet's companion in these deserted towers of Newstead; Margaret Parker had also been his companion there.

The mutual love of Thyrza and the poet was known only to themselves, their smiles being 'smiles none else might understand:' so it was with Byron and Margaret. When 'Margaret coloured through the paleness of mortality to the eyes' at the casual mention of her lover's name, Augusta (his sister) 'could not conceive,' says the poet in his journal, ' why my name should affect her at such a time.'

Thyrza and the poet exchanged love-tokens: Byron and Margaret Parker did the same. The poet wore Thyrza's love-token; Byron wore Margaret Parker's locket next his heart. He *is said* to have shown the locket with vile vanity to Mary Chaworth; but he valued it enough to wear it next his heart in Italy, towards the close of his career.

The mutual affection of Thyrza and the poet was the sentiment of young people, so innocent of desire, that ' even Passion blushed to plead for more.' So was the mutual devotion of Margaret and her cousin.

In her peculiar beauty, alike delicate and evanescent,

'A star that trembled o'er the deep,
Then turn'd from earth its tender beam,'

Thyrza resembled Margaret Parker, who is styled 'one of the most beautiful of evanescent beings' by her lover, who adds in the autobiographic memoir, 'I do not recollect scarcely anything equal to the transparent beauty of my cousin. . . . . She looked as if she had been made out of rainbow—all beauty and peace.'

Besides dying at a distance from her lover, Thyrza dies before the poet has heard of her illness. In like manner Margaret died before Byron had even a hint of her danger. 'I knew,' he says, 'nothing even of her illness till she was no more.'

On the other hand, the poems contain lines that seem to point to some other person than Margaret. At the time of her death, she and her youthful lover (at Harrow) were not 'by many a shore and many a sea divided.' Margaret having been dead for some years, Byron, 'when sailing o'er the Ægean,' can scarcely have thought of her as being alive, and gazing at the moon. And, for the same reason, whilst he was lying ill of fever at Patras, he cannot be imagined to have found comfort in thinking that Margaret knew nothing of his pain. Though some license is permitted to interpreters of poetry, as well as to poets, these touches cannot be construed as pointing to the poet's cousin. They may have no historical significance, and have been introduced only for pathos or mystification. But *if* they point to a girl, whom he hoped whilst in Greece to see on his return to England, the girl so pointed at cannot have been his cousin Margaret.

None the less certain however would it be that the poems point to Margaret Parker, and that she was at least *an* inspiring force of the verses. All the points of similitude between Margaret's story and Thyrza's story being taken into consideration, it cannot be questioned that, if the course of the Cambridge 'passion' resembled in any great degree the course of the poet's passion for Thyrza, its object would be inseparably associated in his mind with the girl whom she resembled so closely in beauty and fate. The two loves would be so linked and blended in his memory, that it would be impossible for him to think of the one without thinking also of the other. The poems inspired by either of the dead girls would be inspired by both. In that case the girl, whose name is unrecorded, would be no less accountable than the girl whose name we know, for the strains of love and desolation. On the other hand, to show that Byron after Margaret's death never loved a girl, whose fate resembled hers, would be to prove that she alone was Thyrza. It yet remains to state the strongest piece of evidence that Margaret was the sole inspiring force of the famous series of poems. One of those curious personal revelations, which escaped the poet during the last months of his existence, was the revelation that the original of Thyrza was one of his cousins who died of consumption. On the voyage from Genoa to Cephalonia (1823), Byron said to Trelawny, 'When I first left England I was gloomy. I said so in my First Canto of " Childe Harold." I was then really in love with a cousin.' [Thyrza, he was very chary of her name], Trelawny observes, 'and she was in a decline.' Byron's cousin

Margaret Parker died of a decline, and was the only one of his cousins to die of that malady after inspiring him with love. True that she died long before he left England; but to his poetic fancy she was still living and fading away when he thought of her on his travels. The mystification and historic inaccuracy of the poet's statement do not weaken the evidence afforded by the words, that Margaret and Thyrza were the same person in *his* mind.

And now, after passing his eyes over a few dates, the reader must consider a remarkable fact which, though pointed to in a previous chapter, has been withheld from prominence, till his mind should have been fully prepared to accept so strange a matter.

In 1797, when he was only nine years old, Byron fell in love with Mary Duff,—his love for her being no ordinary childish fondness for a congenial playmate, but a consuming passion.

In the summer of 1800, when he was twelve and a half years old, he conceived a stronger passion for Margaret Parker, who nine years after her death became a chief (if not the only) inspiring force of the poems to Thyrza.

In November 1802, he wrote Margaret Parker's elegy, just about two years and four months after falling in love with her.

In the summer of 1803, when he was in the middle of his sixteenth year, he fell in love with Mary Chaworth.

In 1804—(and here is the marvellous fact)—when he was still in an early stage of the long-enduring anguish caused by the disappointment of his passion for Mary Chaworth—the news of Mary

Duff's marriage, coming too suddenly upon him through his mother's defective sensibility and want of caution, moved him so strongly that he was within an ace of falling into convulsions. 'My mother,' Byron says in the autobiographic memoir, so often referred to in previous pages, 'used always to rally me about this childish amour; and, at last, many years after, *when I was sixteen*, she told me one day, "Oh, Byron, I have had a letter from Edinburgh, from Miss Abercromby, and your old sweetheart Mary Duff is married to a Mr. Co . . . . ." And what was my answer? I really cannot explain or account for my feelings at that moment; but they nearly threw me into convulsions, and alarmed my mother so much, that, after I grew better, she generally avoided the subject—to *me*—and contented herself with telling it to all her acquaintance.' Out of this incident, and Mrs. Byron's habit of talking about it, arose the absurd cock-and-bull story of Byron's behaviour at Southwell on hearing of Mary Chaworth's marriage.

Hence it appears that Byron had not only survived his first great love sufficiently to entertain a still stronger love for another object, but had also survived the second passion sufficiently to conceive a still more vehement passion for a third object, and was even yet in the anguish consequent on the disappointment of this third passion, when the memory of the earliest of the three precocious attachments so nearly overpowered him.

It will be said by many a reader that all this is very strange,—so unusual and unlike ordinary human nature, as to be almost incredible. Byron's nature, with its feminine sensibility and masculine combativeness, *was* far outside the lines of ordinary human kind. 'Childe Harold,' 'Cain,' and 'Don Juan' could not have come from a mind constituted in the usual way of human nature ; and to understand and know the poet, people must be able to accept unusual things, that are not in accordance with their personal experience of human feelings and actions.

The reader knows how to account for the strong emotion, that was inexplicable to Byron himself, by referring it to the strongly retentive memory, lively imagination, and quick sensibility of the mind that, after heightening the beauty of its recollections by the exercise of poetical fancy, made no distinction between the remembered facts and the loveliness imparted to them by its own action, but with all the results of quickened sensibility dealt with the remembrances, that were partly fictitious, as though they were altogether real. Memory, fancy and feeling were the three forces that enabled the poet to derive a far larger measure of gladness from the remembrances of his native hills than the joy that had come to him in childhood from the sight of the hills themselves,—and rendered the sorrows of former time even more afflicting to his sensibility, when he reflected upon them, and by reflection intensified them, than they were in actual experience. They were the three prime forces of a machine which, though often —perhaps most often—set in action by circumstances independent of its possessor, could also be put in motion, and certainly sometimes was put in motion by his own will. Washington Irving was right in suspecting that the poet in dealing with his memory was the cunning farmer of a fertile soil, and deliberately brooded over the past for the sake of the stimulus which came from the process to his sensibility and creative energy. Whilst thus reviving the past, for the uses to be had of its joys and sorrows, Byron could rearrange and modify his recollections in order to turn them to better poetical account, and could even weave pieces of pure fiction into them.

Examples of the way, in which he would thus manipulate his tenderest and saddest recollections, even to the falsification of his own personal history, may be found in the poems and the passages of poems, which readers are most ready to regard as so many passages of autobiography in verse. To those who, instead of regarding the poet's marriage as a mere affair of convenience, believe that his regard for Miss Milbanke was one of genuine affection, it must appear more than probable that even the most touching of all the unutterably pathetic pictures of 'The Dream,'—the picture which Moore thought himself 'justified in introducing historically' into his account of the wedding—owes quite as much to the writer's imagination as to his memory :—

' I saw him stand

 Before an altar with a gentle bride ;
 Her face was fair, but was not that which made
 The starlight of his Boyhood ;—as he stood
 Even at the altar, o'er his brow there came
 The self-same aspect, and the quivering shock
 That in the antique Oratory shook
 His bosom in its solitude ; and then—
 As in that hour·—a moment o'er his face
 The tablet of unutterable thoughts

Was traced,—and then it faded as it came,
And he stood calm and quiet, and he spoke
The fitting vows, but heard not his own words,
And all things reel'd around him ; he could see
Not that which was, nor that which should have been—
But the old mansion, and the accustom'd hall,
And the remember'd chambers, and the place
The day, the hour, the sunshine, and the shade,
All things pertaining to that place and hour,
And her, who was his destiny, came back
And thrust themselves between him and the light :—
What business had they there at such a time ?'

And how about the account of the wedding in the poet's memoranda, with which these doleful verses are said by Moore to correspond 'in so many of its circumstances.' From the biographer's abstract of the prose account, it appears that on waking on the nuptial morning the poet was held by the 'most melancholy reflections, on seeing his wedding-suit spread out before him ;' that before the ceremony he 'wandered about the grounds alone ;' and further it is told—'He knelt down, he repeated the words after the clergyman ; but a mist was before his eyes,—his thoughts were elsewhere ; and he was but awakened by the congratulations of the bystanders, to find that he was—married.' This is all. Hence, the account in the poet's note-book agrees with the picture of the poem, in some of the unimportant, but in none of the important particulars of the latter. The whole affair was over before the bridegroom could collect his wandering thoughts, and he had a vague feeling of surprise at finding himself married :—The same may be said of fifty out of every hundred bridegrooms. He knelt down and repeated the words after the clergyman :—and he was quite right in doing so. What bridegroom does otherwise? He walked about the garden till he was summoned to the celebration of the marriage :—what better place for walking can be imagined ? or what better way of whiling away the time till the bride should be dressed? He was low-spirited at the dawn of the eventful day :— it is not unusual for a bridegroom to be so, if he is a nervous man. Though he has decided on it deliberately, and may be confident he is about to take a wise step, a nervous man is apt to have misgivings when he is on the point of doing a momentous and irrevocable act. But in what important points does this account resemble the passage of the poem? The prose account had no single word of reference to Annesley and its well-remembered chambers, to the old mansion or to 'her, who was,' the poet's 'destiny.' From the *memoir*, of which Moore talks so absurdly, it does not appear that Byron, either before or at or after the ceremony, had a single thought about Mary Chaworth on his wedding-day. And, as readers will see shortly, there are grounds for a strong opinion that she never approached his mind, to trouble it, at any moment of the honey-moon.

Readers of ' The Dream ' should bear in mind that it was written at Geneva, just a year and a half after the marriage, and about six months *after* Lady Byron left her Lord for ever. It was written (in July 1816) when the poet was in a mood to persuade himself that after all he had never really cared much for the lady, who had dismissed him so unceremoniously ;—and when he was also in the humour to slap the lady's face with a poem, which should tell

her and all the world that another woman had years
before and all through his matrimonial time possessed
his heart. The labour of writing ' The Dream ' was
an effort of art ; the poem is a work of an incomparable art ; the publication of it was an act of
revenge. And after the wont of acts of vengeance,
the deed of spite recoiled on the doer's head,—by
making the world believe he had never loved his wife,
and confirming the world in its opinion·that he had
treated her very badly.

Byron is believed never to have seen Mary Chaworth after dining with her in 1808. Once (whilst
he and Lady Byron were on loving terms) he thought
of visiting her, but was saved from the false and
perilous step by the advice of his good sister—ever
his Guardian Angel. But though he never again saw
Mrs. Musters (Mr. Chaworth had by this time returned
to his old surname), Lady Byron—when she and her
husband were still a mutually loving couple—met
the heiress of Annesley in society. How the two
women eyed one another, what they thought of each
other are matters for the imagination. Men's wives
are apt to think lightly and suspiciously of their
husbands' 'old flames.' On seeing his bride for the
first time, a woman seldom fails to discover her
former suitor has made a poor choice.

CHAPTER IX.

Despondency — Eddleston, the Chorister — Dr. William Lort Mansell — College Friends — Hobhouse on Byron's Nature — Eighteen Long Years Hence — 'Hours of Idleness' — Lord Carlisle — College Debts — Cambridge Dissipations — The 'Edinburgh Article' — Walter Scott's Opinion of the Article — Who Wrote It? — The Poet's Regard for Cambridge — Honour done the Poet by the University.

GOING up to Cambridge reluctantly in October 1805, Byron left the University in the beginning of 1808, after taking the honorary degree to which, as a nobleman, he was entitled.

To account for the heaviness of heart with which he approached the seat of learning and passed his first terms in it, he says that it pained him to quit Harrow, that he had wished to go to Oxford, that his sense of loneliness in the world oppressed him, and that it made him miserable to think he was no longer a boy. The gaiety of his companions only deepened the melancholy of the freshman, who wanted the homage of his Harrow 'favourites,' and was still pining for the bride who was another's bride. Holding aloof from most of the undergraduates, who offered themselves to his acquaintance, as soon as he had taken possession of a set of rooms appropriate to his dignity, the young peer, during his first year at Trinity, spent much of his time in solitude, and most of his other time in the society of his former schoolfellow, Long, or in communion with the sweet-voiced chorister, for whom he conceived a regard that may not be referred altogether to that vulgarest kind of amiable insolence,—the delight of patronising one's social inferiors. Probably it flattered the young lord's self-esteem to take so humble a person under his protection ; and doubtless the fortunate youth, of whom Byron wrote to Miss Pigot, 'I certainly love him more than any other human being,' was at much pains to retain his patron's favour. But arrogance on the one side and obsequiousness on the other would not of themselves have sustained the curious friendship that endured, without any apparent diminution of fervour and steadiness, till Eddleston's death in 1811. Being to an hour two years younger than the poet, this well-mannered and affectionate boy was still in his sixteenth year, when he first won Byron's regard.

Had Byron brought from Harrow enough Latin and Greek to place him creditably with the studious men of his year, he would possibly have come to Trinity with a lighter heart, and left Cambridge on better terms with its Professors. In every race so much depends on 'the start,' it is not surprising that the young peer—who with better preliminary training and a fairer prospect of success might have entertained a desire for academic honours, and justified the ambition by winning them—determined to avoid the course, in which, at the outset of the running, he would have competed under vexatious and humiliating disadvantages with young men, inferior to him alike in rank and natural ability. To his tutor it was soon apparent that the young nobleman, who lived chiefly with an old Harrow schoolfellow and one of the youngest of the college choristers, meant to attend as few lectures as possible, and to hold aloof from the more serious pursuits of the University. After the Long Vacation of 1806, when he had gradually become less shy and more sociable, the peer displayed a purpose of running the usual career of a Trinity nobleman.

As they seem to have heard nothing of his two previous volumes of verse, printed by a Nottinghamshire bookseller for private circulation, it was not surprising that, till he published, for sale to all who cared to buy it, a third book of poetry, containing some equally feeble and saucy satire on his University, Lord Byron of Trinity was mistaken by the Master (Dr. William Lort Mansell) and the tutors of his College for a young man of ordinary endowments, who differed in nothing more important than his lameness from the other lads of birth and affluence, who thought it good fun to make night hideous by roaring in chorus under the Master's bedroom window, 'We beseech thee to hear us, good Lort! Good Lort, deliver us!' Like other young nobles and fellow-commoners, with whom he co-operated in equally riotous and common-place exhibitions of puerile hilarity, Lord Byron occupied luxuriously furnished rooms, gave 'breakfasts' and 'wine-parties,' and 'suppers,' and was waited on by a valet instead of a college 'gyp.' The proprietor of two big dogs,—the superb Newfoundland (Boatswain) and the ferocious bull-dog (Nelson),—Lord Byron of Trinity kept a couple of horses (one of them a large-boned grey animal) on which he rode fairly well, and a coronetted carriage in which he posted to and fro between Cambridge and London, London and Southwell. On returning to the University after the Long Vacation of 1807, he brought up 'the bear,' destined (as he averred with appropriate seriousness) to compete for a Trinity fellowship,—the same bear that two years later guarded one pillar of the chief entrance to the mansion at Newstead, whilst a wolf kept watch at the other post of the stately portal. Of course, at a time when all modish gentlemen were duellists, and the use of deadly weapons was a part of every young nobleman's education, pistol-cases and fencing-foils were always conspicuous in Lord Byron's rooms ; and it being understood at the beginning of the present century that a gentleman should know how to use his fists, as well as 'the hair-trigger' and 'small sword,' it was needless for his lordship's visitors to ask whether he could provide them with 'the gloves,' when it was their humour to have a set-to at boxing on his Turkey carpets. In these and a score other matters Lord Byron of Trinity did like the other young gentlemen who had the *entrée* of his college-rooms. He may, perhaps, have been a little more ostentatious of his fire-arms, and rapiers, and boxing gloves,—for even in his early boyhood he made a favourite toy of the pistol, which he liked to think would put him with his lameness on equal terms with adversaries of the steadiest footing ; and in his constant desire to divert attention from the infirmity, which telling heavily against him in sword-exercise placed him even more at the mercy of competent 'bruisers,' the lame poet was sometimes comically boastful of his prowess with the blunt sword and 'the gloves.' The unquestionable excellence of his swimming was a matter in which he differed from most of his associates at the Univer-

sity. And whilst he was distinguishable from the
other mounted 'gownsmen' by the colour of his large-
boned grey steed, he was still further distinguishable
by the eccentricity of his riding costume,—the *white*
coat' and '*white* hat,' that made Hobhouse regard
the poet with hot dislike, and even brought the two
young men to arrangements for a duel, before they
joined hands in a friendship that survived even the
poet's death. But these trivial shades of difference
could not be expected to affect the judgment of the
college tutors who, having good reason to regard
Byron as a common-place Trinity lordling and still
better reason (after the publication of ' The Hours of
Idleness ') for deeming him a lordling with no very
strong genius for satire, had the best reason for astonishment on finding he ' had it in him ' to produce
such keen, strenuous, scorching and irresistibly comical verse as the best things of the 'English Bards and
Scotch Reviewers.'

But whilst playing, in this common-place way,
the part of a conventional ' Trinity tuft,' and associating with Fellow-Commoners whose chief distinction
throughout life was the honour of having been Fellow-Commoners of so famous a college, Byron had a
small circle of peculiar friends, who would never have
cared to know him intimately had his rank been his
strongest note of introduction to their favour, and
whom he would never have conciliated so studiously
and drawn so closely to his heart had he valued men
chiefly for their hereditary distinctions. Instead of
being the ' snob ' of noble degree that biographers
have represented him, valuing himself less on his
deeds than his descent, and overflowing with secret

disdain for people of ordinary origin, Byron throughout life chose his familiars from considerations altogether pure of the petty patrician insolence, that has
been attributed to him on no better grounds, than
the boyish verses to the glorification of his Norman
progenitors and his occasional exhibitions in later
time of an altogether reasonable and wholesome respect for his ancestral dignity. After Long's withdrawal from the university, the poet's most intimate
friends at Cambridge were—Charles Skinner Matthews, a man of infinite humour and an intellect of
the highest order, who was regarded by all his contemporaries as a person designed by nature for a
career of high achievement; Scrope Berdmore Davies,
a man no less remarkable for elegance of taste than
for a generous high-mindedness; Francis Hodgson,
the exemplary Latinist and future Provost of Eton;
William Bankes, whose letters and enduring attachment to his former schoolfellow are matters of history;
and John Cam Hobhouse (Lord Broughton), who
after holding firmly to his 'fellow-traveller in Greece,'
through good report and evil report, with undiminished affection and admiration for him from this time
of their riper boyhood to the hour that made Missolonghi a name of mourning throughout the whole
world, stood forth the vindicator of his memory, when
twice ten years had passed over the poet's grave.
After declaring that truth was more precious to him
than even his friend's honour, Lord Broughton delivered himself of these words, 'Lord Byron had
failings—many failings certainly, but he was untainted with any of the baser vices; and his virtues,
his good qualities were all of a high order.'

The reader should take to heart the words, thus transferred to this page for a definite purpose. From his early manhood to his premature death, Byron was known more fully and precisely to Lord Broughton than to any other person. His familiar at Cambridge, his guest at Newstead, his comrade in Greece, his constant associate in London, his ' best man ' at his wedding, his confidant at every point and turn of his domestic troubles, John Cam Hobhouse was at the poet's side from the commencement of their friendship at Cambridge to the moment of Byron's withdrawal from England. A few months later Hobhouse joined Byron at Geneva, and after accompanying him on the Swiss trip went with him to Italy. In the years of Byron's exile Hobhouse was with him repeatedly. Every incident that contributed to the poet's estrangement from his wife was known to Hobhouse. With every opportunity for knowing him thoroughly, in every minutest particular of his character and career, it is not conceivable that Hobhouse was uninformed or deceived respecting his friend's nature or respecting any important matter of his friend's conduct up to the time of his withdrawal from his native land ; for whilst the poet's friend was a shrewd, discreet, judicious man of the world,—an excellent man of business, as Byron always called him ; a man, moreover, of the strictest honour and truthfulness, as all his acquaintance knew,—Byron was frankness itself, incapable of keeping either his own secrets or even the confidences of a friend, and ever blabbing to gossipmongers of whom he knew scarcely anything the matters which his own interest required him to keep strictly to himself. Is it likely that the observant

man of the world would not know everything of the
affairs and temper of the friend, one of whose most
charming characteristics was his absolute incapability
of reserve? 'Part of this fascination,' Lord Broughton
remarked, when Byron had been dead twenty years,
'may, doubtless, be ascribed to the entire self-aban-
donment, the incautious, it may be said the dangerous,
sincerity of his private conversation; but his weaknesses were amiable; and, as has been said of a
portion of his virtues, were of a feminine character—
so that the affection felt for him was as that for a
favourite and sometimes froward sister.' Hobhouse
was by no means blind to the serious nature of some
of his friend's failings. He often had occasion to
observe and took occasion to deplore the selfishness,
which he regarded as the dark blot and doleful
blemish of the poet's character. There were occasions,
when Lord Broughton referred sorrowfully to this
serious and incorrigible defect of an otherwise noble
nature after the poet's death; one of the persons to
whom he sometimes ventured to express the regret
being the poet's sister Augusta, whose love of her
father's son never blinded her to his failings. Of this
defect more will be said hereafter.

Eighteen long years hence,—eighteen long years,
during which so many of those who are now living
will have gone from this life,—the world will have
under its eye the book which will afford *the proofs*,
that Byron's college friend was more than justified in
saying what he said well-nigh forty years since, in the
poet's defence against the charges preferred against
him in the House of Lords by the Bishop of London.
If eighteen long years were no more than eighteen

short months, this book would not have been written. But why should hundreds of thousands of people during the next eighteen years be required to live and die under false, hideous, and depraving notions of what is possible in Christian human nature in this nineteenth century,—and all because the evidence, left by Lord Broughton for a happier century, is withheld from them? The time must, however, be waited out; people in the meanwhile comforting themselves as they best can with Lord Broughton's assurance that though ' Lord Byron had failings—many failings certainly, he was untainted with the baser vices ; and his virtues, his good qualities, were all of the higher order.'

Let it not, however, be inferred from what appears on a former page that, in associating himself so closely with the five other members of his particular ' Trinity set,' the young peer can be credited with any sort of condescension, or that it could possibly have entered into the head of any one of those five gentlemen to think of himself, even for a moment, as being honoured by the peer's regard, *because* he was a peer. By birth and circumstances as well as by scholarly attainments and refinement the five men were gentlemen, who would have smiled at the notion that their friend's rank could affect either their opinion of him, or their disposition to be intimate with him. Had it been otherwise, the fact of Byron's ' set ' of six containing no other nobleman would be less satisfactory evidence that he selected his college friends from motives and for considerations altogether disconnected from aristocratic sympathies. For had they been persons of Eddleston's social condition, it might be suspected that, whilst the young nobleman's conduct in the matter was determined by the delight of condescending to his inferiors, the others repaid his condescension with complaisance.   The social condition no less than the intellectual quality of the five men precludes either suggestion.   It was not in the nature of things for Byron to imagine he was descending from his nobility in attaching himself to them.   On the other hand, it was not in the nature of things for his rank to be any considerable attraction to them.   They joined hands with him because they liked him ; and he chose them for his familiars because as men of taste and literary discernment they were congenial to him.

Towards the end of June 1807, when Cambridge was bright with girls from country parsonages, and Cantabs were on the point of 'going down for the Long,' Byron, having kept the terms for his honorary degree, bethought himself whether he should ' come up ' again for further residence in a place of which he was growing weary.   Several of his friends were ' going down ' with no intention of ' coming up ' again.   Eddleston —the well-looking and well-mannered young chorister, whom Byron had christened Cornelian, in reference to the cornelian heart which the lad had given to ' his patron !'—was no longer a member of the Trinity choir, having obtained through his patron's influence a clerkship in a house of business in London.   Under these circumstances it is not wonderful that the poet thought of giving up his handsome rooms, and of withdrawing from the University till the beginning of the year, when he would run up for his degree, and after taking it would bid Alma Mater adieu for ever.   ' I am almost superannuated here,' he wrote to Miss

('Good-bye, Gaby') Pigot, of Southwell, dating from Cambridge, 30th June, 1807. 'My old friends (with the exception of a very few) have all departed, and I am preparing to follow them, but remain till Monday to be present at three *Oratorios*, two *Concerts*, a *Fair*, and a *Ball*. . . . . I quit Cambridge with little regret, because our *set* are *vanished*, and my *musical protégé* before mentioned has left the choir, and is stationed in a mercantile house of considerable eminence in the metropolis. You may have heard me observe he is exactly to an hour two years younger than myself. I found him grown considerably, and, as you will suppose, very glad to see his former *Patron*. He is nearly my height, very *thin*, very fair complexion, dark eyes, and light locks. . . . . The University at present is very gay from the fêtes of divers kinds. . . . . The Masters and Fellows are very polite, but look a little *askance*—don't much like *lampoons*—truth always disagreeable.'

The lampoons, which caused the Trinity dons to look askance at the young poet, were the pieces of by no means strenuous satire on the University, her system of education, her professors, and the Trinity choir, that had recently appeared in 'The Hours of Idleness,'—published by Ridge, the Newark bookseller, with a dedicatory inscription to the Right Honourable Frederick Earl of Carlisle, by 'His Obliged Ward and Affectionate Kinsman, The Author.' Probably the boyish 'lampoons' of this far from contemptible collection of youthful poems were not more to his guardian's taste than to the taste of the dons, who cannot have felt themselves treated with fairness or civility in the following lines,—

' The sons of science these, who, thus repaid,
Linger in ease in Granta's sluggish shade ;
Where on Cam's sedgy banks supine they lie,
Unknown, unhonour'd live, unwept for die :
Dull as the pictures which adorn their halls,
They think all learning fix'd within their walls :
In manners rude, in foolish forms precise,
All modern arts affecting to despise :
Yet prizing Bentley's, Brunck's, or Porson's note,
More than the verse on which their critic wrote ;
Vain as their honours, heavy as their ale,
Sad as their wit, and tedious as their tale :
To friendship dead, though not untaught to feel
When Self and Church demand a bigot zeal.
With eager haste they court the lord of power,
Whether 'tis Pitt or Petty rules the hour ;
To him, with suppliant smiles, they bend the head,
While distant mitres to their eyes are spread.
But should a storm o'erwhelm him with disgrace,
They 'd fly to seek the next who fill'd his place.
Such are the men who learning's treasures guard !
Such is their practice, such is their reward !
This much, at least, we may presume to say—
The premium can't exceed the price they pay.'

But if Lord Carlisle regarded such satire with
disapproval, he never told the author so.   Acting on
Sir Walter Scott's well-known rule for the acknowledgment of ' presentation copies,' and acting on it
probably from a presentiment that after reading the
poems he would find it more difficult to write civilly
to the author, the Earl hastened to thank his ward for
the copy and the dedication, before perusing the
volume, in a letter which, though not devoid of polite-
ness or cordiality, failed to satisfy the poet, who wrote
to Miss Pigot of Southwell from London on 13th
July, 1807, ' Lord Carlisle, on receiving my poems,

sent, before he opened the book, a tolerably handsome letter :—I have not heard from him since. His opinions I neither know nor care about : if he is the least insolent, I shall enrol him with *Butler* and the other worthies.   He is in Yorkshire, poor man! and very ill! He said he had not time to read the contents, but thought it necessary to acknowledge the receipt of the volume immediately.   Perhaps the Earl "bears no brother near the throne," *if so*, I will make his *sceptre* totter *in his hands.*'

The poet's purpose of leaving Cambridge ' for good,' and visiting it again only to take his degree, was relinquished within a week after its announcement to Miss Pigot.   ' Since my last letter,' he wrote to that young lady from Trinity, on 5th July, 1807, ' I have determined to reside *another year* at Granta, as my rooms, &c. &c. are finished in great style, several old friends come up again, and many new acquaintances made ; consequently my inclination leads me forward, and I shall return to college in October if still *alive.*'

On returning to the rooms, which upholsterers had ' finished in great style,' Lord Byron of Trinity was in the gayest spirits, and in the humour to ' lead' the modish undergraduates till next July, just as he had ' led ' the boys at Harrow during his last year upon ' the hill.'   Bringing with him ' the bear,' destined for a college fellowship, Lord Byron had also brought up with him the sense of dignity appropriate to a nobleman of wit, whose poems had been praised in critical reviews and bought by duchesses,—at least, by ' Her Grace of Gordon,' who (as the happy youngster wrote to his fair correspondent at Southwell) 'bought my volume, admired it exceedingly, in common with the rest of the fashionable world, and wished to claim her relationship with the author.' A nobleman of wit and fashion, Lord Byron of Trinity had now only to achieve a reputation for rakishness, to be as famous as he desired. Hazard being a favourite pastime just then with the '*jeunesse dorée*' of the university, Lord Byron of Trinity seized the dice-box, and played away night after night till four in the morning. 'I have thrown as many as fourteen mains running,' he recorded at a later period in one of his journals, 'and carried off all the cash upon the table occasionally; but I had no coolness, or judgment, or calculation. It was the delight of the thing that pleased me. Upon the whole, I left off in time, without being much a winner or loser. Since one-and-twenty years of age, I played but little, and then never above a hundred, or two or three.' When a gamester prates of having 'left off in time, without being much a winner or loser,' it may be taken for certain that he did not leave off in time, or without losing much more than he won. Byron's losses at hazard were doubtless, largely accountable for the enormity of the debts that weighed upon him and harassed him painfully, on his coming of age. '*Entre nous*,' he wrote to his always sympathetic and judicious counsellor, the Rev. Mr. Becher of Southwell, on 28th March, 1808, when only twenty years and two months old, 'I am cursedly dipped; my debts, *every* thing inclusive, will be nine or ten thousand pounds before I am twenty-one.' The twelve or fifteen hundred a-year from the Newstead property after paying some of the charges of the long suit (still in progress) for the Rochdale property, of course, could not afford the young peer a sufficient allowance for what may be called his legitimate expenses.　A youngster,—continually posting in his own carriage to and fro between Cambridge and London and between London and Southwell, keeping two riding-horses, a groom and a valet, and spending money on two editions of poems printed for circulation amongst his friends, and another collection of poems for public sale,—could not be expected to live within an allowance of perhaps a thousand a-year.　But to account for the 10,000*l.* of debt contracted in two years, one must suppose that Lord Byron of Trinity lost more at hazard than he cared to confess in a journal made up for his biographer's convenience.

If rumour of the high play, that went on in his rooms and in the rooms of his more reckless friends, came to the ears of the dons, it may well have made them continue to 'look askance' at the young peer, who wrote to Miss Pigot on 26th October, 1807: 'We have several parties here, and this evening a large assortment of jockeys, gamblers, boxers, authors, parsons and poets sup with me,—a precious mixture, but they go on well together; and for me, I am a *spice* of everything except a jockey.'　The social gaieties of undergraduates are seldom remarkable for orderliness and freedom from noise; and it may be imagined that when the cheers and uproar of the jolly good fellows in Lord Byron's rooms broke in upon the studious hours of serious students, with no turn for jollity and no admiration for the kind of goodness that is best described in the small hours of the morning by 'three times three—and one more!' they must have wished his lordship had not 'come up' for another year. And in this feeling the dons and other grave personages of the learned society must have been confirmed by report, which passed from gownsman to gownsman in the later days of October, that this troublesome and audacious lordling, who had sneered in verse at the Master's 'ample front sublime,' and most irreverently called the college-choir 'a set of croaking sinners,' was already at work on another satire,—and had in fact already turned off three hundred and eighty lines of the new poem, which would exhibit to public ridicule the worthiest of living men. It was thus Lord Byron's friends, and his friends' friends whispered of the poem, that would put an end to Walter Scott's popularity, and make Southey rue his rashness in becoming an author by profession. For though the 'English Bards and Scotch Reviewers' was Byron's answer to the article which did not appear in the 'Edinburgh Review' till January, 1808, and doubtless owed the greater part of its force and most vicious stabs to the anger stirred within the poet's breast by the ludicrously insufficient assault on his reputation, the groundwork of the satire was laid weeks before he received his 'early intelligence' of the rod that had been pickled for his back. Left to himself, Lord Byron of Trinity would have produced a satire, something stronger than the satirical stuff of the 'Hours of Idleness,' something weaker than the satire of the 'Hints from Horace,' that might have caught the public attention for an hour, on its way to the oblivion that claims all satire that does not rise to a high standard of excellence.   Fortunately for the poet, and no less fortunately for countless later sufferers from unjust criticism, the 'Edinburgh Review' came to his aid with an article that stung him to an exhibition of strength, that placed him, boy though he was, amongst the masters of a kind of literature, in which the young so often try to distinguish themselves, and so rarely excel.

It is not easy to sit in judgment on the notorious article, which has proved so prejudicial to the authority and influence of professional critics, without thinking of the satire which gave it enduring notoriety.   And to remember the boyish daring, and malicious sportiveness and irresistible humour of the 'English Bards,' is to lose the power of regarding impartially the outrage that stirred the youngster's wrath.   But when the satire is put as much as possible out of recollection, and the attention confined as strictly as possible to the failings of the 'Hours of Idleness' and the faults of the review, there is little to be urged in palliation of the intemperance and excessive harshness of the latter.   When all reasonable excuses have been made for the reviewer, it remains that he was signally deficient in good feeling, good judgment, and good taste,—that this article is alike reprehensible for its want of kindliness, its want of critical discernment, and its vulgarity.   In sneering at the young lord for being a young lord the reviewer at least showed a curious want of breeding. In striking a youngster so heavily, and at the same moment deriding his modest appeal for consideration on the score of his youth, the censor showed, to put the case mildly, a discreditable lack of sympathy for youthful ambition. In loftily bidding the young aspirant to 'forthwith abandon poetry,' as a field for which he had not a single natural qualification, the critic showed a singular unfitness for his office ; for though they comprised many weak verses, and several exhibitions of boyish, even childish, indiscretion and inexpertness, the poems afforded numerous indications of poetic feeling, and several passages of thoughtful and strenuous writing. Walter Scott, who had already looked through the poems, might well be astonished at the 'undue severity' of the 'offensive article,' which caused him to protest to Jeffrey against its scandalous harshness, and even to think of writing a note of sympathy and consolation to the author. And Scott was not the only reader of 'The Edinburgh' to regard with equal surprise and disapproval its treatment of a book of poems, which 'contained some passages of noble promise,' though 'they were written like all juvenile poetry, rather from the recollection of what had pleased the author in others than what had been suggested by his own imagination.'

It still remains a question with many persons whether Jeffrey or Brougham wrote this unfortunate review ; it being assumed by the questioners that the article proceeded from the pen of the one or the other. As it rests on the assumption, that, if the article had not been of his own writing, he would, sooner or later, have disassociated himself from the discreditable performance by revealing the real blunderer or at least disclaiming the authorship of the essay, the case against Jeffrey is so weak that it should not injure his reputation. Jeffrey had his failings ; but he was not the man to betray a coadjutor, or sneak out of an editorial scrape under cover of an undignified avowal. Moreover, if Medwin's book may be trusted (and on such a matter the 'Conversations' are trustworthy in some degree), Jeffrey disclaimed the authorship in so far as he could do so with dignity, by assuring Byron in confidence that though responsible for the deed he was not its doer. That Jeffrey ever promised (in the manner alleged in the 'Conversations') to put Byron in the way to discover his aggressor is more than improbable. The case against Jeffrey must be allowed to perish. Discredited by various circumstances, the notion that Brougham wrote the article is nothing more than a suspicion, hugged to the last by Byron who, with several good reasons for hating the lawyer, was not unwilling to strengthen them with a poor one. 'I have no loves,' Byron said to Trelawny, as they were sailing to Cephalonia, 'I have only one friend, my sister Augusta, and I have reduced my hates to two—that venomous reptile Brougham, and Southey the apostate.' The poet's opinion that the review proceeded from the venomous reptile, because it contained some legal jargon about 'minority pleas' 'plaintiffs' and 'grounds of action,' was mere childishness. If Brougham wrote the offensive stuff, he wrote it when he was half asleep. It is possible the article—so unworthy of 'The Edinburgh,' and so significantly different in tone and style from the acknowledged compositions of the 'Review's' principal and regular writers—was the production of an occasional contributor who, as. a resident member of the University of Cambridge, seized a tempting opportunity for administering a seasonable chastisement to the young satirist of college tutors. The 'dons,' who looked askance at Lord Byron of Trinity before the long vacation, may well have come to a strong and unanimous opinion in the ensuing November that the young nobleman's presence at the university was neither for his own advantage, nor the good of the young gentlemen who gathered about him. On hearing of the 'new satire' already on the stocks, the tutors may well have wished for some one, enjoying the confidence of a powerful editor, to give his lord-ship a lesson in the art of saying unpleasant things of one's neighbours, and to show him with equal prompti-tude and energy that satire, like stone-throwing, was a game at which two persons could play,—a game in which no one should be allowed to have all the play to himself. And as this view of what would be best for Lord Byron of Trinity and also for his academic superiors grew more general and strong, at the high-tables of the colleges, it would naturally occur to any one of the Fellows, who had friendly relations with the Edinburgh editor, that he would do a good turn to his university and more especially to its junior members, by paying Lord Byron off in his own coin, and showing all undergraduates of a froward and malapert temper that even a young peer of the realm could not ridicule 'dons' and other duly constituted authorities with impunity. Whilst all this appears alike natural and probable, the tone and very structure of the article point to the same conclu-sion. Written throughout in a vein of supercilious 'donnishness,' the review reminds one alternately of a college-tutor who regards sarcasm as the most effective vehicle of instruction, and of a schoolmaster who more in sorrow than in anger condescends to chastise a naughty boy with an implement of torture, far larger and more terrifying than the author's goose-quill. After administering the flagellation to the last cut, the pedagogue forbears to dismiss the humiliated culprit till he has pointed the moral of the incident, for the edification of youthful listeners, by reading aloud some of the weakest verses of his never felicitous satire on academic persons and practices. With this cue to the possible origin and purpose of the review, which caused the poet to drink three bottles of claret at a single sitting, most readers of its insolent phrases will perhaps be inclined to think with the present writer that, though the blow was delivered from Edinburgh, the impulse of the blow came from Cambridge.

If the offensive article proceeded from a Cambridge tutor, chiefly desirous of driving Lord Byron from Trinity before the summer terms, the reviewer had reason for a brief while to congratulate himself on the success of his essay. In London where he hastened from his punishment to his claret, Lord Byron was in no humour to pass another term at Cambridge, where for the moment the laughter was all on the side of the reviewer and the dons. The poet, who in later time could not endure with calmness the speechless obloquy of London drawing-rooms, had not the heart to face the Masters and Fellows who, instead of merely eyeing him askance as they passed him in Hall or Quadrangle, were now prepared to confront him with faces brightened with smiles of triumphant malice. So far as his university career is concerned, the 'Edinburgh Review' snuffed out the poet, who had meant to stay on at Trinity till the following Midsummer. From the date of that number of the 'Edinburgh Review,' Lord Byron ceased to be Lord Byron of Trinity. He 'went up' indeed to take his degree in 1808; but having taken his grade amongst the graduates, he withdrew immediately from the university, to nurse his wrath and bitterness in London and at Newstead,— till he should find verse for their adequate expression.

Referring to his wilder time at Trinity, towards the close of his time on earth, Byron said to Medwin, ' I had a great hatred of College rules, and contempt for academical honours. How many of their wranglers have ever distinguished themselves in the world? . . . I believe they were as glad to get rid of me at Cambridge, as they were at Harrow.' Though they come to us through a no more reliable reporter than Medwin, it can be readily believed that Byron spoke these words, and that they fairly represent the feeling of the Trinity tutors, in finding themselves well rid of so troublesome an inmate of their College.

But though his time at Cambridge ended thus abruptly and ingloriously, Byron bore his university no ill-will. On the contrary, in the darker periods, and also in the brighter periods, of his life he held *Alma Mater* in tender recollection, thanking her in his affectionate heart for the friends she had given him. Towards the close of October 1811, little more than three months after his return from the East, he roused himself from the sorrow of the preceding weeks, and went to Cambridge to pass a few days with Hodgson. Four months later, when he and Hobhouse were thinking of running from London to Cambridge, to look round the old familiar

haunts and exchange greetings with the few of their
former friends, still lingering in them, the poet — now
in the morning of his fame — wrote sadly to Hodgson,
' Cambridge will bring sad recollections to him, and
worse to me, though for very different reasons.   I
believe the only human being that ever loved me in
truth and entirely was of, or belonging to Cambridge,
and, in that, no change can now take place.'   And
whilst Byron loved the university which he left at
the moment of his discord with her chiefs, even as he
loved the school which he quitted under somewhat
similar circumstances, the younger Cantabs were
quick and the older Cantabs by no means slow, to
hail him as one of the brightest ornaments of their
seat of learning.   When Byron went to Cambridge
in October 1814 to vote for Mr. Clarke, the Trinity
candidate for Sir Busick Harwood's Professorship, his
appearance in the Senate House was the occasion of
an outburst of applause from the undergraduates, that
brought tears of joy to his strangely lustrous eyes
and the crimson of sudden gladness to his pale
face.   And just upon thirty years later, Trinity
College conferred honour on herself and rendered
meet homage to the poet, as one of her own great
sons of genius, by placing in her library the statue of
Thorwaldsen, which would not have found a fitter or
more honourable home had it been admitted to Westminster Abbey.

CHAPTER X.

CAMBRIDGE VACATIONS.

In London —'The Noble Art of Self-defence '—Swimming in the Thames — Byron's Life at Southwell — His Quarrels with his Mother — Harrowgate — First and Second Editions of The Southwell Poems —'The Prayer of Nature '— Byron's Scepticism — His Height and Fatness — Starvation and Physic — Their Results — Tobacco and Laudanum.

WHILST keeping his terms at Cambridge, first as a shy, retiring undergraduate, then as a lad of lively humour and sociable disposition, and lastly as one of the most hilarious and unruly men of his year at Trinity, Lord Byron enlarged his knowledge of human nature and human manners by visits to London, where he saw life much as Tom and Jerry saw it, from points of view best known to gentlemen about town, and sometimes with companions whose society was not calculated to inspire him with a generous admiration of his species. Not that he had a morbid preference for unworthy associates, or a keen appetite for any of the grosser vices. On the contrary, eating less than a squeamish school-girl, and seldom drinking more wine than he could carry with composure on his naturally unsteady feet, he found his chief daily enjoyment in reading the best poets and in writing such poetry as may be found in the ' Hours of Idleness.' But though his favourite drink was soda-water, in days when sottishness ranked with the fine arts and it was a point of honour with nine out of every ten Englishmen to fuddle themselves with strong wines and stronger spirits at least once in every four-and-twenty hours, Lord Byron went about town with merry fellows who, instead of emulating their friend's abstemiousness, bantered him on not caring to 'drink like a lord.' In their wanderings about town — wanderings made almost wholly upon wheels, on account of the poet's inability to walk far and freely — Lord Byron and his friends went of course to the theatres, and afterwards to places where the play was high or the dancing wild, and doubtless to other places into which the readers of this page would not care to follow them. In simple truth, they went about and saw life, as young gentlemen of all the social grades from peers to law students, were expected and even admonished by their fathers to go about and see it, in the earlier decades of a century that has grown more virtuous and much more decorous, as it has grown in years. One of the circles they often attended was the gathering of fops and dandies to be found every afternoon at Jackson's (Angelo and Jackson's) School of the Noble Art of Self-Defence.

The friend and correspondent of royal princes, and of dukes who without being of royal degree, were august personages, Mr. Jackson had too many lords on his visiting list to feel himself greatly honoured by the civilities lavished upon him by the nobleman from Trinity College. But the great Professor of Pugilism had too genuine and warm an admiration for 'pluck' and 'bottom,' whenever they came under his observation, not to be touched to the heart by the spirit and address with which the lame peer (who was said to write as fine poetry as 'any man who did it for a living') handled the gloves—striking out from the shoulder, and 'coming up' on his tottering pins for round after round with the best 'millers.' of the school, till he was forced to give in from the unendurable pain that came to his right foot from the violent exercise. And in truth, for a beholder to be stirred with generous emotion at so pathetic an exhibition of courage and resoluteness it was not needful for him to be either a professor or connoisseur of 'the noble art.'

Byron, still in his minority, and Jackson, still at the highest point of his professional eminence, became close friends ; and for a while Eddleston, if the gentle youth was capable of jealousy, must have been troubled to see how much the young lord, who delighted in a chorister's affection, could also delight in a prize-fighter's friendship. When the one was in London and the other in the country, the poet and pugilist wrote letters to one another ; the professor of 'the noble art' being styled 'Dear Jack' by his noble correspondent. Jackson was one of the few greatly eminent persons to visit Byron at Newstead ; and in 1808, when the poet stayed for several weeks at Brighton, the Professor made a weekly journey to the Sussex coast, for the purpose of carrying on his young patron's pugilistic education. In the previous year (August 1807) when Leigh Hunt saw the author of the 'Hours of Idleness,' swimming for a wager from Lambeth to Blackfriars Bridge, he 'noticed a respectable-looking manly person, who was eyeing something in the distance.' The something in the distance was the poet's head, bobbing up and down, as he

rehearsed the part of Leander' in the London river;
and the 'respectable-looking manly person' was Mr.
Jackson, the prize-fighter, who took occasion to inform the by-standers who the swimmer was, and to
expatiate on the virtues of his noble pupil. 'Last
week,' Byron wrote to Miss Pigot on 11th August,
1807, 'I swam in the Thames from Lambeth through
the two bridges, Westminster and Blackfriars, a distance, including the different turns and tacks made
in the way, of three miles.'

But though he spent much of his Cambridge
vacations in London, Lord Byron of Trinity passed
the greater part of the successive holidays at Southwell, where he was singularly fortunate in the neighbours with whom he associated on terms of the closest
intimacy. If it was well for the poet that in his
infancy he made the acquaintance of people placed
only a few degrees above the poor, it was even better
for him that, instead of being brought so soon into
the higher world as he would have been had it not
been for his mother's peculiarities and Lord Carlisle's
consequent distaste for her, he was on the threshold
of his manhood placed into familiar relations with
persons of the gentle middle class,—a class that is
generally too little known to people of noble rank.
In the drawing-rooms of the modest homes of Southwell, which he entered almost daily to sing songs and
gossip with young ladies, who probably in their
whole lives never exchanged words with another peer
of the realm, Lord Byron learnt more of the finer
qualities of human nature, and more particularly of
feminine character, than he learnt a few years later in
the London salons, where dames and maidens of the

highest birth and fashion thronged and pressed towards him, to scan his features and catch his lightest words. It was in those country-town parlours and in the gardens on which their windows opened, that the young Byron, excluded by more benignant than cruel circumstances from the homes of his social equals, encountered men and women whose conversation weaned him from his shyness, relieved his manners of their rusticity, and taught him the art of pleasing. And it speaks no little for the refinement and efficiency of his teachers that on passing from them, after a brief interval of foreign travel, into the brightest and stateliest circles of the English aristocracy, he was not more applauded for his genius than for his noble air and perfect breeding.

At Southwell Byron lived almost wholly with the gentry of the little town. Once in a while he received a call from a gentleman of 'the county,' or an invitation to a 'county house.' But partly from the knowledge that his pecuniary circumstances would not permit him to visit the territorial families of his ancestral shire on equal terms, and partly from a feeling that his mother would be less acceptable to the ladies of the county than to the gentlewomen of the Green, the poet declined the invitations, and sometimes omitted to return the calls,—alleging, in excuse of the incivility of such negligence, either that the calls had been too long deferred, or that the callers should have brought their womankind to see Mrs. Byron. The young man's shyness was also largely accountable for his disinclination to make the acquaintance of his county neighbours. To Mr. Becher's sensible advice that he should go more into

the world, and seek friends beyond the boundaries of
his mother's parish, he replied,—

> ' Dear Becher, you tell me to mix with mankind,—
>   I cannot deny such a precept is wise ;
> But retirement accords with the tone of my mind,
>   And I will not descend to a world I despise.

> ' Did the Senate or Camp my exertions require,
>   Ambition might prompt me at once to go forth ;
> And, when infancy's years of probation expire,
>   Perchance, I may strive to distinguish my birth.

> ' The fire, in the cavern of Etna concealed,
>   Still mantles unseen, in its secret recess ;—
> At length, in a volume terrific revealed,
>   No torrent can quench it, no bounds can repress.

> ' Oh thus, the desire in my bosom for fame
>   Bids me live but to hope for Posterity's praise ;
> Could I soar, with the Phœnix, on pinions of flame,
>   With him I would wish to expire in the blaze.

> ' For the life of a Fox, of a Chatham the death,
>   What censure, what danger, what woe would I brave ?
> Their lives did not end when they yielded their breath,—
>   Their glory illumines the gloom of the grave ! '

But whilst Byron's intercourse with his neighbours of the Green was alike social and salutary, the
Burgage Manor-house was too often the scene of
ludicrous disputes between the mother, who had not
the good sense to relax the reins of maternal authority
as her offspring neared the time for becoming his own
master, and the son who, having never submitted
graciously to his mother's violent temper, became
less tolerant of her vexatious conduct on ceasing to
be a school-boy. With down darkening his lip, and
with a growing sense of what was due to his dignity

us a man and a peer of the realm, it was not to be expected that Lord Byron of Trinity, who had fought Dr. Butler at Harrow, would consent any longer to be rated by his mother in the hearing of her servants, as she used to rate him in his childhood. On the other hand, Mrs. Byron was resolved to forego none of the enjoyment that came to her from the exercise of the most congenial of her maternal privileges. The scandal of this state of things of course spread beyond the walls of Burgage Manor. Even if the servants of the manor-house had refrained from telling what they naturally told to all the other servants of the Green, the Pigots and Leacrofts and the other gentlefolk of the town would have known no less of the unseemly quarrels of the mother and son. For whilst Mrs. Byron hastened with tears in her eyes, after every battle, to tell her neighbours what a wretched woman she was to have so undutiful a boy, Byron—like the Byron of later time—laid his domestic troubles before the world, and entreated society to join with him in weeping over them. An equally farcical and truthful story is told of the way in which one of the South-well apothecaries received early intelligence of a more than usually vehement combat, from which each of the two belligerents withdrew with a strong feeling that the other would commit suicide before the morn-ing. Having good reason to think his mother violent and mad enough to do all her words implied, Byron went off to the apothecary the same night, and begged him on no account whatever to supply Mrs. Byron with the means of putting an end to herself. And the apothecary had scarcely dismissed his patron with an assurance that his wish should be respected, when he received a nocturnal visit from Mrs. Byron, who had come—not to buy poison, but to beg that no kind of deadly stuff should be sold to her son.

Soon after this comical incident, the Pigots were sitting late one evening in their drawing-room—debating possibly what would be the end of these wretched disputes—when Lord Byron came in upon them with a petition that they would give him a bed for the night, as he had resolved to go up to London in the morning, without bidding his mother farewell, and to stay away from Southwell till she had with due expressions of penitence promised to amend her faulty manners.   Only a few minutes earlier a stormy altercation between the two habitual disputants had ended in a manner, that occasioned Lord Byron the less surprise as Mrs. Byron had in former times thrown the fire-tongs at his head.   On the present occasion the eccentric gentlewoman, stirred probably by 'mountain' as well as maternal indignation, had attempted to silence her adversary with the poker. Hence the young nobleman's determination to keep away from Southwell, till his mother should promise never again to have recourse to so dangerous and objectionable a form of argument.

In the morning, before Mrs. Byron had a suspicion of his purpose, Byron was well on his way towards London, having left Southwell under circumstances that caused him to write to Miss Pigot on 9th August, 1806, from his lodgings at 16 Piccadilly: 'Seriously, your mother has laid me under great obligations, and you, with the rest of your family, merit my warmest thanks for your kind connivance at my escape.'   It was the fugitive's desire that his place of retreat should not be revealed to Mrs. Byron, to whom he sent word, through Miss Pigot, that should she venture to pursue him she would do so at the risk of driving him 'immediately to Portsmouth,' —a sufficiently plain hint that to avoid her, till she should have come to a proper view of her behaviour, he was prepared to go abroad. But the young man's wish was disappointed. On learning her son's address (probably through the disloyalty or indiscretion of the groom who was ordered to go to London with the peer's horses), Mrs. Byron went up to town at fullest posting speed, and in due course had an interview with him at his Piccadilly lodgings, from which she retired with a clear perception that her lame brat of a boy had passed out of her government. 'I cannot exactly say with Cæsar, "Veni, vidi, vici," ' the poet wrote to young Pigot,—Miss Pigot's brother, an Edinburgh medical student ; 'however, the most important part of his laconic account of success applies to my present situation ; for, though Mrs. Byron took the *trouble* of " *coming* " and " *seeing*," yet your humble servant remained the *victor*.' Henceforth, so far as his lamentably incompetent mother was concerned, Lord Byron of Trinity was his own master. 'The enemy,' as the conqueror undutifully styled his parent, having retired to her entrenchments in Nottinghamshire, Lord Byron with his servant and horses made a trip to Worthing and Littlehampton on the Sussex coast ; whence he returned in two or three weeks' time 'with all the honours of successful war ' to Southwell, for a brief visit of courtesy to the vanquished 'enemy,' before he set out for Harrowgate, with young Pigot for his companion.

At Harrowgate—whither they posted in his lordship's carriage, and were preceded by his lordship's saddle-horses—the young men found little diversion in the gaieties of an unusually 'gay season.' Whilst the student was thinking more of his Edinburgh studies than of the amusements of the water-drinkers, the poet thought chiefly of his verses when he was not playing with his big dogs. 'Harrowgate,' Mr. Pigot wrote to his sister at Southwell, 'is still extremely full; Wednesday (to-day) is our ball-night, and I meditate going into the room for an hour, although I am by no means fond of strange faces. Lord B., you know, is even more shy than myself.' Twenty years later, on being asked for particulars of the visit that might be serviceable to the poet's authorised biographer, Dr. Pigot wrote, 'We were at the Crown Inn, at Low Harrowgate. We always dined in the public room, but retired very soon after dinner to our private one; for Byron was no more a friend to drinking than myself. We lived retired, and made few acquaintances; for he was naturally shy, *very* shy, which people who did not know him mistook for pride.'

On their homeward journey from the Yorkshire springs, whilst his friend maintained the silence that was asked of him, Byron—as the post-horses covered the distance between Chesterfield and Mansfield, 'spun the prologue for our play' (published in the 'Hours of Idleness'), that was delivered in due course at the dramatic entertainment that took place in Mr. Leacroft's drawing-room towards the end of September; the entertainment at which the poet, in his delivery of the epilogue by Mr. Becher, distinguished himself,

more perhaps to the surprise than the delight of some
of the audience, by an exhibition of the talent for
mimicry that in later time enabled him to play the
part of a racy and irresistibly comic *raconteur*.

Towards the close of November, copies of the
volume of poems, which the young man had been
seeing through the press during the summer and
autumn of 1806, were sent to Mr. Becher of Southwell
and Mr. Pigot at Edinburgh ; but these copies had
no sooner passed from his possession, than the author
was induced to burn all the remaining volumes of the
edition, by Mr. Becher's equally prompt and judicious
expression of his opinion that the sixteen stanzas ' to
Mary ' were disagreeably animated with the spirit of
Little's amatory verses. That the clergyman had
good reason for the protest may be ascertained by a
perusal of the single extant copy of the poem ; but
the justice of the censure detracts in no degree from
the praise due to the poet for the graceful docility
and good temper with which he accepted it. Had he
declined to profit by the good counsel, and laughing
at his friend's squeamishness persisted in sending out
the books on which he had expended so much care,
Byron would only have acted like a youngster of
ordinary wilfulness and self-sufficiency. But in
yielding so readily to the clergyman, whose judgment
he respected and whose affection he valued, Byron at
least justified Dr. Drury's testimony to his manage-
ableness, and showed that, however quick he might
be to pull against the cable of harsh and tyrannical
government, he was still to be led by the silken
thread of wise and sympathetic authority. In truth
his behaviour in a matter, so likely to provoke the

pride and obstinacy of youthful nature, is no slight
evidence that his insubordination to Drury's successor
was more due to the master's want of tact than the
pupil's want of temper, and that the Cambridge
'dons' would have found him less unruly if they had
been better qualified to govern him.   That the young
man's submission to Mr. Becher's judgment involved
a considerable sacrifice of his inclination appears from
the quickness, with which he brought out the second
collection of verses for the amusement of his friends,
and for the gratification of his eager appetite for the
distinction of 'being an author.'

The proofs of this second volume of poems, printed
for private circulation, were undergoing revision, when
Byron, still in his nineteenth year, wrote 'The Prayer
of Nature,'—a composition that shows with interesting clearness the character and limits of the religious
scepticism, which made the young poet an object of
mingled terror and pity to many, perhaps the majority,
of his acquaintance:—

THE PRAYER OF NATURE.

'Father of Light! great God of Heaven!
　　Hear'st Thou the accents of despair?
Can guilt like man's be e'er forgiven?
　　Can vice atone for crimes by prayer?

'Father of Light, on Thee I call!
　　Thou see'st my soul is dark within;
Thou who canst mark the sparrow's fall,
　　Avert from me the death of sin.

'No shrine I seek, to sects unknown;
　　Oh point to me the path of truth!
Thy dread omnipotence I own;
　　Spare, yet amend, the faults of youth.

' Let bigots rear a gloomy fane,
    Let superstition hail the pile,
Let priests, to spread their sable reign,
    With tales of mystic rites beguile.

' Shall man confine his Maker's sway
    To Gothic domes of mouldering stone ?
Thy temple is the face of day ;
    Earth, ocean, heaven Thy boundless throne.

' Shall man condemn his race to hell
    Unless they bend in pompous form ;
Tell us that all, for one who fell,
    Must perish in the mingling storm ?

' Shall each pretend to reach the skies,
    Yet doom his brother to expire,
Whose soul a different hope supplies,
    Or doctrines less severe inspire ?

' Shall these, by creeds they can't expound,
    Prepare a fancied bliss or woe ?
Shall reptiles, grovelling on the ground,
    Their great Creator's purpose know ?

' Shall those, who live for self alone,
    Whose years float on in daily crime—
Shall they by Faith for guilt atone,
    And live beyond the bounds of Time ?

' Father ! no prophet's laws I seek,—
    Thy laws in Nature's works appear ;—
I own myself corrupt and weak,
    Yet will I pray, for Thou wilt hear !

' Thou, who canst guide the wandering star
    Through trackless realms of Æther's space ;
Who calm'st the elemental war,
    Whose hand from pole to pole I trace :

' Thou, who in wisdom placed me here,
    Who, when Thou wilt, can take me hence,
Ah ! whilst I tread this earthly sphere,
    Extend to me Thy wide defence.

> ' To Thee, my God, to Thee I call !
>   Whatever weal or woe betide,
> By Thy command I rise or fall,
>   In Thy protection I confide.
>
> ' If, when this dust to dust restored,
>   My soul shall float on airy wing,
> How shall Thy glorious name adored,
>   Inspire her feeble voice to sing !
>
> ' But, if this fleeting spirit share
>   With clay the grave's eternal bed,
> While life yet throbs, I raise my prayer,
>   Though doom'd no more to quit the dead.
>
> ' To Thee I breathe my humble strain,
>   Grateful for all Thy mercies past,
> And hope, my God, to Thee again
>   This erring life may fly at last.'

In the following year (1807), at a time when he was anticipating speedy death, Byron in his twentieth year wrote,

> ' Forget this world, my restless sprite,
>   Turn, turn thy thoughts to Heav'n ;
> There must thou soon direct thy flight,
>   If errors are forgiven.
>   To bigots and to sects unknown,
>   Bow down beneath the Almighty's throne :—
>   To Him address thy trembling prayer ;
>   He, who is merciful and just,
>   Will not reject a child of dust,
>   Although his meanest care.
>
> ' Father of Light ! to Thee I call,
>   My soul is dark within;
> Thou, who canst mark the sparrow's fall,
>   Avert the death of sin.
>   Thou, who canst guide the wandering star,
>   Who calm'st the elemental war,

> Whose mantle is yon boundless sky,
> My thoughts, my words, my crimes forgive ;
> And, since I soon must cease to live,
> Instruct me how to die.'

Had it been composed a few months later, when Byron was living under the influence of Charles Skinner Matthews, ' The Prayer of Nature' would probably have contained more to shock orthodox readers. Written in the Christmas-tide of 1806, the poem gave utterance to a scepticism that differed in no important particular from the religious opinions he professed less precisely at Harrow, where he fought Lord Calthorpe for accusing him of atheism. Exhibiting abundant faith in the existence of a personal Deity, vigilant of the actions and attentive to the prayers of human beings, and showing no disposition to question the doctrine of man's personal existence after death, the Prayer, in its heterodoxy, is but a cry of revolt against certain of the doctrines imposed on the writer's mind in its infancy ;—doctrines that had become intolerable to a mind, so sensitive and imaginative. Differing from the infidelity of Hume and Gibbon and Voltaire, with whose writings he had already a slight acquaintance, almost as widely as it differs from the devout unbelief of Darwin, this scepticism, whose single aim is to escape from agonizing imaginations, has little in common with the cold doubt of the philosophic thinkers of the poet's own period, and scarcely anything at all with the free thought of recent scientific inquirers. And it will be seen by-and-by that these remarks are not more applicable to Byron's infidelity in its earlier than to his infidelity in its later exhibitions.

The scepticism of ' Childe Harold ' differs notably

from the scepticism of ' The Prayer of Nature ; ' the scepticism of the second instalment of the poet's first great poem is in many particulars out of harmony with the scepticism of the earlier cantos ; and the bolder and cynical scepticism of ' Don Juan ' is in several respects strangely unlike the scepticism of the ' Pilgrimage.'   Although Shelley believed himself incapable of influencing his friend in respect to religious questions, the man who had held daily communion with so fearless and subtle a reasoner was other than the Byron, who loitered with so sober and matter-of-fact a scholar as Hobhouse through the ruins of ancient Athens.   In like manner the pilgrim of the Eastern tour, with Hobhouse at his elbow, was other than the Byron who delighted at Cambridge and Newstead to talk with Charles Skinner Matthews on the mysteries of existence and the perplexities of faith.   And the Byron, with whom Matthews talked, was other than the Byron who in 1806 wrote ' The Prayer of Nature.'   But in all the variations of his unbelief, Byron is always the sceptic of emotion,—never the cold and calmly speculative free-thinker.   More referable to the feminine than the masculine forces of his nature, his scepticism is an affair of sensibility and passion, instead of logic and conviction.   Whether he rails in boyish verse at ' priests ' and ' bigots,' or in a loftier strain compassionates the ' poor child of doubt and death, whose hope is built on reeds,' or exclaims with cynical vehemence,

> ' For me, I know nought ; nothing I deny,
>   Admit, reject, contemn ; and what know *you*,
> Except perhaps that you were born to die ?
> And both may after all turn out untrue ;'

he is the sceptic of feeling and excitement, whose profoundest reasonings are familiar arguments of 'common sense,' and whose confidence in his own conclusions sinks as his pulse subsides. Begotten of anxiety for himself and sympathy for human kind,—the selfish fear being far less powerful in his generous breast than the concern for others,—this feverish, impulsive, timorous scepticism was fruitful of repudiations of unendurable dogmas; but every repudiation was attended by an uneasy feeling that the rejected doctrine might in the end prove a true one. In the agitation which followed his death, people perplexed themselves with the question, whether he had in his later time been a Christian? Answering this question in a way that left the question unanswered, Leigh Hunt remarked, 'He was a Christian by education: he was an infidel by reading. He was a Christian by habit: he was no Christian upon reflection.' But Byron, with his keen sensitiveness and strong memory, was so constituted that his later reading (never severe) could not altogether overcome the influence of early education. Shelley was less powerful over him than May Gray. Hovering and oscillating even in the periods of his boldest scepticism, between Christianity and disbelief, he never after his boyhood rested either on the one or the other. There were moments when he could speak and write as though he had passed altogether from his early faith ; but to the last he was an anxious and hesitating unbeliever, and the religious opinions of the man, who in Italy and Greece was an habitual reader of the Bible given him by his sister on the eve of his withdrawal from England, resembled the religious opinions of the boy who wrote 'The Prayer of Nature.'

The period of the production of this religious poem was also the time at which the young man first set himself earnestly to combat the tendency to corpulence of which Moore speaks so daintily. It was no mere disposition to inconvenient stoutness, but a burdensome and disfiguring grossness of which Byron resolved to rid himself at the commencement of his twentieth year; and as he has been unfairly ridiculed and persistently exhibited to contempt for the vanity, which caused him to sacrifice bodily health to personal appearance, it is but fair to display in all its repulsiveness the extravagance of the disease that made him employ such violent measures for its abatement. The matter is the more deserving of consideration, because the regimen, in which he persisted with a resoluteness and perseverance that may almost be called heroic, affected his temper and happiness, his character and even his genius.

So long as he continued to grow in stature, this vicious habit of body was fruitful of no serious inconvenience. Nor was it attended with humiliating and embittering results. But as soon as he ceased to grow higher, the youth who had been a thick-bodied, heavy-featured lad, expanded with fat till he became ludicrous and repulsive to beholders,—especially to those beholders, the young and lovely of .the gentler sex, of whose approval he was most keenly desirous. Let it be remembered that on attaining its full measure his stature barely escaped shortness. It was his humour and weakness to maintain that he stood five feet and eight *and a half* inches high. In questions of height, it may be laid down as a sure maxim that the man who claims credit for the extra half-inch, claims credit for what he does not possess. In his boots Byron stood a trifle over five feet eight inches; but this was the height of a man—standing on his toes, with heels raised by boots of peculiar make. His actual height was midway between five feet seven inches and five feet eight inches. And on the nineteenth anniversary of his birthday this young man of barely average height weighed fourteen stone and six pounds. Of this burden of flesh more than an average proportion pertained to the trunk and superior limbs, as his inability to take much walking exercise was unfavourable to the development of the legs. The young man, of abnormal girth and large shoulders, tottering unsteadily on spindle limbs and small, distorted feet, had a face swollen to unsightliness with fatty tissue. Is it wonderful that his visage was disgustful to him? and that he resolved to mortify his keen appetite for food, to abstain from fattening drinks, to weaken himself by the daily use of drastic medicines, to quicken his skin's action with hot baths, and to deny himself several of the most important pleasures of sense, in order to escape such hideous disfigurement and to look like other young men? Surely it was more honourable than contemptible in him that he could make such a daily and hourly sacrifice of bodily indulgence and delights for which he had keen zest, in order to emerge from such a swinish state of physical depravity? It is best for a man to be natural in his habits and outward show. But when a man cannot be natural without looking like a hog, he does well to be unnatural for the sake of looking like a man. Let it be granted that the motive was vanity, and that vanity is no heroic quality,—albeit, a quality that is seldom wanting in heroes, and often contributes not a little to their heroism. Still the fact remains that, his only choice lying between the part of a pig and the part of a peacock, it is creditable to him that he declined the part of the pig.

In the April of 1807, he wrote from Southwell to his friend Pigot at Edinburgh, ' Since we met, I have reduced myself by violent exercise, much physic, and hot bathing, from fourteen stone six pounds to twelve stone seven pounds. In all I have lost twenty-seven pounds. Bravo!' On going up to Cambridge he was so changed in shape and show that even his familiars of Trinity did not recognise him at first sight. 'I was obliged,' he wrote to Miss Pigot from Cambridge on 30th June, 1807, 'to tell everybody my name, nobody having the least recollection of my visage or person.' The mild-mannered Eddleston was 'thunderstruck' at the change in his patron. A fortnight later the poet wrote to Miss Pigot from London, 'Though I am sorry to say it, it seems to be the mode amongst *gentlemen* to grow *fat*, and I am told I am at least fourteen pounds below the fashion. However, I decrease instead of enlarging, which is extraordinary, as violent *exercise* in London is impracticable.' Violent exercise, however, can at no time have been a chief factor of the regimen, which owed most of its efficacy to starvation, Epsom salts, and the sweating bath. Such exercise as he could take, he took. In the summer and in the cold seasons he swam for long distances daily; but that is no exercise for the reduction of fat. He was daily for hours in the saddle; but as soon as the muscles, which it affects especially, have accommodated themselves to the strain, horse exercise ceases to be either a violent or a reducing exercise. Were it a remedy for grossness of bodily habit, one would not see so many pot-bellied troopers, and hunting-men who ride sixteen stone. At Cambridge in these later days such a man, if he could bring himself to sacrifice the beauty of his hands, would sweat the fat from his ribs in an out-rigger, and Byron, with his broad shoulders, muscular neck and thewy arms, would have been a superb oars-man, and led the Cam in a sport where his lameness would have put him at no disadvantage. But in Byron's days at Trinity, the Cam knew nothing about eight-oars, and four-oars, and sculling matches. The only violent exercise to be of much service to him in his war against fat was long-continued exercise on foot; —and that exercise was impossible to him. He could rush about for a few minutes at a time in Jackson's boxing-room; but he could maintain the exertion only for short spurts, and at the cost of intense pain.

For the sacrifices, which he made for the attain-ment of his object, Byron was repaid nobly. He sub-mitted to starvation and physic, in order to escape loathsome unsightliness; and besides relieving him of the repulsive aspect, the regimen—to his astonish-ment and delight—endowed him with the beauty of loveliness; beauty that became proverbial. No longer big and puffy, his eyelids and cheeks became fine, and firm, and delicate, with curves as clear in outline as the curves of sculpture. Ceasing to be thick and heavy, his lips and chin assumed the peculiar sweet-ness and softness, that made him in the lower part of his countenance a bewitchingly charming woman rather than a handsome man. The nose—even in his comeliest period something too broad, and having (as Leigh Hunt spitefully remarked) the appearance of having been put upon the face, instead of coming out from it—was relieved of its clumsiness, and refined into harmony with the rest of a profile singularly suggestive of high breeding. At the same time the blue-gray eyes, fringed with dark (almost black) lashes, acquired a brightness and subtlety of expression that had never before distinguished them. His complexion was purified to transparency, and his auburn hair, playing over his brow in short, feathery curls, became richly lustrous. The man, who with the fine touch of a delicate and naturally sensitive hand takes in his fingers a lock of Byron's hair for the first time, experiences a curious surprise from the feather-like softness of the filaments.

Thus much starvation and medicine did for the aspect of his face. The transformation of his figure was no less striking,—a body of grace and dignified elegance being substituted for a body of almost loutish clumsiness. At the same time, the regimen was even more beneficent to his sensations than to his appearance. Relieved of the burden of his superfluous flesh he could walk with comparative ease and security. The body, that had oppressed him, was no longer unwieldy and unmanageable. Obeying his will, it filled him with delight. And what is even more noteworthy than all the other results of the regimen taken together, is that this discipline of starvation and drastic depletives quickened his brain to such a degree, that the man of intellect for the first time knew himself to be something far higher than a man of mere intellect.

The goads and whips of the regimen had affected the nervous system, so that he had become a man of genius. He had gone to drugs and starvation at the instigation of personal vanity. Henceforth he persisted in using them for the sake of the delights of that highest life, to which they had raisèd him, and from which he soon sunk surely and quickly without their assistance.

It is not difficult to show how it was that starvation and medicine affected Byron in so remarkable a manner. Though he may not be aware of the process by which it operates for his immediate gratification and ultimate injury, the absinthe-drinker takes his pernicious beverage for the sake of the mechanical irritation it causes to the lining membrane and nerves of the stomach, and the consequent sympathetic excitement of the brain. Byron with Epsom salts and starvation did for his stomach and brain what the absinthe-drinker accomplishes by means of the essence of wormwood. He kept the mucous membrane of the stomach in constant irritation, and the nerves of the stomach in constant and abnormal activity, the immediate effect of their excitation being a sympathetic action of the brain, alike agreeable to his whole nervous system and conducive to mental sprightliness. The state to which he thus brought himself was attended with the pleasurable sensations of intoxication, and indeed differed chiefly from vinous exhilaration in being followed by no serious depression. 'A dose of salts,' Byron remarks in one of his journals, 'has the effect of a temporary inebriation, like light champagne, upon me.' Wine made him gloomy and savage, as soon as the momentary exhilaration had passed; the irritation of the medicine affected his brain as alcohol affects men whose nerves suffer no painful consequences from it. And to the last, starvation and medicine operated in the same way on his mental forces. 'By starving his body,' says Trelawny, speaking from his observation of the poet in his closing years, 'Byron kept his brains clear: no man had brighter eyes or a clearer voice.'

The sacrifices, which Byron thus made for quickness of brain and freedom from bodily grossness, were too heavy and grievous to be made daily throughout successive years, without reluctance and with no occasional relaxations of the stern discipline. But as soon as he wavered in this ascetic course, so far as to eat and drink like other men, he began to fatten and (in his earlier manhood) wax dull; and it was only by returning to the severe regimen that he could recover his vigour and intellectual brightness. What it cost him in discomfort and effort thus 'to clap the muzzle on his jaws' (to use his own words), 'and like the hybernating animals consume his own fat,' he alone knew. He spent the great part of his manly time under the goads of keen hunger, living for days together on biscuits and soda-water, till overcome by gnawing famine he would swallow a huge mess of potatoes, rice and fish, drenched with vinegar, and after recovering from the indigestion occasioned by such fare would go in for another term of qualified starvation. Fortunately for the man who was constrained to take this ascetic course, the desire for food was not sharpened by an epicurean yearning for delicate flavours. Like Walter Scott, Byron had a strangely insensitive palate. Sir Walter preferred

whisky to wine, and could not distinguish one kind
of claret from another; and Byron thought no dinner
of the rarest viands could surpass a meal of poached
eggs and bacon and bottled beer.

In other matters besides food he was strangely
abstinent.   From a few boastful passages of his
journals, it might be thought that Byron's practice
was to drink freely.   But the evidence is conclusive
that, whilst his excesses in wine were rare and exceptional incidents even in his times of indulgence, his
usual moderation in alcohol would be thought exemplary even in these days when sobriety is the fashion.
The gin-and-water, of which he spoke whimsically as
the source of the wit of 'Don Juan,' was a single
glass of weak,—sometimes very weak—toddy on
nights of unusual weariness and exhaustion.   Once
in a long while he smoked a cigar, to see if he liked
it; but at no time was he 'a smoker.'   Drinking
laudanum, he used also (at times) to chew tobacco, to
stay the pain of hunger biting at his vitals.   In Italy
he was often seen with his tobacco-box in his hand and
a quid in his mouth.   But all through life, from
Southwell to Missolonghi (with the exception of
two exceptional periods of excess), his rule in regard
to meat and alcohol was to 'live low' that he might
'think high.'   'The regimen' of starvation and physic
answered well for a time, but ill in the long run, like
absinthe-drinking which, operating pleasantly for a
time, results in ruined stomach, shattered nerves, and
all the distresses of mind and body that attend failure
of the digestive powers and the nervous forces.

For some months in 1816—the months of his
heaviest domestic troubles—he took brandy in excess,

and was at the same time a laudanum-drinker.   And
at Venice—during his period of depravation—he was
for several months even sottish in his use of spirits.
But these passages of intemperance contrast strongly
with the temperance for which he was at other times
remarkable.   His most vicious and baneful habit in
the way of drinking was the use of laudanum.   The
abundant evidence of his journals and letters that it
was his practice to consume opium in this form, is not
the only extant evidence that, like De Quincy and
Coleridge and several other chiefs of our nineteenth
century literature, he was so much addicted to laudanum, that he may without exaggeration be said to
have been a laudanum-drinker.

CHAPTER XI.

PEER AND PILGRIM.

WHILST he was spending money during his minority at the rate of five or six thousand a-year, Byron looked to the Rochdale property to pay his debts, put the Newstead mansion in habitable condition, and still give him ten, twenty, thirty, or forty thousand pounds, to begin housekeeping with in the seat of his forefathers. Whenever he meditated gloomily on his growing embarrassments, Rochdale with its coal was the mine of wealth that, on the termination of the Chancery suit next year, or at the furthest two years hence, would free him from his little difficulties, enable him to dismiss the money-lenders, and put him in easy circumstances. His notions of the value of this charming property were elastic ; its worth growing with the difficulties it was to dissipate. In August 1806, immediately after a favourable finding at Lancaster Assizes, the property was worth 30,000*l.* ; in February 1807, the value of the estate had risen to 60,000*l.* Fourteen years later, when the young lord's hair was beginning to turn grey, he said to Medwin, ' The

Lancashire property was hampered with a lawsuit, which has cost me 14,000*l.*, and is not yet finished.'

The Rochdale property may therefore be left out of the calculation, when the reader is considering his lordship's sources of income from the attainment of his majority till his residence at Pisa, when Medwin made his acquaintance. On coming of age, the poet was more than 10,000*l.* in debt, whilst his income from Newstead—his sole revenue—was less than 1500*l.* a-year. It was however in his power to sell Newstead,—the picturesque property for which he was offered a few years later 140,000*l.* by a gentleman who forfeited 25,000*l.* on his failure to complete the purchase, and which was eventually sold for 94,000*l.*

Mr. Hanson (the poet's solicitor) told his client, that he should not think of selling the Rochdale property which, pending the litigation, would not bring in a good price, but should lose no time in parting with Newstead, where he could not live in any style whatever. But the young peer would not entertain, still less act upon the judicious advice. His honour was concerned in keeping Newstead ; and for once he and his mother were of one mind. Mrs. Byron was longing to move from Southwell to the Abbey. Her son also was pining to dwell in his ancestral halls. And in his desire to live there, he was so imprudent as to repair some rooms of the dilapidated mansion at a considerable expense, and then to furnish them at great charge (on credit) of 1500*l.*, when he was still in his minority. Taking up his abode at Newstead in September 1808, when he was four months under age, he spent much of his time there till the June of the next year, when he started for Greece. As he would not allow Mrs. Byron to live with him at the Abbey, his establishment was settled for the needs of a bachelor ; but though it was fixed on a modest scale, the household, consisting of an old butler, a valet, the groom, and three or four female servants, was an establishment far beyond his means. Nearly every requisite for this establishment was obtained on credit from tradesmen, who in consideration of risk were entitled to charge their customer at high rates. The wine was sent in on credit ; the coals were supplied on credit ; the money needful for the young lord's current expenses was obtained from lenders at usurious interest ; and soon after coming of age, his lordship borrowed of the Jews—to whom he referred long afterwards in ' Don Juan '—the considerable sum of money for the charges of his Eastern tour, which he made in a style more in harmony with his rank than his means.

In the earlier months of 1808, before going into residence at Newstead, he had spent money freely in London on the ordinary pleasures of a young gentleman of quality ; a chief cause and object of his profuseness being the girl who, living with him in lodgings at Brompton, used to ride about town with him, habited in male attire. Dressed like a boy, this person accompanied him to Brighton, where he had the folly to introduce her to his acquaintance as his ' brother Gordon ;' and a few months later she was at least for a short time an inmate of Newstead. And it shows the difference in certain matters of taste and morality between English society in this year of grace and English society at the beginning of the present century, that instead of provoking loud censure by this display of his intimacy with a saucy ' *fille de joie*,' young Lord Byron was thought to be amusing himself quite within the lines of permissible license, and was even commended for his address in giving an air and flavour of piquant eccentricity to an otherwise uninteresting arrangement. Instead of passing the young peer and 'his brother' on the Brighton Parade without appearing to notice them, the lady of rank and fashion, to whom Moore refers, entered freely into conversation with 'the brothers,' and was vastly amused when, in answer to a complaisant speech about the beauty of her horse, the girl in boy's clothes remarked, 'Yes, it was *gave* me by my brother.'

A still more remarkable illustration of the same difference in taste and morality between the English of to-day and the English of seventy years since is found in the affectionate interest and absolute freedom from dismay, with which the first readers of 'Childe Harold' accepted *au pied de la lettre* the poet's 'revelations' of his way of living at Newstead before he set out for his travels. It shocks the nerves to conceive what thunderbolts of reprobation would be hurled by every newspaper of the land at the young gentleman who, in a book of verse or prose having every appearance of autobiographical sincerity, should now-a-days assure the world that, in chagrin at his refusal by a young lady on whom he had set his affections, he filled his country house with loose women and well-bred *mauvais sujets*, and spent several weeks with them in drunkenness and voluptuous enjoyments, till sated and exhausted with debauchery he came to loathe himself for his abandonment and excesses. But Byron said all this of himself in a way that caused the whole world to take his statements literally; and instead of being horrified by his evidence against himself, the only regret of his readers was that the confessions were not more full and particular. Byron's avowals of surprise and displeasure at his readers' perverseness in taking ' Childe Harold ' for himself, and in regarding the Childe's career at home and on his travels as the author's career, are merely so many laughable examples of the way in which a writer, after describing himself or his friends in a work of fiction, is always blind to his achievements in portraiture. The Childe is a young spendthrift of lineage long and glorious; the Childe has sighed in vain to the heiress of goodly lands; the Childe's ancestral hall is a vast and venerable pile, where superstition once had made her den ; the Childe has a mother and a single sister ; the Childe visits the same places as the author visited ; to fix the Childe's personality yet more closely on himself, Byron had christened the poem ' Childe Burun,' and was not easily persuaded to substitute Harold for his own surname ;—and yet, when he had taken all these pains to identify himself with the hero of the poem, the author was at a loss to understand why he was universally supposed to have been writing about himself. But the disavowals of the identity of the author and the hero do not touch the point, to which the readers of this page are asked to give their attention,—that Byron's contemporaries were universally of opinion that his doings at Newstead resembled the Childe's riotous excesses in his ' father's hall,' and that far from causing them to revolt from him or regard him with disapproval, the opinion disposed most of them to think of him with favour and even with admiration.

The comedy of the whole business is heightened by the slightness of the poet's grounds for the super-sensational description of his naughty behaviour in his own house. The only 'Paphian girls . . . . to sing and smile' at Newstead for the delight of a master 'sore given to revel and ungodly glee' were the cook and housemaid of the bachelor's staff of servants, and the girl whose boyish dress and horsemanship had a few weeks earlier made a stir on the Brighton cliff. Dallas indeed was so completely possessed by the fictions of the poem, as to write seriously of the considerations which determined the young lord to 'break up his harams'; but in sober prose the 'harams' of Byron's worst biographer were the young woman who cooked the poet's frugal meals, the young woman who kept his rooms tidy, and the girl from Brompton who came and went in the garb and under the name of 'brother Gordon.' The 'revellers from far and near' were three or four of the neighbouring clergy, half-a-dozen of the poet's old friends at Southwell, and his former chums at Cambridge—Matthews, Scrope Davies, Hodgson and Hobhouse; the last of these 'heartless parasites of present cheer' being the true and trusty comrade, with whom the poet had already arranged to travel for a couple of years. Unless he had his eye on some of the Southwell folk, who may be suspected of treating him somewhat reverentially when they came to look over the Abbey, it is impossible to conceive who were the 'flatterers of the festal hour,' of whom the Childe speaks so disdainfully. For a week or two the poet thought of having 'private theatricals' in the great hall, and of inviting a lot of people to see the performances ; but if he had not relinquished the project, the young lord would have been compelled to invite his tenants and their children and the villagers from Hucknall-Torkard, in order to escape the shame of playing to empty benches. For till he went abroad, he could have counted on his fingers all the persons he knew of Nottinghamshire 'county families.'

Once only was there any serious effort in the way of hospitality on a large scale. On the twenty-first anniversary of his lordship's birthday, Newstead was stirred ' by such festivities as his narrow means and society could furnish.' An ox was roasted for the farmers and their families and the humbler peasantry of the estate ; and in the evening, there was something of the nature of ' a ball.' But the dance must have been a sorry affair, as Moore was unable to discover that anyone of greater importance than Mr. Hanson (the solicitor) figured amongst the dancers. This ball, without ladies and gentlemen of quality, or a single carriageful of county neighbours, was in truth a dance for the farmers and servants ; and it seems to have been the sole realistic foundation for the lines about 'concubines and carnal companie, and flaunting wassailers of high and low degree.'

When the poet entertained four of his Cambridge friends at his Abbey in May 1809, shortly before his departure for foreign lands, the life of the old mansion went merrily, with good stories and songs over champagne, and just the faintest possible flavour and savour of profanity in the monastic masquerades and mummery with which the young men amused themselves. Rising late from their beds, they breakfasted at noon, and whiled away five or six hours with reading, fencing, singlestick, shuttlecock, pistol-practice, riding, walking, and sailing on the lake, till the time came for the host and his guests to array themselves for dinner,—a repast that always ended with the 'loving cup' of burgundy : the wine being passed round in the big skull, which Byron had exhumed from the burial-ground of the monks of olden time, and put to this rather profane use. At dinner Byron with exquisite humour played the part of my Lord Abbot in full abbatial costume, whilst his friends played the fool no less cleverly in their monastic dresses, with a fitting show of crosses, beads and tonsures, as monks of inferior degree. Doubtless, wild things were said and done in the small hours of the morning ; but the party of five young men ('now and then increased by the presence of a neighbouring parson ') dispersed after a few days of these humorous ' high jinks,' without doing anything to justify the extravagant rumours that went about the country of their impious usages and wild orgies. Men of culture and refinement, these ' heartless parasites of present cheer ' may once and again have ' vexed with mirth the drowsy ear of night,' but the recollection of all their wildest pranks and extravagances would not have plunged the poet in remorse for associating so closely with such a crew of tippling reprobates. Even when he plied his pen in obedience to the stern requirements of his muse, the poet thought of them far better than he ventured to write of them.

In the absence of his few guests, whose visits were rare and brief and at considerable intervals, Byron's life at Newstead was a life of study, meditation, and strenuous labour. Pope had long been his favourite poet, and now he studied the great artist of words and malice, to extort from him the secret of his peculiar department of literary art,—to learn how to produce verse that should inflict the acutest pain on his enemies, and at the same time afford the keenest delight to the witnesses of their sufferings. He was hard at work,—working passionately and yet at the same time calmly,—on the satire that was destined to fill his foes with silent fury, and put him in the front rank of the new generation of men of letters.

On an early day of 1809, he went up to London with his satire, polished and pointed and poisoned for the press ; his guardian being one of the few persons for whom it contained an expression of homage or courtesy. In the author's ' copy ' the Earl was down for this compliment,

> ' On one alone Apollo deigns to smile,
> And crowns a new Roscommon in Carlisle.'

But when the poem came to public view, for this graceful and not undeserved couplet the poet had substituted,

> ' Lords too are bards, such things at times befall,
> And 'tis some praise in peers to write at all.
> Yet, did or taste or reason sway the times,
> Ah ! who would take their titles with their rhymes ?
> Roscommon ! Sheffield ! with your spirits fled,
> No future laurels deck a noble head ;
> No muse will cheer, with renovating smile,
> The paralytic puling of Carlisle.
> The puny schoolboy and his early lay
> Men pardon, if his follies pass away ;
> But who forgives the senior's ceaseless verse,
> Whose hairs grow hoary as his rhymes grow worse ?
> What heterogeneous honours deck the peer ! '

Lord, rhymester, petit-maître, pamphleteer !
So dull in youth, so drivelling in his age,
His scenes alone had damn'd our sinking stage ;
But managers for once cried, "Hold, enough !"
Nor drugg'd their audience with the tragic stuff.
Yet at their judgment let his lordship laugh,
And case his volumes in congenial calf ;
Yes ! doff that covering, where morocco shines,
And hang a calf-skin on those recreant lines.'

One peculiarly offensive line of this attack would not have been penned, had the writer known that his former guardian was suffering from a nervous malady. What had happened since the beginning of the year to account for the change of feeling towards the Earl, to whom the poet was required by respect for himself, and by regard for his own action in the Dedication of the ' Hours of Idleness,' to wear at least a front of formal civility ?

On going up to town to publish his satire, Byron also went thither to take his seat in the House of Lords ; and whilst under the misconception that the etiquette of the House required that a peer on taking his seat should be introduced to the chamber by one of its members, he wrote to Lord Carlisle that he should be of age at the opening of the next parliamentary session. Instead of evoking from the Earl a cordial offer to introduce his young kinsman to the House, this letter only drew from its receiver a cold epistle of information respecting the course the poet must take in the business. The Earl's young kinsman was nettled,—construing the formal note as an intimation that the writer had no wish to be closely associated in the world's regard with the author of the ' Hours of Idleness.' This annoyance was followed quickly by a more serious vexation. On finding that in order to take his seat he would have to produce evidence of his grandfather's (Admiral Byron's) marriage with Miss Trevanion of Caerhayes in Cornwall, Byron directed his solicitor to get the needful evidence at once. But it is sometimes more difficult to obey an order than to give it. At first it was uncertain where the marriage was celebrated ; and when after some delay it was discovered that the Admiral's wedding had been solemnized in a private chapel at Caerhayes, Byron was informed to his dismay that it was necessary to discover the record of the event. Before Lord Hardwicke's Marriage Act the records of irregular marriages, and also of regular marriages celebrated in private chapels, were kept so carelessly, that it was no uncommon thing for people to be without legal evidence of their wedlock. Till the evidence of the Admiral's marriage should be obtained, Lord Byron could not take his seat. Should the evidence be irrecoverable, he would be in a position of discredit. For the world would not believe the marriage had taken place, and Byron, so far as his peerage was concerned, would be accounted as a pretender claiming to enter the House of Lords through a sire of illegitimate birth. The case was so alarming, that the nervous, sensitive, excitable Byron, who never attained the calmness of philosophy or the *sang-froid* of patrician breeding, may be pardoned for showing extreme agitation. Whilst the hunt was going on for the missing evidence, Lord Carlisle was applied to for information about his mother's family,—information which he wouldn't give or couldn't give. To Byron's heated imagination it seemed that he was the victim of his former guardian's cynical insolence and malignity. The Earl was chuckling in his sleeve at the thought that the young man, whom he had disliked from his early boyhood, would be shut out from the House of Lords, and be degraded from the highest place of his ancient family. Thinking all this of the Earl (who doubtless would have given every information in his power to the point, though he may have declined to give information that was beside it) Byron, white with rage, seized his pen for vengeance. Hence the withdrawal of the civil couplet, and the substitution of the abusive verses. If he was altogether in the wrong, Byron could at least plead in palliation of his misbehaviour the fierce and torturing excitement caused by his painful position. That he was very much in the wrong may be inferred from the fact that his sister Augusta thought him so and had the courage to tell him so. With all her devotion to and admiration of her brother, and all her consequent readiness to humour him in matters that involved no sacred principle, the Honourable Mrs. Leigh never shrunk from telling him the truth. She had the daring of goodness, and she displayed it in opposing him when he did ill, no less than in clinging to him when he suffered ill. And in this business of the Carlisle quarrel—on which he felt so bitterly and hotly—she never ceased to tell him that he ought to make the generous *amende* to the Earl. It was long before Augusta succeeded on this point. But at length the *amende* was made nobly in the tribute of affectionate homage to ' young gallant Howard,' with its line,—

'And partly that I did his sire some wrong,'

penned by the baffled exile, when all his kindred had turned against him, with the exception of the brave woman who demanded the atonement to the man he had wronged.

Byron was still in the first fierceness of his rage against the Earl of Carlisle, when, the evidence of the Caerhayes marriage having been obtained, he took his seat in the House of Lords on the 13th March (within a few days of the appearance of the famous satire), going thither for that purpose with his friend Dallas. Had not Dallas called on him accidentally at an opportune moment, Byron would have driven from his lodgings in St. James's Street to Westminster without a companion. It shows how completely he had lived outside the lines of his ' order ' that, when Lord Carlisle failed him, there was no other peer to whom he could look to introduce him to the House. Dallas has recorded how frigidly the young peer touched the Lord Chancellor's (Eldon's) proffered hand, and how on leaving the House he said, ' If I had shaken hands heartily, he would have set me down for one of his party—but I will have nothing to do with any of them on either side.'

At Cambridge Byron had played at being a Whig, and there can be no question that his mind and temperament qualified him for action with the more popular of the two aristocratic parties. Possibly disgust at his treatment by the ' Edinburgh ' was the chief cause of his present coldness to the Whigs. Possibly he was only actuated by a prudent feeling that he had better hold aloof from both parties till he knew more of politics and of himself. Anyhow the words he spoke to Dallas on leaving the House after taking his seat accorded with words spoken by him on the same subject to other people in the earlier months of 1809. To those who sounded him as to his political sentiments and purpose just a week before his coming of age, the young peer, affecting to be neither Whig nor Tory, declared he should take time to think before espousing the cause and committing himself to the policy of either party. In his ill-humour with his former friends, there were occasions when he spoke of them as a weak army, commanded by blundering subalterns. At heart, however, on the eve of his departure for foreign lands, he was more ambitious of figuring amongst statesmen than of out-singing the poets. Nothing was further from Byron's forecast at this time than that literature would be his vocation. Dr. Drury's high opinion of his declamatory address was influential with the young poet, who looked to public life as the arena in which, after a few years of foreign travel, he would achieve greatness.

Having entertained his Cambridge friends at Newstead in the manner set forth on previous pages, dropped a parting tear on Boatswain's grave, gathered together the portraits of his Harrow 'favourites,' signed his will, settled his mother in the Abbey mansion, shaken hands with Dr. Butler, seen his satire into a second edition, and made inadequate arrangements for remittances to foreign bankers, the young lord, whose whole income was by this time insufficient for the payment of the interest of his debts, sailed for Lisbon at the end of June, 1809, with a suite of three men-servants and a wardrobe of gorgeous and costly clothing,—one of the brave habiliments being the ' scarlet coat, richly embroidered with gold, in the style of an English aide-de-camp's dress uniform,' which he wore on occasions of state, and at least once in the bazaar at Constantinople.

Leaving England in the summer of 1809, he was back again in his native land in the summer of 1811, after an absence of two years and three weeks. From Lisbon he rode on horseback through Portugal and the corner of Spain to Cadiz, whence he journeyed leisurely and luxuriously to Malta, Previsa, through Albania to Tepalsen and back to Previsa. Thence to Missolonghi, Athens, Smyrna, Constantinople, and back to Athens, where he had his head-quarters in a Franciscan convent, whilst making excursions through Attica and the Morea. With plenty of time and, during the earlier period of his travels, enough money at his disposal, he moved hither and thither by routes not easily traceable from his letters and memoranda ; but the above-given names indicate with sufficient clearness his way-bills and devious wanderings till he reappeared at Malta, whence he set sail for England on the 3rd of June in the ' Volage ' frigate. In these days of railroads and steamships and sure postal intercommunication, when tourists can name almost to an hour the time for their arrival at any point of their journeyings, and never need to linger for days and weeks at a single place, waiting for more money, the whole tour, with all its supplementary trips and minor excursions, seems a strangely matter-of-course and hazardless business to designate a pilgrimage. Now-a-days it would be the affair of a lawyer's long vacation, and be made at a tenth or twentieth of the money it cost this Pilgrim of the English peerage.

Every month of the year young ladies by the score set out from London on travels of greater distance, interest, and adventure; and on returning to their English homes they do not look to be credited with having done something remarkable. In these matters the world has changed greatly since Byron went on board 'the good ship, Bristol packet.' The long wars of the Napoleonian period, and the revolutionary troubles which preceded them, had disposed our great-grandfathers and great-grandmothers to prefer security and ease at home to the diversions of roaming; and the Childe's 'pilgrimage,' made though it was in the easiest and most enjoyable manner, with congenial comrades and obsequious servants, was sufficiently daring and venturesome to entitle the pilgrim of lordly condition to a modest measure of approval, even if he had not produced so fascinating a memoir of his travels.

To tell again how his intellect and fancy were quickened and delighted by the scenes he visited would be to reproduce in ordinary prose the finest passages of 'Childe Harold.' But the tour was attended with one or two incidents of biographical value to which passing reference may be made in these pages, as the poet omits to mention them in the 'Pilgrimage.' Whilst journeying from Patras in the Morea, he fired at an eaglet and brought it down on the shore of the Gulf Lepanto near Vostizza; when the brightness and beauty of its eyes filled him with pity for the wounded bird, and made him anxious to save it. 'But,' he remarks, with characteristic sensibility in his brief note of the occurrence, 'it pined and died in a few days; and I never did since, and never will, attempt the death of another bird.'   At Patras, near the end of September 1810, he was struck down by a sharp though short attack of marsh-fever,—the malady that assailed him so often in later years, and was no less accountable than the regimen against fatness for his premature death.   And during his second stay at Athens he conceived an affection for a poor Greek boy, that resembled in vehemence and condescending benignity the friendship he hoped to renew on his return to London with Eddleston, and the friendship he had entertained for the farmer's boy at Newstead.   The object of this third outbreak of affectionateness to a youth so far beneath him in rank was the Nicolo Giraud of Athens, to whom he made a handsome gift of money, on bidding him farewell at Malta, and a few months later bequeathed a legacy of 7000*l.*

Having left home with the hope of seeing Persia and India during the course of his travels, Byron, whilst staying at Athens in 1811, took measures for an excursion to Egypt ; but like the schemes for visiting Persia and India, this later and less ambitious project for the extension of his wanderings was given up for want of money.   Instead of the needful remittances the pilgrim received letters from England, which made him see clearly that he must take prompt steps to satisfy his more importunate creditors, and that to satisfy them he had better sell the Rochdale coal-pits or even the Newstead ruins than go to the usurers for another large loan.   Writing to his mother in February 1811, he said, ' If it is necessary to sell, sell Rochdale.'   Seven months earlier he had written to the same lady, ' I trust you like Newstead, and agree with your neighbours ; but you know *you* are a *vixen*,—is not that a dutiful appellation ? Pray take care of my books and several boxes of papers in the hands of Joseph ; and pray leave me a few bottles of champagne to drink, for I am very thirsty :—but I do not insist on the last article, without you like it.' From the ' Volage frigate,' when he hoped with a fair wind to arrive at Portsmouth on the 2nd of July, the poet wrote to Hodgson, ' Indeed, my prospects are not very pleasant. Embarrassed in my private affairs, indifferent to public, solitary without the wish to be social, with a body enfeebled by a succession of fevers, but a spirit, I trust, yet unbroken, I am returning *home* without a hope, and almost without a desire. The first thing I shall have to encounter will be a lawyer, the next a creditor, then colliers, farmers, surveyors, and all the agreeable attachments to estates out of repair, and contested coal-pits.' The *home* for which Byron sailed in this melancholy temper was the house in which there had been an execution in the previous year for the upholsterer's bill of 1500*l*. It was the home of the mother who was a vixen, with a thirst for champagne.

CHAPTER XII.

'CHILDE HAROLD.'

'Hints from Horace'—The Valley of the Shadow of Death—Melancholy
Poetry—Sam Rogers's Dinner—Newstead and London—First Speech
in 'The Lords'—Sudden Fame—Social Triumph—The Poet's Demeanour—The Prince Regent—The Season of 1812—Cheltenham—.
Pecuniary Affairs—Dissentient Voices.

RETURNING to England, with the first two Cantos of
'Childe Harold' and the 'Hints from Horace' almost
ready for the press, Byron reached Portsmouth none
too soon for the exigencies of his affairs, and so late
that he might have been met on landing from the
'Volage' with dismal news. Young Eddleston, on
whom the poet had lavished such affection as his
nature would under other circumstances have expended on a younger brother, was no more. Dead also
was the poet's former schoolmate, the Honourable
John Wingfield of the Guards, who had perished of
fever at Coimbra, meeting a soldier's death but missing its glory. The chorister and the peer's son had
died in the same month. The loss of the former
touched Byron more acutely than the death of his
Harrow friend, whose fate inspired the stanzas of
'Childe Harold,'—

> 'And thou, my friend—since unavailing woe
>   Bursts from my heart and mingles with the strain,—
> Had the sword laid thee with the mighty low,
>   Pride had forbid e'en Friendship to complain :

> But thus unlaurel'd to descend in vain,
>   By all forgotten, save the lonely breast,
> And mix unbleeding with the boasted slain,
>   While Glory crowns so many a meaner crest !
> What hadst thou done to sink so peacefully to rest !
>
> ' Oh, known the earliest, and esteem'd the most !
>   Dear to a heart where nought was left so dear !
> Though to my hopeless days for ever lost,
>   In dreams deny me not to see thee here !
> And Morn in secret shall renew the tear
>   Of Consciousness awaking to her woes,
> And Fancy hover o'er thy bloodless bier,
>   Till my frail frame return to whence it rose,
> And mourn'd and mourner lie united in repose.'

Of the spirit in which the young man of fervid
but placable temper had come by this time to regard
his satire and the provocation that had occasioned it,
a noteworthy indication may be found in the letter he
wrote Dallas, dating from the 'Volage Frigate, at
sea, June 28, 1811.' 'My satire,' he said, 'it seems
is in a fourth edition, a success rather above the mid-
dling run, but not much for a production which, from
its topics, must be temporary, and of course be successful at first, or not at all. At this period, when I
can think and act more coolly, I regret that I have
written it, though I shall probably find it forgotten
by all except those whom it has offended.' Twelve
months later, when he was receiving civilities and
expressions of their generous admiration of his genius
from the very persons who had most reason to resent
the satirist's wrath and injustice, this regret grew so
strong that he stopped the sale of the ' English
Bards ' when the fifth edition was going off steadily,
and took every occasion to make the *amende* to indi-

viduals whom it had outraged.   Calling it one of the
'evil works of his nonage,' he wrote to Walter Scott
on July 6, 1812, 'The satire was written when I
was very young and very angry, and fully bent on
displaying my wrath and wit, and now I am haunted
by the ghosts of my wholesale assertions.'

That Byron thought more highly of the 'Hints
from Horace' than of 'Childe Harold' is less perplexing than curious.   When the fever of composition
has subsided, it is not unusual for the writer of lively
satire and fine sentiment, to prefer the smart writing
that flatters him by its cleverness, to the pathetic
writing that only commends him for right feeling.
Moreover the adverse judgment of the first critical
reader of the greater of the two works was quite
enough to put so sensitive and diffident an author
out of conceit with the performance, that, quickening
the heart by its emotional fervour and charming the
ear by language alike strenuous and musical, stirred
the earliest generation of its readers to a degree not
to be easily realized or accounted for at this distance
of time.   On the other hand, it is no less perplexing
than strange that the first critical peruser of the
manuscript should have failed to see that the poem
was peculiarly qualified to seize the world's attention
and cause what is termed now-a-days 'a sensation.'
Dallas certainly was no prophet; but the novelist
and poetaster (to whose hands Byron committed the
MS. of the 'Hints from Horace' on 15th July, 1811,
and the MS. of 'Childe Harold' on the following day,
at Reddish's Hotel, St. James's Street) had enough
literary feeling and discernment to see at once that
'Childe Harold,' the work of a writer in his twenty-

third year, would prove one of the memorable poems of its period.

Talking about the poems with Dallas, discussing less agreeable matters (one of them being the prosecution of the editor of the 'Scourge' for two libels on himself and his mother) with Mr. Hanson, and receiving visits from callers especially uncongenial to the man who described himself as 'hating bustle as he hated a bishop,' Byron remained at Reddish's Hotel in St. James's Street, London, for a fortnight, when, just as he was on the point of leaving town with his solicitor (Mr. Hanson) for Lancashire, with the intention of calling at Newstead *en passant*, alarming intelligence came to him from the Abbey. His mother was seriously ill. The next day (August 1 1811), before leaving town, he received the announcement of her death. On the morrow (August 2), on the road from town to Nottinghamshire, he wrote a brief letter from Newport Pagnell to his friend Pigot (now Dr. Pigot), giving the intelligence of his mother's death, and saying that the sad event would not affect the measures for punishing the libellous editor of the 'Scourge.' 'I am told,' said the writer, ' she was in little pain, and not aware of her situation. I now feel the truth of Mr. Gray's observation, "That we can only have one mother!" Peace be with her!'

The right feeling of these words is moderately expressed ; but there was no moderation in the grief to which Byron gave way at Newstead for a brief hour, after hearing the particulars of his mother's death : which was the result of apoplexy, caused by a fit of violent rage at the magnitude of an upholsterer's bill. In the middle of night, hearing a noise in the chamber of death, Mrs. By, the waiting-woman of the deceased lady, entered the apartment, where she found Lord Byron sitting by the side of his lifeless mother. 'Oh, Mrs. By,' he exclaimed, bursting into tears, ' I had but one friend in the world, and she is gone.' To account for the vehemence of this grief for a mother, whom he had regarded with an aversion at the same time natural and most unnatural,—the mother of whose cruelty he had spoken with passionate repugnance to the Marquis of Sligo, as they were dressing after swimming in the Gulf of Lepanto,—readers must remember what was said in a former chapter of the way in which Byron's memory, sensibility and imagination acted upon one another. Coarse, harsh, violent creature though she was, the woman, who had nursed her little step-daughter Augusta with affectionate devotion in France, had not been wanting in the same womanliness to her own child in his times of infantile sickness. In a certain way, she had loved him ; and now the recollection of long unremembered and remote exhibitions of maternal tenderness rose to his mind, and unmanned him.

Grief is no precise measurer of its own intensity :— a fact to be remembered in considering Byron's grief by those who would not do him the injustice of questioning the sincerity of its extravagant exhibitions. What he said truly of his early friendships, he could no less truly have said of all the movements of all his affections. They were passions. His loves, hatreds, friendships, griefs were so passionate, that as long as any one of them was in full force and activity, it possessed him completely, and caused him for the moment to imagine he had never loved or abhorred any one else. Touched by grief for the death of his Newfoundland dog, the young man, who could not go abroad for a couple of years without taking miniatures of his Harrow 'favourites' with him, wrote of the animal :—

> 'To mark a friend's remains these stones arise ;
> *I never knew but one*, and here he lies.'

Stirred by sudden tenderness for the mother, whom he had regarded with excusable dislike, he discovered in a moment, *not* that after all he had a lingering fondness for her, *but* that he never '*had but one friend in the world*, and she was gone.' For the moment, whilst thinking of him with tearful eyes, he took the same view of John Wingfield :—

> ' Oh, known the earliest, and esteem'd the most !
> Dear to a heart where nought was left so dear !'

The ink with which these lines were written was not dry,—in truth, they had not been penned (the sentiment of the written words being only recollected emotion),—when the poet's grief for Wingfield's death becomes trivial in comparison with his grief for some one far dearer. ' In Matthews,' he writes to Dallas on September 7, 1811, ' I have lost my " guide, philosopher, and friend ;" in Wingfield a friend only, but one whom I could have wished to have preceded in his long journey.' It is notable also how in the extravagance of passionate sorrow for the loss of a friend, Byron used to tell his surviving friends that their regard for him was something far inferior to real friendship. ' I believe,' he wrote to his true, loving, and grateful friend Hodgson,—thinking probably of

Eddleston, when he penned the words, ' the only human being that ever loved me in truth and entirely was of, or belonging to, Cambridge, and, in that, no change can now take place.'

The violence of his grief for his mother was naturally of no great duration.   Instead of following her coffin to the grave, he watched the hearse and train of mourners from the Abbey door, and, as soon as they were out of sight, ordered his servant (young Rushton) to fetch ' the gloves.'   While the service was being read over Catherine Gordon Byron, her son was sparring with the servant,—throwing, as the boy noticed, unusual force into his blows.   Doubtless in the exercise he sought escape from mental distress, due in some degree to filial affection and also in some degree to uneasiness at feeling so little regret for his mother's departure.   In a few minutes, as though the exercise failed in its object, he suddenly threw down the gloves, and went from the servant's sight.

Byron had scarcely received the news of his mother's death, when Charles Skinner Matthews was drowned whilst bathing in the Cam on August 2, 1811, close upon the very time at which the poet was writing from Newport Pagnell to Dr. Pigot.   A man of brilliant academic distinctions, Matthews was intending to offer himself at the next election as a candidate for the honour of representing his university in Parliament, when an attack of cramp ended his career in all the brightness of its promise.   The second of Byron's Cambridge friends to die of drowning, Charles Skinner Matthews had on the day before his death written the poet a letter, that forwarded from London reached Newstead on the 5th, whither it was speedily followed, if indeed it was not preceded by the intelligence that its writer was no longer with the living. 'Some curse,' Byron wrote from Newstead to Scrope Davies on August 7, 1811, 'hangs over me and mine. My mother lies a corpse in this house ; one of my best friends is drowned in a ditch.' Exactly a fortnight later he wrote to Dallas, 'You did not know Matthews : he was a man of the most astonishing powers, as he sufficiently proved at Cambridge, by carrying off more prizes and fellowships, against the ablest candidates, than any other graduate on record; but a most decided atheist, indeed noxiously so, for he proclaimed his principles in all societies.'

To realise fully the quickness with which these successive blows by Death's cold hand fell on Byron, the reader should know that the poet received the confirmation of the intelligence of Wingfield's death in Coimbra, only a few hours before he left town. 'You may,' he wrote to Hodgson on August 22, 1811, ' have heard of the sudden death of my mother, and poor Matthews, which, with that of Wingfield (of which I was not fully aware till just before I left town, and indeed hardly believed it), has made a sad chasm in my connexions.' The news of his mother's illness came to him on July 31st ; the confirmation of the report of Wingfield's death and the intelligence of his mother's death reached him almost at the same hour on the night of August 1st, or early in the following morning ; on the 7th of August, probably sooner, he knew that Skinner was dead. He was already mourning for his *protégé*, Eddleston ; and it has been told how, in October 1811, he wrote to a friend that between the beginning of May and the end of August of that year, he had lost by death six of his nearest associates.

It can cause no astonishment that after so remarkable a series of bereavements, which would have shaken the fortitude and stirred the feelings of the hardest and coldest nature to transient sadness, Byron was for several months the prey of sorrow that alternated between the agitations of hysterical vehemence and the gloom of profound melancholy. The man of feminine softness and emotionality was not the man to walk with firm step and stoical composure through the terrors and darkness of the Valley of the Shadow of Death. He was still in an early stage of this appalling journey when, in the week immediately following his mother's interment, he gave instructions for the will,—with its legacy of 7000*l.* to the Greek boy (Nicolo Giraud), and its provision for his own interment, by the side of his dog, Boatswain, 'in the vault of the garden of Newstead, without any ceremony or burial-service whatever;' and with its codicil enjoining that his body should on no account be removed from the vault, and providing that 'in case any of his successors within the entail (from bigotry or otherwise) should think proper to remove his carcass, such proceeding should be attended by forfeiture of the estate, which in such case should go to the testator's sister, the Honourable Augusta Leigh and her heirs on similar conditions.' The day on which he gave the first instructions for this will was the day on which he wrote to Dallas, 'It is strange that I look on the skulls which stand beside me (I have always had *four* in my study) without emotion, but I cannot strip the features of those I have known of their fleshy covering, even in idea, without a hideous sensation ; but the worms are less ceremonious.' Two months later, he is dating the first of the poems to ' Thyrza ' (October 11th, 1811) ; and *the* doleful letter to Dallas (October 11th, 1811) ; and the Epistle to a Friend (beginning ' Oh, banish care ' —October 11th, 1811) with the frantic threats and hysterical foolishness of its concluding verses ; and the six concluding stanzas of the second canto of the ' Pilgrimage,' the last of them being also dated October 11th, 1811, whilst the third and fourth of the same stanzas (Stanzas xcv. and xcvi. of Canto II.) are part of the outpouring of song to Thyrza,—

> ' Thou too art gone, thou loved and lovely one !
> Whom youth and youth's affections bound to me ;
> Who did for me what none beside have done,
> Nor shrank from one albeit unworthy thee.
> What is my being ? thou hast ceased to be !
> Nor staid to welcome here thy wanderer home,
> Who mourns o'er hours which we no more shall see—
> Would they had never been, or were to come !
> Would he had ne'er returned to find fresh cause to roam !

> ' Oh ! ever loving, lovely, and beloved !
> How selfish Sorrow ponders on the past,
> And clings to thoughts now better far removed !
> But Time shall tear thy shadow from me last.
> All thou couldst have of mine, stern Death ! thou hast ;
> The parent, friend, and now the more than friend ;
> Ne'er yet for one thine arrows flew so fast,
> And grief with grief continuing still to blend,
> Hath snatch'd the little joy that life had yet to lend.'

Why Byron selected the 11th of October in preference to any other day for the date to be assigned

to the letter and several pieces of song, the writer of
this page can offer no suggestion—unless it may be
assumed that the 11th of October was chosen because
it was the last day of his literary labours at Newstead
—the day of drawing together the threads of sorrow-
ful thought and solitary effort—before he went to
Cambridge and London. It is not to be supposed
that so much work of brain and heart and pen was
accomplished on one day. It is, however, only
reasonable to suspect that literary mystification—a
game in which Byron delighted—was one, if not the
only, object of the fictitious dating.

After spending something more than ten weeks
at Newstead in sad seclusion, Byron went to Cambridge, where (on the 29th of October) he wrote Tom
Moore a letter on the subject of the Irish poet's
reasonable demand for some kind of satisfaction for
the ridicule put upon him in the 'English Bards and
Scotch Reviewers.' From Cambridge he went to
St. James's Street, London, and stayed there till he
returned to Newstead for the Christmas holidays,
when he entertained Hodgson and Harness in the
rooms, whose crimson hangings and cheerful fires
caused Harness soon to lose 'the melancholy feeling
of being domiciled in the wing of an extensive ruin.'
Of the weeks spent in London (where Byron used his
club 'The Alfred,' to which he had been elected
during his absence in Greece) the most memorable
incident was the dinner (a *partie carrée*) at Sam
Rogers's table, where the author of 'Childe Harold'
met his host, Moore and Thomas Campbell for the
first time;—the dinner at which Byron, to the
surprise of his three companions who had heard

nothing of his eccentric diet, declined the banker's fish and meat and wine, and, in default of biscuits and soda-water, stayed his hunger with potatoes and vinegar. At Newstead the poet and his two guests, Hodgson and Harness, spent the hours of their intercourse chiefly indoors, in literary work and literary chat, the weather of the singularly dark and dreary season affording them no inducement to leave rooms ample enough for the mild exercise of carpet-walking. Rising late the trio went to bed late; and after a lapse of more than half a century, Harness remembered how on several occasions their more serious conversation, turning on questions of religion, gave him opportunities for observing how strongly and lamentably the extreme Calvinism of the poet's early religious training in Scotland had affected his regard for the principles of Christianity;—the chief result of the discipline being 'a most miserable prejudice, which appeared to be the only obstacle to his hearty acceptance of the Gospel.' There was of course nothing in the poet's way of entertaining the young Cantab, who was reading hard for his degree and holy orders, to afford a colour of probability to the strange tales told in later time of Byron's wild and voluptuous life in the halls of his ancestors,— tales for which the merry doings in the May 1809 were less accountable than the fictions of 'Childe Harold.' It must, however, be conceded that, if Harness could have looked beneath the decorous surface of life at the Abbey, he would have seen one or two things to disapprove in his old schoolmate's domestic arrangements. To justify its title this book must glance for a moment at unedifying circumstances, that will jar rudely against the feelings of readers who would prefer to think of the poet, during his grief for the vanished Thyrza, or at least so soon after its subsidence, as indifferent to the charms of ordinary womankind. Paphian girls with natty caps and bright ribbons on their servile heads still sung and smiled in the galleries of the Abbey mansion, one of whom (to use Moore's words) 'had been supposed to stand rather too high in the favour of her master ; ' and the Christmas holidays were scarcely over when this young serving-woman and one of her companions were sent off to their relations in consequence of acts of levity and disloyalty duly proved against them. To Moore, holding the views of his generation on domestic morals, which fortunately are not the views of decent people of the present age, this affair was remarkable only for the degree to which ' the young peer allowed the discovery of the culprit's misbehaviour to affect his mind.' After speaking of his weakness in respect to these faithless young women as ' a two months' weakness,' Byron adds vehemently in a letter to Hodgson, ' I have one request to make, which is, never mention a woman again in any letter to me, or even allude to the existence of the sex ; ' — the fervour and extravagance of the entreaty showing that even in so discreditable a business Byron was more influenced by sentiment than most young men would have been.

On the 27th of February, 1812, just eleven days after the date of the last-mentioned letter to Hodgson, the young peer delivered his maiden speech in the House of Lords in the debate on the Nottingham Frame-breaking Bill ; —a speech that made a favourable impression on the crowded assembly, that had been brought together not more by the importance of the subject under discussion than by desire to see the poet, whose verse and travels had already made him an interesting personage. Having prepared himself for the essay, by writing his oration with care, as he had been wont in his boyhood to prepare for the Harrow 'declamations,' he entered the House with sentiments worthy of consideration, and on rising to his feet he soon made it obvious he would fail neither from want of elocutionary address nor from want of presence of mind. There was a generous disposition in the auditors to give him an encouraging reception and a full meed of applause ; and he at least proved himself not undeserving of their indulgence. If not a success, the speech was so nearly successful, that the orator left the house with the elation of triumph. Lord Eldon and Lord Harrowby had paid him the compliment of answering his arguments ; Lord Holland and Lord Grenville had praised him in their speeches,—and commended him still more cordially in private chat. Whilst Lord Holland said, ' You'll beat them all if you persevere ;' Lord Grenville's complaisance went to the length of saying, that in their construction some of the maiden orator's periods resembled Burke's. Sir Francis Burdett declared it ' the best speech by a *Lord* since the " Lord knows when ; " '—a compliment that delighted the Lord of Newstead, though it came from a politician of whom he had often spoken with sincere contempt. Meeting Dallas in the passage to the Great Chamber with an umbrella in his right hand, Byron exclaimed joyfully, ' What! give your friend your left hand upon such an occasion?' To Hodgson he wrote, 'I have had many marvellous eulogies repeated to me since, in person and by proxy, from divers persons *ministerial*—yea *ministerial.*' No wonder that he was delighted with the stir and approving hum of the House, which he had entered three years before without an introducer. No longer faltering in the choice of his party, he threw himself into the arms of the Opposition, and was welcomed to Holland House, Melbourne House and all ' the best Whig houses.'

Having made his *début* in ' the Lords' to his own contentment, though scarcely to the satisfaction of his most sanguine admirers, Byron made a second essay to achieve parliamentary distinction on April 21, 1812, in the debate on the Earl of Donoughmore's motion for a Committee on the Roman Catholic Claims, but without placing himself higher in the opinion of the peers, or in the regard of politicians outside the hereditary chamber. It was felt that his manner was too theatrical and ' stagey,' and that the effect of his fine voice was diminished by ' the chanting tone' in which he delivered his periods ;—the same tone that had so disagreeable an effect in his recitations of poetry. Poets are seldom good reciters of poetry, from their disposition to 'sing' what they ought only to 'say ;' and in this respect Byron was a flagrant offender against elocutionary art. Later in the session, the poet was at the meeting of the Opposition peers, sitting next the Duke of Grafton who, in reply to his question ' What is to be done next?' begged him to ' wake the Duke of Norfolk,'—snoring away in his seat.

Two days after the poet's maiden speech in ' the Lords' appeared ' Childe Harold.' For a month early sheets of the poem had been in the hands of a few favoured persons,—poets of the first rank and people of the highest fashion. A few copies had also been distributed in confidence to critics, who could be greatly powerful in giving the work immediate popularity. Rogers had received his early copy in January, and pleased with the compliment of the gift he had for weeks been telling the drawing-rooms of 'the great' what a treat was in store for them. 'It was,' says Moore, 'in the hands of Mr. Rogers I first saw the sheets of the poem, and glanced hastily over a few of the stanzas which he pointed out to me as beautiful.' Lady Caroline Lamb, then in the zenith of her fashionable celebrity, thus got a view of the poem,—*not* in manuscript (as countless writers have asserted on the authority of the lady herself, who after Byron's death wrote to Lady Morgan that Rogers 'offered her the MS. of " Childe Harold " to read '), *but* in the 'early printed copy,' lent her by Rogers, under strict seal of secresy. Lady Caroline was delighted, and went about her bright quarter of the town, telling every one she had seen the forth-coming poem and was 'in the secret,' though she was bound in honour to tell no one where or how she had seen the book. The novel or poem of which Lady Caroline spoke so highly could not fail to make a stir and run through editions in a single season. 'I must see him,—I am dying to see him!' she exclaimed to Rogers, in her impatience to behold the new poet and hasten to her doleful fate. ' He has a club-foot, and bites his nails,' said Rogers. 'If he is as ugly as Æsop, I must know him,' returned the impulsive lady of irresistible beauty, high birth, highest fashion.

No wonder that the poem, thus introduced to ' the world,'—the poem that coming into the world from the shop of the meanest bookseller and under the most inauspicious circumstances would have made its mark in two days,—was no sooner published (on February 29, 1812) by Mr. Murray, the rapidly rising publisher of ' society,' than it was seen every-where, read by everybody. · No wonder that the author ' awoke one morning and found himself famous,' that statesmen and philosophers wrote him grave utterances of their homage, that the Queens of Society rained *billets-doux* down upon him, that St. James's Street was blocked with carriages pressing to his door, that talk of ' Byr'n, Byr'n,' was audible over the babble of every dinner-table and *salon* of Mayfair. Marvellous stories were told in the literary cliques of the price paid for the poem by its publisher; some of the gossips, who of course had their ' inform-ation on the very best authority,' asserting that Murray had paid at the rate of a guinea a line for the poem. The price really paid by the publisher was 600*l*. (more than six shillings a line); and the poet, who of course could not descend so far from his nobility as to take a bookseller's money for his own use, gave the 600*l*. to his poor relation and literary ' devil,' Dallas, who had negotiated the terms with Mr. Murray and seen the verses through the press with exemplary care and assiduity. At the present time one may well smile at the sensitiveness which made Byron, burdened with debts and clogged with mortgages, decline to spend on himself the earnings of his pen. A few years later he stood out stoutly for the extra shillings of the guineas from his pub-

lisher, counted them carefully, and pocketed them
with complacence. But in 1812 the world still held
to antiquated notions touching the pecuniary obligations of 'noblesse.' A nobleman in those days
would have flushed scarlet at a proposal that he
should become a sleeping partner in a wine business or
a Manchester warehouse, and would have put a bullet
through his head rather than see his name figuring
on the prospectus of a joint-stock company. It was
a question whether a peer could take interest for
money lying at his banker's 'on deposit,' without
sullying his nobility with a taint of trade. Whilst
peers felt in this way, the populace had a strong opinion
that it was unutterably 'mean' for a lord to earn
money in any way but fighting, gaming, political
jobbery, the very highest official employment, and
(through the medium of well-salaried agents) the
clever management of land. Far from being peculiar
on the point of dignity, Byron was not more certain
than the ignoble journalists of his acquaintance that,
as a peer, he could not honourably take to his own
use the pecuniary fruits of his literary toil. No sooner
had the tide turned against him, and the fashion of de-
crying him replaced the fashion of extolling him, than
one of his fiercest assailants in the press charged him
with making large sums of money by his pen, and
spending the money so earned on his own pleasures.
And this monstrous accusation seemed so sure to lower
the poet in the esteem of all right-minded people that,
whilst Dallas wrote a public denial and disproof of the
calumny, Byron's friends went about the clubs and
drawing-rooms, assuring 'the town' that he was quite
incapable of such baseness of spirit and manners.

'Childe Harold,' the poem which people of fashion praised madly, was published on the same day as Lord G. Greville's poem which every one abused badly. On June 7, 1812, Lady Morgan, already 'in the swim' of success and the brightness of butterfly celebrity, wrote to Mrs. Lefanu, ' When I was in London, Lord G. Greville read me a poem of his own on the same subject as " Childe Harold." The rival lords published their poems the same day; the one is cried up to the skies, the other, alas, is cried down to——!' Lord G. Greville was the poet ' to bite his nails ; ' Byron had every reason to be proud and careful of the tips of his shapely fingers.

On entering the great world with the glory of ' Childe Harold ' on his brow, the earnestness of it in his eyes, the melody of it flowing from his lips, Byron was in the perfection of his personal attractiveness. He was not a handsome man,—he was beautiful. The glowing fire overpowered the brownness of his auburn hair, that gradually deepened almost to the deepest and richest brown of auburn, before it turned grey. The blue-grey eyes were eloquent of emotion through their long, fine, almost black lashes. The brow, over and about which the feathery auburn curls played in tiny wavelets, was white as marble ; his usually pale complexion was delicate even to transparency, and at moments of joyous excitement was touched with the faintest sanguine glow. His mouth, with its white and dainty teeth, with its lips of feminine sweetness and something of feminine voluptuousness, and his delicately modelled chin, strong enough for fascination—far, far too weak for moral robustness—were the lips and chin of a lovely sensitive, capricious, charming woman, rather than the lips and chin of a man.   It has been already remarked that his countenance, especially in the mouth and eyes, was remarkable for mobility and expressiveness, —curiously in harmony with the quickness and vehemence of his emotional temperament.   His long broad throat, broad chest, and square set shoulders were, however, abundantly expressive of masculine strength.   The shapeliness of his small, white hands did not escape observation at a time when it was the fashion for modish people to have models of their hands in marble on their drawing-room tables.   In their smallness these delicate hands accorded with the poet's feet, that were not wanting in apparent shapeliness, though they suffered from the lameness which no one could exactly describe or satisfactorily account for.   Sweeter, and richer and more tender even than his verse, Byron's voice was in his ordinary conversation, perhaps, more musical than the voice of any other man or woman of his period.   To the children of the houses, where he was a most frequent and familiar guest, he was the 'gentleman who speaks like music.'

Enough of his looks, for the present. Let something be said of the manner of this young nobleman who had been trained in the parlours of a little country town for conquest in London drawing-rooms. Fortunately he has left us his own account of his bearing and demeanour towards men and women, at this point of his career, in the following stanzas of 'Don Juan :'—

> ' His manner was perhaps the more seductive,
>   Because he ne'er seem'd anxious to seduce ;
>   Nothing affected, studied, or constructive
>   Of coxcombry or conquest : no abuse

' Of his attractions marr'd the fair perspective,
    To indicate a Cupidon broke loose,
And seem to say, ' Resist us if you can '—
Which makes a dandy while it spoils a man.

' They are wrong—that's not the way to set about it ;
    As, if they told the truth, could well be shown.
But, right or wrong, Don Juan was without it ;
    In fact, his manner was his own alone :
Sincere he was—at least you could not doubt it,
    In listening merely to his voice's tone.
The devil hath not in all his quiver's choice
An arrow for the heart like a sweet voice.

' By nature soft, his whole address held off
    Suspicion ; though not timid, his regard
Was such as rather seemed to keep aloof,
    To shield himself than put you on your guard :
Perhaps 'twas hardly quite assured enough,
    But modesty's at times its own reward,
Like virtue ; and the absence of pretension
Will go much farther than there 's need to mention.

' Serene, accomplish'd, cheerful but not loud ;
    Insinuating without insinuation ;
Observant of the foibles of the crowd,
    Yet ne'er betraying this in conversation ;
Proud with the proud, yet courteously proud,
    So as to make them feel he knew his station
And theirs :—without a struggle for priority,
He neither brooked nor claimed superiority.

' That is, with men : with women he was what
    They pleased to make or take him for ; and their
Imagination's quite enough for that :
    So that the outline's tolerably fair,
They fill the canvas up—and ' verbum sat.'
    If once their phantasies be brought to bear
Upon an object, whether sad or playful,
They can transfigure brighter than a Raphael.'

A clever man's manner is always so nearly what he wishes it to be, that one could rely on the general fidelity of this portraiture, even if its testimony were unsupported by other evidence. Fortunately, however, the poet's account of his own demeanour during his brief hour of social triumph is sustained by those of his biographers who knew him in this period, and half-a-hundred other persons of his acquaintance to whom we are indebted for gossip about him,—by Moore, Dallas, Hunt, Hobhouse, Harness, Lady Morgan, Lady Caroline Lamb, and a throng of other sure witnesses. By the men and women, who regarded him from a distance or knew him only slightly, he was thought undemonstrative and taciturn, at times even frigid. That even Lady Caroline was not insensible to the coldness and reserve of his demeanour at their first meeting, appears from the passage of ' Glenarvon ' which says,—' A studied courtesy in his manner, a proud humility, mingled with a certain cold reserve, amazed and repressed the enthusiasm his youth and misfortunes excited.' ' Lord Byron,' Lady Morgan wrote in June 1812, 'the author of delightful "Childe Harold" (which has more *force, fire and thought* than anything I have read for an age), is cold, silent and reserved in his manners.' But Lady Morgan had only met the poet in crowded rooms, and probably had never even exchanged the courtesies of introduction with him. At most she was one of the multitudes of worshipful womankind, who regarded the new poet with reverential curiosity wherever he went. The remains of the poet's constitutional shyness were observable in his coldness and severe formality to strangers. These characteristics of his ordinary bearing in throngs were sometimes—perhaps too often for his advantage—mistaken for indications of pride, never for signs of insolence. In truth, though he was accused of superciliousness after he had begun to fall in social favour, and though he sometimes provoked the accusation by his bearing *to men* whom he held in disesteem or aversion, nothing was more foreign than insolence to his demeanour or temper in the brief summer of his triumph in his native land. Appealing to Time the Avenger, after his banishment, he could exclaim with an unreproving conscience,—

> ' If thou hast ever seen me too elate,
>   Hear me not : but if calmly I have borne
>   Good, and reserved my pride against the hate
>   Which shall not whelm me, let me not have worn
> This iron in my soul in vain—shall *they* not mourn ?'

And whilst bearing himself courteously and modestly, though with guarded speech and a show of coldness to the many of whom he knew little or nothing at all, to the men, with whom he was intimate, Byron was a very fountain of joyousness and genial humour,—brimming with quaint anecdote, bubbling over with frolic and merriment, and not seldom running out into the practical jokes of a jolly schoolboy. ' Nothing, indeed,' says Moore, ' could be more amusing and delightful than the contrast which his manners afterwards, when we were alone, presented to his proud reserve in the brilliant circle we had just left. It was like the bursting gaiety of a boy let loose from school, and seemed as if there was no extent of fun or tricks of which he was not capable.'

With women he was what they pleased to make or

take him for. But he was most pleased with them, when they treated him as nearly as possible like 'a favourite and sometimes froward sister.' The reader may smile but must not laugh :—it was as 'a favourite and sometimes froward sister' that he was thought of and treated by Hobhouse and other men. What then more natural for him to like to be thought of and treated by women in the same way? To be received by them on this footing, he would leave his bed early (say at 11 A.M.) so that he might breakfast with them, open their letters for them, chat with them, fondle their children in their boudoirs, for an hour or two at a time, before less privileged visitors dropt in for luncheon. It was in the character of candidate for the place of a sister in her affections that he sate for an entire hour with Lady Caroline Lamb, nursing her ladyship's babe all the time, without speaking a word above a whisper lest the sleeping infant should be roused to consciousness. As 'a favourite and sometimes froward sister' he hung about the Countess of Oxford's skirts, playing at odd minutes with her beautiful little girl, Charlotte,—precisely of the same age as Margaret Parker, when as a schoolboy he loved his pretty cousin passionately. As the Countess's sister and the little Lady Charlotte's aunt, he wrote the verses to Ianthe, with

> ' that eye, which wild as the gazelle's,
> Now brightly bold or beautifully shy,
> Wins as it wanders, dazzles where it dwells.'

If Ianthe in her innocence had put the forbidden question to her mother's sister, and asked, ' Why to one so young his strain he would commend?' the unspoken answer would have been, ' Because you remind me of my boyish passion for my cousin Margaret, of whom I thought tearfully, and wretchedly, and yet not altogether unhappily, when I wrote my beautiful poetry to Thyrza.' When a young man is allowed to play the part of a sister to a beautiful woman, the position is dangerous both to the one and the other. For the man, who is sympathized with and treated like a sister, whilst feeling and acting like one, may in a moment be stirred by masculine impulses to feel and act like a man :—in which case, he feels and acts like a man without self-control, and the woman remains what she has been all along—an excited and weak woman.

One of the incidents of this London season (1812) was the poet's introduction to the greatest personage of the realm *vice* a person with a more august title, but now in retirement from illness. At a ball given at a great house in July, where the poet was present, the Prince Regent declared the delight it would give him to number the author of 'Childe Harold' amongst his personal acquaintance. Of course Byron was introduced to the Prince, who was still smarting under the 'Lines to a Weeping Lady,' which the poet had thrown off in the previous March. Had he not attributed the anonymous lines to Tom Moore, His Royal Highness would have been less favourably disposed to their author, with whom he now held a long and animated conversation, on poets and poetry, and more particularly Walter Scott's poetry,—a conversation that closed with the Regent's flattering expression of his desire to see his lampooner at Carlton House. It shows how manageable a creature Byron was that, in his delight at the Prince's blandishments, he put his auburn curls into powder and his person into a court-suit, for the purpose of attending a levee, which was postponed at the last moment. If the powder had not been decidedly unbecoming to his style of beauty, the poet would perhaps have grown grey again in homage to the guilty father of 'the weeping lady.' As it was, the accidental postponement of the ceremony, personal vanity and self-respect saved Byron from the mistake of going whither he should not have thought of going so soon after the first publication of the notorious verses.

Another incident of the season was the poet's attendance in May 1812, at the execution of Bellingham in front of Newgate. Coming to the Old Bailey about 3 A.M., with his old schoolfellows, Bailey and John Madocks, he found the house, from which they were to witness the ghastly spectacle, not yet open. Whilst Mr. Madocks was rousing the inmates of the house, Byron sauntered up the street with Mr. Bailey, when his compassion was stirred by the sight of a wretched woman lying on some door-steps. The act of charity to which pity moved him had a startling and painful result ; for, instead of taking the shillings he offered her, the miserable creature sprung to her feet, and uttering a yell of drunkard's derision began to imitate his lame gait. Byron said nothing either to the woman or the friend on whose arm he was leaning, but Bailey felt the violent trembling of his companion's arm, as they walked back to the house. Another story is told by Moore in illustration of the degree to which the poet's lameness was noticeable to casual passers, and his annoyance at the attention they paid to his infirmity.

'This way, my Lord,' cried a link-boy, as Byron was stepping, with Rogers, to his carriage, from the door-way of the house where they had shown themselves at a ball.

'He seems to know you,' said Rogers.

'Know me!' was the bitter reply; 'every one knows me,—I am deformed!'

Apart from such annoyances, from which there was no escape, and the annoyance that came to him from the comparative failure of his second essay in parliamentary debate, Byron could, however, at the close of the London season, review the previous five months with unqualified complacence. To be really worth having, success should come early, before time and trouble have embittered the feelings and blunted the appetite for praise. The author (whether he be peer or commoner) who becomes the idol of society in his twenty-fifth year, and 'going everywhere' never joins a brilliant throng without knowing that every individual of it has read his book with enthusiastic admiration, is an enviable mortal, though he dare not satisfy the cravings of his hunger for food, and whilst overflowing with merriment and frolic is persuaded that he is 'one of the most melancholy wretches in existence.'

Having spent the London season of 1812 in the brightest circles of fashion and dignity, Byron spent the closing weeks of summer and the autumnal months at Cheltenham (never in higher fashion), and in visits to some of the best houses of the country,—the rural homes of the Earl of Jersey, the Marquis of Lansdowne, and other personages of light and leading. Making his head-quarters at Cheltenham, where for several weeks he had a pleasant loitering time with the Jerseys, Melbournes, Cowpers, Hollands, Rawdons, and Oxfords; and returning once and again from the country-houses to his lodgings at the Gloucestershire spa, he passed the greater part of his time there till the end of November,—reading, scribbling letters, writing good poetry and bad poetry (the verse of the latter sort comprising the trumpery satire on 'The Waltz,' which he had no sooner published anonymously, than he disavowed it by means disagreeably near falsehood), and meditating on a disappointment that will be mentioned more particularly in the next chapter.

And how about the pecuniary affairs of the peer, who, living lavishly, had no sufficient revenue for the payment of the interest of his debts? Soon after his mother's death he received from her trustee, Baron Clerk, the residue of the price paid for the Gight estate,—something under 4000*l.*; a sum that enabled the poet to pay a few of his most urgent creditors. Coming to him at a moment of divers difficulties, this modest inheritance was a great relief. But it did not lessen the necessity for measures that would give him an adequate and sure income, after releasing him from money-lenders and clamorous tradesmen. And now that his literary triumph and social success had afforded him superior titles to respect, he could with calmness and discretion think of selling the picturesque estate, to which he had clung for honour's sake, so long as he had no higher position than that of the chief of an impoverished territorial family. The man who had become famous no longer needed some old ruins and a few farms in Nottinghamshire as evidences

of his respectability within the lines of his order. If
the Newstead estate could be sold for 100,000*l*., and
so many thousands more as would wipe out his debts,
he would stand more creditably in the eyes of the
world, than he now stood as the owner of a noble
park and ruinous mansion, without the means to live
in them. With the interest of money at five per cent.,
he would have 5000*l*. of sure yearly revenue, and
retain the still unproductive Rochdale property, to
save him from the discredit of being a landless
lord. Mr. Hanson had for years been imploring the
young lord to take this view of his position ; but the
lawyer begged and preached in vain, till his client
could with reason value himself on his achievements
rather than on being the Lord of Newstead Abbey.
Early in the autumn of 1812 Newstead was offered
for sale at Garraway's, when it was 'bought in,'
90,000*l*. being the highest offer made in the auction-
room for the property. Soon, however, Mr. Claughton
came forward with an offer that even exceeded the
vendor's hopes. 'You heard,' Byron wrote from
Cheltenham to his friend, William Bankes, 'that
Newstead is sold—the sum 140,000*l*. ; 60,000*l*. to
remain in mortgage on the estate for three years,
paying interest, of course. Rochdale is also likely
to do well—so my worldly matters are mending.'
By this contract it was stipulated that the estate
should remain in the vendor's hands till the purchaser should fulfil his part of the agreement, and
that in case of the buyer failing in that respect within
a given time he should forfeit 25,000*l*., and the bar-
gain become void. Two years later the forfeiture
was paid by Mr. Claughton in consequence of his

inability to complete the purchase; and the estate continued with Byron. Enabling him to pay some of his most pressing debts, the 25,000*l.* also enabled him to live in comparative freedom from pecuniary anxieties till his marriage with a lady, whose fortune which had been egregiously magnified by rumour, brought his creditors down upon him at a moment when the concessions of his marriage-settlement had seriously lessened his ability to satisfy their desire for immediate payment.

Whilst the fashionable drawing-rooms were applauding the force, fire, and melody of 'Childe Harold,' the far larger multitudes of thoughtful and devout people living in comparative humility outside the uttermost breast-works of 'society' were considering the religious sentiments of the poem with alarm and abhorrence, and coming to the conclusion that the author was destined to perdition, and that, if his pernicious influence were not counteracted by bold and timely denunciations of his impiety, he would lead countless thousands of light-headed people to the doom of eternal punishment. It is significant of the manners of the period that, whilst these earnest people were quick to detect the poet's infidelity and exclaim against it, they do not appear to have been greatly shocked by his account of his naughty life at Newstead before he started on his travels. The account was in truth too accordant with their conceptions of lordly living, and also with their experience of the less exalted ways of human life, for it to occasion them either astonishment or anxiety. But it was a new and terrifying thing for a poet to write of matters pertaining to religion in

the style of the third and fourth stanzas of the second
Canto :—

> 'Son of the Morning, rise ! approach you here !
> Come—but molest not yon defenceless urn :
> Look on this spot —a nation's sepulchre !
> Abode of gods, whose shrines no longer burn.
> Even gods must yield—religions take their turn :
> 'Twas Jove's—'tis Mahomet's—and other creeds
> Will rise with other years, till man shall learn
> Vainly his incense soars, his victim bleeds ;
> Poor child of Doubt and Death, whose hope is built on reeds.

> 'Bound to the earth, he lifts his eye to heaven—
> Is't not enough, unhappy thing ! to know
> Thou art ? Is this a boon so kindly given,
> That being, thou would'st be again, and go,
> Thou know'st not, reck'st not to what region, so
> On earth no more, but mingled with the skies ?
> Still wilt thou dream on future joy and woe ?
> Regard and weigh yon dust before it flies :
> That little urn saith more than thousand homilies.'

Though he was far from imagining what a storm
of reprobation these words would bring upon him in
the course of a few months, and still farther from
conceiving that the outcry against them would grow
louder and fiercer throughout successive years, Byron
had not been many days at Cheltenham before he
heard the first sounds of the rising tempest. For the
moment he could smile at the letters and verses that
came to him through Mr. Murray's office from good-
natured correspondents 'anxious for his conversion
from certain infidelities,' and could write with more
flippancy than good taste to his publisher on September 14, 1812, 'The other letters are from ladies,
who are welcome to convert me when they please ; and
if I can discover them, and they be young, as they

say they are, I could convince them of my devotion.'
Nine months later, when the protest had been steadily
growing more audible, and the importance of the
protesting voices had become more apparent, he wrote
in a sober vein to the editor of 'The Quarterly,'
'To your advice on religious topics, I shall equally
attend. Perhaps the best way will be by avoiding
them altogether. The already published objectionable passages have been much commented upon, but
certainly they have been rather strongly interpreted.
I am no bigot to infidelity, and did not expect that,
because I doubted the immortality of man, I should
be charged with denying the existence of a God. It
was the comparative insignificance of ourselves and
our world, when placed in comparison with the mighty
whole, of which it is an atom, that first led me to
imagine that our pretensions to eternity might be
over-rated.' When Gifford, whom the young poet
regarded with 'veneration,' and used to term his
'father' in literary matters, urged him to be cautious,
and spoke of rocks and dangers ahead, Byron could
not doubt that he was sailing in perilous waters. And
as the months went by, he saw more and more clearly
the wisdom of his 'father's' counsels.

Of all the many strange mistakes made by clever
men about Byron's career none is stranger than the
error of supposing that the storm, that drove him from
his native land, was brewed in a single hour, and that
it was altogether due to the caprice of fashion and
society's fantastic readiness to visit the sins of many
upon one, and drive that one forth into the desert as a
scapegoat. The sentiment, before which the poet retired in early manhood, almost in his boyhood, into exile

for his remaining days, was a sentiment of slow growth and diverse causes. Not the least powerful of those causes was the general social resentment at his religious opinions, and this cause began to operate before the first edition of ' Childe Harold' was exhausted. No greatly celebrated man ever had a shorter term of unqualified and unbroken applause. The unanimity of praise was the affair of a single day and a single class. It can scarcely be said to have lasted even in that one class for twenty-four hours. The morning's fame, of which he used to speak, had lost something of its whiteness before the evening. Even from the outset of his career, praise and dispraise joined hands to make him in the same moment famous and infamous.

CHAPTER XIII.

THE RIVAL COUSINS-IN-LAW.

The World of Fashion — Lady Caroline Lamb — Her Looks and Nature — 'Mad, Bad, and Dangerous to Know' — Platonic Love — Miss Milbanke — Her Fortune and Expectations — Her Influence over Byron — Lady Caroline 'Playing the Devil' — Love turned to Hate.

IT was a mad world Byron entered at twenty-four years of age, with the honour of his poem fresh upon him; — a wild world strangely fascinating and perilous to the sensitive and excitable young man who, with his reputation for gallantry and genius, his travels in Greece and songs to Eastern beauties, knew no more of fashionable society and the 'high life,' than any son of an English parsonage who, during his education at school and college, has spent his holidays in the parlours of a small provincial town. In his later time he used in his bitterness to declare that in domestic morality Venice would endure comparison with London, and Italy with England; and if any reliance may be put on the chroniclers of English 'society' during the Regency, his words were only by a few degrees less truthful than severe.

It was a wild world, honouring women for their beauty provided it was mated with loose principle, and caring little for womanly virtue that was unattended with personal attractiveness. And of all its wild people none was wilder or more capricious, lighter or more wilful than Lady Caroline Lamb— the Mrs. Felix Lorraine of 'Vivian Grey,' the Lady Monteagle of 'Venetia.' Vivian thought Mrs. Felix Lorraine 'a *dark* riddle.' In respect to her person and character, the Lady was, however, a light riddle. Her eyes, indeed, were dark and her countenance (in repose) was grave ; but her complexion was fair, her figure slight, her hair fawn-flaxen shot with gold. Writers by the score have called her tresses golden,— but they were golden with a difference. Byron rewarded her for writing a book to prove he was satanic, by telling Medwin, with a view to publication, that she had scarcely 'any personal attractions,' and that 'her figure, though genteel, was too thin to be good, and wanted that roundness which elegance and grace would vainly supply.' Byron, however, thought better of the figure in 1812, and he never denied its possessor the merits of 'an infinite vivacity and an imagination heated by novel-reading.' Pressed upon the point, he would have admitted, with her most intimate friend of the literary cliques, Lady Morgan, that she had 'a voice soft, low, caressing, that was at once a beauty and a charm, and worked much of that fascination which was peculiarly hers.' Her voice and all her other charms were at their perfection when, in her twenty-seventh year, she employed them to enthral Byron, only twenty-four years old.

Now that fifty and more years have passed over her grave, and all who cared for her have gone hence, it is time to speak the truth—gently but fearlessly —of this poor Queen of Society. So much has been

said insincerely of the harm Byron did her, it is well
at length to hint that there is another side to the account,—the harm she did him. ' In spite of all the
absurdity' of her behaviour to Byron, Rogers believed her *innocent*. Of what? Surely not innocent
of acting in a way to justify ordinary observers of her
conduct in thinking her guilty of everything of which
she was suspected. And in regard to such a question,
it should be remembered that the greater part of the
social injury comes from appearances. Apart from
the few persons to whom the reality would be especially injurious, the show of wickedness is every whit
as hurtful as the reality. Moreover, what is to be
said of the self-respect, the sense of dignity, the honour
of a woman—descended from half-a-hundred noble
houses, married to the finest-natured gentleman of her
time, and having children to think for—who wantonly
put herself in need of such a witness to character as
Sam Rogers? More than enough having been said of
her wit and genius, the time has come to speak—not
harshly, but soberly and truthfully—of her arrant
silliness. Though they contain a few redeeming passages, her three novels—'Glenarvon,' 'Graham Hamil-
ton,' and 'Ada Reis,'—are the tales of an unusually
foolish lady, notwithstanding the care expended by
skilful ' hacks ' in dressing them for the press. But
writers being often better than their books, it is more
generous to the lady to judge her by her letters. 'The
only question,' she wrote, at a moment when social
disgrace was upon her in a form that should have
startled and scared the lightest woman out of habitual
levity, ' I want you to solve is, shall I go abroad?
shall I throw myself upon those who no longer want

me, or shall I live a good sort of a half-kind of life in some cheap street a little way off, viz. the City Road, Shoreditch, Camberwell, or upon the top of a shop,—or shall I give lectures to little children, and keep a seminary, and thus earn my bread? . . . or shall I fret, fret, fret, and die ; or shall I be dignified and fancy myself as Richard the Second did when he picked the nettle up — upon a thorn?' This to Lady Morgan, when Medwin's book and its immediate consequences had compelled the writer's superb and royal-hearted husband, for his honour's sake, to put her from him in the gentlest and tenderest way! It is simply appalling to turn over Lady Caroline Lamb's letters, and remember that the giddy, light-hearted creature—devoid alike of mental force and moral fibre —was one of those personages whom Lord Beaconsfield used to style 'stateswomen,' and would have been a power in the government of the country, had she lived on good terms with her lord till he became premier!

The woman, so weak in everything but beauty, and temper, and vivacity, and drawing-room tact, could however be irresistibly charming. Her *rôle* in the wild world of which she was a queen was that of the saucy, freakish, impulsive, gushing creature, startling her friends at every turn by her eccentricities and relieving the dullness of every assembly by doing or saying what no one else could do or say with an air of good breeding. Falling into a fit of fury about nothing at her wedding, she stormed at the officiating bishop, tore her dress to pieces, and was carried to her carriage nearly unconscious. The lisp of her tongue gave a piquancy to her startling words.

' Gueth how many pairth of thilk thtockingth I have
on,' she said at a ball to Harness (a rather serious
young Cantab reading for ' Orders '). Seeing by his
blush that he could not answer the nice question, she
answered it for him by saying ' Thicth,' as she raised
her skirts above a pretty ankle, and pointed to a tiny
foot. At Melbourne House this daughter of the third
Earl of Bessborough used to amuse herself in the
drawing-rooms playing ball with her pages. One
of these boys having thrown a detonating squib
into the fire, she punished him by hurling a ball at
his head, so as to draw blood from his temple. ' Oh,
my lady, you have killed me!' exclaimed the childish
servitor; whereupon the lady rushed into the hall,
screaming ' O God! I have murdered the page!' in
so loud a voice, that the words were heard in the
street and were fruitful of half-a-hundred wild rumours
about the town of the horrible tragedy at Melbourne
House. The temper and character of this strange
woman's career were given by Byron in a single line
of ' Don Juan.' She played the devil, and then wrote
a novel. When Byron made her acquaintance she
was in the earlier stage of her story. Just then, and
till he had torn himself from her, it was enough for
her to play the devil.

Madly vain, incessantly thinking of herself, and
seizing every occasion to talk of herself, this absurd
but delightful creature believed that no man could
see her without admiring her, know her without
loving her. Taking seriously the compliments they
paid her in common with hundreds of other women,
she flattered herself that Rogers and Moore were her
lovers,—the cynical bachelor-banker who loved no

one ; and the clever little Irishman who, ready at any moment to sing his sentimental ballads to any woman of fashion till his eyes brimmed with tears of emotion, loved no one but his Bessie. As soon as she had looked through the early copy of ' Childe Harold,' she made up her mind that Byron, even though he bit his nails and were as ugly as Æsop, should also love her. They first met at a ball, where she saw 'the women suffocating him' and 'throwing up their heads at him,'—a ball given by Lady Westmoreland who (as Lady Caroline assured Lady Morgan) had known the poet in Italy,—a country, by the way, in which he had not then set foot. It indicates the kind of homage already rendered to Byron by the highest womankind of the land that, instead of bringing him up to be introduced to Lady Caroline, Lady West- moreland led her up to be introduced to him. On coming within a few paces of the young man, Lady Caroline Lamb eyed him steadily, and without speak- ing a word or making movement of reverence or courtesy to him, turned away from him abruptly :— ' I looked earnestly at him,' she told Lady Morgan, ' and turned on my heel.' A pretty scene,—and one that of course made a stir in the throng of suffocating worshippers. On reaching home she made this note of her opinion of the new poet and hero in these words, ' Mad—bad—and dangerous to know.' The words would have been better placed, had she written them against her own name. If it is bad for a woman to be the slave of caprice and a violent temper, and to be disloyal to a royal-natured husband, she was bad. To palliate her misconduct, her most strenuous and charitable apologists have insisted on her madness.

As for the danger of knowing her:—it was an ill day for Byron (himself a weak and froward woman, in one half of his nature) when he yielded to the charms of the lady who was at best a sensitive and wayward woman.

Two or three days after this scene at Lady Westmoreland's ball in March 1812, Byron and Lady Caroline Lamb met at Holland House in the afternoon, when Lady Holland said, 'I must present Lord Byron to you.' 'That offer was made to you before; may I ask why you rejected it ?' said Byron. If the lady had answered the question truly, she would have said, ' Because I thought it the best way of piquing you into loving me.' The next day, heated and muddy from a gallop in the park (she rode as boldly as she talked, and far better than she wrote) she was chatting with Rogers and Moore at Melbourne House in her bespattered riding-habit, when on the announcement of Byron's arrival she ' flew out of the room ' (as she told Lady Morgan) ' to wash herself.' On her return to the callers, Rogers said, ' Lord Byron, you are a happy man. Lady Caroline has been sitting here in all her dirt with us, but when you were announced, she flew to beautify herself.' To humour the poet, who delighted in children, and to pose herself in the most amiable manner before him, Lady Caroline sent for one of her children ; and Byron did not leave till he had nursed the sleeping infant for more than an hour. Henceforth Lord Byron was for the next year or so an almost daily visitor (when in town) at Melbourne House, which was just then a place of daily meeting for the *beau monde*, for waltzes and quadrilles. Cherishing political ambition and seeing in a close alliance with the Lambs the shortest and surest path to political success, Byron became the tame cat—a *very* dangerous tame cat—of the great home of whiggism. To Lady Caroline he was soon as a sister,—no less so than to Lady Oxford a few months later. The mutual attachment of Lady Caroline and the young poet, who had learnt drawing-room manners at Southwell, was all that a platonic love should be,— fervid enough for jealousy on either side ; enthusiastic with a secret anticipation of the coming embarrassments by both parties ; confidential in the highest degree with reserves on both sides ; and so obviously innocent that people soon began to whisper that mischief would come of it. These remarks are of course equally applicable to the young man's platonic friendship with the Countess of Oxford. Every one was sure there was ' nothing wrong ' in these friendships, but if people had been quite confident the friendships were ' altogether right,' so much would not have been said about them.

One of the first persons to feel that trouble might come of Lady Caroline's vehement liking for the young poet was her ladyship's mother-in-law, who spoke to Byron on the subject with the frankness she was entitled by her years and position to use to so youthful and inexperienced a person, of whose amiability and goodness of principle she had a high opinion ;—for at the beginning of the present century, the fact of his having amused himself, as Byron was believed to have amused himself at Newstead, was not regarded as any serious evidence against his domestic morals, and absolutely no evidence whatever that he would play the libertine to women of his own social degree. ' You need not fear me,' Byron *is said* to have answered to the lady, whom he regarded with filial reverence, and even spoke of as his ' second mother' (no great compliment, by the way, to Lady Melbourne); 'I do not pursue pleasure like other men ; I labour under an incurable disease and a blighted heart. Believe me, she is safe with me!' Lady Melbourne's apprehensions were not however completely dissipated by her *protégé's* assurance, though she had implicit confidence in his kindness, rectitude, honour. Anyhow, she thought the future Lady Melbourne would be safer, if Byron were married, and married also within the lines of the Lamb family. With a clever, idolizing wife to look after him, so gentle and affectionate a young man would be happier and less likely to deviate from his present virtuous course to the ways of Paphian girls. If he married the future Lord Melbourne's first cousin, his intimacy with the future Lady Melbourne would be so much a matter of course that no one would gossip about it maliciously. As a member of the Melbourne connexion, indeed of the Melbourne family, he would have a strong domestic interest in the social honour and credit of the Lambs. If the young lord, who wrote such charming poetry and had given promise of becoming an able debater, could only be led into loving and marrying her niece, he would have a wife with better opportunities for observing his friendship with Lady Caroline, and keeping it within proper limits, than any Lady Byron, taken outside the Lamb family. Lady Melbourne had reason for confidence that her niece—a

young woman with a high reputation for dutifulness
and other virtues—would act with her in keeping
Lady Caroline in order, and be abundantly grateful
to her for helping her to so good a match. What
more natural project for the lady—a woman and
therefore a match-maker, a mother and therefore
anxious for her son's welfare, a 'stateswoman' and
therefore with a taste for managing other people's
affairs—to entertain for the good of her family?

And who was the niece?—Anne Isabella (familiarly styled Annabella) Milbanke, the only child of
Lady Melbourne's brother, Sir Ralph Milbanke of
Seaham co. Durham, and Halnaby co. York, who was
just twenty years of age (three years and eight
months Byron's junior), when her aunt first entertained this scheme for her matrimonial settlement.
That the match would be a good one for Byron either
in money or rank, Lady Melbourne neither imagined
nor tried to persuade herself. She was looking out
for her niece rather than for him, and for herself, her
husband and her son more than for her niece.

One of the wildly wrong notions about Byron is
that he married Miss Milbanke for her money, that
he sought her out because she was an heiress. She
was not an heiress at the time he proposed to her.
She had only a modest, though sufficient, provision
for a young lady of her rank. There is in Medwin's
'Conversations' an absurd story, that on first meeting Miss Milbanke at a London rout in 1812, Byron
mistook her from the simplicity of her costume for a
humble companion, when Moore enlightened him on
the point by saying, 'She is a great heiress, you had
better marry her, and repair the old place, Newstead.'

The story is fictitious in every particular. Byron first met her under Lady Melbourne's wing, well knowing her to be Lady Melbourne's niece; she had at that time no reputation for wealth; and instead of wishing Byron to marry her, Moore was one of the poet's several friends who thought her no fit match for him.

These are the facts of Miss Milbanke's position. She was the only child of a baronet of fairly good estate; but Sir Ralph Milbanke had only a life interest in the property which, on his death without male issue, would pass to the heir under the entail. He was in no position to endow his daughter largely, for he had crippled himself with electioneering expenses. Under these circumstances Miss Milbanke's assured fortune was 10,000*l.*—and no more. From her parents she looked for nothing of importance, apart from this sum. She had however 'expectations' from her uncle, Lord Wentworth, who, at the time of Byron's first offer to her, was sixty-seven years of age and likely to live for many years. She was not this uncle's only niece; and as he had the free disposal of his estate, it was conceivable that, even if she survived him, she would be none the richer for his death. Dying in 1782, one of Lord Wentworth's sisters left a son, Nathaniel Curzon (third Baron Scarsdale, who died in November 1856); a second son, William Curzon, killed at Waterloo; and Sophia Caroline Curzon (Viscountess Tamworth) who died in 1824. Thus at the time of Byron's first offer to Miss Milbanke, Lord Wentworth had two nephews and two nieces. He was known to have natural children whom he regarded affectionately. The expectations Miss Milbanke had from the uncle were not likely to inspire Lord Byron with a mercenary desire to capture her. So much for her money.—Now for her rank. On Lord Wentworth's death in 1815, the viscounty of Wentworth became extinct, whilst the barony fell into abeyance between his lordship's sister, Lady Milbanke, and his nephew the Hon. Nathaniel Curzon, afterwards third Lord Scarsdale, and it was not till this Lord Scarsdale's death in November 1856, that the poet's widow became Baroness Wentworth. It cannot be supposed that Byron was impelled to Miss Milbanke by regard for her uncertain prospect of a peerage, which did not come to her till thirty-two years had passed over his grave,—till a time when, had he survived, he would have been sixty-eight years old. So much has been said to magnify the wealth and grandeur of the lady whom he married, and said moreover for the sake of putting Byron under something more than a suspicion of mercenary and sordid motives, that it is well for people to remember how small her fortune was, and how remote her peerage, when he first sought her hand.

Let it, also, be observed that Byron's first offer to Miss Milbanke was made at the time when Mr. Claughton's offer of 140,000*l.* for Newstead, gave him a good prospect of a sure income of 5000*l.* a-year after the payment of his debts, without selling any part of his Rochdale estate, where things were again looking brighter. Consequently the case of this proposal for marriage stands thus :—a young peer of the realm, the idol of society, the greatest poet of his time, with 5000*l.* of yearly revenue (on the settlement of his affairs), an estate in land which is expected to yield him further income in a short time, and a pen soon to earn more than 2000*l.* a-year, makes an offer of marriage to a baronet's daughter with 10,000*l.* for her immediate fortune, a prospect of something more (not much) from her father, and indefinite 'expectations' from a rich uncle, through whose death she has no hope of any considerable enrichment, so long as her mother (a hale woman, only sixty-one years old) shall be living. And yet Byron has actually been accused of mercenary motives in this business. Can it be questioned that, had he been a fortune-hunter, Byron might have carried off the wealthiest heiress in the kingdom, when he asked a lady with 10,000*l.* and shadowy 'expectations' to become his wife? Instead of being a good one, the match from a pecuniary point of view was a decidedly bad one. Indeed the badness of it was pressed upon his notice by several of his friends. In the course of events, had he lived happily with his wife, it would have proved a fairly good match— though nothing more. On making his first offer, he could not calculate on Lord Wentworth dying in 1815, and leaving between 7000*l.* and 8000*l.* a-year to his sister (Lady Milbanke) for life, with remainder to her child. On the appearance of Medwin's loose gossip, Hobhouse might well be astounded at hearing that the marriage, which proved his friend's indifference to money at that early point of his career, had been a mercenary one. How often had Hobhouse to repeat that 'Byron did *not* marry for money,'—a declaration which came from his lips whenever this meanness was charged in his hearing against the poet.

In her book of strange misconceptions and delusions, Mrs. Beecher Stowe regards Miss Milbanke as a simple maiden of high degree who, passing her life in stately seclusion and benevolent concern for the peasantry on her father's estate, entered womanhood with no experience of the world's wickedness, and gave herself to her husband in ignorance of the sins of his youth. Having read ' Childe Harold,' and like all the other ladies of the period taken much of it as autobiography, Miss Milbanke cannot have been unaware of the difference between his former life and her own. She knew the meaning of the verses about the Paphian girls. It certainly was due to no want of frankness on his part, if she did not think him much worse than he really was. Moreover the morals of 'county society' in Durham and Yorkshire at the beginning of the present century afforded a young lady of the highest quality ample opportunities for discovering there was a morality for men and a different morality for women of their degree. Instead of being shocked by ' Childe Harold ' she admired the poem greatly ; and though she declined the poet's first offer, she was far from thinking him unfit to hold communion with a gentlewoman of her refinement. On the contrary, she refused him in so gentle and flattering a manner that he wished to be to her as a brother ; and he had little difficulty in persuading her to receive letters from him and to answer them with sisterly trustfulness.

Perhaps it will surprise Mrs. Stowe to learn that Miss Milbanke's views of English life and character were not taken altogether from the habits of the Durham gentry and the manners of the poor on her father's estate. Though she was not so considerable a personage as her sister-in-law of Melbourne House, Lady Milbanke had her place in London society and came to town for the season ; and her only daughter saw as much of people of letters, art and science, if not of people of the highest fashion, as her cousins, the Lambs. Lady Milbanke's parties were in good repute ; and when she received her acquaintance, which was often, the visitor found people of mark in her drawing-rooms. Mrs. Siddons, Joanna Baillie, and Maria Edgeworth were her familiar friends. If she had not been Lady Melbourne's niece, Miss Milbanke would have heard all about Lord Byron and Lady Caroline Lamb, his doings and his worshippers from her mother's guests, when all London was talking of the new poet and of the pains people were taking to make him a foolish one. Being Lady Melbourne's niece, Miss Milbanke—a young woman of abundant intelligence—knew well enough why her aunt was so desirous of seeing her Lady Byron.

Without being beautiful, Miss Milbanke was by no means unattractive to those who were not repelled by her formality and coldness. Simple, unaffected, and more likely to think too much than too little of her dignity, she had the air of natural refinement rather than of fashion. Her presence would have gained greatly in effectiveness by two or even three more inches in stature, but "'her figure' (to use Byron's own words) 'was perfect for her height.' Though her countenance was remarkable for the roundness, which suggested to Byron the pet-name of 'Pippin' for her, it had a piquant and sometimes slily humorous expression. If they were wanting in regularity, her features were delicate, feminine and intellectual. There was nothing in her face to indicate hardness of nature, unless it was the placid severity it could wear to those who were distasteful to her. She was known to be clever, and well read, so far as the reading of gentlewomen went in the days of the blue-stockings. Campbell went much too far when he said that her poetry would endure comparison with her husband's. Her best verses *just* missed the goodness that would have qualified them to be compared with his worst verses. Two of the minor poems, however, of Mr. Murray's complete edition of Byron's works, were certainly of her writing. At the same time her slightest and most trivial essays in poetical composition were superior to the average poetry of the ' Keepsakes ' and other fashionable collections of ' *Vers de Société !* '

In their ignorance of Byron, people have wondered how a woman, more remarkable for composure than loveliness, attracted Byron's attention ; and in their misinformation respecting her pecuniary worth, they have escaped from the difficulty by assuming he was drawn to her by her money. In his knowledge of the poet, Harness suggested shrewdly that her coldness had a charm for him ; and there is sure evidence that the suggestion was in a degree a true one. From his knowledge of himself Byron knew that an air of reserve and even of frigidity to comparative strangers did not necessarily indicate coldness of heart. He was precisely the man to be piqued by coldness to curiosity about its cause, and a desire to overcome it. Lady Caroline Lamb began in the right way when she ' turned on her heel ;' two days afterwards he asked for the reason of her conduct, and the next day he called upon her and made love to her. But though she was clever enough to see the right course, Lady Caroline Lamb had not self-control and strength enough to persist in it.

There was little love between Miss Milbanke, who was by nature sincere even to faultiness, and her cousin's wife, who was by nature an actress,—an actress of a flashy and melodramatic kind, with all her high fashion. Whilst she affected to disdain her husband's cousin, as an inferior and lamentably rustic young person, Lady Caroline Lamb secretly feared her quiet manner, calm self-dependence, and unaffected contempt for the artifices and triumphs of fashionable womankind. Miss Milbanke thought Lady Caroline a silly creature ;—she even said what she thought on this point. Two words expressed Miss Milbanke's estimate of her cousin-in-law :—Beautiful Silliness. Another name Miss Milbanke invented for her fashionable cousin-by-affinity was—Fair-seeming Foolishness. And at least on one memorable occasion, Miss Milbanke told Lady Caroline that her affectation of a woe-begone, melancholy visage of Byronic grief marred the effect of her fascinating silliness. It was not long before Lady Caroline found that she had a rival in the young lady from Durham county. Whilst 'the women were suffocating' their idol, 'throwing up their heads at him,' dressing their features and toning their voices with manufactured melancholy, very much in the fashion of Mr. Gilbert's love-sick maidens, Miss Milbanke smiled at the absurdities of the Byromaniacs. When some verses of rather clever satire on the Byronic mania, after being circulated for several days about Mayfair in manuscript, found their way into the newspapers, Lady Caroline was furious, —because Byron applauded the good sense of the verses, which she suspected Miss Milbanke to have written. Whilst his fair idolaters suffocated and sickened him (to a degree Lady Caroline little imagined) with their insane worship, Miss Milbanke was one of the few women to talk to him of his poetry in a way showing they could appreciate it. But her respect for his art was curiously devoid of enthusiasm for the artist. She liked to talk with him of poetry ; and showed him specimens of her own verse. But she respected poetry too much to fall at the poet's feet ; she respected herself too much to become one of the apes, who tried to imitate his feeling and manner. The young man, who plumed himself on his superiority to the herd, naturally honoured the woman who showed herself superior to the mob of fashionable womankind. And as he grew more and more weary of the fantastic caprices and hysterical vehemence of the silly woman of fashion, he was more and more attracted by the composure and tranquil intellect of the clever woman of no fashion.

Byron's journals show how steadily his tender concern for Miss Milbanke deepened and strengthened throughout the two years following her refusal of his first offer, and how much his manly sentiment for her —born of judgment rather than emotion, and fed by experience and reflection—differed from the fierce, fitful, boyish 'passions,' with which inferior women had inspired him. Having induced her to correspond with him (a thing he would not have done, had he not really cared for the lady of small fortune), he wrote in his journal on November 26, 1813, 'Two letters ; one from Annabella, the other from Lady Melbourne—both excellent in their respective styles. Annabella's contained also a very pretty lyric on " Concealed Griefs ; " if not her own, yet very like her. Why did she not say the stanzas were, or were not, of her own composition ? I do not know whether to wish them *hers* or not. I have no great esteem for poetical persons, particularly women ; they have so much of the "ideal" in *practics* as well as *ethics*.' Four days later (November 30th, 1813) he has another letter from Miss Milbanke, and writes in his journal, ' Yesterday, a very pretty letter from Annabella, which I answered. What an odd situation and friendship is ours!—without one spark of love on either side, and produced by circumstances which in general lead to coldness on one side and aversion on the other. She is a very superior woman, and very little spoiled, which is strange in an heiress — a girl of twenty—a peeress that is to be, in her own right —an only child and a *savante*, who has always had her own way. She is a poetess—a mathematician — a metaphysician, and yet, withal, very kind, generous, and gentle, with very little pretension. Any other head would be turned with half her acquisitions and a tenth of her advantages.' Most readers will detect the workings of love in this memorandum,—and all the more clearly, on account of the writer's disclaimer of every ' spark of love.' In February 1814, Lady Melbourne, still hopeful and wishful for the match, that would place her staid and dutiful niece between Byron and her flighty daughter-in-law, is writing with maternal kindness to the young man about his melancholy. 'Had a note,' he jots down in his journal on February 18th, 'from Lady Melbourne who says, it is said I am "much out of spirits." I wonder if I really am or not.' On Tuesday, March 15, 1814, the diarist jots down this significant note, 'A letter from Bella, which I answered. I shall be in love with her again, if I don't take care.' On September 15, 1814, he made his second offer to Miss Milbanke;—the offer she accepted.

Moore says that just before this offer was made, Byron was strongly urged by a lady, on whose judgment and care for his interests he relied, to propose to another lady than Miss Milbanke,—'remarking to him, that Miss Milbanke had at present no fortune, and that his embarrassed affairs would not allow him to marry without one; that she was, moreover, a learned lady, which would not at all suit him.' On the pecuniary ground, the advice was certainly good; and that the lady called Byron's attention to the question of money is evidence that in marrying Miss Milbanke he was not thought by 'society' to be making a fortune-hunter's match. Mr. Claughton's undertaking having by this time dropped through, and the 25,000l. of forfeit-money having been nearly all spent, Byron was again in trouble for money—with a revenue that still barely covered the interest of his debts, and nothing wherewith to defray his current expenses, except the literary earnings which he still declined to apply to his own needs. Under these circumstances, the match with Miss Milbanke was, in respect to money, a bad match. There were persons who thought it an almost ruinous match. But he made it;—because he was in love.

Writing from his uncertain memory (the biographer's words are '*as far as I can trust my recollection*') of a passage in the destroyed 'Memoirs,' Moore says that even at the last moment Byron relinquished his purpose of proposing to Miss Milbanke, and by the hand of his fair counsellor proposed to a lady of better fortune, and that he did not resume the relinquished purpose, and send his second proposal to his Annabella, till this mercenary offer had been declined. If the 'Memoirs' contained any story so discreditable to Byron, its presence strengthened the reasons for destroying them. It is only fair to Byron and reasonable to assume that Moore's memory (*so far as he could trust it*) was no memory at all. The anecdote, so inconsistent with the poet's contemporary memoranda and letters,—the anecdote, so vaguely recalled after several years from papers that were destroyed because they were unreliable and foolish—the anecdote, in respect to which the reporter admits he cannot trust his memory altogether, does not weaken the abundant evidence that Byron's marriage was a love-match. On the contrary, even to those who believe it, the story rather confirms the evidence that the match was *not* a *mariage de convenance*.

It is not wonderful that Byron—no callous, hardened, aged *roué* (as his calumniators insist), but a highly nervous and emotional young man (a boy, *ætat.* 24, 25, 26), with no sure knowledge of the world or of himself—revolted from the hysterical fervour and emotional extravagances of the fashionable ladies, and conceived that in choosing a companion for life he had better select a woman as unlike Lady Caroline Lamb as possible. For a month Lady

Caroline, with her beautiful silliness, her fair-seeming foolishness, was delightful to the young man, who in the spring of his twenty-fifth year was of course flattered, even intoxicated, by the preference shown for him by so famous a Queen of Society. At the end of six months, he had seen enough of her tears and swoonings, her caprice and gusty passionateness, her jealousies and spites, her hot fits and her hotter fits, to feel terror at imagining what would become of him were he to be linked for life to a woman of her unruly kind. Another six months, and, instead of affording him social distinction, her devotion was alternately making him ridiculous and menacing him with disaster. What more natural, than for the youthful student of life and character (with Lady Melbourne for his sympathetic adviser and 'mother') to think that, instead of mating with an impetuous and ungovernable woman, he had better mate with a woman of serene temper and well-balanced mind, who could govern herself?

All London was talking of Lady Caroline Lamb's friendship with the poet! How could it be otherwise, when from the day of her first letter to him,— an epistle in which she had offered him all her jewels, if he were in want of money,—she had seized every occasion for letting all the world know everything of the matter? As soon as he entered a room in her presence she pounced upon him as though he were her peculiar possession. On leaving one party, at which she was present, for another to which she was invited, Byron could not seat himself in his carriage without having the lady on the opposite seat of the '*vis-à-vis*.' On leaving parties, to which she had not been invited, he found her waiting for him in the street. More than once on returning home from his social diversions after midnight, Sam Rogers found Lady Caroline Lamb walking in the garden of St. James's Place, and waiting for him ; her purpose being to entreat him to make up her last quarrel with Lord Byron.   People asked how her husband could allow her to behave in such a way.   This question could be answered only by those who knew the temper of the man (whose favourite maxim of statecraft, when he had lived to be a great statesman, was embodied in the question, ' Why can't you leave it alone ? ')—and who knew also the great-hearted husband's confidence in his wife's devotion to his honour. Though he knew her to be wilful, wayward, vain, wildly passionate, insanely extravagant, it never occurred to him to suspect her of disloyalty to him,— still less to imagine her capable, even in thought, of the most shameful wickedness.   The Byromania was only her last mania ; —like previous manias it would work itself out, if people would only leave her alone. To him it was only one of Caroline's pretty ways when, at Lady Heathcote's ball in June 1813, she vented her fury, arising out of words with Byron, first by trying to throw herself out of a window, and then by stabbing herself—slightly (just for the scene's sake) with a supper knife, or (as another account says) rather badly with a piece of a broken glass.   It was not in every one's power to judge her so leniently as she was judged by her husband. Lady Melbourne ventured to entreat her daughter-in-law to be more careful.   Lady Bessborough begged her daughter to accompany her for change of scene to

Ireland.   Advice so insulting, an invitation so cruel, were unendurable indignities to the lineal descendant of Sarah, Duchess of Marlborough.   Hastening to Byron she told him all the barbarities done to her, simply because she loved him.   The story told, she implored him to fly with her to some distant scene of tranquillity. Till she rushed in upon him with this entreaty, Byron had never fully realised what perils might arise, what an appalling catastrophe might ensue from his Platonic friendship with an extremely excitable and romantic woman of fashion.   It was his duty to repel this piece of Beautiful Silliness firmly, but with such kindness and flatteries as should preserve to her a few rags of self-respect;—with kindness and flatteries that should prevent the needful repulse from overpowering her weak and heated brain, and driving her to suicide.   At the interview he played a part, that made her inveigh against his coldness and sternness. Having sent her back to Melbourne House, he sent the following note after her :—

'My dearest Caroline,—If the tears, which you saw, and know I am not apt to shed ; if the agitation in which I parted from you—agitation which, you must have perceived through the whole of this most nervous affair, did not commence till the moment of leaving you approached—if all I have said and done, and am still but too ready to say and do, have not sufficiently proved what my feelings are, and must ever be, towards you, my love, I have no other proof to offer.   God knows I never knew till this moment the madness of my dearest and most beloved friend. I cannot express myself, this is no time for words—

but I shall have a pride, a melancholy pleasure, in suffering what you yourself can scarcely conceive, for you do not know me. I am about to go out, with a heavy heart, for my appearing this evening will stop any absurd story to which the events of the day might give rise. Do you think *now* I am cold and stern and wilful? Will ever others think so? Will your mother ever? That mother to whom we must indeed sacrifice much more, much more on my part than she shall ever know, or can imagine. " Promise not to love you? " Ah, Caroline, it is past promising! But I shall attribute all concessions to the proper motive, and never cease to feel all that you have already witnessed, and more than ever can be known, but to my own heart—perhaps, to yours. May God forgive, protect, and bless you ever and ever, more than ever.

' Your most attached,

' BYRON.'

' P.S.—These taunts have driven you to this, my dearest Caroline, and were it not for your mother, and the kindness of your connexions, is there anything in heaven or earth that would have made me so happy as to have made you mine long ago? And not less now than then, but more than ever *at this time.* God knows I wish you happy, and when I quit you, or rather you, from a sense of duty to your husband and mother, quit me, you shall acknowledge the truth of what I again promise and vow, that no other, in word or deed, shall ever hold the place in my affections which is and shall be sacred to you till I am nothing. You know I would with pleasure give up all here or beyond the grave for you : and in refraining from this must my motives be misunderstood? I care not who knows this, what use is made of it—it is to you, and to you only, yourself. I was, and am yours, freely and entirely, to obey, to honour, love, and fly with you, *when, where, and how* yourself might and may determine.'

The copy of this letter, different in two or three particulars from all other published copies of the epistle, has been made from the original manuscript. The erased ' devoted '—erased by a single fine line—is a notable feature of the letter. It was by striking out the word ' devoted ' (left clearly legible), and substituting the colder word ' attached,' that Byron defined his attitude towards the receiver of the epistle in an unmistakable manner. Was ever woman repelled more firmly and gently? Declining to fly with her, he does his utmost to make her feel as though she were declining to fly with him. Yet more, in his generosity he puts himself in her power, to the extent of enabling her to prove against him the villainy of which he had not been guilty. To relieve the repulse as far as possible of the humiliation most likely to pain her in the coming time, he penned the last sentence of the postscript (a sentence inconsistent with and contradictory to all that precedes it), so as to enable her to say truly (should she be ever taunted with the matter) that he had declared his readiness to fly with her, *when, where,* and *how* she pleased. What written words to put in such a woman's keeping ! Henceforth, by showing the concluding words of the postscript and at the same withholding the rest of the epistle from perusal, it was in Lady Caroline Lamb's power to make any one conceive that the poet had entreated her to elope with him. What words, what a writing for her to have at hand, should she ever wish to give that impression to man or woman!

Lady Caroline Lamb told Lady Morgan, that whilst she was in Ireland with her mother, out of the way of the English hubbub about her escapades, she ' received letters constantly,—the most tender and amusing' from Byron ;—the fair interpretation of the words being that she wrote Byron many letters, and he answered some of them, as civilly as he could. Certainly the last of his letters was neither amusing to her ladyship nor tender to any one.   By her statement of the case in ' Glenarvon,' the letter ran thus, —' Lady Caroline Lamb,—I am no longer your lover; and since you oblige me to confess it by this truly unfeminine persecution, learn that I am attached to another, whose name it would of course be dishonest to mention.   I shall ever remember with gratitude the many instances I have received of the predilection you have shown in my favour.   I shall ever continue your friend, if your ladyship will permit me so to style myself.   And as a first proof of my regard, I offer you this advice : correct your vanity, which is ridiculous ; exert your absurd caprices on others ; and leave me in peace,—Your obedient servant, Byron.'—Of course, in the novel this epistle opens with ' Lady Avondale' and ends with ' Glenarvon.'   That Byron actually sent some such letter is certain; for Medwin (an honest though foolish reporter) says that Byron remarked to him of ' Glenarvon,' ' The only thing belonging to me in it is part of a letter.'

The letter came to Lady Caroline's hands in Dublin, as she was on her way back to England. 'There was,' Lady Caroline told Lady Morgan, 'a coronet on the seal. The initials under the coronet were Lady Oxford's. It was that cruel letter that I have published in " Glenarvon ; " it destroyed me ; I lost my brain. I was bled, leeched ; kept for a week in the filthy "Dolphin" at Rock.' As she recovered her brain, and was able to continue her journey in a week, the lady's illness was not very severe. The letter is not a letter one likes to think of the poet and peer writing to a gentlewoman; but Byron's excuse is that, having vainly tried to escape from her persecution by courteous ways, he was driven to violent measures. That the words were none too harsh was proved by her behaviour after her return to London. Driven as he was, Byron may be pardoned for writing roughly to this lady of fashion, who was capable of throwing herself into his rooms in the disguise of masculine attire (in the manner described by Lord Beaconsfield in 'Venetia') when she found his valet had been ordered to deny her admission.

But though she resented the letter, which she published under the impression she would injure the writer more than she would hurt herself by doing so, Byron's most grievous offence was that he married her cousin. For that insult she could not forgive him, till he had himself bitterly repented the imprudence. It tortured the fashionable lady's pride to think how her insignificant and lamentably rustic cousin, with her reputation for virtue and propriety and other homely qualities, had carried off the poet from all the Byromaniacal women of the great world.

It exasperated her to know that this hateful match (approved and favoured by Lady Jersey) had been desired from the first and brought about at last by her mother-in-law. Of course, Lady Caroline saw the motive and end that had actuated Lady Melbourne in the business, and was properly grateful to her mother-in-law.

After Byron's fall, it was the cant of 'good society' to say that he had trifled cruelly with poor Lady Caroline's feelings. Ten years later, when she had broken her nerves by drinking brandy and laudanum, people of mode used to sigh and say, 'Ah, poor thing!—it was all that wretched Byron!' Certainly the Lambs were slow to discover that the poet trifled with this lady of their house. All through Lady Caroline's extravagant behaviour to him, Lady Melbourne treated the poet with maternal kindness. Months after the stabbing scene at Lady Heathcote's ball, Lady Melbourne is found writing to him with undiminished confidence and affection. On escaping from Lady Caroline's persecutions he married the only daughter of Lady Melbourne's brother. Lady Melbourne's treatment of the poet, and his marriage within the lines of the Lamb connexion are evidence that he was not regarded at Melbourne House as having failed in honour or right feeling towards Lady Caroline Lamb. Nor were there any better grounds for attributing the eccentricities of the lady's behaviour in her later time to Byron's maleficent influence. She was a vain, flighty, violent creature long before she knew him. Miss Milbanke, rated her as a piece of fair-seeming foolishness long before Byron saw either of the cousins. In her thirty-fifth or fortieth year she was just what she promised in her earlier and brighter time to become in her middle age. Byron had no more to do with her later than her earlier follies. She failed early, as women of her temperament and training are wont to fail.

CHAPTER XIV.

THE TURNING OF THE TIDE.

Bennet Street — Mrs. Mule — 'The Albany' — The Poet's Clubs — 'The Giaour' — The Marquis of Sligo's Testimony — Horsemonger Lane Gaol — The Seasons of '13 and '14 — 'The Bride of Abydos' — 'The Corsair' — 'Anti-Byron' — Disgust for Literature — Renewal of Industry.

INSTEAD of returning to the rooms in St. James's Street, where he awoke one morning to find himself famous, Byron, on coming up from Cheltenham to London, entered the lodgings in Bennet Street, which he occupied till the end of March 1814, when he moved into the Albany:—the precise date of the commencement of his residence in the 'college of bachelors about town' being given in one of his journals in these words, 'Albany, March 28.   This night got into my new apartments, rented of Lord Althorpe, on a lease of seven years.   Spacious, and room for my books and sabres.   *In* the *house*, too, another advantage.   The last few days, or whole week, have been very abstemious, regular in exercise, and yet very unwell.'   Elected a member of 'the Alfred' before his return from Greece, the poet joined Watier's Club, somewhere about the time of his migration from Bennet Street to the Albany.   In one of his books of memoranda, quoted by Moore, Byron wrote after his withdrawal from England, ' I belonged, or belong, to

the following clubs or societies :—to the Alfred ; to
the Union ; to Racket's (at Brighton) ; to the Pugilistic ; to the Owls, or " Fly-by-night ;" to the *Cambridge* Whig Club ; to the Harrow Club, Cambridge ;
and to one or two private clubs ; to the Hampden
(political) Club ; and to the Italian Carbonari, &c. &c.
" though last not least." I got into all these, and
never stood for any other—at least to my own knowledge. I declined being proposed to several others,
though pressed to stand candidate.'

It was at Watier's, soon after he joined the club,
that Byron made a characteristic fish-supper on May
19, 1814, after going with Moore to 'see Kean.'
Bitten and goaded by hunger (which he had been
quickening rather than appeasing for two days with
biscuits and bits of gum-mastic) he came into the
club, faint and famished, to devour two or three lob-
sters (to his own share), which he washed down with
four or five ('near half-a-dozen' is Moore's expression) small liqueur-glasses of strong white brandy,
drunk neat, with a draught of hot water after each
dram of the spirit. ' After this,' says Moore, 'we had
claret, of which having despatched two bottles between
us, at about four o'clock in the morning we parted.'
This may be taken as a fair example of one of the
' outbreaks '—one of the concessions to appetite—
that varied at considerable intervals the poet's brave
and suicidal persistence in the regimen, by which he
kept down his fat and destroyed his stomach.

The reader has already been told that Byron
sometimes appeased the famine, ever preying on the
delicate membrane of his stomach, by chewing something less cleanly than mastic. Writing to Harness

on December 8, 1811, he says—'You will want to
know what I am doing—chewing tobacco.' On the
same day he writes to Hodgson, 'I do nothing but
eschew tobacco ;' a curious mistake as to the meaning
of eschew, which he repeated some ten years later in
' Don Juan ' (Canto xii., stanza 43) :—

> ' In fact, there's nothing makes me so much grieve,
> As that abominable tittle-tattle,
> Which is the cud eschewed by human cattle.'

That Byron was an occasional (if not a regular)
tobacco-chewer in Italy we know from Leigh Hunt's
base book. Guilty of the unpleasant practice during
his severe fasts, for the purpose of mitigating the pangs
of hunger, from 1811 to 1824, he was, chiefly for the
same purpose, a consumer of opium.

At Bennet Street Byron found the hideous old
woman, Mrs. Mule, whom he took under his protection
in a manner so agreeably illustrative of his affectionateness and also of his habitual kindness to his servants. During one of his transient illnesses in
Bennet Street, this aged person, whose ' gaunt and
witchlike appearance ' made her a thing of dislike and
dread to most beholders, waited on the lordly tenant
of the best rooms of the Bennet Street lodging-house
with a show of sympathy, that stirred his grateful
nature. The particulars of her services are unknown.
Possibly in Fletcher's absence, she had on a sudden
emergency of spasms from indigestion, to which he
was liable, come opportunely upon the scene with
wet cloths for hot fomentations, and had ventured
to soothe the sufferer by saying ' Dear my lord, your
lordship will be easier soon!' That would have been

quite enough to make the young man regard her tenderly and feel she had a claim upon him for ever. To
the surprise of his friends, who hoped to be quit of
the ugly old body when he had left Bennet Street,
Mrs. Mule appeared in better clothes at the Albany
Chambers. A year later she shone forth in a black
silk dress in the Piccadilly house, where Lord and
Lady Byron played their parts in a domestic drama
that will never perish from the annals of literature.
On being asked by an intimate friend what on earth
induced him to carry this ancient body about with
him as one of his household gods, Byron answered,
'The poor old devil was so kind to me.'

Having been instructed by 'Childe Harold' to
look for personal revelations in his literary productions, the readers of 'The Giaour' (published in May
1813) were quick to discover the author in one of the
personages, and an episode of the poet's own history
in the principal incident and positions of the 'wild
and beautiful fragment' (as Moore calls it) that, containing in the first edition about four hundred lines,
grew with its success till it became a poem of nearly
fourteen hundred verses. It is still to be shown that
the poem was based on one of the poet's adventures
in Greece. The probability is that the underlying
story relates to some affair, of which Byron heard
when he was in Athens, and about which he made
inquiries in a way that caused him to be confounded
in local gossip with the heroic actor in the melodrama.
Could Byron have truthfully told *of* himself the story
which the Marquis of Sligo reported as being current
about him after his departure from Athens, he would
have certainly told it *for* himself with full particulars

on his word of honour, instead of inviting the Marquis (a mere reproducer of hearsay gossip) to stand forth as sponsor for the truth of the romantic fable. The Junius mystery had produced a general appetite for literary mysteries; and to gratify this appetite popular writers, from Walter Scott to very humble fabricators of romance, were exercising their ingenuity in feats of literary mystification. The time was not far distant when Byron could without compunction send to the journals of Continental capitals pure fictions about his own doings, — fictions by the way that redounded to his dishonour instead of his credit. But though he already delighted in mystifying his readers with misleading dates and other light touches of his pen, and delighted in 'bamming' and hoaxing his hearers with piquant inventions, he had too much regard for truth and his own honour to be capable of exceeding the wide license accorded by fashion to humorous *raconteurs*, so far as to make on his honour a statement which he knew to be false. He could mystify his readers, hoax credulous quidnuncs, 'bam' dull and impertinent questioners, within the limits of the license accorded to humorous talkers. Misled by heated fancy he would misstate matters of fact. But he was incapable of lying. To persons who asked whether he really saved the wretched damsel from execution, whether he really pulled out his pistol and threatened to shoot the chief of her escort at the very jaws of death, he could not reply, 'Yes, I did.' But, having no wish to contradict the stories that exhibited him in so interesting and heroic an attitude to his Mayfair idolaters, he bethought himself of an ingenious way of avoiding the question and leaving the stories to do their work.   He could say to questioners, 'You must excuse me for declining to speak of that matter, as it is a business on which I do not like to speak more than I can help.   If you really wish for the particulars, go to Sligo, who will tell you all he heard of the affair immediately after I left Athens.   Or, if you like, I will show you what Sligo has written to me on the subject.   But you must permit me to hold my tongue on the matter.'   By this means, without avouching the stories, or telling any positive untruth, he could leave his questioners under the influence of the delusions and misconceptions, in which he wished them to remain.   To the last, Byron thus used the Marquis's letter, which merely states what the writer heard of certain loose and unsifted rumours.   He offered to show Medwin the letter.   But he never committed himself by an assertion that the rumours, mentioned in the letter, were substantially true.

Though it was no work to raise a new writer to the eminence Byron had achieved by ' Childe Harold,' the new poem was precisely the performance to enlarge the young poet's popularity and intensify the general admiration of his genius.   Giving the novel-readers a romantic story, and tickling the ears that preferred to loftier and more thoughtful song the particular kind of musical verse, the poetry of sweet and delicate sounds, of which Moore was so perfect a master, ' The Giaour ' was a great success.   The enlarged editions followed one another rapidly ; the poet throwing into each of them more and yet more verse, of animating lilt and lyric lightness.   But the poem's success could not extinguish certain indications that the enthusiasm for the poet was already subsiding in that central and exclusive circle of the polite life of the capital, which claimed to be 'society' (*par excellence*, and in inverted commas). No man of his day had a finer hand or more sensitive touch for feeling the pulse of this 'inner circle' than its favourite piano-poet, Tom Moore ; and on coming to town for the season of 1813, he detected signs of a disposition in certain sets and coteries of 'society' to think less cordially of the author of 'Childe Harold.' 'In the immediate circle, perhaps, around him,' says Moore, 'familiarity of intercourse might have begun to produce its usual disenchanting effects.' If the change had been only the slightest, Moore's nice discernment would have apprehended it. But if it had been only a very slight change, the biographer, retained by Byron's publisher and the world's voice to re-dress and re-paint and re-varnish the battered poet, would have been silent about the matter. It must have been a change so considerable and obvious, that the biographer felt he could not forbear from referring thus lightly to it, without exposing himself to critical censure. Moore's words are even more remarkable when he goes on to account for this change. 'His own liveliness and unreserve,' says the biographer, 'on a more intimate acquaintance, would not be long in dispelling that charm of poetic sadness, which to the eyes of distant observers hung about him ; *while the romantic notions, connected by some of his fair readers with those past and nameless loves alluded to in his poems, ran some risk of abatement from too near an acquaintance with the supposed objects of his fancy and fondness at present.*'—In other words, Byron was found no more a Byromaniac than John Wilkes was a Wilkeite. On coming to know him intimately, persons who would have preferred him to resemble his melancholy poetry, were disappointed at finding him so merry, droll and loquacious; and he was at the same time suffering in the esteem of the best drawing-rooms from his devotion to Lady Oxford, and still more from his devotion to Lady Caroline Lamb. The many ladies with good reasons for disliking the Countess questioned the taste of the young nobleman who had made so poor a choice of an especial object of adoration. The *very* many ladies with *better* reasons for disliking Lady Caroline were beginning to think meanly of him for his submissiveness to the caprices of the woman, who was doing her best to make him as ridiculous as she was making herself. That the universal favour, shown to Byron by society in his first season, should have waned thus perceptibly at the outset of the second season, is re-markable. It is part of the evidence that society did not, as Lord Macaulay imagined, make up its mind all in a single moment to pitch the poet away like an old glove.

The season of 1813 closed with the famous 'Dandy Ball,' at which Byron was present as one of 'the dandies.' It was the season, in which he dined with Leigh Hunt in Horsemonger Lane Gaol, where the minor poet was undergoing his term of punishment for the libel on the Prince Regent. It was also the season, that heard (on June 1st) his third, least successful and last speech in the House of Lords, in the debate on Major Cartwright's Petition. Just as the first speech was in fact a tame success (though circumstances made him for a moment think it a brilliant one), this third speech was a tame failure (though circumstances blinded him to its completeness); a failure that was another slight indication of the turning of the tide of triumph. On the occasion of the maiden speech people wanted to see and hear him; on the occasion of the third speech, the lords and their friends, without being antagonistic to him, had ceased to be curious about him, and therefore in a mild way showed they had seen and heard enough of him—at least in their chamber. Combative on the masculine side, just as he was alternately yielding and froward on the feminine side of his double nature, Byron would have justified Dr. Drury's opinion and become a great parliamentary debater, had he in his first forensic essay encountered such humiliation as would have stung him to assert his natural superiority to other men. Baffled at the outset like the younger Disraeli, he would have conquered like Beaconsfield. But in 1812 and 1813, things went smoothly with Byron, and it was only in troubled waters that he found his strength. Moreover his literary triumphs made him indifferent for the moment to political distinction. So his parliamentary career ended almost as soon as it had begun. Some one (surely, a humourist!) asked him in the November of this year to present the Debtors' Petition, and he declined to do so. 'I have', he wrote in his journal, 'declined presenting the Debtors' Petition, being sick of parliamentary mummeries. I have spoken thrice; but I doubt my ever becoming an orator. My first was liked; the second and third—I don't know whether they succeeded or not. I have never yet set to it *con amore;*—one must have some excuse to one's self for laziness, or inability, or both, and this is mine. "Company, villanous company hath been the spoil of me;"—and then, I have drunk medicines, not to make me love others, but certainly enough to make me hate myself.'

During this year of 1813 (and also the next) he was often at theatres, kept up his boxing and friendship with Jackson, dined with wits and statesmen, and was seen in the best of good society,—showing no disposition to go into any society, that was not good in some sense or other. In need of money for himself he always had money for others; doing several deeds of munificence to people who had only the slightest claim, or no claim whatever, upon him,—one of these latter recipients of his bounty being the paltry fellow, Ashe, whom he assisted out of pity for him, and pitied out of disgust. At the same time, though upbraiding himself in his journals for laziness, he worked much—sometimes at high pressure. Each of the new editions of 'The Giaour' might be called a new poem. 'The Bride of Abydos' was published in December 1813; 'The Corsair' (with the padding of trifles at the end of the pamphlet) followed it quickly upon the turn of the year.

What-induced him to put 'Weep, daughter of a royal line,' in that padding is unknown. The avowal of the lines could not heighten his reputation, could serve no good end, was sure to make him many dangerous enemies. Yet he reproduced them thus obtrusively;—perhaps out of generous sympathy with the other libeller of the Prince Regent, with whom he had dined in Horsemonger Lane gaol. If the act was done out of concern for Leigh Hunt, generosity was never more completely wasted. The

reckless act had the consequences he might have foreseen. Forthwith abuse of the most passionate and
even virulent kind was poured upon him by newspapers especially jealous and zealous for the honour
and interest of the Prince Regent. Day after day
throughout successive weeks of February and March
1814, these journals poured the vials of their wrath
out upon him. He was a mean creature, who had
eaten his own words, in order to curry favour with
powerful writers whom he had assailed in the 'English
Bards.' He was a scribbler of poor verse, to be
placed low in the list of minor poets. He was a
venal poetaster, guilty of the meanness of 'receiving
and pocketing' large sums of money from his publisher;—the rapid and prodigious sale of the last poem
being pointed to as a justification of the charge. He
was no less deformed in mind than he was in body.
The Prince Regent almost shed tears of regret, on
finding that the offensive lines, which he had attributed
to Tom Moore, had been written by Byron. In his
alarm at the outcry, which was no less surprising than
the sale of the poem, Murray begged the poet to omit
the lines from future editions of the pamphlet, and
even ventured on his own authority to issue copies
without the naughty verses. But Byron would not
yield to the man of business. He would not withdraw the verses, and seem to be 'shrinking and
shuffling after the fuss made about them by the
Tories.' Macaulay wrote of Byron that 'he lampooned the Prince Regent; yet he could not alienate
the Tories.' This was true in a limited sense,—but
in a *very* limited sense. As a 'ladies' man,' as the
dandy and poet especially acceptable to women of rank,

Byron still went to certain of the great Tory houses. But if he continued to receive cards from great ladies to their routs, and had not yet provoked the Tories of high society into dropping him, he had most certainly so far alienated powerful organs of the Tory press, that they felt it their duty to educate the great body of their readers to regard him with fierce animosity. They had in truth become a great force for his overthrow.

Whilst powerful papers were denouncing him for the lampoon, another thing happened in this third season of his fame, to show Byron how the tide was now setting against him. Murray sent him the manuscript of 'Anti-Byron,' which had been offered to the publisher. No work of reckless abuse, or angry flippancy, or dull fanaticism, but a thoughtful performance, attacking the poet (as he himself wrote to Murray) 'in a manly manner and without any malicious intention,' 'Anti-Byron' was a serious exhibition of what its author deemed pernicious in the religious sentiment and in the moral and political influence of Byron's writings. 'It is not,' Byron wrote of this work to Moore on April 9, 1814, 'very scurrilous, but serious and ethereal. I never felt myself important, till I saw and heard of my being such a little Voltaire, as to induce such a production. Murray would not publish it, for which he was a fool, and so I told him ; but some one else will doubtless.' In the autumn of 1812 serious ladies wanted to convert the poet to righteousness. In the spring of 1814, a book had been written to demonstrate that he was a teacher of evil.

Having no doubt that this manuscript would find

a publisher, Byron cannot have supposed it would be the only book produced to discredit him. He must have foreseen the approaching storm, and felt that he was nearing the troubles predicted by Gifford. But instead of disheartening him and shaking his nerve, the prospect of the tempest seems to have inspired him with new zeal and energy. Anyhow, the man,—who at the end of April 1814, in a sudden fit of pique at the insults of certain of his anonymous assailants, and of distaste for labours that were rewarded with their abuse, had actually resolved to withdraw from literature, and ordered his publisher to stop selling his books,—now found courage to go to work on another poem. Begun towards the end of May, 'Lara' was ready for the printer,—indeed in the printer's hands and almost ready for publication—at the beginning of July. To think of the rapidity with which 'The Giaour,' 'The Bride of Abydos,' 'The Corsair,' the Napoleon 'Ode,' and 'Lara,' came from his pen, whilst he was in the quick stream of the social excitements of a man of pleasure and the world, is to be amazed at the fecundity of his genius, and of its power to achieve its ends amidst countless distractions.

CHAPTER XV.

BYRON'S MARRIED LIFE.

Byron's spirits during the Engagement—The Wedding at Seaham—
Art of 'Bamming'—Duck, Pippin, and Goose—Quiet time at
13 Piccadilly Terrace — Lord Wentworth's Death — Matrimonial
Felicity—The Poet's Will — Commencement of Bickerings—'An
Unhappy sort of Life'—'Causes of Quarrel.'

ENGAGED to Miss Milbanke in September 1814,
married to her in January 1815, Byron in July 1816
wrote the poem, which made the whole world think
that during his engagement to Sir Ralph Milbanke's
daughter his heart was in his cousin's (Mrs. Musters's)
keeping,—that at the very moment when he took his
bride for better and for worse, he was thinking of the
Mary who ten years before had become 'another's
bride.' Byron's journals and letters of 1813, 1814,
and 1815, afford conclusive evidence that the autobiography of 'The Dream' was, in that matter, mere
romance. Having cared enough for Miss Milbanke
in 1812 to wish to make her his wife, he learnt to
love her during the next two years ; and having by
assiduous addresses won her love in the autumn of
1814, he married her—not in a frenzy of boyish
passion, but with the steadier sentiment of manly
devotion.

On September 20, 1814, he writes to Moore in
high spirits, ' I am going to be married—that is, I

am accepted, and one usually hopes the rest will follow. My mother of the Gracchi (that *are* to be) *you* think too strait-laced for me, although the paragon of only children, and invested with " golden opinions of all sorts of men," and full of " most blest conditions " as Desdemona herself. . . . She is said to be an heiress, but of that I really know nothing certainly, and shall not inquire. But I know she has talents and excellent qualities ; and you will not deny her judgment, after having refused six suitors and taken me. . . . I must, of course, reform thoroughly ; and, seriously, if I can contribute to her happiness, I shall secure my own.'— To the Countess of ——, he writes from the Albany on October 5, 1814, ' I am very much in love, and as silly as all single gentlemen must be in that sentimental situation ; . . . all our relatives are congratulating away to right and left in a most fatiguing manner. You perhaps know the lady. She is niece to Lady Melbourne, and cousin to Lady Cowper and others of your acquaintance, and has no fault, except being a great deal too good for me, and that I must pardon, if nobody else should. It might have happened two years ago, and, if it had, would have saved me a world of trouble.'— Again to his intimate friend, Moore, he writes on October 14, 1814, averring that he has chosen from love, not money, ' I certainly did not address Miss Milbanke with these views, but it is likely she may prove a considerable *parti*. All her father can give, or leave her, he will ; and from her childless uncle, Lord Wentworth, whose barony, it is supposed, will descend on Lady Milbanke (his sister), she has expectations. But these will depend upon his own disposition, which seems very partial towards her. She is an only child, and Sir R.'s estates, though dipped by electioneering, are considerable. Part of them are settled on her ; but whether *that* will be *dowered* now, I do not know,—though, from what has been intimated to me, it probably will. . . . I certainly did not dream that she was attached to me, which it seems she has been for some time. I also thought her of a very cold disposition, in which I was also mistaken—it is a long story, and I won't trouble you with it. As to her virtues, &c. &c., you will hear enough of them (for she is a kind of *pattern* in the north), without my running into a display on the subject.'—To Henry Drury, he writes on October 18, 1814, ' I am going to be married, and have been engaged this month. It is a long story, and, therefore, I won't tell it,—an old and (though I did not know it till lately) a mutual attachment.'

Are these passages (which fairly represent the tone of the letters from which they are taken) indicative of selfish greed or despondency? Would a fortune-hunter have written so carelessly and contentedly of the lady's small present fortune and uncertain expectations, and of the probability that her present fortune would be settled upon her? Would a man, dropping in a faint-hearted way into a *mariage de convenance,* have written so proudly and affectionately of the lady's virtues, of his love of her, and of his pleasure at finding that her love of him was no younger than his love of her ? Moore speaks of finding the poet melancholy and despondent and restless in December, shortly before his marriage :— speaking, be it remembered, fourteen years after the marriage from memory, when events had trained the biographer to regard the wedding as a doleful business from first to last. The poet, however, may well have been anxious and troubled just then. The nervous man had cause for discomfort, on the eve of his marriage at a time of pecuniary embarrassments that made him foresee his bride's home would be besieged by bailiffs. His marriage would put him in a worse position than ever for dealing with his creditors. For he had agreed to make a large settlement on his wife, whose trustees under the deed of settlement would for the performance of the trust have control over 60,000*l.* of the capital that should come from the sale of Newstead. Whilst Byron made this large settlement on his bride, her fortune of 10,000*l.* (which Byron is so generally believed to have squandered) was also settled upon her. Hobhouse knew all about this matter ; and in answer to one of the most serious of the two or three hundred misrepresentations of Medwin's book, he wrote in the 'Westminster Review,' 'The whole of Lady Byron's fortune was put into settlement, and could not be melted away.'

Byron, with Hobhouse for his 'best man' and his travelling companion from London to the north, set out for Seaham co. Durham at the end of December 1814, and was there married to Miss Milbanke on January 2, 1815. Enough has been said to show that 'The Dream' has no autobiographical value, except as evidence of the way in which the poet was pleased to regard certain passages of his life, eighteen months after the wedding. A dream, it was as false to fact as dreams usually are. The ceremony over, and the breakfast a thing of the past, the happy pair started for Halnaby, Sir Ralph Milbanke's place near

Darlington. Hobhouse handed Lady Byron to her carriage, and saw her drive off with the poet by her side ; her parting words to the 'best man' being, 'If I am not happy, it will be my own fault.' Of course there was no lady's-maid in the carriage, sitting 'bodkin' between the bride and bridegroom ; though Byron, no doubt, said to Medwin at Pisa in 1821, 'After the ordeal was over, we set off for a country seat of Sir Ralph's ; and I was surprised at the arrangements for the journey, and somewhat out of humour to find a lady's-maid stuck between me and my bride. It was rather too early to assume the husband ; so I was forced to submit, but it was not with a very good grace. Put yourself in a similar situation, and tell me if I had not some reason to be in the sulks. I have been accused of saying, on getting out of the carriage, that I had married Lady Byron out of spite, and because she had refused me twice. Though I was vexed at her prudery, or whatever you may choose to call it, if I had made so uncavalier, not to say brutal, a speech, I am convinced Lady Byron would instantly have left the carriage to me and the maid (I mean the lady's). She had spirit enough to have done so, and would properly have resented the affront.' On reading this piece of literature in Medwin's book, Hobhouse exclaimed fiercely, that Medwin was an infamous impostor. He had himself handed Lady Byron into the carriage and could swear there was no maid in it ! And Hobhouse was not mistaken on the point of fact. But he was wrong in thinking Tom Medwin an impostor. How did this invention come into Tom's book ? How came Byron to put it there ?

When he spoke to his especially confidential friends of Byron's most serious faults, Hobhouse used to put high in the list the poet's readiness to gossip with sycophants about his private affairs,—a failing which, though it had a show of amiability, was in truth a most hurtful weakness. Whilst the habit fed the selfishness which (according to Hobhouse) was Byron's worst and most deplorable characteristic, it was prolific of absurd stories that darkened the poet's fame. To Hobhouse it seemed that Tom Medwin was one of the sycophants who by humouring Byron's vanity led him to talk loosely; and an impostor who deliberately vamped up the poet's imprudent statements with bits of fiction, so as to impose the gossip more readily on the public.

But Shelley's familiar connexion and schoolmate —poor Tom Medwin, whilom of the 24th Light Dragoons, and in 1821 and the two following years living in Italy on insufficient means—was neither knave nor toady. A man of gentlemanly address and puerile simplicity, he was a good-tempered fool. If he had disliked this relative and hanger-on of the Shelleys, Byron—living in close intimacy with Shelley—could not have treated him with open rudeness. But Byron had a tenderness for the young man who was just then no less unfortunate than unwise. Warned by Trelawny that this inquisitive prattler was taking notes with a view to printing them, Byron answered lightly, 'So many lies are told about me that Medwin won't be believed.' And having said thus much and a little more to Trelawny, Byron took care that Medwin should not be believed :—took care that the 'notes' should comprise so large a proportion of obvious fictions, that cautious readers would not know what of their statements they might believe, would be doubtful whether they contained a single pure and unadulterated fact. In a word, Byron 'bammed' Medwin; and Medwin was a very easy man to 'bam'!

'To bam' was to hoax with a humorous fiction. The old slang word 'bam' meant a story which none but a simpleton would believe. It occurs in 'Sam Hall,' the convict's ditty that used to be encored loudly in the Cave of Harmony, when Arthur Pendennis was a young man,—

> 'The parson, he did come, he did come,
> And talk of " kingdom come ; "
> But then it was *all bam !*'

In the days when Kit North's friends wrote their convivial articles for 'Blackwood' over their tumblers, and sometimes under them, a reference to the art of 'bamming' was often seen in the columns of that polite magazine. At the same time the Prince Regent, a consummate master of the elegant art, made 'bamming' a favourite pastime with the gentlemen of his *entourage*. When George the Fourth entertained a dinner-table by describing gravely how he commanded-in-chief at Waterloo, he was not mad or tipsy; he was telling 'a bam' for the fun of seeing how it would be received by one of his guests, the Duke of Wellington. 'Bamming' was 'lying with a difference.' It was necessary for 'a bam' to be humorous; it might not be uttered for the teller's pecuniary benefit or for his material advantage in any way; it was needful for it to be so egregiously absurd that no one but a dullard

would believe it. Byron's story about the lady's-maid
was 'all bam.' Medwin having swallowed the invention, and gravely put it away for use, it is not wonderful that Byron found him a diverting companion
in idle hours.

The marriage, on which Lady Melbourne had set
her heart, was an accomplished fact. For the moment
she could breathe freely, whilst her daughter-in-law
meditated mischief and brooded over schemes of revenge. She could breathe the more freely because she
sincerely believed that her niece was precisely the wife
for the young man, for whom she felt genuine affection. And for a while it seemed that events would
justify her opinion. The evidence of ' The Dream '
notwithstanding, Byron passed his time so agreeably
at Halnaby, with the lady who had carried him off
from the Byromaniacs, that in the very heart of the
honeymoon he could write gaily to Moore (Jan. 19,
1815) 'So you want to know about milady and me?
. . . I like Bell as well as you do (or did, you villain!)
Bessy—and that is (or was) saying a great deal.' On
his return to Seaham, he writes to the same friend
(February 2, 1815), ' Since I wrote you last, I have
been transferred to my father-in-law's, with my lady
and my lady's-maid, &c. &c., and the treacle-moon is
over, and I am awake, and find myself married! My
spouse and I agree to admiration. Swift says "no *wise*
man ever married;" but, for a fool, I think it the most
ambrosial of all possible future states. I still think
one ought to marry upon *lease;* but am very sure I
should renew mine at the expiration, though next
term were for ninety and nine years.' On February
10, 1815, again writing from Seaham, he says to

Moore, 'Bell desires me to say all kinds of civilities, and assure you of her recognition and high consideration. . . . By the way, don't engage yourself in any travelling expedition, as I have a plan of travel into Italy, which we will discuss. And then, think of the poesy wherewithal we should overflow, from Venice to Vesuvius, to say nothing of Greece, through all which — God willing — we might perambulate in twelve months. If I take my wife, you can take yours; and if I leave mine, you may do the same.' On the day before leaving Seaham for London, with the intention of visiting Colonel and the Hon. Mrs. Leigh, at Six Mile Bottom, near Newmarket, on the road to town, he writes to Moore (March 8, 1815), 'Bell is in health, and unvaried good-humour and behaviour. But we are all in the agonies of packing and parting ; and I suppose by this time to-morrow I shall be stuck in the chariot with my chin upon a band-box. I have prepared, however, another carriage for the abigail, and all the trumpery which our wives drag along with them.' If Byron was melancholy in the first nine weeks of his wedded life, and pining for ' another bride,' he hid his grief under a smiling face.

Writing to Moore from Six Mile Bottom on March 17, 1815, the young husband, touching a delicate question, says, 'To your question, I can only answer that there have been some symptoms which look a little gestatory. It is a subject upon which I am not particularly anxious, except that I think it would please her uncle, Lord Wentworth, and her father and mother. The former (Lord W.) is now in town, and in very indifferent health. You, perhaps, know that his property, amounting to seven or eight thousand a-year, will eventually devolve upon Bell. But the old gentleman has been so very kind to her and me, that I hardly know how to wish him in heaven, if he can be comfortable on earth. Her father is still in the country. We mean to metropolise to-morrow, and you will address your next to Piccadilly. We have got the Duchess of Devon's house there, she being in France.'

The brief sojourn at Six Mile Bottom, under Colonel Leigh's roof, was especially agreeable to the newly-wedded couple,—Lady Byron conceiving a strong affection for Augusta Leigh, whom she approached with a strong predisposition to love as if she were really her sister, whilst Byron was delighted to see how cordially and sincerely the two women 'took to one another.' The house was none too large and the children were noisy, but the stay was enjoyable in the highest degree to both visitors. Byron had never seen much of his little, plain, dowdy-goody sister. Whilst he was on his travels and after his return to England fully occupied with literary labours, in which she felt no concern beyond a sisterly pride in their success, and with social distractions in which she was no participator, Augusta had her Cambridgeshire home, her husband, and children to engage her attention. Hence it was that, on July 8, 1813, Byron wrote from Bennet Street to Moore, 'My sister is in town, which is a great comfort,—for, never having been much together, we are naturally more attached to each other.' Till October 16, 1814, Miss Milbanke had never either seen or written to Augusta, of whose amiability and womanly sweetness of nature she had however heard much from a common friend.

At Six Mile Bottom, Mrs. Leigh and the newly married couple addressed one another by pet names. Whilst Byron called his wife 'Pippin' and she called him 'Duck,' they both fell into the habit of calling Augusta 'Goose,' who addressed her sister-in-law by her husband's pet name for her, but in speaking to Byron persisted in her old practice of calling him 'Baby.' Their use of these pet names—Pippin, Duck, Goose and Baby—may be taken as an indication of the affectionate heartiness and freedom from formality that characterised the intercourse of the trio.

Coming to town on March 18, 1815, in good spirits and undiminished affectionateness for one another, they settled down in the Piccadilly house, which had been lent to them by the Duchess of Devon, and had a very quiet time throughout the season. In his 'Westminster Review' article on the mis-statements of Medwin's 'Conversations,' Hobhouse said, 'Lord and Lady Byron did not give dinner-parties; they had not separate carriages; they did not launch into any extravagance.' Hobhouse's accuracy on these points is demonstrated by abundant evidence. The new chariot, which conveyed the bride and bridegroom from Durham to London, was never seen on the London pavements after that journey, until it was brought out of the coach-house on January 15, 1816, to convey Lady Byron to Kirkby Mallory. Lady Byron had this carriage at hand during her residence in 13 Piccadilly Terrace, but she never used it between her arrival at and final departure from Piccadilly. She drove about town in her husband's carriage: often driving about town *with* him, and waiting good-temperedly for the hour at a time at the doors of houses, whilst he was making calls on people whom he did not care to introduce to her, as on the occasion of his visit to Leigh Hunt at Paddington Green, when, after going by herself to buy flowers at Henderson's Nursery Ground, she sent up twice to remind her lord that she was waiting.

Several circumstances combined to make them live thus quietly. In the middle of April they went into mourning for Thomas Noel, second Viscount and ninth Baron Wentworth, who died on the seventeenth of that month, leaving the bulk of his property (from 7000*l.* to 8000*l.* a-year) entailed on his sister, Lady Milbanke, for life, with remainder to Lady Byron and her issue ; and whilst she was in mourning for so beneficent an uncle, the eventual heiress of his estate and barony could not with propriety have thrown herself into the gaieties of the London season, even if she had wished to do so. She had of course no disposition to go much at present to houses, where she would be almost sure to run across Lady Caroline Lamb. She was already in a state of health that gave her hope of becoming a mother. ' Lady Byron,' her husband wrote to Moore on June 12, 1815, ' is better than three months advanced in her progress to maternity, and, we hope, likely to go well through with it. We have been very little out this season, as I wish to keep her quiet in her present situation.' Moreover, for a peer and peeress, housed in Piccadilly, with a sufficient establishment of servants, the Byrons were as ' poor as mice.' Living with economy in Piccadilly as a married man, Byron lived at a greater cost than he had done as a bachelor of the Albany ;

and about 500*l*. a-year was all the immediate growth of his income from his marriage. Newstead was again in the market; but a good purchaser for so considerable an estate was not to be found in a day; and on its sale, it would devolve on the trustees of the marriage-settlement to determine how 60,000*l*. of the money paid for the property should be invested. Duns ran in upon the poet at every turn and from every quarter. Confirming them in their misconceptions respecting the change effected in their debtor's pecuniary circumstances by his marriage, Lord Wentworth's death made the poet's creditors louder and more urgent in their demands for immediate payment. How matters went in this respect at 13 Piccadilly Terrace may be conceived from the fact that there had been nine executions in the house before Lady Byron left it on January 15, 1816. No wonder that the Byrons forbore to give dinner-parties, lived economically, and did as they best could with a single pair of carriage-horses.

Annoyances and humiliations from want of money notwithstanding, the young husband and wife lived as young married folk should for four and even five months in the Duchess of Devon's house without quarrelling, or even bickering. In society Byron played the part of an idolising and triumphant husband; at home he found in Lady Byron a thoughtful and sympathetic wife, who throwing herself into his literary interests was delighted to act as his amanuensis and secretary;—her service in this respect being of great convenience to the poet who wrote a poor hand, and on his nervous days disliked the drudgery of penmanship. During these months she wrote several small poems, some of which he corrected,—very much of course to their improvement. They had no altercation, dispute, or difference of a serious kind, or indeed of any kind, till August.

This was the time when he was habitually so cheerful, and sometimes so hilarious in her society, that he was surprised to find her of the same opinion as those who regarded him as the victim of deep and incurable melancholy. He had been more than usually gay and brilliant in society, when his wife declared her pleasure at seeing him in such high spirits.

'And yet, Bell,' he said, 'I have been called and miscalled melancholy—you must have seen how falsely, frequently.'

'No, Byron,' she answered, with the fine perception of wifely sympathy, 'it is not so; at heart you are the most melancholy of mankind; and often when apparently gayest.'

If Byron had been so gloomy at his wedding as 'The Dream' represents, he could scarcely have been so surprised at his wife's detection of his melancholy.

An incident of the time closely preceding the weeks in which they began to differ, deserves especial notice, as it shows how pleasantly they dwelt together up to the very threshold of their discord. Events having occurred to make it desirable that better provision should be made for the Hon. Mrs. Leigh and her children,—the lady's husband having lately sustained losses,—Byron made the will that was proved at Doctors' Commons, London, after his death. Disposing of the residue of his estate, after the performance of the trusts of Lady Byron's marriage-settlement, for the benefit of his sister and her issue, the testator uses these words, ' I make the above provision for my sister and her children, in consequence of my dear wife Lady Byron, and any children I may have, being otherwise amply provided for.' A few days after making this will Byron told his wife the contents,—telling her at the same time of his reasons for doing so much for his dear Goose, and talking of his dear Goose's financial anxieties and her goodness, till the tears came to his eyes, and also to the eyes of his sympathetic listener. He expressed a hope that his action would have Lady Byron's approval, in consideration of the fact stated in the above-quoted words of the testament. The will was cordially approved by 'Pippin' on that ground, and for other reasons also. Despite the coldness and reserve of her manner, and notwithstanding the hard things said of her temper, Lady Byron had a warm and generous heart, at this period of her story ; and in her delight at Goose's good fortune, and also at her husband's display of brotherly affection, she declared her purpose of writing to Goose, telling her what a superlative brother her Baby was, and how cordially Pippin approved the will. It was on this occasion that Lady Byron (the cold, and stony-hearted Lady Byron, as she has been called by her detractors) thanked her husband for giving her the desire of her heart,—a sister whom she could love as thoroughly as she could have loved any sister given her by her own parents. Come what might, she promised always to be kind to Augusta ;—the promise of which she was in later time reminded by strange and impressive incidents, that bit the words too deep into her memory for time to be ever able to erase them from the tablet. From the day of Byron's withdrawal from England to the hour of Augusta's death, and onwards to the hour of her own death, the words lived in Lady Byron's soul. They were a living part of it. No fire of anger could kill them, no force of hatred could pluck them out of the heart into which they had grown. Again and again at critical moments of her career those words struck her with awe. They were visible to her in luminous letters in the darkness of sleepless nights. She heard them even in her deep slumber, when her spirit could not sleep.

Another incident of this point of Byron's life with his wife must be mentioned;—an incident showing how nicely considerate he was for her happiness shortly before the time when he began to show strange indifference to her feelings. Having assumed the surname of Noel, in accordance with the requirements of Lord Wentworth's will, and taken up their abode at Kirkby Mallory, Sir Ralph and Lady Milbanke (now Noel) offered Seaham to their daughter and her husband for a country residence. Made in July, this offer was accepted thankfully; and forthwith Lady Byron began to think of going to Seaham for her accouchement. Byron at the same time, with his wife's hearty concurrence, asked Tom Moore and Mrs. Moore to stay at Seaham in the course of the autumn. 'If so,' he adds, 'you and I (*without our wives*) will take a *lark* to Edinburgh and embrace Jeffrey;'—this postscript of the invitation being probably withheld from Lady Byron. A few weeks later (at the beginning of August, 1815) Byron asked his wife to invite Lady Noel to stay at Seaham in November, so as to be there during the accouchement. 'You see,' Byron added, 'at Kirkby Mallory your mother will be so miserable about you.' Even more pleased by this nice thoughtfulness for her mother than by the suggestion itself, Pippin was a truly happy wife for a few days. And it shows the cordiality and completeness of her affection for her sister-in-law, that even in her delight at Byron's delicate mindfulness for her mother, she liked to think that Goose had suggested to him that he should put the proposal in this peculiarly agreeable way. Feminine instinct causing her to attribute to feminine influence the alleged reason for the proposal, she was *pleased* to regard Augusta as the woman who had said to him, 'To give your wife the most pleasure, you must make her think your thoughtfulness is due to your thoughtfulness for her mother ; she will be more gratified by the show of consideration for her mother than by another display of consideration for herself.'

At the same time, fearful of ruffling him, possibly even of vexing him into rebellion, by any premature or indiscreet exercise of wifely authority, the young wife hoped to govern him *through* her influence over the sister who had so much influence over him. In this hope she began a practice of hinting to Mrs. Leigh what she might say to Byron on certain delicate and troubling matters. A good example of this practice is found in the way, in which she confided to her sister-in-law that the frequency of Byron's visits to Melbourne House caused her uneasiness. Of course, on his coming to town, Byron went quickly to call on his wife's aunt, Lady Melbourne, his 'second mother.' He went there repeatedly. He was continually calling there. Of course, the niece had no reason to resent his dutiful and affectionate attentiveness to her aunt. But the cousin was troubled at his frequent visits to a house, where he would be so sure, or likely, to see Lady Caroline Lamb. She was jealous, but pride and prudence combined to make her desirous of concealing the jealousy from her husband. If she even hinted that he was troubling himself overmuch about her aunt, he would detect the motive of the hint, and cut her to the quick by retorting, ' You mean, your aunt's daughter-in-law. You are jealous! You distrust your husband!'—But she would escape this suspicion and imputation, and yet carry her point, if she could induce Goose to say to her Baby, ' Take care you don't go so often to Melbourne House, as to make Pippin think you have a lingering weakness for Beautiful Silliness.' And in Lady Byron's uneasiness about the visits to Melbourne House, the reader sees the first rising cloud over her domestic happiness :—a cloud from which many drops were soon to fall. When Lady Caroline Lamb called on Lady Byron after Byron's withdrawal from England, she was received by her cousin with these words, ' I know all, Lady Caroline. He has told me all, and you could have saved me from all my misery.' It was natural for Lady Byron to take this view of her cousin's part in the dismal drama ; but she probably attached too much importance to the mischief done by the mischievous woman of fashion.

But though they had no differences before August 1815, the month did not close without bickerings, and by the beginning of September the husband and wife

were in the 'some time' of 'an unhappy sort of life,'
described in the First Canto of 'Don Juan,'—

> 'Don Jóse and the Donna Inez led
>   For some time an unhappy sort of life,
> Wishing each other, not divorced, but dead;
>   They lived respectably as man and wife,
> Their conduct was exceedingly well-bred,
>   And gave no outward signs of inward strife,
> Until at length the smother'd fire broke out,
> And put the business past all kind of doubt.
>
> 'For Inez call'd some druggists and physicians,
>   And tried to prove her loving lord was *mad*,
> But as he had some lucid intermissions,
>   She next decided he was only bad;
> Yet when they ask'd her for her depositions,
>   No sort of explanation could be had,
> Save that her duty both to man and God
> Required this conduct—which seem'd very odd.
>
> 'She kept a journal, where his faults were noted,
>   And open'd certain trunks of books and letters,
> All which might, if occasion served, be quoted;
>   And then she had all Seville for abettors,
> Besides her good old grandmother (who doted);
>   The hearers of her case became repeaters,
> Then advocates, inquisitors, and judges,
> Some for amusement, others for old grudges.'

It is needless to say that in thus describing his
domestic troubles, the poet was not severely accurate. In his talk with Medwin, Byron admitted that
the spies employed to watch and gather evidence
against him were Mrs. Clermont, acting on her own
account, and persons obeying Mrs. Clermont's instructions. In the same talk, though he charged Lady
Byron with sending the epistles to the writer's husband, he pointed to Mrs. Clermont as the person,

who had broken open his writing-desk, and taken from it the letters he had received from a married woman before his marriage. He expressly acquitted Lady Byron of being accountable for the visit of Dr. Baillie and the lawyer to ascertain whether he was insane. 'I do not, however, tax Lady Byron with this transaction : probably she was not privy to it,' he is represented as saying to the reporter who, though a simpleton, was an honest gentleman.

It is certain that Lady Byron and her husband separated on account of reasons covered by the familiar and elastic phrase 'incompatibility of temper,' —a phrase that may cover serious unkindness, scarcely a hair's breadth short of legal cruelty. It is certain that no one of the various kinds of flagrant immorality charged against her husband by scandalous rumour was the reason why Lady Byron determined to leave him. It is certain *if* he was guilty of any one of the charges so made by report, the sin was done with a secresy, that saved it from being an insult to his wife, and made him certain neither she nor any of her friends knew of it. On all these points fortunately for human nature there exists conclusive evidence, that will sooner or later be published to the world.

It is certain also that she did not determine to repudiate him for trivial reasons ; but for reasons so serious and weighty, that they will not be deemed positively insufficient for her justification, even by those who may on hearing them be disposed to deem them scarcely sufficient to justify her action. It is certain that from the beginning of September to the date of her accouchement,—a time when it was especially incumbent on him to make sympathetic allowance for the unevenness of her spirits, and to show her extraordinary kindness ; and afterwards from the day of her child's birth to the day of her journey to Leicestershire, he treated her with extraordinary unkindness for which her conduct afforded no sufficient excuse. It is certain that she had good reason to think he might be insane; and instead of being singular in attributing his strange behaviour to mental disease she was countenanced in this view of his case by the poet's sister Augusta and his cousin George Byron, who were both of opinion that his conduct might possibly be due to trouble of brain, falling within the term of ' mental derangement.' On all these points, fortunately for human nature there exists evidence.

No doubt, Harness heard nonsensical stories of the poet's ill-treatment of his wife ; but however absurd they may have been in their details or from the peculiarities of the narrator, the stories about the discomfort of the lady's meals pointed to no slight matter, but to a constant source of daily and serious annoyance. Byron's alleged dislike to see women eating was probably nothing more than a poetical way of stating the fact that it irked and irritated him to see them enjoying their food, whilst he, with an ever keen appetite pinching and biting his vitals, resisted the cravings of appetite. And he was not the man to pretend day after day at his own table, that he liked what he disliked extremely. He was not the man to put himself to the discomfort of ' making believe ' that he enjoyed his dinner and chat with his wife, when he was all the while longing for the meal to be over.

The consequence was that, after the earlier months of her married life, Lady Byron usually breakfasted alone, lunched alone, and dined alone,—or, what was even less cheerful, had the solitude of her meals broken by a husband who came in for a few minutes in the middle of a repast, or after showing himself at the outset of dinner ran off at the second course. Just as life's happiness is made up largely of small, daily, unremembered enjoyments, the misery of human existence is made up in a great degree of countless petty, daily, and too often bitterly remembered vexations, any one of which may be fairly termed insignificant. It follows therefore that the comfortlessness, coming to Lady Byron's life from her husband's regimen of diet, is a matter not to be overlooked, in the consideration of her position at a time, when—as a young wife, looking forward to the perils of child-birth, at a distance from the mother and father whom she loved vehemently— she had especial need of her husband's tenderest consideration and most soothing speech.

One of the earliest causes of discord between the young husband and his younger wife was his determination to leave England as soon as possible,—to breathe a warmer air, and live under bluer skies ; to escape from the duns and fogs of London, and be at ease and freedom in a sunny clime. Four years since he had returned from Greece in submission to the tyranny of circumstances, with the intention of leaving England again as soon as he should settle his affairs. On February 28, 1811, he had avowed this purpose to his mother in the letter from Athens, in which he says, ' I feel myself so much a citizen of the world, that the spot where I can enjoy a delicious climate, and every luxury, at a less expense than a common college life in England, will always be a country to me ; and such are in fact the shores of the Archipelago.' In the following June, he wrote to Hodgson that, 'after having a little repaired his irreparable affairs,' he would be off again to Spain or the East, where he could at least have ' cloudless skies and a cessation from impertinence.' He had no sooner relinquished his purpose of accompanying the Earl and Countess of Oxford to Sicily in the summer of 1813, than he began to lay plans for an expedition to Abyssinia. Immediately after 'the treacle-moon ' at Halnaby, he invited Moore to join him in a year's tour through Italy, adding significantly, ' If I take my wife, you can take yours.' Any annoyance in England made him restless ; and with him restlessness quickly shaped itself into a yearning to go abroad, to a land of sunshine, blue skies, and freedom. Moore knew there was trouble at 13 Piccadilly Terrace, on the morrow of January 5, 1816, when he read the letter ending, ' But never mind,—as somebody says, " for the blue sky bends over all ! " I only should be glad, if it bent over me where it is a little bluer ; like the "skyish top of blue Olympus," which, by the way, looked very white when I last saw it.'

Lady Byron opposed this wish to roam. She did not oppose it warmly or with excessive firmness. She only let him see that if his heart was in the East, hers was in old England, where she had a father and mother, and would soon have a nursery with a child in it. Now-a-days, with railroads and steamboats and telegraphic cables, to live in Madrid or Cairo or Athens is only to live in a rather out-of-the-way part of England. But in 1815 foreign travel was temporary expatriation. Tourists of pleasure returned from southern Europe to London, to be shocked at the gaps made in the ranks of their home-loving kindred. On preparing for his Eastern tour Byron had told his mother he had better roam the world at once, as his marriage would probably end his days and opportunities for roaming. But now that he had been married some eight or nine months; now that his young bride was on the point of giving birth to her first child, he thought it preposterous that she should expect him to curb his passion for roaming, out of regard for her feelings. After Byron's death Hobhouse, who loved him dearly in spite of his failings, used to say that selfishness was the grand defect and blemish of his character; and it was not in the power of the poet's closest friends to gainsay the severe judgment. It was a curious failing for a young man of vivid sensibility and generous impulses, who could not see pain or sorrow without weeping over it, who in his most urgent pecuniary straits would give a struggling author, a miserable widow, a group of wretched orphans, half his rapidly sinking balance at his bankers; — for the young man who won the love of men, women and thoughtless children by the completeness of his sympathy with them. But selfishness *was* Byron's grand failing. He would concede, he would give away anything except the one thing on which he had for the moment set his heart; but as soon as any one denied him that one thing, or tried to take it from his hands, the selfishness overpowered every generous force of his nature.

Lady Byron had no sooner declared her disinclination to travel in countries far away from England, than she became a person, set on denying him enjoyment for which he yearned, a hard and unsympathetic creature to whom he was linked for ever by that rash, fatal act—his marriage. He told her he did not wish for her company in his journeyings by sea and land. She could have her own pleasure and remain in England, whilst he would please himself at a distance from her. As she preferred her mother and father to her husband, he would not imitate her example and hinder her from pursuing happiness in her own way. But he would not be her slave any more than he would be her tyrant. He and Hobhouse would go abroad together ; and before Lady Byron went to Leicestershire with her babe, Byron and Hobhouse had arranged to leave England together in the spring. The young wife saw that she was not necessary to her husband's happiness. The pleasure of touring was greater to him than the pleasure of living with her; the delight of visiting new scenes, keener than his delight in her society. All this as the time drew nearer and nearer for the birth of her child !

This difference having arisen between them, Byron and his wife daily drifted farther apart. Ceasing to trouble himself about her poetry, he was seldom present at her meals. Taking little note of her proceedings, he spent more time at the Drury Lane Theatre, where it devolved upon him (as a member of the Sub-Committee of Management,—or Mismanagement, as malicious censors averred) to confer with dramatic authors, peruse bad comedies and worse tragedies, take counsel with actors, and arbitrate on the disputes of actresses.

Working hard on his poems ('The Siege of Corinth' and 'Parisina,' written as his troubles grew thicker, passed through the printers' hands when his troubles were at their thickest) he was annoyed when his wife disturbed him at his work by coming into his room. 'Byron, I am in your way?' she inquired on one occasion, when she entered the room, and found him standing before the fire, musing on his troubles: —the answer was 'Damnably!' After admitting that he made this unmannerly reply, the poet observed to Medwin, 'I was afterwards sorry, and reproached myself for the expression; but it escaped me unconsciously—involuntarily; I hardly knew what I said.' But he said things far more brutal and inexcusable. In her hearing he inveighed against his folly in marrying her, and vowed to extricate himself from the unendurable bondage of the union. He did worse, he himself told her that he had persisted in wooing her till he won her—not from motives of love and devotion, but from resentment and a thirst for vengeance:—an absolutely false statement that in his passionate incontinence of speech was probably made to other people. From this mad and utterly untrue speech came the revolting reports of the brutal words said to have been spoken by him to her during the journey from Seaham to Halnaby, and in the subsequent weeks when he was overflowing with affection for her. At Venice Byron confessed to Moore that there were occasions during his life with Lady Byron, when he had 'breathed the breath of bitter words.' From these examples of his more violent utterances to his young wife, it may be seen that the poet told Moore in that respect no more than the bare truth against himself. When Byron breathed the breath of bitter words, the breath was hot indeed and the words were very bitter. It has been suggested by successive writers that he frightened Lady Byron with wild fables of his wickedness. It is conceivable that he was guilty of such freaks of morbid humour, but no satisfactory evidence that he terrified her in this way has come to the writer of this page.

At other times, instead of cutting her with sharp and burning speeches, he punished her with silence. In his childhood he had been given to fits of what he styled 'silent rage;' and now, sulking and scowling all the while, he maintained an insulting and exasperating taciturnity to the victim of his wrath for days together. His violence, also, expressed itself in other ways than speech. In a sudden rage at an incident, arising out of his distress for money, he threw a favourite watch on the hearth, and then smashed it to pieces with the poker. Readers will be the better able to account for all this maniacal behaviour — the rages of false words, the rages of stubborn silence, the outpouring of wrath on a favourite watch, as though it were a living creature — when they are told that Byron was at this time (no less than in later times of his career) a laudanum-drinker.

The man, who chewed tobacco to deaden the pain of his rigorous fasting, may have had recourse to opium for the same purpose. But the practice of taking opium in some form or other was so common in the higher classes of English society from the

opening of the present century till De Quincey's
'Confessions of an Opium Eater' (1822) called attention to the pernicious effects of the indulgence, that
the poet may have taken his first dose of the drug at
the advice of Lady Caroline Lamb (who is known to
have been an habitual laudanum-drinker in her later
time), or at the suggestion of some other person of
fashion. The habit may have been formed in the
East, and brought home with him, together with the
two cantos of 'Childe Harold.' Anyhow there is
the very best evidence that Byron was taking
laudanum at this point of his story.—Another fact
to be borne in mind respecting his condition, when
other persons besides his young wife watched his
eccentricities with anxious suspicion, is that just at
the opening of 1816 he was visited with jaundice. With an over-wrought brain, nerves shaken
by laudanum, temper incessantly irritated by his
creditors, digestive organs impaired by fasting, a
liver undergoing constipation, and a mind torn
and oppressed by matrimonial misadventure, he
may well have said and done things for which
charity would be slow to hold him accountable.
People have made merry over the folly of Lady
Byron's advisers in regarding his hysterical emotion,
at witnessing Kean's impersonation of Sir Giles
Overreach, as a matter worthy of mention in the
list of sixteen symptoms of insanity; but to those
who were unaware of the nervous peculiarity referred
to in previous pages of this work, his overpowering
agitation from so inconsiderable a cause may well
have seemed worthy of medical notice.

There were numerous good reasons for his wife, in

common with his sister and cousin, to attribute to
mental derangement the symptoms which the men of
medicine accounted for in another way. Three or
four months earlier the patient had given every
indication of contentment with his lot and of delight
in his wife's society. Now, though she was about
to present him with offspring and *by his own admission* had treated him with consistent affectionateness,
he regarded her with aversion and addressed her with
harshness and insult. At the beginning of August
he could reflect on the previous seven months as a
period of unruffled harmony, and was exulting in her
generous acquiescence in the will he had made for the
advantage of Augusta and her children, to the injury
of his own future offspring. And now in October he
was assuring her with every appearance of sincerity
that he abhorred wedlock, and had married her solely
from resentment and for revenge. What kindlier or
more rational view could a young woman take of
such behaviour than that her husband's quick and
subtle genius had broken down the thin partition
that was understood to divide great wits from madness? From the outset of his manly time Byron
recognised an element of insanity in his mental constitution, and was now and again apprehensive that the
madness would eventually conquer all the other forces
of his great genius. And yet he and his friends
affected to think Lady Byron guilty of monstrous
impertinence in thinking him mad when he certainly
behaved very much like a madman.

Shunned and harshly used by a husband, whose
aversion for her caused him to look away from her or
down on the carpet more often than at her when they

met, Lady Byron was glad to welcome to her house
her old governess, Mrs. Clermont, who came to stay
with her former pupil in the midst of her trouble and
anxieties.   It would not be surprising if it could be
shown that, in her want of sympathy and in the
absence of a more suitable confidante, Lady Byron
told Mrs. Clermont too much of her griefs, and was
in other respects imprudently communicative to the
person, whom Byron came to regard as the principal
cause of his wife's resolve to repudiate him.   Evidence there doubtless is to support the general
opinion that Lady Byron was guilty of a weakness,
inconsistent with her abundant self-respect and
habitual regard for her own dignity ; but the evidence is by no means conclusive.   Before one could
give a confident opinion on this point, it would be
necessary to know the exact time and other circumstances of the withdrawal of the letters from the
poet's desk, the way in which they came to Lady
Byron's hands, and the time when she sent them to
the writer's husband.   Byron, as readers know, acquitted his wife of, or at least forbore to charge her
with, being an accomplice to the withdrawal of the
letters.   Moreover there are grounds for believing
that at least till she went into Leicestershire, Lady
Byron maintained a proper reserve to her former
preceptress.   Lady Byron was certainly under the
impression that her parents knew nothing of her
domestic troubles, when she arrived at Kirkby
Mallory in January 1816 ; and she could scarcely
have been under this impression, had she talked
freely of her griefs and cares to her mother's especial
and confidential dependant.   That Mrs. Clermont

was a vigilant, busy, prying, meddlesome, scheming, mischievous woman, as women of her years and way of living often are, is conceivable though not quite certain. Reasons altogether distinct from Byron's vulgarly abusive ' Sketch ' of the woman, whose activity in his affairs caused him to say at the moment of signing the deed of separation, ' This is Mrs. Clermont's work,' make it probable that she deserved her odious name of ' the Mischief-maker.' She certainly did Byron an ill turn. But it does not follow that she was so dangerously influential over Lady Byron before the middle of January as the poet wished people to imagine. Nor does it follow that she was so completely without a natural right to be curious about his doings and meddlesome in his concerns, as he caused the world to think.

CHAPTER XVI.

THE SEPARATION.

Ada's Birth — Augusta, the Comforter — Lady Byron's Withdrawal
from London — Her case against her Husband — Written Statement
for Doctor and Lawyer — Lady Noel's Interview with Dr. Lushington — Lady Byron's 'Additional Statement' — Mrs. Clermont,
the Mischief-maker — Jane Clermont, Allegra's Mother — The 'Fare
Thee Well' — Results of its Publication.

THE discord between Lord and Lady Byron had not
diminished, when their daughter,

> ' The child of love — though born in bitterness,
> And nurtured in convulsion,'

was born on December 10, 1815, and soon afterwards
was christened Augusta Ada, the former of the two
names being given to her in compliment to her aunt,
the Hon. Mrs. Leigh, who was one of the babe's
sponsors at the baptism. In those darkest days of
December 1815, and January 1816, Mrs. Leigh was
in her sister-in-law's house, nursing her, comforting
her, encouraging her to take a hopeful view of Byron's
state of health, which caused the comforter no less
anxiety than it had caused the wretched wife and
mother. George Byron was a frequent caller at
13 Piccadilly Terrace, and in his astonishment at the
poet's recent treatment of his wife, concurred with the
two ladies in thinking that the behaviour, so perplexing to persons of no medical experience, was or at

least might be referable to mental illness. Bailiffs were in the house, and the post kept bringing letters to quicken Byron's anger and humiliation at his pecuniary embarrassments. On one point, at least, he showed his good sense. A house occupied by bailiffs and besieged by clamorous tradesmen being no fit abode for his wife, he begged Lady Byron to be off with her babe as soon as possible to her mother in the country;—the request being made in writing on January 6, 1816; so made possibly on account of the husband's desire to avoid a personal interview with the woman who six months since had been the delight of his heart.

Lady Byron forthwith made her arrangements for the journey to Kirkby Mallory, which she deferred no later than January 15th, though it was questionable whether her strength would be sufficiently restored by that time for the fatigue of travelling in so cold a season. Mrs. Leigh, who after paying her sister-in-law a long visit wished to return to her husband and children in Cambridgeshire, was entreated by Lady Byron to remain yet a while in Piccadilly. Augusta had been her grateful sister's best comforter; Augusta could control her brother in his fits of anger; if Augusta would remain with the invalid in London, his wife at Kirkby Mallory would receive regular and reliable news of the progress, for good or ill, of affairs in London. It was by such arguments that Lady Byron induced Augusta to postpone her return to Six Mile Bottom. On January 8, 1816, after talking the matter over with Augusta and George Byron, Lady Byron consulted Dr. Baillie about her husband's state of health; but this visit to the physician was not the cause of the call he made at a later date (in the company of a lawyer) on the poet,—for which intrusion on his privacy Byron believed his wife to have been in no way accountable. The doctor's advice was that Lady Byron should go into the country in accordance with her husband's desire, and during her absence from town should write him bright and animating letters. It was arranged between Lady Byron and Augusta that they should correspond daily; so that whilst the one would know every change in her husband's case and every incident of the life in her London house, the other would be informed of every matter of Lady Byron's intercourse with her parents, having any relation to the poet's interests. The agreement of these ladies to write thus frequently and fully to one another, demonstrates the completeness of their mutual confidence, and of their wish for the greatest possible measure of sisterly intercourse at a time of the keenest anxiety to both of them. Of the affectionate warmth of their correspondence a notion may be formed from the scraps and extracts of some of Lady Byron's letters to her dear sister, that were published in 1869 by the ' Quarterly Review ' in the article on the Byron Mystery :—one of the most sagacious and judicious, and in every respect ablest articles, ever contributed to a Review, where literary adroitness and strength are matters of course.

Taking her child with her, Lady Byron left London on January 15, 1816, and entered her father's house on the following day, with the hope of having Byron with her in Leicestershire before the middle of next month. The hope cannot have been a confident one ; for the view she took of his illness necessarily made her apprehensive that a month hence he might be no fit inmate for her mother's house. One of her apprehensions was that he would commit suicide. She and Augusta had more than once spoken apprehensively to George Byron about the invalid's laudanum-bottle, their fear being that he might take an overdose of its contents. Still she left town with the hope of seeing him at Kirkby Mallory in the middle of February ; for he had promised to come to her before he should go abroad :—the promise being accompanied with a very remarkable and important statement of the poet's main purpose in determining to join his wife in Leicestershire, and to stay with her there for some weeks.

Like most young husbands, with hereditary dignity to transmit to their descendants,—indeed, like most newly married men of every social degree,—Byron had set his heart on having a son. On October 31, 1815, he had written to Moore, 'Lady B—— is in full progress. Next month will bring to light (with the aid of "Juno Lucina *fer opem*," or rather *opes*, for the last are most wanted), the tenth wonder of the world—Gil Blas being the eighth, and he (my son's father) the ninth.' His child's sex had therefore caused Byron much disappointment, in which Lady Byron sympathised. As the peerage, to which she had a prospect of succession would descend in the female line in case of her death without male issue, Lady Byron was less troubled than her husband at having a daughter, when a son would have been more welcome. She was however disappointed by the domestic incident, and before she left London for

Kirkby Mallory was comforting herself with the hope that her next child would be a son. Byron was touched far more acutely by the misadventure; and as he was not given to hide his feelings out of regard for the feelings of others, it is not wonderful that he allowed Lady Byron to see his vexation. It is less an affair for surprise than regret that he allowed his annoyance to express itself in petulant words. Like Lady Byron he hoped for better fortune in the coming time; and on announcing his purpose of joining her in Leicestershire, he told her that he would remain there in her society until she should be in the first stage of another progress to maternity:—an assurance that afforded her the liveliest gratification. In confidence Augusta was informed of Byron's intention to visit Leicestershire in the ensuing month, and also of the chief purpose of the visit. After her sister-in-law's departure, it devolved on Mrs. Leigh to use her influence over her brother to make him follow his wife to Kirkby Mallory; and for the achievement of this end, she took occasion to influence Le Manu (Byron's apothecary), through her cousin, George Byron, who received a hint that he should instruct the medical attendant to urge his patient to go into the country for his health's sake. It follows therefore that, when she left London for Leicestershire, Lady Byron was animated by a hope, which could not have occupied her breast had she not still regarded her husband affectionately. On her way from town to Kirkby Mallory, Lady Byron wrote her husband a tender and cordial letter (beginning with 'Dear Duck' and signed with the pet name 'Pippin'), and on the following day (January 16) after her arrival at her parents' house she wrote him another epistle in the same vein of humorous fondness. This second letter was written by a wife still hopeful of seeing her husband in the course of a few weeks, in order that an heir might be born to the Byron barony. And Lady Byron continued in this hope until she received intelligence from London that her husband, though seriously out of health, was *not* insane. Seventy years since people neither knew nor troubled themselves so much as they do now-a-days about the transmission of malady from parents to offspring. Participating in every anxiety, Mrs. Leigh was cognizant of every hope that occupied Lady Byron's mind during this season of their common trouble. 'There is no one whose society is dearer to me, or can contribute more to my happiness,' Lady Byron wrote, at the moment of leaving her husband to his sister's care, in one of her letters to Augusta, published fourteen years since in the 'Quarterly Review.' The mutual confidence of the two sisters-in-law was perfect. Eloquent of their affection for one another, the confidence was no less eloquent of the high opinion Byron's wife had of his sister's womanly discretion and womanly goodness.

When Lady Byron appeared before them at Kirkby Mallory on the 16th of January, Sir Ralph and Lady Noel saw from her looks that she was far from well. She was pale and thin ; but till she spoke to them about it, they knew nothing of the anxiety that had been oppressing and fretting her for weeks and months. Before she went to bed she had told them her whole story,—withholding from them nothing of the cares she had brought with her to Leicestershire. Though she made a full statement—*a statement without a single reserve*—Lady Byron said nothing to move her parents to indignation against their child's husband. Byron was ill in body and mind, especially in mind. He was set on going abroad when he was unfit for travel. His wife was possessed by terrifying apprehensions for him. After hearing her story, *from which nothing was withheld*, Sir Ralph and Lady Noel said that Byron must be induced to come to Kirkby Mallory, where he should be considered and humoured in everything. The knowledge of the cause of any perverse humour he might display would make it impossible for Sir Ralph and Lady Noel to resent the perversity. Lady Noel, a kindly and well-intentioned woman, though excitable and passionate, made sensible suggestions of measures to be taken for the sufferer's advantage. Before their talk ended, Lady Byron and her parents came to several conclusions. It was decided that Lady Noel should write to Byron, entreating him to come to them. Respecting Byron's project for going abroad with Hobhouse, it was decided that, should it appear that the poet was in no fit state for the enterprise, it would be well for Sir Ralph and Captain Byron to wait upon Hobhouse, and give him their reasons for feeling strongly it would be hurtful to Byron to travel for the present,—hurtful to him in respect to his domestic peace and reputation as well as his health. In the face of such a representation from Lady Byron's father and Lord Byron's nearest kinsman, Hobhouse it was thought would not venture to persist in encouraging the invalid to go abroad.

The 17th of January, 1816—the day on which Lady Noel with her daughter's concurrence wrote the kind and sympathetic letter to Byron, inviting him to Kirkby Mallory—was a day of pain and distress to Lady Byron. She had of late suffered severely from acute headache; and on this day the headache assailed her with unusual vehemence, and put her to extraordinary torture. It cheered her to know that the invitation had been despatched to Byron ; and in the intervals between the neuralgic paroxysms she could look forward to the time when Byron would come to her. The next morning's post brought news from London that troubled her ;—news that her husband was not insane. Le Manu's report was that he detected nothing of mental derangement in his patient. The apothecary was confident that the symptoms, which had occasioned Lady Byron, Augusta and Captain Byron, so much alarm, were referable to the combined excitement and exhaustion of an overwrought brain, the excessive vexation to the patient's temper from the action of his creditors, the melancholy arising from domestic annoyances, and the disorder of the liver, now declaring itself in manifest jaundice.

On receiving this intelligence of her husband's mental soundness, Lady Byron declared that she would never live again with the man who, being sane, had treated her in a way, for which insanity alone could be pleaded as a sufficient excuse. Even yet if it could be proved that he was insane, she could live with him and love him ; but should Le Manu's opinion be confirmed, she would never again put herself in the power of the man who had treated her so ill. Thus the case stood on the 18th of January, when Lady

Noel was making ready for her journey to London,—
in the first place to consult Dr. Baillie ; and then, in
case Byron should be found of sound mind, to take
counsel with Dr. Lushington. For the information
of the physicians, and, if needful, for the instruction
of the lawyer, Lady Byron made with her own pen a
statement of her reasons for thinking her husband
mad ;—a statement that was a repetition of the
matters she had told her father and mother on the
16th instant. Notwithstanding what Lady Byron
wrote and published to the contrary, fourteen years
later, this statement comprised (without reserve of
any kind) Lady Byron's whole case against her
husband, as it then stood. Thus instructed and
authorised to act for her daughter, she set forth on
her mission ; and for several days after their arrival
in London, Lady Noel and her companion (Mrs.
Clermont—the mischief-maker) were busy.

The first notable consequence of the activity of
these two ladies was the visit, which Dr. Baillie and
the lawyer paid Lord Byron, whose treatment of them,
however wanting it may have been in courtesy, satisfied the intruders that he was no madman. The
physician and lawyer having no doubt on this important point, the ladies went off to Dr. Lushington,
to learn whether Byron's treatment of his wife would
entitle her to the benefit of judicial separation. After
hearing and considering the case submitted to him by
Lady Noel, who showed no disposition to exaggerate
the facts, the counsel was of opinion that, though the
poet's misconduct would entitle his wife to judicial
separation, it was not of so heinous a kind as to
render separation indispensable. It was a case for

reconciliation ; and the counsel wished to be of service in bringing the quarrel to an amicable conclusion. This opinion was given on what was then the whole of Lady Byron's case against her husband. The evidence is more than sufficient that she *withheld nothing* of her *original* case from her parents.

In the absence of her mother and Mrs. Clermont, Lady Byron spent doleful days and wretched nights at Kirkby Mallory. There were moments when, in alarm for her own mind, she felt she was in no fit state to have the management of herself. One day she was seen riding about the Kirkby Mallory Park at her horse's fullest gallop. On the morrow she could not leave the room, where, racked with head-ache and burning with fever, she alternately lay on a couch or paced over the floor,—crying to God for help, declaring she had done nothing why he should desert her. Of Byron she thought by turns bitterly and tenderly, resentfully and relentingly. To lessen her distress of heart and brain, she took pen and wrote her husband a letter of vehement feeling (the letter mentioned by previous writers about Byron), which she withheld at the last moment from the post. Had Byron come before her, with the gentlest of his smiles, the richest tones of his irresistible voice, and the light of love in his eyes, when she was penning that letter, there would have been an end to their discord. This passage of softening emotion was followed by hard moods, and gusts of anger. On being told that to get judicial separation it would perhaps be necessary for her to endure the scandal and indignity of a trial, she declared she would endure any shame rather than the misery of living with the man who had treated her so badly. When she talked vindictively of her husband, Lady Byron's words of wrath were somewhat seasoned with self-righteousness. As for Byron's sensibility and the pain and shame, that would come to him from the scandal of separation, Lady Byron thought it was better his pride should be broken and punished in this, than in the next world. It was hard she should be made the instrument of his correction. But God's will must be done. She must do her duty. When Lady Byron had begun to think in this wild and insolent and self-righteous way, the chance was small for the speedy reconcilement of the angry husband and resentful wife.

In all this miserable business George Byron and Augusta were wholly in Lady Byron's confidence, if not wholly on her side. George Byron indeed was completely on her side. In his opinion the fault was altogether with his cousin,—none of it with his cousin's wife. And though she clung fondly to her brother, Augusta was brave enough to tell him the fault was chiefly, if not wholly, with him. Byron never in his heart forgave his cousin for siding with Lady Byron in this bitter contention ; but he admired and honoured his sister more than ever, for the steadiness and courage with which she defended his wife and censured him. To the last hour of her sojourn at 13 Piccadilly Terrace, Augusta never humoured her brother by speaking a single word in censure of his wife.

One result of Lady Byron's perfect confidence in Mrs. Leigh and George Byron, was that they knew much more than the poet of his wife's doings and purposes, after the 15th of January. Byron did not know of his wife's intention to repudiate him till the 2nd of February, 1816, when he received Sir Ralph Noel's letter of proposal for an amicable separation. On that day Mrs. Leigh and her cousin, Captain George Anson Byron, R.N., had been in possession of Lady Byron's purpose for more than a week; but the cousins forbore to give Byron a hint of the course affairs had taken, thinking it best in every way that the poet should get his first knowledge of his wife's determination from her father. Consequently Augusta, still her brother's guest at 13 Piccadilly Terrace, and George Byron, a daily visitor at his cousin's house, were aware of Lady Byron's decision on this grand question some eight days before it was communicated to the person whom it concerned most deeply.

The exact date of Lady Noel's conference with Dr. Lushington is not known to the writer of this page. But the conference seems to have taken place on January 22, 1816. It cannot well have been earlier. It certainly was not later. A fortnight or three weeks later ('about a fortnight or perhaps more,' said Dr. Lushington in 1830) Lady Byron was in London with her father on business touching the separation. It has been assumed by most of the many writers about this business, that Sir Ralph Noel was throughout the affair a mere cypher in the hands of the over-bearing Lady Noel and the artful Mrs. Clermont,—and had no strong feeling on the subject. In this last respect, at least, he has been misrepresented. He was the first to cry out for the lawyer. And as soon as he had reason to think Byron sane, he became the stern censor of his only child's husband. On learning that the poet certainly was *not* mad, the baronet was pugnacious in the highest degree and would not hear of reconciliation. Lady Byron probably took her own course in the matter from first to last. But if her action was influenced by parental authority, the influence came from her father rather than her mother. If Byron knew this, he never admitted it. He preferred to attribute his domestic troubles and consequent social disgrace to the rancour of two deceitful women rather than the judgment of an honourable and sensible man. Writing to Moore on February 29, 1816, when he was in the fiercest period of his first fury against Lady Noel and Mrs. Clermont, Byron said, 'My little girl is in the country, and, they tell me, is a very fine child, and now nearly three months old. Lady Noel (my mother-in-law, or, rather, *at* law) is at present overlooking it. Her daughter (Miss Milbanke that was) is, I believe, in London with her father. A Mrs. C. (now a kind of housekeeper and spy of Lady N.'s) who, in her better days, was a washerwoman, is supposed to be—by the learned—very much the occult cause of our late domestic discrepancies. In all this business, I am the sorriest for Sir Ralph. He and I are equally punished, though *magis pares quam similes* in our afflictions. Yet it is hard for both to suffer for the fault of one, and so it is—I shall be separated from my wife ; he will retain his.' This was Byron's way of putting his case against the women, and showing his disposition (possibly sincere) to regard Sir Ralph as his friend.

Whilst Lady Byron was in town with her father, she had an interview with Dr. Lushington, ' about a fortnight, or perhaps more, after the advocate's first interview with Lady Noel.' At that interview Lady Byron informed Dr. Lushington of facts, which the lawyer in 1830 was of opinion could not have been known to Sir Ralph. These additional facts had such an effect upon the lawyer, that, instead of continuing to regard the case as one for reconciliation, he declared that reconciliation was impossible. On receiving the same additional information, Sir Samuel Romilly underwent the same change of opinion and declared it no case for reconcilement. Writing in 1830, fourteen years after the events, Lady Byron spoke of these additional facts, as matters she had reserved from her parents, when penning the statement for her mother to submit to medical and legal advisers in January 1816. 'She,' Lady Byron wrote in 1830 of her mother's part in the affair, 'was empowered by me to take legal opinions on a written statement of mine, though I had then reasons for reserving a part of the case from the knowledge even of my father and mother.' Writing so long after the affair with insufficient memoranda Lady Byron may well have imagined that these additional matters were part of her original case against her husband, when in truth they came to her knowledge at some time subsequent to 15 January, 1816. The memory of the most honest witnesses is so treacherous and unreliable, that to suggest Lady Byron made this mistake in 1830 is to raise no suspicion of her general veracity, or of her *bona fides* on that particular occasion. After making her statements (of January 16 and January 18, 1816) to her parents, Lady Byron believed the statements had been explicit. Affecting to take her parents wholly into her confidence, and causing them to think themselves so treated, Lady Byron cannot have been innocent of deceit, if whilst professing to tell them everything she withheld the chief fact from them. Disregard for truth certainly was not one of Lady Byron's failings at this early stage of her career or (though she lived to say things strangely untrue) at any time of her passage through life. There is other evidence that Lady Byron's original statement to her parents was the whole of her case against her husband up to January 15, 1816. But of this evidence there is no need to give the particulars.

The additional statement, that had so great an effect on Dr. Lushington and Sir Samuel Romilly, was either a false statement (which is in the highest degree improbable), or a statement of matters that came to Lady Byron after her first communication to her parents. As the poet was living more or less under espionage, circumstances to his greater discredit with Lady Byron may well have come to her ears in the course of three or four weeks. What was the statement? By those, who gave their credulity to the monstrous invention set forth in Mrs. Beecher Stowe's book, it has been assumed that this mysterious and additional statement to Lady Byron's counsel was a communication which could not have failed to inspire the lawyer with unutterable repugnance to the Honourable Mrs. Leigh, and to make him think her unfit for the society of any Christian woman. Had the mysterious statement been what the writer of that lamentable book fancied it to be, Lady Byron would scarcely have told Dr.

Lushington, only a few days later, that she was longing to have an interview with her dear sister Augusta—her child's godmother—for the purpose of conferring with her on their domestic interests. Nor would even so courteous a gentleman as young Dr. Lushington, on receiving this piece of information, have merely advised Lady Byron to keep away from Ada's godmother, till the business of the separation was settled, lest their necessarily emotional conversation at so critical a moment should have a prejudicial effect on their future intercourse. Moreover, had the mysterious statement been what Mrs. Stowe was induced to imagine it, Lady Byron could scarcely have continued for many years to live on terms of close and affectionate intimacy with her sister-in-law, and at the same time have been able to retain the cordial sympathy and chivalric admiration of her famous lawyer.

What was the mysterious statement of which so much has been written? What were the words, spoken in strict confidence by Lady Byron to Dr. Lushington, that made the advocate take another and altogether different view of his client's case? What were the facts—or the allegations which two hard-headed lawyers were content to receive as proven facts—that, besides working so great a change in the lady's legal adviser, determined the counsel on the other side (Sir Samuel Romilly) to return the fee with which he had been retained, on the ground that Lady Byron had a right to the privileges of separation, and that under the newly discovered circumstances of the case Byron had no right to resist her demand? What were the facts or the allegations that affected Byron's own counsel in so remarkable a manner? Before an attempt is made to answer these questions, or rather to indicate the right answers to them, something must be said of two women who exercised no small influence over the poet's career.

Two ladies named Clermont are memorable personages of the Byronic story; Mrs. Clermont, the Mischief-maker, the mature woman of proverbial infamy, and Jane Clermont, the sparkling girl of fervid temper and melancholy fate, the mother of Allegra. Whilst Mrs. Clermont appeared at Lady Noel's receptions as the whilom governess of Miss Milbanke, and the gentlewoman ever in faithful attendance on Lady Byron's overbearing and rather hot-tempered mother, Jane Clermont shone as one of the beauties of a literary set, some of whose members Lady Noel condescended to favour. Of Mrs. Clermont the Mischief-maker every one has heard from the satire Byron poured upon her, almost as much to his own discredit as to her infamy. But the poet's biographers have hitherto been strangely and suspiciously reticent about the charming girl who gave Byron his natural daughter. The surname of these two ladies has been spelt in various ways. One comes upon it in the form of Claremont, Clairmont, and Charlemont as well as Clermont.—Jane Clermont (as her name is rightly spelt in the British Museum Catalogue), the clever and brilliant daughter of William Godwin's second wife, had no liking either for her Christian name or her surname. Dropping Jane (either because it was Christian or unromantic), she cut the second syllable from her surname, and adapting the first syllable of it to her sense of the fitness of things, called herself—Claire. A beautiful brunette, with fine though irregular features, this girl of a wayward spirit and Italian aspect called on Byron, as a person of power in the Drury Lane Theatre, when he was in the midst of his domestic troubles. Claire's purpose in the visit was to ask the poet to introduce her as an actress to the stage. The girl's name caught the ear of the poet, whose pulse always quickened at the sound of his old schoolmate's name (Clare); and the brightness of her beauty charmed his fancy.

Why Claire's application for employment on the stage was unsuccessful does not appear. Possibly Byron saw she would not make a good actress. Possibly he thought she would do better by becoming his mistress. Any how the poet conceived a passion for Claire; and Claire, 'holding' (as Mr. Rossetti expresses it) 'independent notions on questions such as that of marriage,' fell in love with the poet,—love that changed slowly to detestation. The day of Claire's first interview with Byron is unknown; the precise time at which she yielded to his addresses is of course unknown. Circumstances however point to some one of the earlier days of February 1816,— some day closely following on Sir Ralph Noel's announcement to Byron of his wife's desire for separation,—as the time at which the poet's brief association with William Godwin's step-daughter began. It is not very probable that it began earlier. It certainly did not begin before Lady Byron's departure from Piccadilly Terrace; though there is reason to believe that Lady Byron was ere long induced to imagine it began whilst she was in town. Partly because he felt that greater communicativeness would weaken the case against Lady Byron and put discredit on the 'Fare Thee Well,' and partly because he wished to spare the feelings of Godwin and Mrs. Shelley, Moore skates very lightly over the dangerous surface of Byron's scarcely edifying friendship with Allegra's mother. After insisting that Byron's official connexion with Drury Lane Theatre afforded nothing at which his wife could fairly take umbrage, he observes, 'The sole case in which he afforded anything like real grounds for such an accusation did not take place till after the period of the separation.' The *period of separation* is an elastic expression. It may be taken as covering only the time between Lady Byron's journey from Piccadilly to the second day of the following month, the day on which Byron was informed of his wife's purpose to keep away from him ; or it may be taken as covering the far greater time between Lady Byron's journey to the country and the 22nd of April, on which day the deed of separation was signed. In his own breast Moore used the expression in the smaller sense; whilst he intended his readers to construe it in the larger sense. Feeling it would be imprudent to make no reference to a matter which was imperfectly known to a large number of people, Moore thought it best to refer to it in a manner which would cause his readers to infer that the matter was of a time subsequent to the publication of the verses on the unforgiving wife.

Born at least as early as January 22, 1817, Allegra was no offspring of a premature birth. Leaving England on April the 25th, Byron saw nothing more of Claire till the 27th of the following month at Geneva, whither she travelled in the company of the Shelleys. Allegra's birth was due to nothing that took place after Byron's withdrawal from England. Byron had taken Claire for his goddess, and she had enjoyed his patronage for several weeks before he crossed the water from Dover to Ostend. The 'Fare Thee Well' (published in the middle of April 1816) did not set the sentimental women weeping, till the poet had for a considerable period found consolation in Claire's smiles for the cruelty of his unforgiving wife.

Whilst the poet's liaison with Jane Clermont was a new arrangement, it came to the knowledge of Mrs. Clermont, the Mischief-maker, who rendered Lord Byron the considerable dis-service, and her former pupil the questionable service of informing Lady Byron of the affair. The intelligence could not fail to incense Lady Byron. It did incense her. For though Byron could have urged in his defence, that he had not knelt to Claire till he had been discarded by his wife, the quickness with which he had found material consolation for her severity was peculiarly calculated to pique Lady Byron's self-love, quicken her animosity against him, and confirm her in her purpose of having nothing more to do with him. On coming to her knowledge, the liaison may well have been regarded by Lady Byron as a demonstration that he had never really loved her. An unsuspicious woman, in Lady Byron's position, would have been almost certain to assume that the liaison had begun before the separation, even to assume that her husband had sent her into the country, in order that he might enjoy the society of his mistress with greater security from detection. Being of a suspicious nature, Lady

Byron necessarily leapt to the erroneous conclusions to which an unsuspicious woman would have come.

Having taken this view of the liaison, it was natural for Lady Byron to place it amongst her original grounds of displeasure with her husband,—to think and speak of it as part of her original case against him.

It misses several barley-corns of certainty that Lady Byron's ' additional statement ' to her counsel had reference to her husband's intimacy with Jane Clermont ; and in the absence of the several barley-corns of positive evidence—likely to appear at any moment, almost certain to appear on the publication of the Hobhouse papers—that would either convert a considerable body of circumstantial evidence into a perfect historic demonstration or exhibit its fallaciousness, no personal historian would be justified in offering the present suggestion as anything more than a reasonable hypothesis, countenanced by a variety of facts. Readers are therefore cautioned to take the suggestion as nothing more than a reasonable hypothesis pointing to what will probably be found in due course the true explanation of matters that have caused the world much perplexity.

The strong evidence that Lady Byron's first statement (of January 16) of her case against her husband was a full and unreserved statement, the sufficient evidence that Lady Byron's written statement (of January 18) was no less explicit and complete, and the abundant evidence that Byron's marital behaviour up to January 15 had not been faulty in any important particular (discoverable to his wife) over and above the matters set forth in the two statements, are three several bodies of testimony justifying the strongest opinion that Lady Byron's additional statement [*if* a true one,—and the lady was not at that time at all likely to make an intentionally untrue one] must have related to some matters that, besides coming to her knowledge had taken place since her departure from London on January 15, 1816. Though the precise date of its commencement is unknown and most likely undiscoverable, Byron's intimacy with Jane Clermont *certainly* followed so closely on Lady Byron's journey to Kirkby Mallory, that it was probably known to her before she came up to town towards the middle of February to confer with Dr. Lushington. Byron knew that Lady Byron's 'additional statement' to Dr. Lushington (made towards the middle of February) was the cause of the advocate's new view of his client's case,—and the cause of Romilly's determination not to act professionally against Lady Byron's demand for a separation. Knowing this he regarded Mrs. Clermont as the person chiefly accountable for his domestic troubles; —as the person really accountable for the 'additional statement' that had operated so seriously to his disadvantage. The period of Byron's wildest wrath against Mrs. Clermont lay midway between the middle of February, when the 'additional statement' was made, and the middle of April, when the ignoble 'Sketch' was published. On February 29, 1816, he wrote to Moore the letter of coarse abuse of Mrs. Clermont, and he dated the satire on the obscure gentlewoman March 29, 1816. He regarded Mrs. Clermont as the author of the 'additional statement' made a fortnight before the railing letter. She was

the channel through which Lady Byron sooner or
later gained her knowledge of her husband's intimacy
with Jane Clermont;—an affair that incensed Lady
Byron long after she had heard of it. If the 'additional statement' had reference to the Jane Clermont business, Dr. Lushington could only say to
his client, 'That being so, and your feelings being
what they are, I will no longer advise you to think
of reconciliation;' and as a man of fine feeeling
Romilly could only say to his client, 'I will not be
used as an instrument for forcing Lady Byron to
return to a husband who knows so well how to make
himself happy without her.'   Regarding her husband's
intimacy with Jane Clermont as an affair of older
standing than January 15, 1816, Lady Byron (for
reasons already indicated) may well have come to
regard it in 1830 as part of her original case against
her husband; as something withheld from her parents
in January 1816; as something kept back from the
oral statement of January 16, and the written statement of January 18, although her first knowledge of
the matter was considerably subsequent to those days.
It is not difficult to imagine reasons why Lady Byron
felt herself bound in honour to withhold her knowledge of the Jane Clermont affair from her parents.
If the information, which Lady Byron withheld from
her parents, related to that business, it was doubtless
so withheld out of respect to the feelings and wishes
of its giver, Mrs. Clermont. Several motives are
conceivable, anyone of which would dispose the mischief-maker to bind her former pupil to withhold the
information from her father and mother. Care for
Jane's welfare and dread of her displeasure, concern

for Jane's reputation and concern for her own
advantage, may have made Mrs. Clermont urgent
with Lady Byron to keep from every one but her
lawyers a matter so discreditable to the girl and her
connections. The Mischief-maker's natural preference
for secrecy may have been stimulated by regard for
Godwin's feelings. She may have been actuated by
fear of Byron, and a nervous desire to avoid the
very disrepute he put so ruthlessly upon her.—The
large body of facts and considerations indicated in
this long paragraph no doubt fall short of an historic
demonstration, that Lady Byron's mysterious statement to her lawyer referred to the Jane Clermont
business. But they are facts and considerations to
justify a strong opinion, that a perfect exhibition of *all*
the circumstances and consequences of the poet's
intimacy with Jane Clermont would probably put an
end to all uncertainty respecting his wife's ' additional
statement ' to Dr. Lushington.

Though the new love followed so closely upon the
old, that prosaic persons will be disposed to think the
poet cannot have suffered severely from the loss of the
wife, for whom he so speedily found a substitute, it
would be a mistake to regard the ' Fare Thee Well ' as
an altogether insincere and theatrical performance, by
which Byron hoped to win sympathy for himself, and
cause antipathy to the wife, against whom he was so
incapable of ' rebelling.' That it was published for
such ends is more than probable. That it went to the
press without his authority or knowledge, through the
action of an officious friend, as he meant to inform
the world in his posthumous ' Memoirs,' is very much
less than probable.

It can, however, be readily believed that the verses, which should have been seen by no one save the writer and the person to whom he addressed them, were the result of genuine emotion. The wife, whom he had wooed with a persistence foreign to the impetuous and gusty passions of his earlier time, may have occasioned him the disappointment that is the usual sequel of extravagant expectations ; but their intercourse had been fruitful of endearments and mutual tenderness. Though she was not one of the few women, whose love is more likely to be quickened than extinguished by unkindness, she had unquestionably married him from affection. The mere vanity, which has been declared her only motive in accepting him, would in so temperate a woman have been satisfied by a suit that was no secret in her circle. The offer which she declined had given her all the triumph she doubtless coveted over her rival at Melbourne House. Mere rivalry would have disposed her to decline the second offer, even as she had declined the first, rather than to accept the suitor who was not likely to revert to her married rival. On the other hand, though selfishness caused the poet to repent his marriage as soon as he was required to sacrifice his own wishes to his wife's happiness, and had chafed for a brief while under the petty vexations of conjugal bondage, it is no less certain that he also married from affection. Of course there were contributory motives and influences. But on either side the predominant motive to this luckless union was sentimental preference. On Lady Byron's side the feeling may have been deficient in fervour and intensity, qualities not to be looked for in a woman of her tranquil and comparatively unemotional nature. On Lord Byron's side the feeling was certainly devoid —perhaps *ominously* devoid—of the tempestuous rage and sweet turbulence, which three years later made him sing on the river's brink, as he journeyed towards Bologna,

> ' My blood is all meridian ; were it not,
>   I had not left my clime, nor should I be,
> In spite of tortures, ne'er to be forgot,
>   A slave again of love,—'

But it was no marriage of 'convenance.' It was as much a love-marriage on both sides as ninety-and-nine out of every hundred marriages done and celebrated with all honesty in love's name, and without a hint heard from any corner to their sentimental discredit. Lady Byron was no woman to promise to love a man, without regard to the importance of the vow. Pliable though he was in a clever woman's hands, Byron was not the man to marry a woman he didn't really care for, simply because Lady Melbourne (old enough to be his mother, as he called her :—indeed old enough to be his grandmother) wished him to do so. His letters before and after his marriage, all the circumstances of his suit to the lady, and the superabundant evidence of the harmony of their tempers during the earlier half of their term of union, put it beyond doubt that he loved her on the bridal morning, and delighted in her for several months. That she was really acceptable to him during this period of their closest intimacy is shown by his reluctance to sign the deed of separation, and shown yet more strongly by his futile attempt to lure her back to his embrace soon after his withdrawal from England, notwithstanding all the embittering humiliations which their dissension and severance had occasioned him. Had he not still felt a strong attachment to his wife, it is inconceivable that within three months of putting his hand to the deed he would, in accordance with Madame de Staël's counsel, have made overtures through a friend in England for a reconcilement. Of those overtures nothing is known positively, with the exception of their failure and his vindictive annoyance at their failure. But they must have been based on a frank admission that Lady Byron had much to forgive, and must have proceeded from a sincere yearning for restoration to her favour and companionship. They cannot have resulted from mere arguments and considerations of prudence. It is marvellous and perplexing that they should have been made so soon after the rupture which had been fruitful of so many exasperating incidents. It was absolutely impossible for Byron to have made them, had he not found her a congenial companion, and persisted in loving her.

In the first three months of his separation from the woman for whom he felt thus strongly, memory cannot have failed to stir his sensibility with words and looks she had given him,—with pathetic scenes in which they had been the sole actors. His sensibility cannot have failed to rouse poetic fancy to play on these pictures of remembrance. Acting upon one another in their customary manner, remembrance, feeling, and imagination may well have produced the flood of tender and subduing emotions that found utterance in the valedictory verses. But though the

poem may have been an outpouring of genuine feeling, it was published with a mean and malicious purpose. Given to the world as a fair statement of his
case against his wife and of her case against him, it
became a falsehood. The act of publication was, in
truth, a crafty attempt on the poet's part to catch
applause at her expense, to get advantage to himself
by lowering her in the world's regard. It was an act
of public war upon the woman he had injured, that
changing her regard for him, determined her to
change her course towards him,—and henceforth to
be silent in behalf of the man who was so well qualified to be her assailant and his own defender.

On reading the pathetic verses, which brought
their writer much sympathy and caused thousands of
people to imagine he had been more sinned against
than sinning, Madame de Staël exclaimed, ' How
gladly would I have been unhappy in Lady Byron's
place!' Had this woman of wit been in Lady
Byron's place—had she been Lady Byron instead of
Madame de Staël—she would have regarded the
verses as coming from a husband who, after wooing
her for two years and a half assiduously, had in nine
short months found her society tame and wearisome ;
a husband who after living in harmony with her for
seven or eight months had made her feel that his
delight in possessing her was merely the delight of a
child playing with a new toy; a husband who, whilst
recognising her conscientious desire to please him, had
told her she wasted her pains on an enterprise beyond
her power ; a husband who, passing abruptly from
tenderness to harshness, had poured cruel speech upon
her at a time when her health gave her a peculiar

title to his most delicate consideration; a husband who within a few weeks of her accouchement had told her she must choose between travelling with him, or staying at home with her mother, whilst he pursued his pleasure in distant lands, where he would find life enjoyable without her; a husband who, whipped to wild fury by her reluctance to assent to either alternative, had declared his union with her the one disastrous step of his life; a husband who in moments of calmer malice had said he never loved her, and indeed wooed her out of spite from the date of his first offer to the date of his second proposal; a husband who, passing from noisy rage to silent rage, had lived with her for days together in speechless gloom, and whilst persecuting her with morose taciturnity had never encountered her glance, without instantly dropping or averting his eyes in a manner eloquent of aversion. Had she been Lady Byron, and seen the verses for the first time in the author's own hand-writing, Madame de Staël would have had reason for thinking it probable he had not sent them to her without first reading them, in a voice of cynical drollery, to Jane Clermont. Had she been Lady Byron, and seen the verses for the first time in a newspaper, she would have read them as an ingenious composition sent to the press for her injury by the man who, no long while since, had spoken of her as breaking her marriage-vow. Had she been fully instructed in the case, the Frenchwoman of a proud spirit and exacting temper would have been less ready to change places with Lady Byron, and less hopeful that the unforgiving wife would be induced by a few submissive and conciliatory phrases, to pillow herself once more on the breast 'where her head so oft had lain.'

Had the verses been sent by their writer to Lady Byron for her sole perusal on the 17th of March (the date assigned to them by their author), they might have made her falter, at least for a few moments, in her purpose. It is even conceivable, though improbable, that surrendering herself to their influence, she might (the Jane Clermont business notwithstanding), have answered the verses in a way that would have saved her from the imputation of 'wanting one sweet weakness — to forgive.' But their *publication* in the middle of April was an outrage she had good reason to resent. To receive such an insult tamely, to endure unresentfully so undying an injury—a wrong repeated daily throughout the world—a woman must be either the equal of the angels or much lower than sensitive and self-respecting womankind. To Lady Byron the outrage was the more offensive on account of what she regarded its meanness. Heretofore she had admired, loved, feared, and pitied her husband. In the season of his triumph she had regarded him with admiration, whilst holding aloof from the crowd of Byromaniacs who suffocated him with their white shoulders and foolish flatteries. In the days of his tenderness to her she had worshipped and loved him for treating her so tenderly. His outbreaks of anger and 'the breath of his bitter words' had made her fear him. Whilst she thought him mad, she watched him with compassionate anxiety. On being assured that his violence and moodiness were not referable to insanity, she had parted from him in perplexity and dismay

rather than with repugnance. In her mental narrow-
ness she had thought him possessed by the demon of
impious insolence. In her spiritual arrogance she
had for a few days been disposed to regard herself
as an instrument chosen by the Almighty for his
humiliation. But it never occurred to her to despise
him till he tried to divert from himself the unantici-
pated storm of obloquy, which he had provoked by
his own action. She felt that if the storm had broken
in thunder over her head, she would have borne all
the infamy of it uncomplainingly. She scorned him
for trying to turn the fury of the hurricane upon her;
and in her disdain of the meanness of his design she
thought, to his shame, precisely what he wrote a few
months later to her discredit,

‘ I would not do by thee as thou hast done ! ’

CHAPTER XVII.

THE STORM.

'Simple Causes'—Lady Byron's Justification—Her abundant Frankness—The 'Quarterly Review' Letter—Byron's Surprise at his Wife's Resolve—His First Action on the Intelligence—His subsequent Behaviour—Extravagances of Social Sentiment—Observations on the 'Remarks on Don Juan'—'Glenarvon'—Lady Jersey's Farewell Party—The Poet's Withdrawal from England.

USING the word 'simple' in the sense of 'ordinary and common,' Byron remarked shortly before his death to a gentleman, who was pressing him for an avowal of the causes of his separation from Lady Byron, ' The causes, my dear sir, were too simple to be easily found out ; '—words by which he wished to intimate that to discover Lady Byron's grounds for dissatisfaction with him and her reasons for repudiating him, people should seek them in matters that are the usual sources of discord to newly married couples, instead of imagining that the rupture resulted from extravagant crimes and improbable incidents. When their association has survived the first delights of novelty, it is not unusual for a newly married couple to bicker and even to quarrel bitterly from causes that, without being trivial and altogether fanciful, are remote from the outrages which afford a young wife the strongest justification for withdrawing from uncongenial wedlock.

Though it may be a question whether Lady Byron was justified by the circumstances of her case in breaking from her young husband, when she was aware that by doing so she would compel a man of his temperament to a life of more or less flagrant libertinism, no holder of the nicely balanced scale can accuse her of taking so serious a step without serious provocation. As she acted from prudent and selfish care for her own comfort and happiness, she can claim none of the admiration and gratitude, that would have been her proper and glorious reward, had she preferred her husband's welfare and dignity to her own advantage. The sympathy due to her for the wretchedness, which came to her from the alliance she had not sought, is weakened almost to extinction by the recollection of the alacrity, with which she retreated from the position of trial and misery.

Finding him no worse in any other particular (probably finding a better man in *all* other particulars) than she expected to find him, she had no sooner made acquaintance with what Hobhouse used to style the poet's morbid selfishness, and the gusty violence of his temper, and ascertained those defects to be no results of insanity but the chief and incurable failings of an otherwise noble nature, than she determined to be quit of him. Wanting the sympathetic large-heartedness and moral breadth of temperament, that would have enabled her to refer his wild speech to the maddening heats of constitutional irritability, she was stung to resentment by his outrageous and absolutely truthless assertions that he had never really loved her, and had pursued her from motives of resentment and vengeance. Instead of taking these extravagant utterances seriously, and weeping over them in her solitary hours, Lady Byron would have received them with cheerily ringing laughter, would have rallied him about them with sly humour and pleasant irony in their privacy, and would even have chattered gaily and with piquant drollery about them in his hearing and presence (*never* behind his back) to her more volatile acquaintances, had she been a woman capable of controlling the humours of her lord, and 'managing the devil' that lurked in his nature, —a nature good and ill by turns. The woman is conceivable who would have made Byron a happy and good man, and won unutterable happiness to herself from the service of successful devotion to so marvellous a master; but she would have been 'the one woman of ten thousand,' and greatly unlike Lady Byron in intellect and temper. Being a fairly good woman, Lady Byron should not be blamed for not being other than she was. On the contrary, she is rather to be compassionated, like all persons who have come through circumstances, rather than by voluntary intrusion, to high places for which they are singularly incompetent.

It remains, however, that she retreated from the place of trial and difficulty to please herself, *not* because she was under a clear and imperative obligation to leave it. If Byron was morbidly selfish, his wife cannot be credited with perhaps the rarest virtue—absolute unselfishness. To her advantage it may be declared on sufficient evidence that, on withdrawing as far as possible from the distasteful union, she was convinced no good would ensue to Byron from her self-sacrifice, should she constrain herself to remain with him. Recognising her complete impotence to make him happy, and believing that his grief at losing her would at the worst be nothing more serious than a transient annoyance, she resolved to escape from a companionship that, affording him no comfort, could yield her nothing but grief. Under these circumstances it certainly is not obvious that she was wrong in reverting from wedlock to singleness, and in falling back on her natural right to pursue her own happiness. Though it can never rise to rank with the virtues, selfishness is within certain limits the salutary and even sacred privilege of all human creatures. And it does not appear that Lady Byron's selfishness exceeded these limits, when she determined for her pleasure to leave for ever the husband, who for his own mere pleasure was preparing to leave her for a considerable time.

Nothing having occurred since 1816 to enlarge his knowledge of his wife's reasons for parting from him, it is remarkable that Byron spoke so confidently and precisely in 1824 of the nature of the matters, respecting which he had for years pretended to want clear and definite information. In spoken words and in written words it had for eight years been his complaint against Lady Byron and her advisers, that they had refused to tell him in what particulars he had wronged her, when he was at length moved to remark that the causes of the separation were too simple to be easily found out. Having for so long a period affected inability to account for a matter, so hurtful to his happiness and reputation, it is strange that in a sudden fit of candour and communicativeness he should almost at the last moment have admitted his sufficient knowledge of the mysterious business.

Of course there never was a moment when he needed any enlightenment on the affair. After worrying a fairly sensible woman into thinking him a madman, no sane man needs to be told why she thinks him mad. The husband, who has whipped and goaded his wife into disaffection by malicious words and aggravating taciturnity, does not need to be informed why and how she has come to regard him with aversion. If he asks for the information, he does so from some freak of humour, from some notion of policy, from an appetite for further disputation, or from curiosity respecting her feeling on particular points of the contention ;—*not* from a genuine inability to account for her disapproval of his treatment of her. When Byron, after perusing his father-in-law's letter of the 2nd of February, 1816, begged his wife to state her reasons for desiring a separation, he knew both her reasons and the reasonableness of them. And it is only fair to Lady Byron, of whose silence so much has been said by her censors, to put it upon record that in reply to the requirement she gave the needless information with abundant frankness. To the letter, in which Byron made the request for the first time by his sister's pen, Lady Byron replied in a letter published in 1869 in the ' Quarterly Review,'—

' *Kirkby Mallory, Feb. 3rd*, 1816.

'MY DEAREST AUGUSTA,—You are desired by your brother to ask, if my father has acted with my concurrence in proposing the separation. He has. It cannot be supposed that, in my present distressing situation, I am capable of stating in a detailed manner the reasons which will not only justify this measure, but compel me to take it; and it never can be my wish to remember unnecessarily those injuries for which, however deep, I feel no resentment. I will now only recall to Lord Byron's mind his avowed and insurmountable aversion to the married state, and the desire and determination he has expressed ever since its commencement to free himself from that bondage, as finding it quite insupportable, though candidly acknowledging that no effort of duty or affection has been wanting on my part. He has too painfully convinced me that all these attempts to contribute towards his happiness were wholly useless, and most unwelcome to him. I enclose this letter to my father, wishing it to receive his sanction.

'Ever yours most affectionately,

A. I. BYRON.'

It may not be inferred from the least perspicuous sentence of this epistle (penned under circumstances sufficiently trying to account for its occasional obscurities of expression) that Byron declared his purpose of escaping from wedlock almost from the very moment of its celebration, or that it was the writer's purpose to accuse him of having done so. His gravest offence (which would have been received with laughter instead of dismay by 'the one woman in ten thousand') against his wife was that, on coming to quarrel with her some eight months after their wedding, he declared that he *had entertained* a purpose ever since his marriage of freeing himself from its bondage. As Lady Byron cannot have intended to make Mrs. Leigh and her brother a statement, whose untruth would be obvious to both the one and the other, it may be taken for granted that on this point she only wished to inform her sister-in-law and remind her husband, that on declaring his intention to escape from domestic thraldrom, he declared the resolution to have been formed at the very beginning of their union. Augusta being no less aware than her brother of the harmony of the marriage throughout the earlier months of 1815, it cannot have been Lady Byron's purpose to represent that the grossly offensive speech was made in the honeymoon. An editorial interpolation of four words (as an obvious omission) after 'he has expressed,' would give no more than the thought of the writer who must have meant to write, 'I will now only recall to Lord Byron's mind his avowed and insurmountable aversion to the married state, and the desire and determination he has expressed *himself as having entertained* ever since its commencement to free himself from that bondage.' The propriety of this emendation appears also from the fact that the letter represents the offensive speech to have been made at a time, when its utterer could speak of himself as 'finding the bondage quite insupportable,' whilst 'candidly acknowledging that no effort of duty or affection had been wanting' on the part of his wife;—a time that must have been, from the terms of the statement, considerably subsequent to the wedding. Written for persons who can 'read between the lines' and catch the precise meaning of vague and inexact expressions, domestic letters are seldom so carefully worded as official epistles. Whilst its frankness and directness indicate how little cause Byron had to charge his wife with stubbornly withholding her grounds of offence from his knowledge, the freedom and inconsideration of this epistle will prepare readers for the assurance that she was at the outset of the quarrel no more chargeable with caution than with uncommunicativeness.

Instead of returning from London to Kirkby Mallory without seeing her sister-in-law, in accordance with Dr. Lushington's prudent advice, Lady Byron sought and had a meeting with Augusta. Greeting one another with undiminished affectionateness and cordiality, the two sisters-in-law after their conversation parted in perfect friendship. Certainly Mrs. Leigh had no reason to complain of Lady Byron's dogged uncommunicativeness; and it is not conceivable that Byron ventured to charge this fault upon his wife in his sister's hearing. Alluding to the smaller vexations she had endured since her marriage, in a manner to make it obvious that mere considerations of comfort and discomfort were in some degree accountable for her original determination not to return to an uncongenial association, Lady Byron admitted that she had not come to the resolve without a struggle and passages of sentimental vacillation, which of course would not have troubled her had circumstances left no other course open to her. Acknowledging her weakness in not coming to the final resolve directly and unhesitatingly, she expressed sorrow for causing Augusta and several other friends much uneasiness, which she might have spared them by action less wavering and uncertain. Of what she had suffered from Byron's ebullitions of temper and manifestations of selfishness, there was no need for her to speak to Augusta, who had been a witness of some of them, and was well aware of her brother's intention to go abroad with Hobhouse. Speaking thus frankly, she spoke with a singular appearance of freedom from the bitterness to be looked for in a person moved to a momentous conclusion by a strong sense of insult and injury. It comforted her to believe that the separation would cause Byron no acute sorrow or enduring discomfort,—that, instead of regretting her as a lost delight, he would remember her only as a former burden and incumbrance. She declared that, though she might not refer his ill-treatment of her to mental derangement, which would have made it altogether blameless, she thought of all that had passed between them without resentment, and almost without a sense of injury. If there was any subject on which Lady Byron was otherwise than frank in her communications to her sister-in-law, the subject was Byron's intimacy with Jane Clermont;—the one subject on which Byron was probably most desirous for her to be free of speech. There are reasons for the opinion that Byron's first disposition to accuse his wife and her advisers of stubborn and mysterious reticence originated in his vexation at their avoidance of the matter, which he may well have thought chiefly accountable for his wife's displeasure. But this is no question on which the present writer can speak authoritatively. Possibly the publication of the Hobhouse papers will remove it from the field of mere conjecture.

Another proof of Lady Byron's disposition to

think generously of her husband and to act justly towards him, at a moment when she might be pardoned for regarding him vindictively, is found in her determination to do everything in her power to lessen the injurious effect which her action in withdrawing from him could not fail to have on his reputation. On being told that rumour was dealing hurtfully with her husband's reputation, she resolved to give the lie to any slander that should be uttered against him in her hearing. This was certainly her spirit and purpose for some time after she decided on separating from him. And there is reason to believe that she remained in this temper and resolve, till that disastrous act of publication two months later, by which he dragged her from her privacy, and exhibited her to universal reprobation as an unforgiving woman, who, having quarrelled bitterly with her unrebellious lord on trivial matters, refused to give him again the love he longed for.

Though his wife's silence, persisted in for several days—a silence his sister could have fully accounted for, had she cared to do so—must have forewarned him of the coming trouble, and prepared him in some degree for the staggering blow, the first effect on Byron of the announcement (February 2, 1816) that his wife had resolved neither to return to him nor receive him again, was supreme and unqualified astonishment. The silence had told him that mischief was brewing. By the mysterious silence he had doubtless been caused to anticipate expostulation, and exhibitions of censure from his father-in-law and mother-in-law, with all the other disagreeable incidents of a domestic difficulty, that would not issue in an amicable arrangement, without occasioning him many vexations, much disturbance of temper, and some humiliation. But till the post brought him Sir Ralph Noel's demand for an act of separation, Byron had neither conceived nor suspected the seriousness of the situation. In his first surprise, he could not believe Lady Byron had authorised the astounding letter. Sir Ralph Noel (whom the poet regarded as a good-natured old fool) was surely the mere tool of Lady Noel and Mrs. Clermont, who had exceeded their instructions, possibly had acted without any instructions from Lady Byron, in making their puppet pen the marvellous ultimatum. This was Byron's view of the situation. It was inconceivable to him that 'Pippin' would take such extreme measures without a few preliminary intimations through the post of her serious displeasure with her 'Dearest Duck.' In a moment Augusta was ordered to write to Lady Byron in his name to ascertain whether she had authorised her father's action; and as she had for more than a week been fully informed of Pippin's purpose, and had for several days been looking for Sir Ralph's declaration of war, Mrs. Leigh may well have felt some compunction for her duplicity, if without a previous avowal of her knowledge of the real state of the case to her brother, she wrote the letter which drew from his wife the epistle set forth on a previous page of this chapter.

Dispersing the mist of egotistic moodiness that had darkened his moral vision for several months, and lifting him for a season above the depraving influence of his morbid selfishness, the shock of Sir Ralph

Noel's letter startled Byron out of his meaner nature, and in a trice raised him to his better self. On realising the situation, he saw and confessed that the pain and humiliation of it were the natural consequences of his own folly and wrong-doing. Losing sight of his imaginary grievances he took a just view of his serious misconduct. At the same time he took a manly and even generous view of his wife's resentment and resolve. Without overstating the case against himself, as he was apt to do in seasons of hysterical contrition and remorseful self-introspection, he confessed that he had behaved badly, very badly, and had only himself to thank and upbraid for his misfortune. Instead of pretending that he could not account for his wife's revolt, or talking miserable nonsense about her impious violation of her matrimonial vow, or accusing her of obstinately withholding the motives and considerations of her conduct, as he did with no ordinary meanness and dishonesty a few months later, he avowed that he had treated her worse than ill, and that she showed proper spirit in rebelling against his tyranny. If he stopt short of declaring her *fully* justified for her extreme measures of retaliation, he averred stoutly that she had been driven to them by great provocation, and forbore to hint that the justification was less than complete. Forbidding his friends to offer him a suggestion to her discredit, he was no less imperative that they should urge nothing in his defence, or even in palliation of his flagrant misbehaviour.

On February 29, 1816, he wrote to Moore, 'Don't attempt to defend me. If you succeeded in that, it would be a mortal, or an immortal, offence.' To the same correspondent, who had suggested that his friend's matrimonial misadventure was due to his injudicious choice of a wife, he wrote on the 8th of March, 1816, ' The fault was *not*—no, nor even the misfortune—in my " choice " (unless in *choosing at all*)—for I do not believe—and I must say it, in the very dregs of all this bitter business—that there ever was a better, or even a brighter, a kinder, or a more amiable and agreeable being than Lady Byron. I never had, nor can have, any reproach to make her, while with me. Where there is blame, it belongs to myself, and, if I cannot redeem, I must bear it.' No person saw more of him during this period of heavy trouble and exasperating annoyances than Rogers : no one was more certain than Sam Rogers to have heard the ungenerous talk had Byron in the time of tribulation been betrayed into speaking of his wife with animosity or disparagement ; and yet he could write fearlessly and confidently to Samuel Rogers on March 25, 1816,—' You are one of the few persons, with whom I have lived in what is called intimacy, and have heard me at times conversing on the untoward topic of my recent family disquietudes. Will you have the goodness to say to me at once, whether you ever heard me speak of her with disrespect, with unkindness, or defending myself at *her* expense by any serious imputation of any description against *her?* Did you never hear me say, " that when there was a right or a wrong, she had the *right?*" The reason I put these questions to you or others of my friends is, because I am said, by her and hers, to have resorted to such means of exculpation.—Ever very truly yours, " B." ' It being in the nature of family quarrels to

produce bitter and angry speech, one can readily
believe that Lady Byron's nearest relations and
warmest partizans spoke ill and unjust words of
Byron. In doing so they only did to his injury
what he himself did to their discredit. The poet who,
in the very letter of his testimony to his wife's irreproachable goodness during their familiar association,
described her 'nearest relatives' by epithets too violent
and gross for Moore to venture to publish them, was
in no position to express surprise and indignation
on hearing that they spoke of him with similar extravagance.   But though her closest friends doubtless
thought and spoke of Byron much worse than he
deserved, it is improbable that Lady Byron — ever
mindful of her dignity, even to the vigilance of a jealous
concern for it—was ever guilty of the same offence.
Far from joining in the outcry, hourly becoming more
violent against her husband, she was still in the mood
to protest against its excesses of injustice.   The time
had not yet come for her to make the contribution of
' speechless obloquy ' to the clamour of monstrous
slanders.   Byron's note to Rogers should not be produced in evidence against her.   It is however good
evidence to the time when the poet, reverting to his
former animosity against her, and dropping away
from his better to his baser self, passed to the state of
feeling that resulted in the publication of ' The Farewell,' the ' Dream,' and the subsequent satires on
the woman, about whom he should, for his own
honour's sake, never have allowed himself to pen a
single bitter verse or utter a single angry word.

It has been suggested by several of his censors
that, whilst he spoke justly and even generously of

the wife who had repudiated him, the poet was playing the part of a specious hypocrite, with a view to
restoring himself to her favour,—that the fair words
were false words, spoken only that they should be reported to her, and dispose her to condone his offences.
But the suggestion can be accepted only by persons
who have still to apprehend the elementary forces and
the structure of Byron's mental and moral constitution. To men of his acute sensibility and vehement
temperament such hypocrisy is impossible. Insincerity might within certain limits be charged against
Byron. He was capable of saying untrue things at
the instigation of anger, pique, jealousy, spite,—like
his monstrous assertion to his wife that he had never
loved her and had married her from a vindictive
motive. Sincerity was by no means an ever-present
characteristic of his art. But it was not in his power to
play the hypocrite consistently for any length of time.
The creature of impulse and the slave of emotion he
could neither mask his stronger feelings nor even express them temperately. His insincerity was an affair
more of show than reality. The natural vehemence,
which made him too essentially honest for a hypocrite's
career, was associated with a mobility of thought,
fancy and feeling that often had the appearance and
the mischievous consequences of insincerity when it
was altogether devoid of falseness. A man so constituted passes quickly from mood to mood ; and the
inconsistencies of his speech and action in the course
of successive moods, instead of being indications of
falseness and superficiality or even fickleness, are
signs of his sincerity to the impressions and feelings
of the moment. Such a man may be untruthful for

an hour ; he may be a hypocrite for a single day,—
but not for weeks together. So constituted Byron
passed quickly from love to hate, from anger to pity,
from cynical hardness to cordial benevolence. In
regard to his wife he went suddenly from justice and
generosity to mean and malignant animosity. But
he was not more genuine in the later than in the
earlier stage of feeling. When he spoke of her justly
he thought of her with justice ; and when he spoke
of her bitterly he thought of her with bitterness.
Had he in February and March been the dissembler
many people have been induced to think him, he
would have acted more cautiously in several particulars, and dissembling a little longer would probably
have compassed what he certainly desired—reconcilement with his wife. He would have avoided the
intimacy with Jane Clermont,—an affair which could
not fail to confirm Lady Byron in her opinion that he
had never really loved her. He would have persisted
in generous speech about her for another month. He
would have gone abroad without insulting her before
the whole world by the publication of 'The Farewell,'
and speaking in violent terms, certain to come to her
knowledge, of her violation of her marriage-vow.

For some days, even for some weeks, after Sir
Ralph Noel's demand for an agreement of separation,
Byron was hopeful that his wife would be silent.
Knowing that, so long as she remained with him, he
had done her no wrong greater than the unkindness
described in previous pages of this work, he could
not believe that she would persist in her resolve. He
was even disposed to question the sincerity of the
demand, and to regard it as a mere device for bring-

ing him to a perfect sense of his misconduct, and a proper state of contrition. On finding his wife so much in earnest as to have already taken steps for a suit in the Ecclesiastical Court, should he decline to sign the deed of liberation, he saw that he must yield to her request. It has been urged by half-a-hundred writers before Mrs. Beecher Stowe meddled so miserably with the matter, that had he not been guilty of some extravagance of immorality, far more heinous and revolting than the serious misconduct of which he had actually been guilty, he would have refused to join in the private arrangement, and insisted on a public statement and public investigation of her complaints against him. And could he have conceived all that slander would soon be saying loudly or whispering secretly to his infamy, he would probably have taken the course which, painful and inexpressibly humiliating though it would have been to him, would have revealed to the world the precise number and nature of his offences. Unforeseeing the violence of the coming storm, and the disadvantage that would come to him from the secresy of a private submission, it is not wonderful the poet consented to liberate his wife by the process that seemed least likely to occasion enormous scandal. The circumstances of the case forbade him to hope that his wife's suit would be unsuccessful should her case go to trial. The evidence would expose him not only to the censure of rigid moralists, but to what he dreaded far more than their reprobation,—the ridicule and contempt of ' society.' Instead of being exhibited as a gay and irresistible libertine, triumphing over the virtue of women of the highest rank and fashion, he would be found guilty of the most unromantic offences, bad temper and pitifully bad manners,—would be pilloried as the ill-conditioned fellow who had worried his young bride into rebellion from spite and peevishness begotten of a disordered liver.   One of the chief witnesses against him would be his own sister.   Another of them would be his nearest kinsman.   What could he urge against their testimony?   That he had not railed at his wife, and told her he had never loved her, without provocation ; that she had not been so cheerful as she ought to have been; that she had murmured occasionally at the solitariness of her meals and the discomfort of a home besieged by bailiffs ; that the squabbling had not been all on one side.   Was it possible for a man of sensibility and pride to go into court with no better defence than this,—no better grounds for insisting that the woman, who had found him an unendurable companion, should return to him and his ill-humour? How could a gentleman, a man of honour, a poet, go into court with such a case to resist his wife's entreaty for liberation from insufferable bondage?   There being no alternative but the private deed or the public trial, he chose the former.   Clinging to the hope that his wife would relent if she had a longer time for consideration, he delayed to do what was required of him. He parleyed with Sir Ralph Noel and wrangled with the lawyers.   He asked them for particulars of Lady Byron's grievances ; a request that of course only elicited the assurance that the particulars (known of course to him, quite as well as they were known to the lawyers) would be produced in Doctors' Commons, should the case go to trial.   He wished for the ' specific charges in a tangible shape ;' not because he needed further information respecting the charges, but because Lady Byron's sufficiently communicative letter *to* her sister-in-law and *through* her *to* him, was no such document as he could use in literary and open warfare against her advisers. At length, yielding to the force of cruel circumstances he put his hand to the deed on the 22nd of April, 1816, at a moment when he may well have felt that by forbearing to force the Noels into the ecclesiastical court he was giving up his best and last chance of checking the turbulent and seething flood of slander, that was sweeping over his reputation, and carrying away all his just claims to sympathy.

To account for that flood of wild and clamorous calumny, several things must be taken into consideration, some of them being at the first glance matters of such small moment that it is not wonderful they have escaped due attention. In its brightest hour, when no dissentient voices were audible in the acclamations rendered to the poet's genius, shrewd and calm observers of the social ferment would have predicted that so enthusiastic a triumph would be followed at no distant date by a reaction of feeling,— a reaction in which the multitude would be as quick to detect the failings as it had been zealous in magnifying the virtues of its former idol. The qualities of the man and his writings, the circumstances of his personal career and the peculiarities of the promise of his genius intimated that praise so passionate would ere long be succeeded by wilder and even more violent blame. The receiver of this tempestuous worship was a satirist, a dandy and a poet. He was a satirist who had wounded the self-love of an army of writers, greedy for applause, hungering for the homage lavished on the competitor whose fame was the growth of a single morning, and longing for a safe opportunity to wreak their resentment on the wit who had exhibited them to derision. He was a dandy who, though he could not dance, had captivated women of fashion and become the ball-room star of his particular season, before the peerless Brummell had declared him 'incomparable.' He was a poet who had questioned the immortality of the soul and hinted that Christianity was a delusion. Satirists are universally hated. Tolerated only in their own small and super-elegant coteries, the dandies even in their palmiest time were the aversion of ordinary Englishmen. Poets are the objects of masculine distrust in proportion as they are the objects of feminine confidence and approval. Was it possible for such a satirist, dandy and poet as the author of 'Childe Harold,' to escape enmity, jealousy, dislike and suspicion?

Too young to be acceptable to men of years and experience, too triumphant not to be envied by men of every age, too great not to be cordially detested by the small and ignoble of his own sex, Byron rated ordinary men at less than their proper worth, and without intending to treat them insolently, on the contrary whilst often going out of his way to please them and do them good service, allowed them to see he held them of small account. Whilst so considerable a man as Hazlitt was nettled by the young poet into styling him 'a sublime coxcomb,' hundreds of inconsiderable men were piqued into calling him 'an arrant puppy.' Byron's eccentricities were peculiarly irritating to large numbers of men who ridiculed them

all the more roundly and with easier conscience, because they had so strong an appearance of being
affectations. Even in this era of universal tolerance
and indifference, when wine-drinkers and water-
drinkers tipple together with gushing good fellowship, and vegetarians live in charity with devourers
of venison, antagonisms spring from difference of
taste in trifles more often than from difference of
opinion on matters of importance. In the 'port-wine
and beef-steak days' of 'the Regency,' social feeling
was apt to run strongly against gentlemen who fed
sparingly, and either would not or could not carry
their two bottles daily from the dinner-table to the
whist-table. Byron's system of diet (carried out with
needless ostentation and aggressiveness) was scarcely
more injurious to his stomach than it was to his
character with honest gentlemen, who sniffed treason
and every form of social mutiny in the pale poet,
capable of sustaining life on biscuits and soda-water.
On questions of amusement Byron was at war with
men of every country-house he visited. The sentimentalist, who shed tears and wrote poetically about
the eye of a wounded eaglet, detested field-sports for
their cruelty. Riding fairly well (on such horses,
by the way, as provoked Trelawny's derision) Byron
seldom rode to hounds. A good marksman with the
pistol he fired away in the garden at five-shilling
pieces, whilst the barbarians were slaughtering the
pheasants. Under any circumstances such a young
lord would have been unacceptable to the men who
rose every morning from their beds to exclaim 'Go
to, let us kill something.' Whilst these men—a
powerful factor of social opinion in the aristocratic

classes of English society—regarded the poet coldly or with positive antipathy for disliking the sports in which they delighted, the favour shown him by their womankind made him an object of their jealousy and suspicion.   Whilst the women pressed towards and thronged about him in the drawing-rooms, the men scowled at him, and muttered deep curses on the folly of his idolaters and on the arts by which he maintained his power over them.   Ponsonbys and Lambs were not the only men to wish devoutly that some breeze, ill for him and good for them, would blow the verse-writing dandy to the devil, and rid them of the sentimentalist who made their wives and sisters so ridiculous—so heedless of their dignity and even of their honour.   Worrying the men by his method and address with their women, Byron at the same time exasperated them by his political views, sympathies, and preferences.   Whilst nine out of every ten Englishmen regarded Buonaparte as the incarnation of evil, the poet declared in the very teeth of foaming patriots his admiration for the Corsican adventurer. In days when nine out of every ten Englishmen were ready on the slightest provocation to call Washington a successful traitor and the American republic a federation of rebellious planters, Byron rated the American 'Pater Patriæ' as the greatest, brightest, and loftiest of heroes.   Worse still, at a time when for the sake of social order people of good breeding and loyal nature were required to look away from the failings and magnify the virtues of all persons in supreme authority, the peer of Great Britain, who exulted in Napoleon's escape from Elba and worshipped the Cincinnatus of the West, had ventured to exercise his dangerous faculty of verse in lampooning the Prince Regent. It has been shown how that lampoon alienated from the poet certain powerful organs of the Tory press, that had previously commended the productions of his genius. For more than two years those journalists had been educating their readers—no small or powerless portion of the entire community— to underrate his poetry and exaggerate his political maleficence. And now that the scandal of his rupture with a young wife, who had long enjoyed a singular reputation for feminine excellence, gave them a convenient occasion and safe pretext for breaking from his acquaintance and excluding him from their houses, men of high rank and influence in the Tory connexion were quick to reveal how completely they also had been alienated from him by his political indiscretions and extravagances. At the same time he was regarded with coldness, or warm hostility by the Whigs to whom he had for some time been an embarrassment, and now promised to become a source of serious scandal. Several of the Whig families wished him out of the way,—at least for a time. Lord Beaconsfield was fully justified in representing in ' Venetia ' that at the very moment of the poet's fall, there was less disposition within his own party than in the ranks of its opponents to moderate the catastrophe.

Religious organizations are not readily moved, and when put in movement they are not soon brought to rest. Religious opinion is not formed in a day. On the contrary it requires so considerable a period for its gradual development, that four years were all too brief a term for the ferment, which the theology of

' Childe Harold ' could not fail to occasion throughout the country—the ferment, whose first indications reached Byron in the autumn of 1812—to find adequate expression. The religious circles of the provincial towns and rural villages were still forming their judgment on the poet's greatest literary achievement, were still moving to their universal verdict that the book was supremely mischievous, when it was announced that its writer, whose dissoluteness was paraded in his poisonous verse, had returned to the profligacy which he had described himself as quitting from transient satiety rather than from sincere penitence. And in considering how the general disapproval of the poet's religious heterodoxy affected the general view of his domestic troubles, the reader should remember how closely scepticism and immorality were associated in the popular imagination throughout the earlier decades of the present century. In these days we have amongst us a small though considerable minority of people, not unwilling to think, and not incapable of thinking that moral rectitude is quite as likely to prevail in persons, whose strongest hope of future happiness depends on their present devotion to goodness, as in persons who are likely to be inspired by misapprehended doctrine with a notion that it matters little how wrongly they act towards their neighbours, provided they think rightly on matters of creed. But when ' Childe Harold ' was new literature, the Englishmen who held any such opinion could be almost counted on the fingers of a single hand. In respect to its influences on human affairs in this world, creed was valued by the poet's contemporaries as a power disposing people to be good for the sake of the future rewards of goodness, and restraining people from evil through dread of the future punishment of wickedness;—one of their prime theories of human nature being that man was so strongly disposed to evil,—especially to the indulgence of the vindictive passions and sensual appetites,—as to be incapable of living righteously on being liberated from the terrors of orthodox theology. In escaping from orthodox creed the unbeliever escaped from the motives and considerations that withheld men *from* evil, and was bound sooner or later to surrender himself to his natural propensity *to* evil. When this opinion was so general as to be almost universal in English society, it followed from the evidence of his writings that the poet of free thought was a person, not only capable of flagrant immorality, but certain to distinguish himself sooner or later by sinful excesses.

In the Observations on the ' Remarks on Don Juan,' written in 1820, Byron urged that his fellow-countrymen can have had no sufficient grounds for the almost unanimous verdict which drove him from their presence, as they knew literally nothing of him and his affairs except that he was a nobleman who had written poetry, and after becoming a father had quarrelled with his wife and her relatives from causes that had not been revealed to the public. Speaking of the same verdict Macaulay insists that the poet was the victim of something worse than Jedburgh justice in the proceedings, which opened with the execution and closed without an utterance of the articles of accusation. But in truth the public knew more of the culprit's affairs than the poet cared to admit, and more of his misbehaviour than the essayist cared to allow. Besides knowing that he had written poetry, the judges had read the poems in which he had proclaimed himself a sceptic and a libertine. And though people were altogether in the dark as to the particulars of his misdemeanour, the notorious and indisputable fact of Lady Byron's refusal to live with him any longer placed him at the tribunal of social opinion under a general accusation of disloyalty and misbehaviour to a wife, whose irreproachable fame forbade the world to think it possible for her to have repudiated him for light and trivial offences. Under these circumstances it cannot be fairly alleged that the poet was condemned without indictment, or that his judges were altogether without grounds for declaring him guilty. The accusation was wanting in particularity ; and the merciless sentence was wildly disproportionate to the culprit's considerable offences ; but the verdict was a just one. During a long distemper of selfishness and irritability and splenetic savagery he had treated his wife ill ; though he was absolutely innocent of the more serious offences of conjugal disloyalty, and absolutely incapable of the atrocious excesses of which many—indeed, the majority of his judges imagined him to have been guilty. However culpable he may have been to his conjugal partner every man, who consents to a private deed of separation from his wife on mere considerations of incompatibility of temper, is likely to suffer in reputation from the privacy of an arrangement, which by withholding the nature and particulars of the dissension from the world's knowledge may be almost said to invite the malicious and the idle to discover worse causes than the real ones for the severance. In credit and happiness Byron suffered heavily from such secrecy. Had it been the result of a suit and decree in the ecclesiastical court, the poet's separation from his wife would have been nothing worse than a transient inconvenience and momentary trouble, instead of being a perpetual poison to his nature, an enduring disfigurement to his fame, and an unwholesome mystery to the students of his story. Had he driven the Noels into Doctor's Commons, he would not have lived to exclaim in anguish, impotent for everything but the expression of its own intense bitterness,

> ' Have I not suffered things to be forgiven ?
> Have I not had my brain sear'd, my heart riv'n,
> Hopes sapp'd, name blighted, life's life lied away ?'

By defining his wife's grievances, putting precise limits to his own misbehaviour (for which he was to be compassionated rather than blamed), and telling all the evil that could be justly said of him, the investigation would have given him a security from the spite of lying tongues and the inventions of morbid fancy, that would have been cheaply purchased by the humiliations of the exposure and ridicule accruing to him from the one day's suit and nine days' scandal.

Resembling the majority of sudden storms in being heralded by sure signs of atmospheric disturbance, the storm, that swept the poet from the pedestal of national honour, exceeded all tempests of its kind known to biography in the copiousness of the calumny, the virulence of the denunciations and the diversity of the slanders it poured upon the object of universal detestation. It was not enough for his assailants to deride the man of fine sensibility for lacking the tem-

per of men of gentle breeding, to ridicule the poet
for failing in chivalric considerateness towards his
young wife, to taunt the nobleman with having displayed the most offensive qualities of a churl and
boor. Words of truth, however scornful and scalding,
were too weak for the passion and frenzy of the
hour. To give expression to the ferment and the
sincere convictions of society it was necessary for
journalists and pamphleteers to charge him with
crimes foreign to his nature, and vices to which he
had no inclination. It was alleged that he had struck
his wife, brought profligate women to her house, and
fired off pistols in her bedroom in the hope of frighten-
ing her into premature labour and fatal child-birth.
It was even whispered that he had offered her indignities too nauseous and revolting to be mentioned in a
book written for general circulation. Whilst poet-
asters wrote doggerel about the unbeliever's 'guilty
mind' and 'unhallowed eye,' notorious libertines
spoke of his impurity with virtuous repugnance. 'I
was accused,' the poet observed four years later without exaggeration, ' of every monstrous vice by public
rumour and private rancour; my name, which had
been a knightly or a noble one since my fathers helped
to conquer the kingdom for William the Norman, was
tainted. I felt that, if what was whispered and
muttered and murmured was true, I was unfit for
England; if false, England was unfit for me.' As
though he were stricken with a loathsome disease, to
be caught from the touch of his hand, the exhalation
of his body, or the baneful light of his evil glance,
the world fell away from the man of blasted fame, to
whose door carriages used in former time to roll in

such numbers as to block the way of St. James's
Street. With the exception of letters from angry
tradespeople, dunning lawyers and anonymous slan-
derers, few epistles came now to the tables which no
long while since were covered with cards of invitation
from the Queens of Fashion.

Murmured and muttered against, if not loudly
hooted, when he drove through the streets, or walked
across a public pavement to his carriage, the man of fine
sensibility and turbulent temper, whether he moved
about the town or stayed within his own doors, saw
and felt the infamy that had come upon him, —
saw it in the stony coldness of averted faces, felt it
in the silence of his solitary rooms. He still went
to see Kean in his best characters ; but the half-dozen
of his oldest and trustiest friends, who still had the
courage to cross his threshold, would fain have dis-
suaded him from visiting the theatre, where an actress
of singular beauty and cleverness had been recently
hissed from the stage, because she was suspected
of intimacy with the poet, to whom she had never
even spoken. He still dared to show himself and
vote in the House of.Lords, but he went thither at
the risk of being insulted by the way, and with the
knowledge that whilst the populace regarded him
with furious disfavour the peers regarded him with
contemptuous coldness. The mob never mobbed the
poet, in the fashion of the mob through which Lord
Cadurcis cuts his way in the pages of ' Venetia ; ' but
Hobhouse and Rogers had good grounds for their
lively fear that a riotous crowd would give the poet
a rough farewell, on his departure from London for
Dover. The curious and angry people, who gathered

about the poet's travelling-carriage whilst its roof was being loaded with his luggage, and scowling viciously at him breathed deep curses on all wicked lords and false husbands, as he took his seat in the vehicle when he had first regarded them with proud composure, were an assemblage that any untoward accident would have converted to a mob of rioters. Possibly the poet's aspect,—something in the air of his delicate and lovely features, something in the tranquil beauty of his firm and fearless face, something in the grandeur of his brow, something in the sorrow and courage of his terribly luminous blue-grey eyes,—may have restrained them from premeditated violence, by inspiring them with doubt whether a man so young and fair to view could be so old in vice and hardened in crime. Anyhow they forbore to wreck his carriage, and let him go his way without provoking him to use his pistols.

It was the opinion of persons, familiar with Byron and shrewdly observant of the circles in which he was an idol for barely four years, that the outcry against him within those circles proceeded from the men who disliked him for his eccentricities, envied him for his success, resented his occasional superciliousness, detested him for his political extravagances, and loathed him for their own wild misconceptions of his immorality;—and that the majority of the women only acquiesced from sheer terror in the verdict of their furious lords, which they dared not resist and could not have reversed. And it can be believed that not a few of the women who looked away from their former friend in public places, and drove past his carriage in the streets without bowing to him,

were at heart on his side rather than on his wife's
side.   On the other hand it is certain that there were
not a few women amongst the people of fashionable
light and leading who, throwing themselves with
passionate vehemence into the mad war against his
honour and happiness, became his most malignant
traducers even as they had formerly been his noisiest
adulators.   Exemplifying the truth of Congreve's
lines,—

> 'Heaven has no rage like love to hatred turned,
> Nor hell a fury like a woman scorned ;'

the woman, who in the poet's hour of triumph had
thrown herself at his feet, hunted him from house to
house, forced herself into his presence in male attire,
implored him to fly with her, thought no sacrifice of
feminine dignity and delicacy too high a price to pay
for his preference, was the woman who, on seeing the
world turn against him, hastened to exult over his
downfall and to stimulate with monstrous calumny
the passions which she had done so much to evoke
for his destruction.   To make him appear more
shameful she was even capable of confessing much of
her own shame, in the pages of the novel that, doing
nothing for the accomplishment of the author's
malignant object, wrought *her* reputation greater
injury than the book was meant to inflict on *his*
honour.   Writing 'Glenarvon' with murderous purpose, Lady Caroline Lamb published it with suicidal
result.   Sufficiently clever and coherent to show that
she was not mad, the book with only half its malignity and falsehood and shamelessness would have
been sufficiently malicious, untruthful and shameless
to prove her a bad as well as a foolish woman.   It

was her boast that it took her only a month to write the book which followed Byron to Geneva. Even if the boast were truthful, the fact would tell nothing of the time and labour expended on the performance by the hack who dressed it for the press. Like the author's other novels 'Glenarvon' was less the work of the frivolous woman of fashion, who was incapable of the labour of writing a flimsy romance without professional assistance, than of the person who *re-wrote* it and put it together for the printer. The parts, however, of the story for which Lady Caroline Lamb was personally accountable comprise the matters which would be most discreditable to her, had she written every line of the production which, whenever it was begun, was pushed through the press, to consummate the ruin of the man whom she had loved and adored,—and whom she professed to adore—and in a wild, crazy way, *did* adore—when death had released him from the troubles which she had done so much to create and aggravate.

Whilst Lady Caroline Lamb was correcting the proof sheets of 'Glenarvon' and ordering the superb cover for the copy of the novel which she meant to send to Byron, Lady Jersey was sending out her cards of invitation for the party, at which the poet took farewell of English society. If she resembled many women in sympathising with the poet, and wishing him well out of his troubles and well away from his persecutors, Lady Jersey was almost singular in having the courage to declare the friendly feeling. But though her generosity and daring were exemplary, it is questionable whether the Countess chose the best way of expressing her benevolent regard for the victim of social injustice when on the eve of his departure from England she invited him to an entertainment, given expressly in his honour. For though it was in the power of so momentous a personage to fill her drawing-rooms with people, ready to humour her generous whim and amuse themselves by taking a last look at the departing poet, she could not constrain them to treat him with reassuring heartiness. After a lapse of years the guest of the evening could write with drollery of the various ways in which Lady Jersey's friends indicated their various degrees of coldness towards or compassion for him ; but at the time it must have caused him more mortification than amusement to discover in hardened features and frigid words and looks of obvious embarrassment only too conclusive evidence that he was regarded as the black sheep and discredit of his order even by the persons who, being (as Moore expresses it) habitually ' tolerant of domestic irregularities,' were the persons of all England most likely to take a charitable and lenient view of his real misdemeanours and alleged offences. One can imagine what fun was made in the destroyed ' Memoirs ' of the equally absurd and vexatious incidents of a scene, that would doubtless have been turned to good account in one of the concluding cantos of ' Don Juan,' had the poet lived to finish the great satire. Some of the matrons were severely ceremonious, whilst others were loftily forgiving. Ladies of the gushing sort plunged into amiable familiarity, and then fearful of committing themselves too far bridled their impetuosity and withdrew into coldness and reserve. Besides Lady Jersey with her smiles of summer sunshine, the only woman to delight the culprit with frank and fearless cordiality was Miss Mercer (afterwards Lady Keith), of whom he wrote gratefully in one of his diaries: ' She is a high-minded woman, and showed me more friendship than I deserved from her. I heard also of her having defended me in a large company, which *at that time* required more courage and firmness than most women possess.' The men were hard, frigid and suspicious. Some of them barely exchanged the civilities of the *salon* with the chief guest. Some of them slipt to another room, in order to avoid the necessity of greeting him. Speaking of the poet's disgrace and the acuteness of the pain it occasioned him, Harness says, ' He would have drawn himself up, and crossed his arms and curled his lip, and looked disdainfully on any amount of clamorous hostility ; but he stole away from the ignominy of being silently cut.' Even in Lady Jersey's drawing-room, where no one could venture to show him open incivility, he was troubled by ' the altered countenances of his acquaintances ' and endured the ignominy of being treated with magnanimity. A few days later he stole away from the land of his birth,— the land he never revisited.

END OF VOL. I.

LONDON:
Printed by STRANGEWAYS & SONS, Tower Street, Upper St. Martin's Lane.

www.ingramcontent.com/pod-product-compliance
Lightning Source LLC
Chambersburg PA
CBHW021544110726
47902CB00004B/1010